SHADOWHEART

BOOKS BY MEG GARDINER

Ransom River
The Shadow Tracer
Phantom Instinct

UNSUB NOVELS
UNSUB
Into the Black Nowhere
The Dark Corners of the Night
Shadowheart

JO BECKETT NOVELS
The Dirty Secrets Club
The Memory Collector
The Liar's Lullaby
The Nightmare Thief

EVAN DELANEY NOVELS
China Lake
Mission Canyon
Jericho Point
Crosscut
Kill Chain

BY MICHAEL MANN & MEG GARDINER
Heat 2

SHADOW HEART

AN UNSUB NOVEL

MEG GARDINER

BLACK STONE
PUBLISHING

Printed in the United States of America

First edition: 2023
ISBN 978-1-9826-2752-2
Fiction / Thrillers / Suspense

Version 1

Blackstone Publishing
31 Mistletoe Rd.
Ashland, OR 97520

www.BlackstonePublishing.com

For Dominic

I pay in blood, but not my own.

—Bob Dylan

1

Deputy Marius Hayes was standing behind the front desk at the sheriff's station, blowing on the night's sixth cup of coffee, when he heard it. Four forty-two a.m., a Wednesday sunrise heading his way, less than two hours left in his shift.

The night had been dead quiet. That didn't spook Hayes, because this was rural Tennessee, not Khost Province, Afghanistan. In Spring River, quiet wasn't eerie. Most nights were so still he could hear his hair grow. But Marius Hayes believed in watching out for the people in this town, and even on peaceful nights, malice didn't sleep. Trouble breathed in the dark. Violent abusers, meth traffickers. Ghosts, even—or so he thought when he'd had too much coffee and the fluorescent lights flickered. He wished he were on patrol tonight instead of staffing the station. The scanner squawked irregularly, the two other deputies on duty periodically reporting in as they drove Jessup County's back roads. Beyond the windows, the drone of crickets and katydids filled the dark.

The blare of a car horn shattered the calm.

Outside, the station's motion-sensing floodlights lit up. Headlights crawled across the front windows. Hayes put down his mug and stepped from behind the desk.

An old sedan was wallowing across the empty parking lot at walking speed. The floodlights revealed it as a rusting Chevy Impala, early eighties, faded blue. Listing to one side on soggy shocks, it veered toward the bollards that kept vehicles from ramming the station entrance.

"No, you don't," Hayes said.

He holstered his duty weapon. The Chevy nosed into the bollards with a metallic crunch. That stopped it dead, horn raging, headlights blasting the station doors. Hayes saw a man slumped over the wheel. Dark hair. White. Head turned to the side, chest pressing against the horn. Possibly a drunk, maybe someone having a heart attack. But you never know.

Hayes picked up the radio handset. "All units."

He alerted the deputies on patrol that he was responding to an incident at the station. Then he headed for the doors.

The horn went silent.

Hayes ducked away from the glass. Putting the station's brick wall between himself and the doors, he raised his hand to block the glare of the headlights and peered out. The Chevy's door was open.

The engine was still running. The driver was staggering across the parking lot.

Hayes pushed through the doors. "Wait."

The man didn't acknowledge him, just kept lurching toward the road.

The sheriff's station sat on what passed for a main street in Spring River—a state highway along the railroad tracks, dotted with stores, an auto wrecking yard, the Baptist church, and a Dairy Queen. The cool night was lit by the station's floods and the Chevy's headlights and, across the tracks, the red neon sign for the Flying T Motor Court.

That was where the man was aiming himself. He looked to be in his forties, six three, built like a heavyweight, shoulders thick beneath his dirty white T-shirt. He faltered ahead with a bull's momentum.

"Sir," Hayes called out. "Stop."

The man merely waved, raising a hand overhead, and kept walking. "It's all yours."

Not on my watch, Hayes thought. *I'm not the parking valet. And this guy doesn't get out of a DUI by dropping off his car and heaving himself across the highway.*

Hayes raised his voice. "Sir, halt."

The man stumbled into the street. "I don't have anything to do with it."

The hairs on the back of Hayes's neck prickled. *It?*

He turned toward the Chevy. He shined a flashlight through the car's windows.

He spun toward the man. "*Stop.*"

The guy continued shambling toward the motel, nearly tripping over the railroad tracks. Hayes ran toward him.

"On the ground. Hands behind your head."

The night felt creepy-crawly, full of flying bugs, a supernatural shrieking, their clicky buzz a fuse, ready to set off an explosion.

On the back seat of the Chevy lay a woman. Small enough that she was stretched out full length. She wore a peasant top and low-cut jeans and had tattoos that were growing indistinct against her skin, because she was—she'd been—white but now was bloody, blue, and long past dead. Her eyes had clouded.

Her hands, feet, and mouth were wrapped with duct tape.

The driver zigzagged into the parking lot of the motel, a congregation of whitewashed 1950s cabins with red roofs. VACANCY on the sign by the road, the office dark. All the cabins dark.

Hayes ran toward him. Under the beam of his flashlight, he saw that the man was sweating profusely. Breathing heavily.

Hayes drew his Taser. "*Now.*"

The man walked a few more unsteady steps toward cabin 3. Then, swaying, he sank calmly to his knees. He raised his hands, his boxer's shoulders rising, and laced his fingers haphazardly behind his head.

Hayes approached and cuffed him. He got a look at the man's face. The guy was glassy-eyed, reeking of whiskey.

"You're under arrest," Hayes said.

The man looked up at him from beneath greasy hair. He struggled to focus. Then his eyes sharpened. His gaze swept up and down.

Hayes tensed, thinking the guy might fight, or trash-talk, that a white man was reacting to the sight of a Black deputy standing over him. But something swam in the man's eyes, slippery and sharp. Hayes thought this man knew why he was being arrested, and that it wasn't for drunk driving. This man was closely reading Hayes's distress.

Spring River, Tennessee, didn't get duct-taped bodies in the back of big old Chevys. Not ever. The man seemed to find that . . . amusing.

His words came slowly. "She ain't nothing to do with me."

Hayes's eyebrows rose as far as they could go. He grabbed the man by the biceps to pull him to his feet.

The man nodded at cabin 3. "Them, neither."

Deputy Marius Hayes froze.

The room key was in the man's hip pocket. Hayes locked him in the station's holding cell and called one of his patrol units to return to the station ASAP. He set his shoulders square and headed for the doors.

From the cell, the man shouted, "*Not mine!*"

Hayes crossed the tracks to the Flying T. The air felt cloying. Dawn seemed a million years away. The locusts, a dark presence in the trees, buzzed like a downed live wire.

Hayes drew his gun and put the key in the lock of cabin 3. Old-fashioned metal key on a plastic tag. A flimsy plywood door. It creaked open. He stood back, using the door frame as cover. His blood rushed in his ears. He thought of his wife at home and his baby boy. He raised his flashlight and swept the beam across the interior of the cabin.

His flashlight caught a dull silver glint.

"Jesus wept."

On the bed, three more bodies lay side by side. They were wrapped head to toe, like duct tape mummies.

The insect hum abruptly died. The silence seemed to settle in Hayes's chest.

He knew that it would be a long time before Spring River got another quiet moment.

New York City

A yellow sun perched in the afternoon sky, baking the Manhattan streets.

"*Arrested early this morning in a small Tennessee town . . .*"

Noise caromed through the building—people talking and laughing, a beer delivery truck unloading on the street with a clatter. Hot air blew through the propped-open back door, smelling of onions and grease. A woman stood in a hallway and watched the desktop television in the back office. She bit her thumbnail—a bad habit she had quit years ago.

She kept cool, kept her face blank. Midthirties, sandy hair, heavy kohl around her eyes, too many tattoos to count, trendy clothes from a discount store, stylish but cheap. Nothing cheap about the look in her eyes. The look in her eyes was diamond etched, sharp enough to cut. She knew she was staring, that if anybody passed by and got a look at her face, they'd think the future of the world depended on what she was watching on-screen. The news coverage of the Tennessee murders was frenzied.

"Three victims wrapped in duct tape . . ."

Duct tape.

She clenched her fists. The memory flared.

That night—that freezing Brooklyn night. She had run. Christ, holy fucking Christ, how she had run.

Past graffiti-covered warehouses along the East River. The lights of Manhattan reflecting from the black surface of the water.

Don't look back, she'd told herself. *Look back and they'll see my face. They'll know it's me.*

They'll know that I saw.

I saw and did nothing. That I ran.

The wind sliced her. She hadn't meant to see. Bad timing, worse luck. *Oh, God. Don't look back. Don't. Jesus, help me.*

She looked back.

The pier was a hundred yards behind her. And a hundred years old. It was abandoned, lit only by the dim glow of a streetlight and the gray-white sparkle of the East River. The wood was rotting, planks missing, pilings sticking out of the muddy riverbank like the broken teeth of a monstrous beast.

Near the pier's edge, a thin woman sat bound hand and foot and mouth with duct tape. A shadowed figure loomed over her. Pacing. Ranting.

"Slut. Filthy succubus, stealing a man's lifeblood."

Unbelievable.

Too believable, inevitable, *Jesus God oh hell* . . . She could hardly see in the dark, through her shock, the fear. She tripped on a break in the sidewalk and went down, noisily.

On the pier, two faces turned to stare intently in her direction. She flattened herself into the weeds.

The duct-taped woman bucked and tried to shout from behind the gag, but nothing came out. The shadow held still for what seemed an endless time, maybe sniffing the air, sending a sonar ping like a bloodsucking bat. Then seemed to relax.

"It's rats. Sorry they can't bibbidi-bobbidi-boo you out of here like Cinderella."

And laughed. The sound was hard and shrill.

The shadow turned back to the duct-taped woman, arms wide. "Last chance."

The captive raised her hands, begging.

"What's that?" the shadow said. "I can't hear you."

In the weeds, she shrank into herself, inching backward.

The shadow's arms were spread wide, taunting the captive. Then a shrug. Stepping up, ripping the tape off the woman's mouth.

The woman's words spilled out. "Please. I have a kid. I'm all she has."

"Not anymore."

"What . . . No, God. I'll do anything. You can hurt me. Just don't—"

Raising a boot, the shadow kicked the woman off the pier into the river.

The splash was muffled. For interminable seconds, there was no sound. Then came a weak shout, swallowed as the woman sank into the murky, freezing water.

Now, on the TV, a news chyron read, DRIFTER ARRESTED IN QUADRUPLE SLAYING.

Back then—2008, that bitter February—she had stifled a sob and crawled away through the weeds, then run through back streets toward the diner where she washed dishes. *Get gone*, she thought. Cadge some cash from the register, then split. *Ghost yourself, or you're next.*

She turned into the vacant lot behind the diner. Outside the back door, huddled by a pile of trash bags, she saw the girl.

Her throat caught. The girl stared straight at her.

She looked over her shoulder toward the pier. Streetlights illuminated corrugated walls splashed with graffiti. Shadows flickered across a spray-painted red heart. Nobody seemed to be coming for her.

Taking a breath, she hurried across the lot and crouched by the girl. "Hush. Not a word." She extended her hand. "Come with me."

So cold, so unbelievably cold she'd been. Now, in the May heat, a shiver rippled through her once more.

On the television, reporters jostled to film the perp walk.

A phalanx of Tennessee deputies pulled him from a sheriff's van— men in tight tan shirts, one of them a tall young Black guy whose tense, haunted face made her think he was the arresting officer. That he'd found the victims. He'd seen it. Flanking the prisoner, they came toward the cameras. An orange jumpsuit hung loosely on that powerful frame. Black hair lank. Hands shackled to chains around his waist. His handsome face, that tight jaw, those twinkling, empty eel's eyes. The shudder rolled between her ribs, down to her heart.

SUSPECT IDENTIFIED AS EFREM JUDAH GOODE.

He walked with his back straight, his expression flatter than slate. Like this wasn't happening to him; like he was gliding through a mirage. But she knew that behind that silent confidence, the man's mind was writhing. Efrem Judah Goode was heading into the maw.

"I see you, you goddamned fraud," she whispered.

It had been a long wait, but the whirlwind was finally coming.

2

Caitlin Hendrix held her Glock 19M at her side, barrel pointed at the concrete floor. She moderated her breathing. Her ballistic vest and baseball cap said "FBI" in bright yellow letters. Around her, up and down the long hall, gunfire echoed. Her earmuffs deadened the sound.

Turning to face the target, Caitlin raised the gun, assumed a two-handed grip, and fired. She focused, making sure she held steady and didn't anticipate the pistol's recoil. She emptied the magazine and lowered the gun. Even from across the hall, she could see that she'd shot a tight grouping.

The firing range satisfied her competitive urge. She was thirty-one and extraordinarily fit but was happy to leave the obstacle course to the bright-eyed trainees across the campus, at the FBI Academy in Quantico, Virginia. The range, where she'd fired thousands of rounds since joining the Bureau, provided straightforward, instant validation. You hit the mark, or you didn't.

She ejected the empty magazine and inserted a full one. Chambered a round. You hit the mark, but it wasn't a game. Every trigger pull released lethal force. Train like this is real. Then, if the time ever comes, reality won't surprise you. Drawing from concealed, she fired three rounds with her strong hand, the right. She switched hands and fired three rounds with the left.

She felt a tap on her shoulder. Lowering the Glock, she turned.

Her unit chief in the Behavioral Analysis Unit, Supervisory Special Agent C. J. Emmerich, stood behind her. She holstered the gun.

"Boss," she said.

Emmerich was hawklike—sharp and smooth and liable to swoop out of the blue. He wasn't dressed for the range but for the office, in a black suit that emphasized his slide-rule posture. He nodded toward the exit. Pulling the ear protection down around her neck, Caitlin followed him out.

The din of gunfire faded. Emmerich's gaze was quicksilver, bright and impenetrable.

"Goode's talking."

That made her take a mental step back. "He finally confessed? Now?"

It had been years since Efrem Judah Goode was arrested with a body in his backseat and three more on his motel bed. Six months since a jury convicted him of the Spring River murders. In that time, Goode had never admitted his guilt. When the verdict was read, he yelled, "Morons!" and was hauled from the courtroom.

Emmerich shook his head. "He refuses to discuss the Spring River slayings. He's confessing to *other* killings."

"No damned way."

"Thirteen, to be exact," Emmerich said. "The local cops have asked for BAU interrogators. Saddle up."

She ripped the Velcro on the ballistic vest, abruptly eager and anxious. "I'm halfway to Tennessee already."

Emmerich turned solemn. "Goode's sly. Find out if he's telling the truth."

Caitlin quickly swung by her town house, which was a straight shot up the interstate from Quantico. Virginia springtime popped with daffodils and cherry blossoms. Hickories shaded the building from the slanting orange sun. As she climbed from her Highlander, a soccer ball rolled her way from a kids' pickup game on the lawn. An eight-year-old boy ran toward her, face flushed. Caitlin kicked the ball back with a wave.

The boy picked it up. "Thanks, Ms. Hendrix."

He knew her name. She guessed she was at home here now. Home—a three-bedroom town house that had french doors to the balcony, built-in white bookcases, high ceilings upstairs, and most importantly, the man she shared it with, ATF special agent Sean Rawlins.

She opened the front door and heard small feet pound on the hardwood. Sadie Rawlins skidded around the corner into the entryway.

"Is it six thirty?" Sadie said. "It's not. *Sesame Street's* still on."

Sadie, Sean's four-year-old daughter, lived with them half-time. Brown eyes wide, she hurtled into Caitlin like Jackie Robinson stealing home. Despite the thud, the collision felt like joy. Caitlin was in a hurry but let her urgency abate. If she didn't want to spend time with Sadie, she should have gone straight to Dulles Airport. She kept a go-bag at the office.

She bent and kissed the top of Sadie's head. "Not six thirty. But I have to go on a trip, so I'm here to pack."

"On a plane?" Sadie said.

"A big silver jet. But I'll get you dinner first."

Caitlin's dog, Shadow, bounded out of Sadie's room. Black with white paws, Shadow was Caitlin's boon companion. She'd undoubtedly been curled up, against house rules, on Sadie's Disney Princess comforter. But her wagging tail and guileless gaze earned instant forgiveness, as always. Caitlin scratched her behind the ears.

Sadie jumped up and down. "Mac and cheese?"

"Let's see."

In the living room, the babysitter, a college junior, was picking up toy dinosaurs. Caitlin paid her but asked her to stick around. In the open-plan kitchen, she scooped together a meal for Sadie, then clipped on Shadow's leash and took her out.

A real home life. She was getting used to it. She didn't know how long she'd be at Quantico, with the BAU. The FBI assigned agents to multiple rotations, and if she wanted to advance at the Bureau, diversifying her résumé would be important. But she didn't want someone up the food chain to rip her out of the BAU before she was ready to go. She had her hands deep into the work and felt that it was where she was meant to be.

On the hiking trail behind the complex, Shadow strained against the leash. Caitlin said, "Chill, kid," but the mutt turned to her with pleading eyes. Caitlin surrendered and unclipped the leash, and Shadow caromed down the path under dappled sunlight. She reminded herself she was lucky to know a creature who was always excited to see her.

When they returned, Sean's F-150 was parked beside her SUV. Inside, she found him leaning against the kitchen counter holding a Perrier, listening fondly as Sadie narrated her day. Caitlin gave him a lingering kiss hello.

His eyes were dark, his features raw, his gaze acute. Tall and calm, he had a raider's stare that Caitlin liked to think reflected the boldness of his Apache ancestors. Composure was a requirement for his job: explosives specialist for the ATF, the Bureau of Alcohol, Tobacco, Firearms, and Explosives. She thought he was the best-looking thing she'd ever seen.

Sadie spun in a circle. "Caitlin's going on a trip."

Sean slid an arm around Caitlin's waist. "She texted me."

"She likes going on trips," Sadie said. "I do too. I want to go to Jurassic World."

"When you're tall enough for the rides."

Caitlin squeezed Sean for a second. "I should be back tomorrow night."

"You know where to find us."

They'd been together nearly four years, half of those lived on opposite sides of the country. They'd moved into the town house that winter, after Sean was promoted to the ATF's Washington Field Division. And after Sadie's mother—his ex-wife, Michele Ferreira—took a job as head of emergency nursing at a DC area hospital.

It was a juggling act, with chainsaws and flaming axes. Caitlin loved Sean, adored Sadie, and maintained a friendship with Michele. She found it rewarding. And exhausting. And she still sometimes forgot to childproof the house. She suspected that her therapist would have thoughts on that.

She ran a thumb across Sean's bristly cheek. "Just have time to grab some chow and change my clothes."

"Need help?"

"Yeah. It's tricky. Buttons. Shoelaces. Please."

Despite the time crunch, she told herself that this was where she should be. That she didn't need to beat herself up over taking these minutes with her man and his little girl.

Cognitive behavioral therapy had been great—it had quelled any urge to cut herself. For too long, she had ignored the ways the stress of her job might lead her to self-harm. A nightmarish case in Los Angeles had taken her over that edge. In the aftermath, she sought a referral to a stress psychologist.

Dr. Silverberg worked with cops and federal agents, military and first responders. Caitlin wasn't afraid of therapy—she'd had plenty in high school, when cutting seemed badass, seemed goth, when she convinced herself that inflicting pain meant *she* controlled her fear and despair. Once she sat down in Dr. Silverberg's office, Caitlin discovered that she was ready to shed some destructive tendencies. It helped that Miriam Silverberg was practical and matter-of-fact. And that cognitive behavioral therapy worked by getting her to recognize negative beliefs about herself, see how they sabotaged her, and jettison them.

Caitlin was a good student. Ask her FBI firearms instructor. Now she was working to replace damaging attitudes with positive ones. Learning how to fine-tune the edge—to open herself empathetically to cases without becoming emotionally overwhelmed—was a skill she needed to hone. It took her a month to slow down, reboot, and absorb what the doc was telling her: that mindfulness techniques would truly help her in the *present*. For a woman whose job focused on psychological profiling, on close observation, on interpretation and analysis of criminal behavior, that was invaluable.

"You're a tough chick," Dr. Silverberg told her. "You've got that covered. Now we're going to improve your general well-being."

Fuckin' A.

Of course, examining herself with a longer view—backward and forward—felt like pulling her own teeth, because Caitlin knew damn well that she resisted looking deep into her life. If she dived deep, she would confront the Hendrix family legacy. The relentlessness she inherited from her father, the belief that it was on her to protect everyone from darkness and death, the fear that she was destined to screw everything up. *No thanks.* She kept telling herself that, instead, she should work on stress management. Because if she didn't take care of herself, she could break down like an overworked machine.

Sean had been terrific, but he wasn't letting her slide. "You're doing the emotional work it takes to keep from damaging yourself again," he had said. "Consciously. Beware of risks that unconsciously put you in harm's way. Suicide by cop doesn't always take out just the people who provoke a deadly confrontation."

It was the first time he had dared to raise a taboo subject. Death, the black nowhere. Fear of its lure had more than once brushed the back of Caitlin's neck in the empty hours after midnight. As if death were one end of a magnet and she the opposite pole, irreversibly attracted to it according to the immutable laws of nature.

No longer. She now understood that she was not bound to annihilation.

"No," she had said. "I'll take managed risks when warranted. I won't be reckless. No more than you."

Sean had pulled her into an embrace. And Caitlin felt herself unwinding the tight spots around her heart a millimeter at a time.

She was working on how to love but not parent Sadie. And to deal with her low-voltage anxiety that Sean, Michele, and Sadie formed a family—one she wasn't part of. She now understood that Michele had felt that same anxiety, exponentially magnified, about Sean, Caitlin, and Sadie after Michele was critically injured in a bombing at Temescal Hospital in Oakland last year.

Life was a dark river. It sparkled with sunlight but was turbulent beneath, rife with eddies and rips and sharp rocks. Caitlin was trying to figure out how to ride it.

She poured Sadie a glass of milk and caught Sean's eye as she walked out of the kitchen. He followed her upstairs. She closed and locked the bedroom door.

"Given traffic, I have seven and a half minutes before I need to hit the road."

"All right," he said. "Sex, then snacks, then sex again?"

They fell on the bed, tangled, laughing, hot.

3

The sun rose early in Nashville. The sky was acrylic blue when Caitlin and Special Agent Brianne Rainey, her BAU colleague, headed out in the morning. Caitlin drove through the shiny city center, past the NFL stadium and the Tennessee state capitol. The place pulsed with modernity and ambition. New development overran long-standing neighborhoods.

"I was expecting bigger, blonder hair," Caitlin said.

Rainey looked up from the file she was reading. "Music City. Crank up that twang."

Rainey's face had its usual cool dispassion, but her eyes were lively. In her early forties, African American, she was one of Caitlin's lodestars in the Bureau. And she was more likely to listen to Jessye Norman singing *lieder* than to any Nashville hits.

"A tough fed like you can deal with country music for a few hours," Caitlin said.

"Country music's great. Give me Rhiannon Giddens playing fiddle with the Carolina Chocolate Drops. Give me Robert Johnson. You think Delta blues aren't country?" Rainey closed the file. "Spare me middle-class boys who stick 'dirt road' at the end of every verse to sell listeners on their authenticity." She shrugged. "I'll order biscuits baked with *real* lard, thanks."

West of the city, the Riverbend Maximum Security Institution was surrounded by rolling green hills and razor wire. In the distance, the Cumberland River meandered around a wide bend. When Caitlin parked and killed the engine, Rainey turned to her.

"Your first time in a maximum security prison?" she said.

"Yes."

Caitlin had been in plenty of county jails when she worked with the Alameda County Sheriff's Department. She had interrogated dangerous suspects in dingy backcountry police stations. She considered herself savvy and situationally aware. But she didn't pretend to be tougher than she truly felt. She knew that Rainey was about to drop knowledge on her.

"Do exactly what the guards tell you to do," Rainey said. "And pay attention to how they carry themselves. They're part of the ecosystem here, adapted. They're attuned to predator and prey. They twitch, even subliminally, you prepare."

"Got it."

"Easy peasy," Rainey said, getting out. "We're going to lull this critter into rolling over and showing us his belly." She shot a look at Caitlin. "With a verbal punch, if necessary."

Inside, they surrendered their weapons and were buzzed through a series of locked doors. A corrections officer led them down an empty concrete corridor to a windowless interview room. The metal door had an eye-level window with polycarbonate detention glazing. The harsh overhead bulb was encased in a metal cage.

"Can you turn the lights down?" Rainey said.

A less severe atmosphere might help encourage conversation. Murderers who asked to talk sometimes thought, in a twisted way, that they and the cops were working the case together. Dennis Rader, alias BTK, told the officers who arrested him that he'd always hoped they could sit down together and discuss the killings collegially. He was shocked to learn that the detectives didn't regard him as a colleague—after all, he was the expert on the case.

The guard shook his head. "Your choice of on or off."

Rainey half laughed.

"Precautions we should know of?" Caitlin said.

"No. He's been as docile as a house cat. But he'll be shackled."

"I wasn't going to suggest otherwise."

He said the prisoner would be in soon. Caitlin clenched and unclenched her fists.

The Behavioral Science Unit, precursor to the BAU, had famously developed the FBI's understanding of criminal behavior by interviewing imprisoned serial killers and mass murderers. Ed Kemper. David Berkowitz. Charles Manson. Caitlin wondered if the man they were here to speak to was as prolific as those slayers, or merely a wannabe. The table was positioned so she and Rainey had a clear path to the door. They sat side by side, dressed in dark suits with white blouses, hands on the table as a gesture of openness and honesty. Noise ricocheted through the building. She caught echoes of men's voices. Weights clanging in the exercise yard. The room smelled of bleach and sweat. The green hills beyond the razor wire felt distant.

They heard the clink of approaching chains. The door opened. Outside it, flanked by guards, stood Efrem Judah Goode.

He was powerfully built, fit, and, at forty-five, undeniably handsome. His blue cotton prison shirt could have been mistaken for a doctor's scrubs. His eyes were charcoal gray. In his cuffed hands he held a folder.

The guards brought him in, sat him down, and shackled his feet to the floor. He moved with disarming smoothness and ease, but his presence felt ominous. Caitlin continued to lean forward. She wasn't going to give a millimeter, though she sensed that Goode wanted to back her and Rainey away from him.

Caitlin and Rainey usually built a behavioral profile by assessing crime scenes. From that, they pieced together the personality of an unknown offender—the unsub. Though they weren't here today explicitly to profile Goode, they would form their questions through that lens.

Today, across the table, their subject regarded them coolly, his chest expanding, shoulders rising as he inhaled, seeming fully present.

He smiled affably. "The FBI. Finally."

A nomad, Goode had spent his life working odd jobs and committing armed robbery. And, he now admitted, beating vulnerable women to death. Addicts. Runaways. Hookups who looked at him the wrong way. Then, most often, dumping them in rivers and storm drains to wash away evidence. Sometimes wrapping their mouths with duct tape, to keep them quiet on those occasions when he wanted them alive a while longer. But never, he insisted, turning them into the mummies who were found lined up on his bed at the Flying T Motor Court.

He had recently given provocative details to the Jessup County Sheriff's Department but withheld dates and locations. The Tennessee detectives thought his memories were too vivid to be true.

"He's lying to beat the band," one had told Emmerich. "Jerking our chain."

Caitlin had a detective's skepticism and assumed that Goode was a skillful liar. But she knew that serial killers were unique offenders. Whether driven by compulsion, fantasy, or rage, they reveled in committing murder. Afterward, they savored their crimes. Even decades later, they could relive slayings in astonishing detail.

She also knew that serial killers didn't come clean out of remorse. Especially not Goode, who rolled up at the Spring River sheriff's station with one body on the back seat and three more laid out like Tootsie Rolls on his motel room bed—and who still proclaimed that he'd been framed.

What was his motive for talking about other murders *now*?

She lifted her chin. "We hear you have a lot to tell us."

"Depends," he said. "I could say a lot. I could talk for *years*. Telling it to *you*, though—that comes down to how bad you want it."

His open confidence set her on edge. Goode had a forceful presence— what psychologists called fearless dominance. It was an attractive trait that could signal boldness and leadership. Generals, adventurers, and business titans often had it. So did psychopaths. It helped them manipulate people. And Caitlin suspected that Goode wanted to manipulate her and Rainey.

Caitlin had become an adept profiler but was loath to burrow too deep inside an unsub's mind. She feared falling into the depths of the abyss. But with Goode, she would have to tunnel deep. Because she sensed that he was after something besides publicity.

Sure, he reeked of narcissism. He would revel in being a true-crime celebrity. But her instincts warned that Goode wanted something more. Something insidious. His genial smile had a venomous tinge. Emmerich's words rang in her ears: *Goode's sly.*

She said, "What we want is to get to the truth. Let's work on making that happen."

"The truth? No, you want to figure out how come I'm talking. You want me to give you some big *why*." Goode leaned in. "Maybe I want the world to see how the law got everything wrong about me for twenty years. How the law put me in prison over women I explained weren't mine, but it missed thirteen who were." He eyed her and Rainey. "Maybe it's just time I exposed your failures."

The air in the room felt heavy. Goode's weaselly use of the word "maybe" reinforced Caitlin's feeling that he was lying, and hiding something. She didn't react.

Rainey said, "And maybe we flew down here for the barbecue. But bring it. Happy to listen."

Goode hung his gaze on her. Then, theatrically, he opened the folder he'd brought, and took out a set of drawings. He spread them across the table like a poker hand.

They were portraits of women.

Caitlin and Rainey held still, deliberately eyeing the drawings with calm half interest. But Caitlin's heart began to thump.

The faces of the women in the drawings were vivid, haunted, full of longing and fear. Their eyes were sharp, shadowed, and incredibly lifelike. These weren't generic faces. These had personality. All of them had a sense of hurt or shame or want or foreboding.

She didn't recognize any of them. She would ask the unit's technical analyst to perform a reverse image search for every single one. But something ineffable, and dreadful, seemed to leach from the paper these were drawn on. As if Goode had captured, every time, a unique, intimate moment with these people. Something individual, honest, and now, she feared, gone.

Rainey straightened the drawings and perused them impassively, but Caitlin saw her fingers pressed sharply against the tabletop, nail beds white.

"Names, dates, locations," Rainey said.

"Don't know the names of all my beauties." Goode's voice brightened. "Plenty else though."

Caitlin spoke evenly. "Your beauties."

"They were angels who wanted to fly away home. Half dead already. I set 'em free."

She stayed deadpan. Rainey tapped the drawings. Goode leaned back.

"I want to write a book. You okay it, hook up a ghostwriter," he said.

Caitlin managed not to openly scoff. Did he actually think the FBI would act as his literary agents? He had to be putting them on. Or was he really that narcissistic?

"Do that, I'll lay it all out." He brushed his fingertips across the sketches. "These'll prove I ain't lying. You'll see."

Rainey said, "We can look into it. *If* you give us information we can corroborate. Otherwise, you're trying to sell fantasy, and nobody's going to buy that, including us."

He nodded at the drawings. "Corroborate them."

"These are stunning, but we need information to go with them. Names. Dates. Locations."

He raised his hands and tapped his chest. "But you got the source right here. I am the font of all information."

Self-aggrandizing and glib. Caitlin wanted to jerk his chain. On his right forearm was a striking black tattoo: an elaborate Gothic letter "L." She nodded at it.

"Is that information?" she said. "Is it one of your beauties?"

He didn't glance at it. "Yeah. Long gone, baby."

Caitlin's tone turned deliberately caustic. "Baby. Family?"

"Mine, I said."

Rainey said, "Killing something doesn't make it yours."

His eyes darkened. "Blood means mine."

Caitlin picked up the drawings. "Names, locations, dates."

Goode glared. Rainey adopted a jaunty tone. "You give, you get."

Caitlin set the drawings in front of him along with a Sharpie. After a long pause, Goode took it. He annotated various drawings. *Tiffani North Carolina 2005. Liv NYC 2008. Truck stop hooker Paducah Kentucky 2003.*

Caitlin took the Sharpie from him. "We'll get back to you."

"Do that." He turned to the door. "*Guard.*"

Then he leaned back in the chair and stared at Caitlin. "I'd love to draw you."

They walked out of the sally port behind a ringing buzzer, through a chain-link passage topped with razor wire, to the sunshine. With her Glock back on her hip, Caitlin felt more in control.

She kept herself chill until she and Rainey got in their rented car and drove away from the prison. Half a mile down the two-lane road, she rounded a bend and pulled into a turnout.

She killed the engine. "What in the fuck-stained hell?"

Rainey shook her head. "Subtle. Not."

"I've talked to some real shitheads in my life," Caitlin said. "And I don't just mean killers or horrible bosses, or my nasty aunt who told me my prom dress looked cheap. I've told assholes to screw off. Once, a tweaked-out wife beater bit me, and I *headbutted* the guy." She nodded back toward the prison. "But I've never met anything like *that*."

"That's it. Barf it all out." Rainey looked cool but was shaking her head. "We find out if his 'beauties' are real, or figments of his imagination."

"Why does he still insist that the four women he was convicted of killing weren't his victims? I mean, if he's now going to claim this bizarre kill count?"

"That's down the road," Rainey said.

"Right." Caitlin started the engine and pulled out. "First things first."

It didn't take long. Caitlin and Rainey phoned the police in Paducah, Kentucky. Within six hours, they had photos, an autopsy report, witnesses' and officers' statements, and had spoken to the supervising investigator and the county prosecutor. Paducah had a suspicious death on the books that matched—a Jane Doe found facedown in the mud along a creek leading to the Ohio River. She died in 2003. Her autopsy photo was a flattened, cold version of the drawing Efrem Judah Goode had nudged toward Caitlin. A bruise on her temple, caused by a blow with a closed fist, bore a cut from a class ring. Under high-resolution imaging, the cut matched the high school ring worn by Goode when he was arrested in Spring River.

"Kentucky murder's corroborated," Caitlin told Emmerich on the phone.

"Keep going."

He didn't seem surprised. But he had learned to plane his emotions to a flat, thin shine while on the job. Maybe off, too.

"Work with the Tennessee detectives to corroborate or eliminate the other claims."

"They're planning to issue a press release," Caitlin said. "These victims—if the others actually exist—might never have been identified, either. They may be listed as missing. If their bodies were exposed to the elements before they were found, the manner of death might be undetermined. The cops want to put out the drawings."

Emmerich paused. "It's a risk at this point."

"Because Goode could still be shining us on about these other killings. Yeah. He could have made these victims up out of whole cloth. We could play into his hands, look foolish, frighten the public, waste resources, upset a lot of people who have missing relatives."

"You'll make a good field manager one day, Hendrix."

She smiled. "The local investigators think it's time to make this public. The murders Goode claims he committed are at least a decade cold. This information might jog memories."

"You think the Bureau should signal boost?"

"I'm open to it," she said. "The information's going to go public within the day. It's our choice whether it stays on a local server or maybe gets national attention. I see the locals' reasoning. It's a solid call."

"Send me scans of the drawings," Emmerich said. "I'll talk to Media Affairs. If this is going to be out there, let's shape the information best we can and ask for the public's help."

4

Early evening light filtered through the curtains in the farmhouse. On the living room TV, a game show ended and the network news came on. The woman in the back bedroom put down her glue gun and set aside the scrapbook. 'Nuff was enough, for today. She smoothed her jeans as she eyed the photos in the album. Artwork was soothing to her—this kind, anyhow. The news music dwindled to the anchor's movie-star baritone. She stretched and headed up the hall. The old wood floor groaned beneath her feet.

She glanced at the television as she headed to the kitchen. She stared absently into the fridge, annoyed that there weren't any leftovers. Sighing, she poured herself a glass of water and stood at the window, squinting out at the dusty driveway, the distant barn, the heavy trees, and the cornfields. She caught a glimpse of her reflection in the window. Bedraggled. That was the word—she'd seen it in her crossword puzzle book last week. Dilapidated, like this shitty farmhouse. Country charm, my ass. A red rooster on the mailbox didn't make this place Field of Dreams. She poured the water out. Flat, warm, dull, full of nothing.

In the living room, the anchorman's voice took on a buzz-saw edge.

"Dramatic new claims today in the case of convicted serial killer Efrem Judah Goode . . ."

She spun toward the television.

". . . Authorities in Kentucky confirmed Goode's confession to a 2003 cold-case murder. This is only one of several slayings Goode has now claimed he committed over a twenty-year nationwide slaying spree."

Magnetized, she walked into the living room and stood before the television, scalp tingling. She saw what she'd been dreading. His picture appeared on the screen.

"*Goode, forty-five, was convicted last year of the Motel Mummy killings . . .*"

The photo was a harsh mug shot that highlighted dark circles beneath his eyes, made him look heavy and tired and beaten. But she knew he wasn't. She knew.

A contact email replaced Goode's photo on the screen—an FBI tip line. Then a series of sketches. Women Goode said he'd ended. Five of them. One was a strung-out teen with goth-black hair and burning eyes.

The woman pressed a fist to her forehead. "Christ have mercy."

In New York City, an eighteen-year-old girl hunched over her phone, reading the press release. Traffic on the street outside McCarren Park was muffled by the spring trees, but she heard music from car stereos, footfalls of a big group on the track, the North Brooklyn Runners trying to sweat themselves to death training for the next half marathon. Mothers with kids in strollers lolled past. Finch Winter dropped onto a park bench and kept reading.

She had been walking home from her after-school job at the coffeehouse, scrolling social, when she saw the headline. She wanted to get to the apartment—she had an hour of homework at least. Which she wanted to finish so she could play some *Zelda* before her mom got home from work. But she sat on the bench, riveted by the information on her phone screen.

CONFESSIONS OF A KILLER
Convicted murderer Efrem Judah Goode has now claimed responsibility for thirteen additional slayings.

Finch's heart beat against her ribs. The article was crammed with photos of the killer. Mug shots. High school yearbook pics. The newest shot was his intake photo at the Tennessee prison where he was now proclaiming himself a major-league mass murderer.

Bragging his way into the spotlight like some reality TV star. It was creepy disgusting. A snarl hovered in the back of her throat. But what caused her heart to thud were the drawings.

Unmatched confession. "Tiffani," North Carolina, 2005.

Unmatched confession. "Liv," New York City, 2008.

New York. She pored over that one. Goth chick, black lipstick, X-ray eyes. Finch felt a flicker but suppressed it. She always felt a flicker when looking at strangers' photos or at people on the street. Hope, hunger—she knew that it was irrational, but she couldn't extinguish it. She wondered who in the city she might be related to.

Finch had only the barest memory of her birth mother. Three years old. A freezing night, a kiss on her cheek, a feeling of dread.

An adoptee, Finch had always feared that something bad had happened to her mom. She zoomed in on Goode's eerie drawings. The next one was also from New York.

Possible match to confession. Jane Doe, Brooklyn 2008.

Her gut knotted.

Goode says he encountered a white female in a transient area of Brooklyn, New York City, in the winter of 2008. He recalls it as a snowy night. He describes the woman as twenty to twenty-one years old, 5'1"–5'2", and approximately 100 pounds. Goode "hung with her" for approximately a week. He alleges that he shoplifted with the woman and that she sold the merchandise to buy drugs. He also claims that they had sex recurrently and that he paid her in drugs as well.

Goode alleges that he took the woman to a pier in a run-down industrial zone along the East River, where he tied her up and kicked her into the water.

Below the text was a drawing of the woman. Pale, fragile, with devilment in her eyes, and maybe hunger—for food or love or meth. Silky blond hair tied up in a twist on top of her head, a nose ring. Something cagey and desperate, but tough.

Finch had always thought her birth mom must have been tough.

The memory hit her again. The cold kiss on her cheek on a freezing night. The sense of foreboding.

Goode's description included a winter's night. Said he'd hung with the woman for days before he killed her. That would have been long enough for him to know she had a kid. Long enough to give that kid a feeling of dread.

Finch had been adopted in 2008. She ran her thumb across the drawing on her screen. Could this portrait show her mother's face?

She clicked the link to the tip line and started typing.

Back at her desk at Quantico, Caitlin read tip-line messages from people whose loved ones had been missing for years. Her in-box spilled over with hope, desperation, and pleas for help from families across the country who were racked with anguish. She could read only a few at a time before needing to step away and breathe.

Whether or not Goode was responsible for the thirteen deaths he claimed, he had already caused wounds to tear wide open. He had conjured a vast upwelling of unresolved grief.

Outside the windows, Caitlin took in the view of the FBI lab, the vast grounds of the FBI Training Academy, and the green Virginia woods. She gave herself a minute, then turned back to her desk.

Pinned above the desktop was a composite sketch. White male, late twenties, five ten to six feet tall. The FBI's sketch artist had captured his cold menace and dismissive stare. He remained at large. He was the reason she could never allow herself to break down like an overworked machine.

The Ghost.

He was the accomplice of the serial killer known as the Prophet. He had nailed Caitlin's hand to a wooden beam with a nail gun, lured Sean to his near death, and slunk away, leaving Caitlin's father to face the Prophet alone. She and Sean suspected that he was behind the string of bombings that had culminated in the fatal explosion at Temescal Hospital.

She'd seen him once, face-to-face, in a California biker bar. Caitlin could still hear his voice on the phone the day he called her here at Quantico. The day he sent her black lilies. Rasping as if he'd been punched in the throat. Promising that she couldn't live forever, couldn't escape him forever. That he'd find her.

She took him at his word.

She turned back to her computer screen and faced the latest tips—wrenching pleas—from families fearful that one of their own had fallen prey to Efrem Judah Goode. The first came from Kansas.

Subject: My cousin could be Goode murder victim.

The writer, a Topeka woman, said that her teenage cousin had fallen off the radar in 2007 when she took off for New York City. Looking at the timeline, Caitlin saw that story fit with Goode's travel history. The missing teen's name was Rhiannon Griffith. Photos showed a strawberry-blond girl, scrappy, about seventeen, baby fat in her cheeks, wearing a rebellious expression. The possibility that she was one of Goode's victims was slim but greater than zero. Caitlin read between the lines in the email, filling in fifteen years of not knowing, of sadness, of the horror that families of the missing slept with, and woke with, every day.

Just one, she thought. *Let just one of these lost lights be found.*

She forwarded the information to the NYPD.

The next confirmation came a day later. A Maryland cold-case unit matched Goode's confession to an unsolved homicide.

The next week, a North Carolina sheriff tied unidentified remains to one of Goode's drawings and matched Goode's DNA to the suspect's.

Goode wasn't lying. He had left a trail of murder across the country.

In Semora, North Carolina, the late afternoon sun gilded the treetops. The town was barely a wide spot in piney woods north of Hyco Lake, near the Virginia border. Clapboard houses were surrounded by red azalea bushes. Flying bugs jittered in the spring heat. At a bait shop, the air conditioning blew hard.

A GMC Yukon with tinted windows turned off the state highway at a leisurely roll and cruised past the bait shop. ICE BEER WORMS, the sign outside promised. Disgusting but sensible. Fishing was this town's bread and butter. In the distance, the green countryside dipped toward the lake.

The bait shop parking lot was empty. Heat writhed from the asphalt. Inside the shop, a bored cashier leaned against the counter, texting. Even from the road, her tattoos were visible. Modern America. Youth today. The driver snickered. The Yukon rolled on.

When night fell, the cashier locked up. Hoisting a purse over her shoulder, she headed around the side of the building toward her car, lighting a cigarette as she walked. Her shorts revealed a tattoo that hadn't been visible when she was behind the counter: a red scorpion just above the low-cut waistline. Claws up, stinger poised.

She was twenty feet from her car when she spotted the hulking Yukon parked beside the dumpster. She slowed, checking to see if anybody was at the wheel.

From behind her came a voice. "Look at you."

She turned. She was lightning fast, streetwise, cigarette coming up, ready to flick it in self-defense. Her eyes went wide.

A stun baton jabbed her in the chest.

5

The morning dawned cool, cloudless, and full of promise. Caitlin was early to the unit's team meeting. This was a regular daily kickoff, where Emmerich gauged the temperature of everyone's cases and caseloads, and unit members shared information, consulted, and brainstormed. She sat down at the gleaming conference table, files in front of her, laptop open, phone pinging, coffee in her left hand.

The BAU didn't initiate homicide investigations. They weren't street cops. The unit was a department of the FBI's National Center for the Analysis of Violent Crime, which was a branch of the Critical Incident Response Group. Caitlin was one of eight agents and analysts working in BAU-4, Crimes against Adults. They provided investigative support for unusual or repetitive violent crimes—sometimes cases that had gone long unsolved, other times cases that erupted with sudden urgency. That meant the unit responded to requests for assistance from law enforcement, prosecutors, US Attorneys' offices, and FBI divisions and field offices nationwide. As the daughter of a homicide detective, Caitlin found fulfillment in that.

Rainey arrived, sleek and chic, with her braids spun into a high chignon. She put a slide up on the conference room's flat-screen TV: an update on Efrem Judah Goode. Two more cases had gone from *Unconfirmed* to *Confession matched to Jane Doe*.

Agents Frank Horner and Noriko Sato came in, followed closely by Emmerich. He scrutinized the screen.

"Pennsylvania, 2005, and Maryland, 2006," he said.

Horner eyed the data. "Goode's the real deal, huh?"

Rainey, typing on her laptop, said, "Real as the devil and a better liar."

"And these confessions were all spontaneously offered? Self-generated?"

Emmerich sat down. "He wasn't offered anything to begin talking postconviction, no."

"Out of the blue. Weird."

Weird fucking shit, Caitlin thought. *WFS*. But she said, "Something sparked it. Spontaneous mental combustion—I mean, decompensation? I doubt it. He has reasons."

Technical analyst Nicholas Keyes arrived, tossing and catching a baseball with his right hand. He nodded a greeting.

Toying with her pen, Caitlin said, "Four of the killings Goode's claimed have now been confirmed. None have yet been disproven. The drawings . . . they're incredibly close matches to photos of the victims. It's eerie, frankly. Each time a family member has spoken to us, they say, 'The portrait gave me chills.' Or, 'It made me burst into tears.'"

Emmerich took his seat. "I sense a *but*."

She paused. Emmerich was good. Good at reading everyone—unsubs, agents, his daughters. It could be spooky and sometimes infuriating. Caitlin didn't like being read.

She straightened. "But I can't shake the feeling that Goode wants more than a book deal and the fame that would follow. Rainey and I have discussed this."

Rainey closed her laptop. "He has to know that his request is preposterous. He's not going to get money out of anybody while he's in prison. Maybe he's parlaying for true-crime TV fame, but getting a book deal? Pie in the sky."

"And that's not all," Caitlin said. "He's a stone killer. And he's working us."

Sato said, "He's a psychopath. He wants manipulation, domination, and control."

Across the table, Keyes looked thoughtful. "Maybe . . ."

He tilted his head. Keyes was the youngest member of the unit, not yet thirty. He was tall and gangly, especially in his skinny black jeans and slim-fitting H&M dress shirt. His dark hair poodled over his forehead. His glasses, black horn-rims, gave him a hipster gravitas. He had a PhD in mathematics from Caltech and had worked for NASA's Jet Propulsion Laboratory before jumping tracks and joining the FBI. He was fidgety and brilliant, and his mind worked on fractal planes that Caitlin could glimpse only tangentially. She loved him to bits.

"Maybe Goode wants to sow chaos," he said.

Caitlin nodded. "Traditional psychopath's goal."

"He could be claiming an exaggerated kill count, hoping law enforcement will fall for it, like Henry Lee Lucas did."

Emmerich thought about that. "Giving us legitimate cases, getting us to buy in, before he starts claiming every unsolved case east of the Mississippi?"

After being convicted of murder in Texas in the 1980s, Henry Lee Lucas confessed to dozens more killings across the country. Then hundreds. Detectives flocked to Huntsville to interview him. With great fanfare, police departments closed homicides that had been on their books for years. Lucas gained fame as the most prolific murderer in American history, extolled—with disgust and delicious horror—as the all-time champion killer, Jack the Ripper on 'roids.

But it wasn't true. Lucas invented most of his confessions. In return, he gained not just infamy but also a chance to leave prison to visit crime scenes in several states. In the end, most of the six-hundred-some cases that had been declared solved had to be reopened, to the humiliation of police departments across the nation.

Investigative techniques had improved since then. In Lucas's case, numerous officers drove him slowly past crime scenes, almost vibrating with eagerness for him to tell them that yes, *this* was where he'd dumped a body. Which, inevitably, he did. They learned the hard way that giving away too much information to a suspect always bit them in the ass.

When asked why he did it, Lucas said he wanted to show everyone how stupid the cops were.

Caitlin said, "If he's pulling a more sophisticated play than Lucas— next-gen trickery—we should keep an ear out. It's possible. But that doesn't negate the fact that he has given up four confirmed murders. For what?"

"A transfer?" Keyes said. "To a prison with a view, maybe of the beach?"

"Just giving us those bodies without first getting a deal? It doesn't track," she said.

"What, then?"

"When Rainey and I were across from him, he thought he was controlling the interview. Clearly."

Rainey nodded. "His ego was so overweening there was barely any space in the room for the rest of us."

Horner shook his head. He was in his early forties, a former SEC football player now fighting mightily to keep to his playing weight. "It amazes me that a killer whose future relies on federal agents will behave like he's the king of the Holy Roman Empire and you're supplicants."

"If we wanted to deal with the meek, we should be working with puppies," Caitlin said. "For most of the interview, he thought he had the upper hand. And we let him think so to keep him talking, get his guard down, let him hook himself. But one thing threw him off." She looked around the table. "Mentioning family."

"Absolutely," Rainey said.

"It spurred an unfiltered reaction. He stated, 'Blood means mine.'"

"What was he implying?" Keyes said. "Does 'blood' mean death? DNA?"

Caitlin said, "He may think spilling blood gives him ownership. He considers victims *his*. Or he could be talking about blood relations." She glanced at the file folders on the table in front of her. "Though as far as we know, he has no surviving family."

"Bottom line?" Rainey said. "You bleed for me, you're my family."

"I hear you," Sato said. A former paramedic, she knew about blood.

Keyes had put down the baseball and was drumming with his thumbs on the tabletop. "I want to run Goode through SKS."

Emmerich said, "Definitely."

SKS was Keyes's computer program that looked for patterns in homicides. It stood for Serial Killer Software—a highly unofficial name. The software analyzed the locations and methods of thousands of murders and pinpointed unusual clusters above what was "normal" for an area. It could detect the presence of an active serial killer.

"I'm going to run Goode's life through the algorithm," Keyes said. "His confessions, his employment history, criminal history, travel records. Scour death records in every town where he's lived. We'll see."

"Good," Caitlin said. "Because there's too much that's going on under the surface, and right now we're not seeing it clearly—or at all."

Dillsboro, North Carolina, felt like God's playroom to Darryl Cullen. Near the foothills of the Great Smoky Mountains, it had that clean blue country sky overhead. But what made the place wonderful was the embracing bend in the Tuckasegee River where Cullen loved to fly-fish. When he arrived from Charlotte on Saturday morning, the light was popping from the surface of the water. It was early. He hoisted his gear and hiked upstream past a train trestle.

The river sparkled. *Come to Papa*, Cullen thought, and waded in.

Twenty minutes later, with the sun warming his back, he flicked his line toward a dark pool where willows arched over the bank. Within a couple of seconds, he felt the tug on his line.

Gotcha. He readied for the game.

But the line didn't move. Didn't swivel or head for deeper waters. He waded around willow branches that draped the surface.

He stumbled back and dropped the rod. "*Lord on high.*"

In the shallows past the willow, Cullen's hook was embedded in a woman's shirt. A woman whose body bobbed against a gravel bank, face-down.

"Almighty *shit*," Cullen shouted.

The wind shifted, the water lapped, and the smell hit him. His mind seemed to dissolve. He knew she was dead. Her skin was gray; the shirt was a tight T, swollen, her shorts digging into her lower back. And what he saw—all he would see for days, for nights—was the tattoo, the scorpion on her back, claws raised, stinger up, looking like it was begging for release.

The county sheriff stood on the riverbank while uniformed officers scoured the woods for evidence. A photographer snapped shots of the woman in the water. The coroner, decked head to foot in a white coverall, crouched and examined the body in place. Nearby, the fisherman who had hooked her leaned against the trunk of a patrol car, as pale as a trout's belly.

The coroner, heavyset and ruddy, splashed up the bank. "Can't tell yet what caused her death. She could have drowned. Autopsy will tell us whether she has water in her lungs." His face was drawn.

"But?" the sheriff said.

"But she has a depressed skull fracture." He inhaled. "And electrical burns."

"Lord. What kind?"

The coroner made a circle with his thumb and forefinger. "Impressions on her skin—shoulder, midback—show the impression of an object with dual prongs. I'd say she was hit multiple times with a stun baton."

"She was tortured?"

"Those devices aren't law enforcement issue." He pulled off his gloves. "Though with the skull fracture, she might have been unconscious when she went into the water." He glanced back at the body. "Would have been a blessing."

The sheriff shifted, his utility belt groaning. A wormy sensation crawled beneath his skin. "No ID?"

The coroner shook his head. "Her tattoos might help us."

From the sheriff's cruiser, the radio crackled. He trudged over and grabbed the transmitter. "What's up?"

The dispatcher said, "Putting you through to the office." A moment later, the sheriff's assistant came on. "Checked missing-persons reports. There's one out on a woman from Semora."

"Send it," the sheriff said. A moment later, the report appeared on his computer screen.

A driver's license photo showed the woman. Amber Roark, forty. She was skinny and tired looking. She worked at a bait shop in Semora, a tiny burg a couple of hundred miles east. She'd last been seen at the shop a little over twenty-four hours earlier. The report listed identifying marks as multiple tattoos, including a scorpion.

The sheriff walked back to the water's edge. The coroner's team lifted the body from the shallows onto a gurney. When they turned the body faceup, the sheriff kept still. He'd been at this job twenty years and had watched other corpses pulled from this river. He knew what he was going to see. Still, it made him ache. Her face was barely recognizable, but he would have bet money that it was the missing cashier.

But that wasn't what had the sheriff feeling nauseated and uneasy. What was tipping him off balance was his disturbing sense of déjà vu.

He'd been here before.

Several hundred miles northeast, the Yukon with the tinted windows rolled through green countryside near Shenandoah National Park. Plenty of gas, cruise control pegged at the speed limit, music on the stereo. Hot coffee in the cup holder. Roll of duct tape on the back seat.

A perfect day. Putting the Tuckasegee River far below the horizon in the rearview mirror.

The driver crumpled the Post-it note with "SEMORA, NC" written on it, threw it out the window, then punched a new set of coordinates into the GPS.

6

Slinging her computer bag over her shoulder Monday evening, Caitlin waved good night to Rainey and Sato. Beyond the windows, a glorious sun burnished the lawn and treetops. She was eager to get home and go for a run. But as she stepped into the elevator, Keyes called to her.

"Caitlin. Hold up."

She stopped the door as it slid shut. When it opened again, Keyes was standing outside, looking ready to catch fire.

"You have to see this," he said.

She stepped out. "What?"

He rushed toward his office, brushing his hair from his eyes, urging her to keep up.

"SKS," he said.

Serial Killer Software. She jogged after him. "Keyes."

"It found murder spikes that match Goode's travel and arrest history." He rounded a corner and unlocked his office door. "But there's more."

Caitlin followed him in. His office wasn't exactly a lair, more an electronics closet. Multiple computers, some air-gapped. His encryption was above and beyond. And because he had clearance to access certain classified databases, he was the only member of the unit besides Emmerich who rated an office with a door that locked. Caitlin might have envied him, but the cave lacked a window. His desk was an inch deep in printouts, his monitor throbbing with graphics in sharp-etched primary colors. On a shelf in the corner were framed photos of his parents, his boyfriend, and Pluto—the dwarf planet, not the Disney character.

"Dr. Keyes," Caitlin said. "What's the buzz?"

He dropped into his desk chair and spun to face her. "There's a second spike—*now*."

"A second spike. In what—deaths?"

"Yes. Places where Goode killed years ago are seeing repeat homicides." It stopped her cold. "You're positive."

"Kentucky. North Carolina. Maryland." Turning back to the monitor, he brought up a news story. *Body of Woman Discovered in Williamsport.*

"Maryland, a creek leading to the Potomac," he said.

On-screen were photos taken from a bridge overlooking a crime scene. *Homicide Suspected in Woman's Death.*

Caitlin scanned the story, sensing something off. The look of the deputies' uniforms, maybe. No—the age of the cars. She checked the dateline. July 2006.

Keyes clicked to a fresh headline. "*This* is today's paper. Same vantage, same creek, some of the same officers searching the weeds. It's a total repeat." His eyes were wide. "There's a copycat."

Williamsport, Maryland, 2006

The air conditioning blasted Efrem Judah Goode when he came through the automatic doors into the grocery store. The summer sun was broiling. He took off his sweat-stained Cowboys cap, wiped his brow with the back of his forearm, and walked directly to the rear of the store, the refrigerator units. Not actually wanting to buy a gallon of milk. But he opened the fridge door and stood in front of it for a tidy minute, basking in the flow of chilled air.

A young woman swanned past him down the aisle. He didn't bother pretending not to look. Those hips—darlin', did they sway. As if pulled by gravity, he followed her. Watching, breathing, *scenting* her. Boy, howdy.

The woman had a flaming head of hair, a huge dollop of it, sprayed and bouncing. Like an Olympic torch. She wore skintight jeans and a skimpy halter top. Goode stayed twenty feet behind her, hands empty. Squeezing and clenching his fists, pumping blood to his arms.

Without even slowing, the woman slipped a bottle of Southern Comfort from the shelf into her roomy shoulder bag. She rounded the corner to the meat aisle. Two seconds later, a T-bone steak went into her purse as well.

Goode smiled admiringly.

At checkout, he let another customer get between them. The gal sashayed out with a pack of gum and a *People* magazine. Goode bought Tic Tacs with a sweaty, wadded bill.

Outside, he sank back into the heat, feeling it as a goad now. The woman, the torch, the *goddamned smell of her, Christ on a pogo stick*, cut through the oven-hot air in a straight line—a hip-swinging, Lord-did-she-want-it beeline—toward a gold 1982 Cadillac Coupe de Ville.

Dirty gold, Goode thought. *Like her.*

She took a set of keys from that bottomless mystery purse and twirled them on her fingers. He could hear her humming. Something distant, a song. Women singing—that was ungodly, his grandmother would have said. Humming. Wasn't she wicked.

She didn't even turn as he approached.

7

C aitlin and Keyes found Emmerich turning out his office lights.

"Something?" he said evenly. Then his gaze sharpened. "It's Goode, isn't it?"

"More than," Caitlin said.

Emmerich flipped the lights back on. Keyes opened his laptop and explained what the SKS program had discovered: new murders that duplicated Goode's confessions.

Emmerich listened, scanning the news stories and police reports Keyes queued up. SKS had identified a clear pattern: women were being slain and dumped in running water, all within a hundred yards of where Goode had discarded his victims.

"Things have changed," Caitlin said. "This is no longer an assessment of Goode's claims. It's a hot case."

Emmerich glanced out the window. Sunset was coming on.

"We're losing the light. Caitlin, call the detectives running the new Maryland case. I think it'll be the Washington County sheriff. Williamsport is less than a two-hour drive from here. Ask if they'll meet us first thing in the morning."

They got there at 8:00 a.m. The breezy morning promised heat to come. The crime scene echoed many of Goode's dump sites. Off-ramps, trash, a graffiti-marred bridge. A storm drain.

A Washington County Sheriff's Office detective met them, sipping coffee with an unsettled expression. "We obtained identification on the victim while you were on the way." He looked at his phone. "Kimmie Koestler, thirty-seven, of Glasgow, Kentucky."

"Not local," Caitlin said.

He shook his head. "She dropped her son off at day care on her way to work. Maid at a motel. She never clocked in."

He led Caitlin and Emmerich through weeds to a muddy outflow channel from the storm drain. Above them, an overpass rang with freeway traffic.

"Teenagers found her," the detective said. "They probably came down here to smoke weed. Scared them so bad they were still shaking when the state troopers pulled up."

He handed Emmerich eight-by-ten crime scene photos. Emmerich examined each one and handed them to Caitlin. Her jaw tightened. The photos showed a woman in her midthirties, white, faceup at the edge of the storm drain. Her hair and clothing were caked with mud. Head downstream, arms spread wide. A posture of crucifixion.

Emmerich perused the creek. "The killer placed her body intentionally. After dragging her through the mud. Possibly to eliminate forensic evidence. Certainly as a message."

Caitlin spoke softly. "Posing the body may or may not be religiously symbolic, but it's deliberately evocative. Outstretched arms—it's like a performer basking in applause. The killer meant to shock. They're saying, 'Take a look at *this*.'"

She eyed dozens of messy footprints in the cakey mud. "Any way to single out the killer's?"

The detective shook his head. "The teens approached and checked her for a pulse, unfortunately. Contaminated the scene. Stupid, brave kids."

"How long do you think she was here before they found her?"

"Less than a day."

Caitlin glanced over the now empty scene. The place where the body had lain still bore a negative impression where the mud was smoothed out. A cold void seemed to attenuate the light in the sky.

Death. Disdain. Degradation. Treating human beings like filth.

Mimicking Efrem Judah Goode.

She had sat two feet from the man. She'd cajoled and listened to him. His utter lack of connection, his contempt, his seeming amusement at his victims' suffering and death had left her feeling as if she'd climbed from a beast's jaws. Now this. A woman taken. A little boy left motherless. For what? As an homage? Performance art? As a game?

A spectral energy seemed to seep through her. A negative force, one that wanted to drain light from anyone who attended the scene and leave chaos in its place.

That was an effect the copycat sought to evoke.

Remember that. Caitlin refocused. Scanning the site, she tried to take in not just the fine details of the scene, but the overall aura. The trees and weeds were dense, thick with trash. The killer could easily have parked and dragged or carried the body down here without being seen from the freeway.

The morning sun heated her back. "Tire tracks or trace found between here and the road?"

"Nothing worthwhile."

"Were you here in 2006, when Goode's victim was found?"

The detective nodded. "Trees and brush were thinner." He turned. "Less rust on that chain-link fence above the storm drain. More graffiti. And we'd had lots of rain. The first body was covered with silt and debris."

Emmerich said, "Was the original victim found in the same position as this one?"

"Looked like she'd been dragged and dropped into the outflow channel. There wasn't the same . . . care."

Caitlin and Emmerich exchanged a glance.

The detective gave a final look around, as though wanting to get away from this haunted location. Emmerich nodded, and they climbed the bank back to their cars.

Traffic rushed past on the overpass. Emmerich said, "How long after Ms. Koestler went missing was her body discovered?"

"Just over twenty-four hours."

The woman found in the Tuckasegee River in North Carolina had also been missing for twenty-four hours before turning up dead.

"MO," Emmerich said to Caitlin.

"Yeah." She turned to the detective. "The copycat's victims have all been missing for twenty-four hours before death. That's unique to the new murders."

"Goode didn't do that?" the detective said.

Emmerich shook his head. "He sometimes hooked up with a woman and got rid of her within the span of an evening. Other times, he went on long benders with victims, spending a week or two with them—some sort of fling—before killing them. None of his victims were taken and held like Ms. Koestler before being murdered."

"What's this killer doing, then?"

"That's what we can analyze, if you'll let us," Emmerich said.

"Analyze away. Please."

The detective's phone rang. He answered, talked, and ended the call.

"Medical examiner," he said. "Cause of death was ligature strangulation."

Emmerich's gaze didn't shift so much as harden. "That's more personal than blunt-force trauma. It requires more discipline and a longer time in close—sometimes nearly intimate—proximity to the victim. Were there other injuries?"

"Electrical burns. Discrete, about the size of a half-dollar, on her abdomen and thighs."

"Stun baton," Emmerich said.

"Yes."

Caitlin stared down the bank at the brush and weeds of Kimmie Koestler's cruel dumping ground. "The unsub's holding on to victims for some reason. Torture? Submission?"

Despite the sunshine, a cold thread dragged across her skin. She took a second and looked at Emmerich. "This killer works on a countdown."

Kentucky, North Carolina, Maryland.

"The killer's on the move, and I can guess where," she said. "Goode says he dumped bodies in the East River. One from Manhattan, the other in Brooklyn."

As they headed for the car, Emmerich got out his phone and called the NYPD.

8

In a sleeping town along the Monongahela River, deep in the coal-creviced hills of western Pennsylvania, the Yukon cruised a snaking two-lane road. Headlights off. No streetlights on this country stretch, asphalt a dark ribbon, stars visible then swallowed by trees reaching overhead. Half a mile outside what passed for the town of Weatherby, the Yukon rolled by an isolated house. Not really set back from the road, but dark, with a driveway along the side that led to a detached garage around the back. The detached garage was a good sign. It meant privacy. Under a sliver of moon, under a curl of breeze, it became apparent that the porch of the house was decorated with wind chimes and a "Coexist" flag. Looked like a woman's crib.

A lone woman.

Turning into the driveway—rolling dark and low, away from the street—the driver parked outside the garage. Exiting softly, gently shutting the Yukon's door. Grass along the driveway meant a quiet trek to the back door. Flimsy, with panels of glass in a wood frame. Clearly a kitchen door. Simple to hammer out one of the small panes, reach through, and unlock it.

The old linoleum on the floor was a little creaky, a little sticky. A cat's metal food dish reflected the moonlight, but pussy wasn't anywhere to be seen. Probably in bed with Mommy. The driver pulled a chair from the table, sat, and waited.

It took ninety seconds. Deeper in the house, a hall light clicked on. A shadow rose, and the homeowner appeared in the kitchen doorway.

Coming to investigate the sound of shattering glass, no doubt. She stepped into the kitchen and flipped the light switch.

She gasped and stumbled back—a woman nearing the bend toward forty, in men's boxers and a camisole, sleep fleeing from her face.

One more step back. The driver stood and kicked the chair away. "Nope."

The woman froze, confronting the barrel of the gun aimed at her head.

Her face pale, her eyes watery, blinking. She grabbed the door frame to steady herself, or to keep her feet from bolting.

"Just hold still," the driver said.

The woman began wheezing, breathing like a racehorse who had been run into the ground. Her knees sagged. She ran her gaze over the gun barrel. Over the driver's eyes and tattooed arms. She stiffened.

No mask, nothing covering the ink.

No fear of being identified.

The woman plainly knew what that implied. The driver smiled. "Like what you see?"

"I hit a silent alarm," the woman said. "The cops are coming."

"Good. They can start the clock."

The driver shoved her out the door.

It was a flawless spring morning—light winds, soft blue skies, a ferry chugging up the East River past Williamsburg, toward the Manhattan ferry port. The pedestrian path was empty aside from the young man walking his dog. He let her off the leash to run, just briefly.

Thirty seconds later, as he scrolled on his phone, Bodhi began barking. The dog stood at the edge of an old pier, hackles up, barking at the water. The young man's ordinary day ended.

The body was jammed against the rotting pier pilings, bobbing up and down in the ferry's wake, bound tightly, hand and foot, with duct tape.

Caitlin got the call before breakfast, phone ringing as she stood in the kitchen with her hair wrapped in a towel turban from the shower, pouring herself a cup of coffee. Sadie sat at the kitchen island, nibbling toast and video-chatting with her mom. Caitlin walked past, waving at Michele, who was dressed in scrubs and climbing into her car. Michele flashed a peace sign.

Caitlin grabbed her phone. *EMMERICH.*

"Chief," she said.

"There's been another killing. New York."

The victim had disappeared from her Pennsylvania home after hitting a panic alarm, just over twenty-four hours before her body was discovered in the East River.

"Same MO?" Caitlin said.

Sean came in, wearing a button-down shirt and jeans, credentials clipped to his belt, duty weapon holstered. He was pulling on a sport coat. Catching Caitlin's expression, he raised an eyebrow.

"Multiple electrical burns," Emmerich said. "River dumping. There's no question this was prompted by Goode's claim that he killed a woman in Brooklyn."

"You want me to go?"

"ASAP. I've already spoken to the NYPD."

Caitlin kissed Sean goodbye, hugged Sadie, and caught the next flight to New York.

Forty miles north of New York City, the Yukon rolled along the old highway that skimmed the bluffs above the Hudson River. Sunlight poked through the leaves of the trees. It was a lazy spring morning, a good time to listen to talk radio and laugh inwardly at the barking Chihuahuas who presented themselves to the world as public intellectuals. The Yukon had half a tank of gas—plenty to make it the rest of the way without stopping. It was sparkling clean, had been since New Jersey, when a car Wash-N-Vac had conveniently presented itself—out of the way, no cameras, lots of other cars, nobody paying any attention to one more driver prepping their vehicle for a road trip.

Everything taken care of. No leftovers, no stale smells, no whiff of fear or blood or death. Just a refreshing scent of Evergreen from the Wash-N-Vac's selection of car deodorizers. Evergreen, the scent of every childhood road trip. The sunlight flashed off the spotless hood of the Yukon. Sparkle, sparkle, lovely SUV.

Rounding a slow curve, the wide blue expanse of the river peeped into view. What a glorious day. On a day like this, when the mission was going flawlessly, anything was possible. Turning down the yapping Chihuahuas on the radio, the driver powered up a cell phone, hit speed dial, and spoke with easy cheer.

"Hi, Mom."

9

It was midafternoon when Caitlin arrived at the Brooklyn waterfront. She parked the SUV she'd rented at LaGuardia and stepped into the hazy sunshine.

She'd been to New York only twice, never for work. The city felt overpowering. A roiling, constantly self-inventing beast. New York was America's ur-city, an exponentially more intense version of anywhere else. The energy, the excitement, the sheer audacity of the city riled her up, imbued her with energy. She would need that energy to analyze the crime scene.

She pulled on her jacket and walked toward the East River. The water glittered, slate blue. Across the river, Manhattan skyscrapers were back-lit by the sun. The Freedom Tower rose huge and imposing, topped by its immense spire. As she neared the river, the traffic noise reduced to a background rush. She could feel a bare breeze, smell the water and hear it lap against the pier pilings.

Before driving here, she had stopped by Federal Plaza in Manhattan, headquarters of the FBI's New York Field Division, to genuflect and offer *oohs* at the stunning view of Midtown skyscrapers before skipping the gift shop. She had also visited the Ninetieth Precinct of the NYPD, a squat white brick building on a busy corner. There, at the Brooklyn North Homicide Squad, she'd met the detective assigned to the murder case.

Greg Tashjian was a seasoned investigator with a low-key manner, who wore a tailored suit and a trilby with a red feather in the band. He wasn't about to let Caitlin interfere in his case. He barely let her approach the homicide squad room, a cramped corner packed with computers, file cabinets, a TV playing Fox News, and men smelling of aftershave and gritty enthusiasm. But his ears pricked up when she laid out what Keyes's SKS program had found. Seeing that the information put this killing in context, Tashjian offered to share information.

"In exchange for everything you find," he said. "And when you profile this killer, I get it as soon as the words come out of your mouth."

The crime scene tape had already come down. Caitlin walked along the edge of the pier.

The latest victim, Chely Ann McKee, had been found near the spot where an unidentified woman washed up in 2008, also wrapped in duct tape. That unidentified woman's autopsy photo was an eerie match to Goode's drawing labeled *Jane Doe, Brooklyn 2008*.

Caitlin compared old and new crime scene photos.

The location had been gentrified. The waterfront pedestrian path was landscaped. Warehouses had been joined by an auto repair shop and co-working spaces. Bus tours now cruised by to view graffiti that featured rainbows and uplift instead of broken hearts and gang tags. Blue glass condos had gone up. She had passed a high school on her way here, just letting out, across from a leafy park. She absorbed the atmosphere, then walked to the spot where the victim's body had been pulled from the water.

Chely Ann McKee had been transported here from the small town of Weatherby, Pennsylvania. She suffered multiple jolts from a stun baton.

Why? To subdue her? To force information from her? For sadistic gratification?

Caitlin turned in a slow circle. How did the killer dump the body here without being seen? It was a lower-rent industrial corner, but she saw security cameras on several buildings. She knew that Detective Tashjian was putting in shoe leather, gathering CCTV footage. But the body had been dumped sometime within an eight-hour window. So far, they had nothing. They needed something. From Brooklyn streets, from a Manhattan camera a hundred yards across the water, maybe showing a vehicle driving slowly along the waterfront and stopping here . . .

Caitlin could hope. She couldn't imagine that killer had hauled the victim across town thrown over one shoulder in a firefighter's carry or wrapped up in a blanket and wheeled to the pier on a dolly. Or brought downriver on a speedboat.

Stop, she told herself. Don't speculate. She was here to analyze the crime scene and draw inferences about the unsub's behavior.

But she had a cop's instincts, honed during her years with the Alameda Sheriff's Department before Emmerich recruited her to the FBI. Joining the BAU had meant studying forensics and victimology and learning to interpret crime scene evidence to construct a profile of the perpetrator. It was her job to uncover how an unsub thought. Everything at a crime scene told a story. Even the choice of location revealed something about the offender.

This location told her the killer was determined and willing to risk discovery in order to leave the body in a place that held special significance. Whether it held significance as fantasy, as fetish, or as a message was a question she had to answer.

When she turned from the water, she saw the girl.

Tucked in the shade by the corner of a warehouse was a youngster in red jeans and a black Kangol cap.

For a second, the girl shrank back. Then, like a bobcat assessing an open space, she stepped into the sunlight.

She wasn't as young as Caitlin had first thought. Not a tween, but a high schooler. She was simply petite. Her strawberry-blond hair flowed from under the Kangol cap in messy curls. She had a backpack slung across one shoulder and wore a *Mandalorian* T-shirt. Caitlin got the sense that she hadn't just wandered by the scene.

Caitlin gave her a long look, waiting to see what she might do, giving her an opening. The girl didn't move. Caitlin turned back to the water.

"Excuse me?"

The voice was light. When Caitlin turned back around, the girl had jammed her hands in the back pockets of her red jeans and stuck one hip out. She was blinking rapidly. Her attempt to look cool and disinterested was failing miserably. The kid was nervous.

Caitlin gave her a break. "Hello."

She couldn't be more than five feet two. She hupped a breath. Caitlin guessed that approaching an FBI agent wasn't something this kid had ever done. She stepped nearer. Her fingernails were painted midnight blue. She smelled unmistakably of coffee—so strongly, in fact, that Caitlin guessed she must have a job as a barista. The girl glanced at the credentials clipped to Caitlin's belt and at her holstered Glock. Then she met Caitlin's gaze and didn't look away.

Her heel jittered. "You're here about the body, right?"

Caitlin kept her voice mild. "Do you know something about what happened here?"

The girl gazed past Caitlin's shoulder to the pier. Her posture tightened. Almost comically, she put her shoulders back.

"Maybe." She was trying to stand as tall as possible. Five two and one sixty-fourth. "But not what happened this week."

"Miss?"

"What happened in 2008." Her eyes darkened. "The woman who drowned—who was murdered here. The one all tied up in duct tape. The first one."

She stared at the pier pilings. The girl was nearly vibrating. Caitlin sensed that coming out of the shadows, speaking about this out loud, had required nerve. She didn't think the girl felt any sense of personal danger, but it seemed that her fears were being exposed.

"I contacted the tip line," the girl said. "I emailed. A long message."

Caitlin recalled reading it. She had taken a hundred calls, read another hundred emails, but she remembered that one.

She put out her hand. "I'm Special Agent Hendrix."

After a moment's hesitation, the girl shook. "I'm Finch Winter."

"Ms. Winter. Why don't you tell me what's going on?"

The girl blew out a breath.

Caitlin said, "Because you worked up your courage to stop lurking and speak to me. Might as well lay it out. You could help me, you know."

"Okay."

"How old are you?"

"Eighteen. I'm a junior at Marshall." She nodded over her shoulder.

"Marshall High School, by the park." She took another breath. "I wasn't lurking."

Caitlin couldn't help but smile. "You were observing. Silently, from the shadows. Surveilling."

"I heard about this killing. On the news." Her face drew taut. "I had to come. I think the Jane Doe who was killed here in 2008 might have been my mother. My birth mother."

"Why do you think that? The 2008 victim hasn't been identified. Do you know her name? Have you spoken to the police?"

"I know the victim hasn't been identified," Finch said. "That's exactly why I have my suspicions. I saw the drawing that was on the FBI website. The information that man . . . Goode . . . gave. Nineteen or twenty years old. Kicked into the water right . . . right . . ." She pointed. "There."

"Do you have photos of your birth mother?" Caitlin said.

Finch shook her head.

"Documentation? Her name, history—"

"None of that. But I just . . ."

Her face scrunched. For a second, Caitlin thought she was going to cry. Then she seemed to plant herself more firmly. Despite her nerves, she was holding her ground.

"I was three when I was adopted. I have a few sketchy memories. But that's all. My mom—my adoptive mom—shields me from everything. From any knowledge of what she calls my 'tough early years.' I *know* she knows something, but it's like she thinks I'm still a baby. And I'm not, I'm a legal adult."

"Have you contacted the NYPD? You could at least add your name to their tip database."

"I emailed them and got zero in reply. They ignored me."

Caitlin kept her face neutral, listening politely. Finch bristled, as if sensing a brush-off.

She spread her hands beseechingly. "You can't know who you are if you don't know where you came from."

This girl was a pint-size hurricane. All passion, no proof. But Caitlin was struck by her heart and grit.

"Here's what you do," Caitlin said. "Get evidence. Adoption records, photos, mementos, a DNA profile. Do that, and I'll listen. Do that, I'll take it to the NYPD cold-case unit, check ViCAP and the National Missing Persons Database."

Finch looked as if she'd been about to pounce but brought herself up short. "For real?"

"Of course."

"Do you have, like, a card?"

Caitlin smiled. She took out her wallet. Finch held out her hand, ready to snatch the card like a snapping turtle. Caitlin held off a second.

"Actual, real evidence," she said. "The hard stuff. Not vapor."

"Wouldn't dream of it."

Caitlin handed over her card. Finch held it tight in both hands, as if memorizing it. She looked up.

"I'll get back to you," she said. "Count on it."

Caitlin might have handed her a communion wafer, or an Infinity Stone. She watched the girl hurry up the street.

Turning back to the water, she pictured the killer lowering the victim's body into the river. Wrapped, silenced, shrouded, as if for a grotesque antibaptism. Washing away evidence instead of sin. It was ritualistic yet riven with rage.

She texted Detective Tashjian.

This unsub is recreating Goode's confessions as if walking the Stations of the Cross—with a stun gun. The dump site named in Goode's next drawing will be the killer's next stop on the trail. Watch out.

10

When Caitlin got home from New York Saturday morning, she and Sean took Sadie to a kids' soccer game at a local park. Rainey's sons were playing—boys Sadie idolized, who treated her like a little sister. Rainey's husband, Charles Bohannan, coached the team. The sky shone blue, and the air smelled of freshly mown grass.

On the sideline, Caitlin let Sadie hold Shadow's leash. The ten-year-old players raced up and down the field, all coltish legs and grass-stained energy. Bo paced in a Nationals cap and a Howard University T-shirt. Parents sipped coffee and—mostly, Caitlin was glad to see—cheered encouragement.

Rainey walked by in jeans and a US Air Force T-shirt, carrying a box full of snacks. She beamed. "Thanks for coming."

League playoff. The entire office knew how pumped Rainey was about the game.

"You bet." Caitlin followed to help her unload the box. "Special Agent Snack Mom."

A cheer went up, and Rainey turned to the game, eyes keen. Twenty boys ran hard downfield. In goal, her son, Dre, bounced on his toes, hands spread, achingly focused on the ball. He looked as if he were preparing to throw himself in front of an artillery shell. A striker drilled toward him, lining up to take the shot.

From the left side, a gangly defender came flying. As the ball left the striker's foot, he deflected it. The shot flew out of bounds.

Dre stopped bouncing. The defender—his twin brother, T. J.—slowed to a jog, nodding at him, then slid a glance toward his parents.

Rainey clapped. So did Sadie, jumping up and down. Bo gave a thumbs-up. He was a criminal defense attorney and former Air Force JAG, whose solemn demeanor kept the kids on the team calm and determined. Caitlin thought it must also serve him well in the courtroom. With his deep-set eyes and stoic bearing, he struck her as a sage.

He gave Rainey a smile of pure pride and childlike glee. She grinned back.

It was bracing, a breath of literal fresh air, for Caitlin to enjoy a day off. She set out snacks, watching Dre pace in front of the net, shaking his shoulders loose. He seemed more internal and self-contained than his brother. T. J. was a mustang colt, bolting around with unruly energy.

"They're real individuals, aren't they?" she said.

Rainey tore open a box of protein bars. "You thought they were clones?"

"No, but . . . I notice how different they are."

"They have that twin connection, sure, but they're not Children of the Corn."

"I didn't mean . . ."

"You're an only child, aren't you, Hendrix?"

Caitlin rolled her eyes. "Your boys are great. Your husband's great. Shove a protein bar in my mouth and shut me up."

Rainey tossed one to her. "You're obsessed with duplicates is what I'm thinking."

"We're off the clock."

"Federal agents are never off duty. That's why Bo and I have Friday Fed Cosplay Night."

Caitlin snorted but stifled a reply because Keyes walked up, hands stuffed in his pockets.

"What are you two laughing about?" he said.

"Ammunition and its penetrating ability," Rainey said.

He blinked, uncertain if she was joking. "NATO spec? I prefer armor-piercing, personally."

"That's sweet. And I appreciate y'all turning up to cheer."

On the field, a whistle blew. Bo called time-out, and the boys jogged to the sideline.

Rainey crossed her arms. Sotto voce, she said to Caitlin, "Seriously though. You're looking for echoes between Goode's killings and the copycat's. Duplications."

"I'm looking for reasons."

Caitlin had woken up before dawn bristling with disquiet, mystified and alarmed by the copycat killings. The look on Keyes's face, eyes somber behind his horn-rims, suggested he felt the same. He stepped closer and lowered his voice.

"Motive?" he said.

"And triggers," Caitlin said. "What kicked this campaign off? Are the copycat killings a twisted fan's homage to Goode?"

"Or an attempt to outdo him?" Rainey said. "Competition, rather than compliment?"

"It seems both weird and obvious that the copycat's killings started so soon after Goode's new confessions were published."

"That says something about the killer's behavior."

"What though? What does it say about . . ."

She nearly said *him*. Statistically, the copycat was likely to be male. But probability wasn't proof, wasn't enough for a profile, and could lead her to unwarranted assumptions.

"What, exactly, does the swift launch of the copycat's campaign say about the killer's motive? Or internal fantasy? Or their needs?" she said.

"This unsub is methodical and orderly," Rainey said.

"And well informed. But not a compulsive copycat—the new killings are close but not exact copies."

"What's exact, and what varies?" Rainey said.

Keyes bounced on his toes. "I can dive into the data on that."

Caitlin nodded. "We need to know why the killer holds captives alive for twenty-four hours and tortures them with a stun baton. And why the copycat transports some victims long distances to Goode's dump sites."

"What's the killer's victimology?" Rainey said.

"The copycat's victims are all white and forty at most," Caitlin said.

"So were Goode's."

A mom walked past, giving a wave. Rainey smiled back.

Then she lowered her voice further. "But what's the difference?"

"Goode's victims were killed in alleys, along back roads, or behind truck stops. The copycat's victims have been attacked at work and home. They aren't runaways or street addicts."

"That's a starting point."

"I'll dig into their backgrounds. I know . . . look for connections, commonalities, red flags—anything that can illuminate why the copycat chose them."

Up the sideline, Bo eyed them. He knew they were talking shop. He wagged a finger and raised a whistle toward his lips. Rainey raised her hands in surrender. Shaking his head, but fondly, Bo turned back to the field.

Caitlin said, "Sorry, Snack Mom."

"Go be with your family," Rainey said. "But cheer hard for the boys."

Caitlin walked back to Sean.

"Solve the case?" he said.

"Piece of cake." She could feel her pulse in her fingertips.

He slid his arm around her waist. Sadie ran up, cheeks pink, with Shadow at her side. Caitlin's mind buzzed. *Duplicates. What's different? What's driving this killer?*

11

That night, while Sean drove Sadie to Michele's apartment, Caitlin changed into sweats and a hoodie. She put Janelle Monáe on the stereo. Then she sank into the sofa with a cold beer and a notepad and wrote out a list that compared Goode's victims with the copycat's.

According to his confession, Goode became friendly with everyone he killed—over two weeks, two days, or a nightlong hookup. They drank, danced, maybe shared a shoplifting expedition or a bump of cocaine in a gas station bathroom. They had consensual sex. Goode's surface attractiveness—the shady charm, his classically handsome features—would have offered an illusion of safety. Claiming that victims were "his"—his beauties, his angels—was patently narcissistic. Asserting that the murders were mercy killings was a shallow lie. If he actually expected people to believe it, his emotional intelligence was more rudimentary than the earthworm Caitlin had dissected in high school biology lab.

Those worms had been soaked in the death-sweet pong of formaldehyde. If only Goode had radiated such a repulsive smell, it could have served as a warning.

His victims were, on the whole, runaways, street addicts, women fleeing domestic violence, impoverished and living on the edge of safety.

She wrote down the victims who remained unidentified.

Jane Doe, Brooklyn, 2008. Approximate age: 20. Cause of death: drowning. She had abrasions and bruising, which indicated she had been physically attacked before being bound with duct tape and kicked or thrown, alive, into the East River.

Caitlin underlined *Jane Doe.*

Goode's sketch of the victim was plastered on the FBI website. Goode had been featured in national news stories and on at least one nightly news broadcast. Yet the FBI tip line had received only one inquiry about this victim—from the teenager Caitlin had met in Brooklyn, Finch Winter. And Finch had nothing except a teenager's enthusiasm to back up her claim.

No, that was wrong. Finch had conviction and anguish and a righteous hunger for justice. That meant something, even if only that Caitlin should pay respect to the girl's concern for the unnamed victim.

At Caitlin's feet, Shadow lay curled. The dog glanced up, ears pricking. Caitlin messaged Rainey.

Goode's Brooklyn Jane Doe. Nobody ID'd her in 2008, even though it's not every day that a young woman—a young, blond, white woman, prime tabloid fodder—washes up bound in duct tape. Same today, even with the sketch. Why not? What are we missing? How can we get the public to take another look at this?

A minute later, Rainey replied. Reframe the request for help on the tip line.

Caitlin mulled, then typed. NYC is a city of immigrants, transients, and tourists, as well as native New Yorkers. The press release seeks witnesses who recognize this woman as someone who went missing *in NYC* in 2008. But . . .

A minute later, Rainey's reply arrived. But she might not have been from NYC. Could have arrived in the city as a passenger in Goode's car. What we need to do—

Caitlin was already typing. We need to ask the public if the drawing reminds them of someone they haven't *seen* in a long time. She could be from anywhere. Maybe her family filed a missing-persons report in Wisconsin. Alaska.

Right, Rainey replied. She could have been from Romania. She could have climbed in Goode's car in Arkansas two years earlier.

Caitlin sighed. Somebody must know who she is. Somebody holding out hope.

Maybe, Rainey replied. Hate to break it to you, kid, but some families never file a report

"Jesus," Caitlin muttered.

Shadow whimpered, concerned, and set her chin on Caitlin's knee. Caitlin stroked the dog's ears. Rainey's message continued.

Sad to say, some families figure their daughter or son ran off, and good riddance. The authorities are not informed, and help never comes. Bad times, bad outcomes. People simply vanish.

Rage bloomed behind Caitlin's ribs, and a sharp ache for a young woman left so long in limbo, unclaimed, unavenged. She typed, This one's been found. I'm going to put a name to her so someone can bring her home.

Rainey signed off with I believe you.

Caitlin finished her beer and got Shadow a dog biscuit. She picked up the notepad again and wrote: *Spring River, Tennessee, April 2018.*

Those four murders had put Efrem Judah Goode behind bars for life. Caitlin suspected he had escaped the death penalty because the victims were from the margins of society. The woman in the back seat of his car had run a shotgun-shack bordello outside town. The victims wrapped like mummies in his motel room were small-time thieves and meth traffickers. Witnesses testified to seeing Goode with them in Nashville bars. His DNA was found on their bodies, and their DNA in his car. CCTV from a Spring River gas station had captured Goode driving up the back road that led to the brothel and returning hours later, the night of the murder.

Why Goode continued to deny his guilt in those four murders, Caitlin didn't yet know. Because he got caught? Psychopaths, infamously, would confess to dramatic acts of violence if it made them look good—good, by their lights, meaning powerful and frightening. They would deny petty crimes that they thought made them look weak.

Maybe Goode was embarrassed that he'd been captured. Maybe he thought his fetish for wrapping women in duct tape marked him as a weirdo when he wanted to be seen as a sex god—so desirable that women literally sought him out and begged him to fulfill their sexual dreams before sending them into the netherworld.

Something other than the truth: he'd been so staggeringly drunk that he busted himself. It remained a question mark.

She drew a line down the middle of the page. Second column: the copycat's victims.

Look for connections, commonalities, red flags—anything that can illuminate why the copycat chose them.

Amber Roark, 40. Last seen working at a bait shop in Semora, North Carolina, on the evening she disappeared. Found in the Tuckasegee River outside Dillsboro, North Carolina, twenty-four hours later. Identifying marks: a scorpion tattoo. History: checkered. Rap sheet for possession, petty theft, fencing stolen property. That ended when she turned thirty, was sentenced to a diversion program, and got clean.

Kimmie Koestler, 35. Disappeared from Glasgow, Kentucky. Found dead twenty-four hours later in Williamsport, Maryland. Body posed, cruciform, at the exit of a storm drain.

Chely Ann McKee, 36. Abducted from her Weatherby, Pennsylvania, home, kept alive twenty-four hours, then strangled. After death, McKee was bound with duct tape and placed in the East River. Time not established, but it must have been late at night, when nobody was nearby to witness it.

Caitlin paused.

None of the copycat's victims were sexually assaulted. None showed evidence of having vaginal sex in the time between their disappearance and discovery.

The difference needled Caitlin. It went to the copycat's motive, which remained obscure.

Goode's victims ranged in age from eighteen to thirty-three; the copycat's from thirty-five to forty. Why target a distinctly older demographic? Did the copycat seek victims who were settled, with predictable schedules, easier to pin down in homes or traveling to and from work? Did the copycat surveil and track them ahead of time? That difference needled her too.

She stared at the ceiling, frustrated. This new slayer was focused, driven, and cycling at a rapid rate. She fully expected them to strike again. Soon. A wire of dread ran down her back. She needed a way into the copycat's mind. Now, not later.

Slow down. Think.

Like other copycats, this one would obsessively seek details about the killer they were imitating. How else could a copycat duplicate—and perhaps outdo—the original's work?

This unsub had sprung into action soon after Goode's story went big. To Caitlin, that spoke of a long-term interest in murder, Goode, or both.

The copycat had likely followed Goode's Tennessee arrest, trial, and conviction closely. Likely knew every detail of the case and had accumulated copious information about Goode. They would have a voluminous search history. They might have gone to the crime scenes, attended victims' funerals, attended the trial.

And that wouldn't be all. The copycat was almost certainly researching, following news reports, and perhaps joining online discussions of Goode's crimes.

This unsub was an obsessive. To fully exploit, indulge, and enjoy that obsession, the copycat would feel an overwhelming need to ingest all available information about Efrem Judah Goode. Caitlin sat up straight, abruptly filled with anxious energy.

Twenty minutes on her laptop turned up a host of articles, armchair-detective podcasts, and comment threads about Goode. She browsed a few, snorting at misconceptions people held about the FBI, serial killers, and criminal law. Still, she read closely. In her experience, some amateur sites were repositories of useful information that official databases didn't have.

The problem in many serial cases, Caitlin knew, was linkage. Information existed in silos. That was one reason the FBI had created ViCAP: to offer law enforcement agencies access to information on cases from all over the country. That was why the Bureau had created the Highway Serial Killing Initiative.

But what she needed right now was a singular window into Goode's story. Something that was vivid and bright and drew the attention of groupies and ghouls. A glittery cesspool.

She found it on the Efrem Judah Goode Facebook fan page.

"Hoo boy," she said.

The page featured a photo of Goode taken at his trial, talking to his lawyers. He wore an easygoing smile and looked engaged and vital. The header photo was a snapshot of him as a young man, leaning against a pickup truck. He was tan, his jeans tight, his eyes cool and sexy.

How had this page gotten the photo?

Caitlin checked. The page was run by a woman who had become Goode's prison pen pal.

Tonya Pappas was the page admin. According to her greeting, she posted messages she'd received through the mail or on phone calls from Goode. Caitlin knew that prisoners were denied direct access to social media sites. But a contact on the outside could post on an inmate's behalf. Pappas had created the page after Goode's arrest in Tennessee. Initially, she posted anguished paeans to Goode's innocence, slathered with barely submerged lust. Pappas railed that the justice system was prejudiced against "lords of the open road." She wrote, "Efrem is a truly free man, and that scares THE MAN."

Unsurprisingly, when Goode was convicted, Tonya seamlessly shifted from championing his innocence to supporting him in his suffering.

She posted, "Hard time. But Efrem Judah is a man who can bear up to it."

Caitlin had studied cults and doomsday sects. When Judgment Day arrived—and departed without a peep—the most fervent disciples almost never turned against their false prophets. They blamed themselves for failing to believe with sufficient zeal. They dug their fingernails into their holy texts to understand how they had miscalculated the hour and the day. Sometimes, they did this on the street, bankrupt and homeless. Sometimes, they did it at the graves of fellow believers who had swallowed poison at the rising of a comet, certain that its ascension would be theirs as well.

What they didn't do was snap out of it. They decided that the *next* comet was the one they were actually waiting for and that their messiah was still the One. They bought in, bet the farm, and metaphorically ice-picked their brains to avoid facing reality. They circled a new date on the calendar for the freshly rescheduled apocalypse.

Superfans struck Caitlin as having the same dynamic. Their fantasy depended on buying what their hero was selling. So they went all in.

Denial and delusion were real things. She didn't need her therapist to teach her that.

Tonya Pappas's photo showed a thin woman in her late forties, with a smoker's pallor and sunken cheeks. She lived in New Jersey, and from what Caitlin could gather, her interactions with Goode were entirely virtual. She hadn't attended his trial or visited him in prison.

Tonya, it seemed to Caitlin, was a lonely true-crime junkie who was getting a thrill from being Goode's "voice" online. Her posts read like a fifteen-year-old girl's diary entries about a boy she had a crush on. Some sounded bubbly, breathless, nearly giddy. They conveyed an unmistakable sense that maybe, at last, Tonya Pappas felt *special*.

She had posted dozens of personal comments from Goode, photos of notes he'd scrawled to her, so followers of the page could see that her transcriptions were accurate. They left Caitlin cold inside.

She shuddered at Tonya's fixation on Goode—and at the underlying assumption that a man in prison was harmless. Putting a killer like Goode behind bars didn't defang him. He may be a drifter and self-described lone wolf, but that didn't make him a complete loner. Men like Goode almost always had proxies on the outside.

Tonya herself was a proxy. If she thought she was the only one or that Goode wouldn't manipulate his others, perhaps to harm her, she was a fool.

But it wasn't Caitlin's place to warn every fool in America that making friends with killers could be unwise. What she knew was that this fan page was a public source of fresh, personal revelations from Goode. It would be like candy to someone obsessed with him.

Someone like the copycat.

Caitlin set an alert to notify her when anyone followed the page or commented on it. Right now it was all she had. The copycat was killing at a fearsome pace.

And could strike anywhere.

12

Finch Winter drummed her thumbs against her thighs and waited for the light to change. She was walking home from school with her boyfriend, Zack Arcega. Traffic around McCarren Park was picking up—delivery trucks and bikes, people walking dogs in the breezy afternoon, music pouring from apartment windows, the sound of a bat hitting a softball at the playing field.

"It's making me insane," she said. "Everybody ignores me."

"Not fair. The world, and this in particular," Zack said.

He gazed down at her. He was a foot taller than Finch—most people were, but Zack *acted* tall, carried himself through the streets with easy confidence, which endeared him to her. (He was secretly hot. She didn't think he knew how she *swooned* when he walked toward her.) And he had expressive hands and a smile that truly popped when those mischievous eyes landed on her. He also had major senioritis since he'd been admitted to Stony Brook, but that meant he had plenty of time to hang with her.

Traffic cleared. They crossed and turned into her neighborhood, where the streets were quiet and trees brushed the rooftops. At her building, Finch dug her keys from her backpack.

"There has to be evidence of my birth mother's identity. I just can't find it."

She unlocked the front door and led Zack into the building's tiled hallway. Their feet and voices echoed as they climbed the stairs. In her apartment, she dropped her backpack on the hardwood floor. The place was cozy, right-sized for her and her mom, with heaving bookshelves and

Rothko reproductions on the wall, big bumps of red. The back window overlooked the building's courtyard and gave her a slice of greenery to admire when she flopped on her bed. But right now she didn't want to flop. She was boiling with exasperation.

"You have to be able to do something about this," Zack said.

"I'm figuring out what that is."

She grabbed two cans of La Croix from the fridge. The aroma of peaches and that stinky Gorgonzola her mom was trying out bloomed across the kitchen. High-end pots and pans hung from a rack over an island. Expensive knives gleamed in a wooden rack beside the sink. Cookbooks lined the wall.

She felt like bursting. Didn't want to stay inside. "Come on."

She tossed Zack a sparkling water and led him up to the roof. The wind and sun spanked her in the face. She took in the view over the East River, to Manhattan.

"I can't legally get hold of my original birth certificate," she said. "The one that named my bio-mom and maybe a dad. When I was adopted, the certificate was amended. It lists Annie Winter as my mother." She shook her head. "That's the way adoptions work."

"That sounds like lying," Zack said.

"I understand it," she said. "Once you're adopted, you're part of your new family. Your adoptive parents are listed on your birth certificate because they *are* your parents, your real parents, now and forever. Your legal documents reflect that so there will never be any questions going forward. In a way, it feels supportive."

"Except it's an erasure of the whole story," Zack said.

She smiled. He wasn't just cute, but also smart. Everything about him just hit her so perfectly. College bound. Into theater, but not in a weird way. Played guitar in a band. Uncomplicated but serious. Even his name was right. *Zack*. It could have been Trevor or, *ugh*, Clifford, like that guy in trig class.

He frowned, watching her watch him. "I say something wrong?"

She shook her head and held out her hand. "You said something caring."

Across the rooftops, beyond treetops and the water tower off Franklin Street, the apartment buildings and brownstones petered out, giving way to industrial buildings and warehouses. She couldn't see the street where she had lurked, watching the FBI agent.

"Why don't you talk to your mom?" Zack said. Then, when she eyed him, frowned. "That's not out of line of me, is it?"

She could barely see the river. Beyond it, the Manhattan skyline was blue-hazed and shadowed, a charcoal silhouette backlit by the white sun. Due west was Union Square and the restaurant where her mom worked.

"No, it's not out of line."

"Do you think she knows who your birth mother is? That it was, what do you call it—"

"An open adoption. I do think that." *Suspect.* That was the word she almost used. She suspected that her mom knew the whole story.

She was, in fact, convinced that her adoptive mom, Annie Winter, knew the facts and was keeping them from her. Finch deeply loved Annie, who had worked her butt off to make a good life for her. But now it wasn't enough.

She turned to Zack. "Annie overprotects me."

"You're all she's got."

"Don't say it like that."

"Sorry . . ."

She stepped away. "Annie devotes herself to me. Sure, she's got her job, her cooking, her friends at work. She has this whole life, but she always puts me at the center of it."

"I didn't mean anything bad. Jeez, Finch . . ."

She threw up her hands. "Yes, she overprotects me. I'm *eighteen.* I'm not a baby!"

"What, exactly, do you think she's keeping from you?" Zack said.

"She has to at least know the circumstances I was living in when . . . when . . ."

"When your birth mom abandoned you?"

"Don't say that."

His eyes popped, this time with hurt. "Finch, c'mon, I'm trying here. This is all new to me."

"Of course it is."

Zack had parents who were married, and an older sister and brother, and they went to mass on Sunday mornings at the redbrick church on Manhattan Avenue, even though it was mainly a Polish parish. Zack had grandparents who lived within walking distance, and cousins, aunts, uncles—a whole network of family.

Finch had Annie—the warm, tough, funny entirety of her world—who had saved her from a black hole.

"All Mom's told me is that I had a rough start in life. That's just so vague. She'll never go deeper, never tell me whether she heard that from a foster family or an adoption agency or whether she knows more. I think she has to. She must know the circumstances I came from."

"Like, she heard the story and doesn't want to tell you? Or . . ."

"Or she knows what happened to my birth mom firsthand. She might."

"Finch." Zack stopped being skittish and now looked frustrated. "Ask her. Just do it."

Down on the street, car horns honked. Music floated up from a window.

"Yeah." She sighed. "I need to know. And there's more at stake now than just me."

She took out her phone.

"What are you going to do?" Zack said.

"What you just told me to."

It was five fifteen. Not the start of the dinner rush, but people would be stopping by for happy hour at Axis, the restaurant where Annie was a chef. Finch texted.

I need the truth. My birth mother deserves justice.

Hands shaking, she lowered the phone.

She listened to the noise of the neighborhood. A brace of pigeons took off from a nearby roof, flapping and cooing. A jet scored the air overhead, on approach to LaGuardia.

Ping. Her mom had replied. Finch checked the screen.

You're on the wrong track. We'll talk tonight but OMG, DON'T get involved in a mess involving a convicted killer!

Finch groaned. Zack leaned in and read the message. He said nothing but rubbed her shoulders.

"I'm not 'getting involved' in a mess with a convicted killer," Finch moaned. "I'm trying to bring the truth to light."

"Of course you are," Zack said. "Is there some other way to get the information?"

"Adoption agencies won't even hint at it. No way."

She felt a hard knot in her chest.

Why was this getting to her now? She'd always known she was adopted. Her mom never kept it from her, like some big shameful secret. It was only in the past few years that an undercurrent had started building. When she started high school maybe. It had come from Annie too. A strange secrecy, the way Annie shut down when Finch mentioned her adoption. No—when she mentioned her birth family. Annie turning off the television or stereo when certain stories came on the news. Finch remembering, more regularly, that singular memory of the night when . . .

What? When her birth mother left her?

For a long while, Finch had assumed she was either dropped at an orphanage or found by social services, neglected in some horrible, filthy hovel. But the memory—of the cold, the sense of fear, of danger and dread . . . When she found Efrem Judah Goode's confession, a bolt of lightning had hit her. Something was there. She knew it.

She felt torn. What she didn't feel was frightened. This was a festering sore, and it was time somebody ripped it open and exposed it to sunlight.

The wind scored her face. "I have to be able to do something."

"Your mom's coming home when?" Zack said.

"It'll be eleven thirty by the time she gets here. I'll wait up, but she's not going to want to talk about this," she said. "You saw her text. She's going to tell me to back off. Wants to keep everything locked in the dark."

"That's not what I meant," Zack said. "She won't be home all evening."

Finch turned. He had his hands in his pockets, shoulders scrunched up. His black hair was falling over his eyes. He tossed his head.

"She has to have information, right?" he said. "All the stuff she got when you were adopted. The adoption people didn't just shoot you out of a T-shirt cannon at a Mets game and let whoever caught you take you home."

She was too surprised to laugh.

Zack said, "That file cabinet, and her desk. What's in there?"

His eyebrows rose. Finch took a deep breath.

Back in the apartment, she dug through Annie's desk. She lifted out notebooks, a checkbook, putting everything back as precisely as she could. Finding nothing surprising, aside from her mom's tax return, which had *lots* more pages than she'd ever imagined. In the bottom drawer, she came across a folder containing pictures she had drawn in kindergarten. Bright colors, faces with eyes that were unevenly sized. *MoM aND mE*, one was labeled.

"Cute," Zack said.

Feeling a pang of guilt, Finch replaced the drawings and moved to the file cabinet in the corner. When she reached to open the bottom drawer, she was surprised to find it locked.

"Huh."

"Not huh. *Yeah*," Zack said. "Where's the key?"

Finch went through the desk again, and the kitchen drawers. Her heart was kicking against her ribs. With trepidation, she pushed open her mom's bedroom door.

"Wait here," she told Zack.

Creeping inside, she went to the nightstand. The key was inside the drawer.

Her eye caught the framed photo on top of her mom's dresser: the two of them, laughing, heads pressed together, on the observation deck at the Empire State Building. Heat bloomed on Finch's cheeks. The key was hot in her palm.

Mom, do you have secrets?

When she came out of the bedroom, Zack was leaning against the wall, biting his thumbnail. She walked past him and slid the key into the bottom drawer of the file cabinet. It turned smoothly in the lock. She pulled the drawer open.

Zack leaned over. "Whoa."

Inside were things she recognized: a bedraggled stuffed lamb that she'd slept with when she was little. A lock of her hair, from when it was fine and light, tied with a pink ribbon. And a battered green metal lockbox. She hesitated. Zack reached for it.

"No." She pushed his hand away. He was too eager. This wasn't some Disney adventure film. "Let me."

She sat cross-legged on the floor and lifted the lockbox from the cabinet. Setting it on her lap, she wiped the sweat from her palms and pressed the latch.

"Oh."

The box contained a faded snapshot of three young women leaning against a wall outside a diner. Finch picked it up. Her hand trembled.

She didn't know any of the people in the photo. Why would her mom keep an old photo that didn't even include herself?

But that wasn't the thing that made Finch's stomach knot.

One of the young women resembled Goode's Brooklyn Jane Doe drawing. The resemblance wasn't just clear—it was uncanny.

Zack's Scooby-Doo enthusiasm collapsed. His voice turned deadly serious.

"Call the FBI agent," he said.

Finch shook her head.

"This is what she wants. This is it. Proof. The first evidence you've found. This is no coincidence, Finch."

Finch stared hard at the photo. The streets in the background looked like New York. This photo was at least ten, maybe fifteen, years old, judging from the hairstyles and clothes. The three women in the photo were young, leaning together, not that much older than Finch was now. Eyes vivid, full of snark and something dark, despite their smiles. The one on the left had a superintense glare, as if she automatically got suspicious about anybody who turned their attention on her. The one on the right had apple cheeks and brown, stringy hair. The one in the middle had blond hair, crooked teeth, something eager and hungry in her look.

Zack squeezed her shoulder. "She wanted evidence. What else could this be?"

Finch shook her head. "It is. But it's not enough. There's no identifying information, and from my dealings with the cops and FBI, that's what they want. I'll talk to Special Agent Hendrix, but I have to nail this down first—one hundred percent."

"What's one hundred percent?"

She stood up. "DNA."

"Are you going to the police?"

"They won't take my DNA to test. I have to do that."

Heading to her room, she slid the photo into a shoebox at the back of her closet. She put the lockbox back, locked the file cabinet, and replaced the key in her mom's nightstand.

On her phone, she checked her bank balance. She had enough saved up from her coffeehouse job. She logged on to a commercial ancestry site and ordered a DNA test kit.

13

Gum on the sidewalks, graffiti tags on bus benches and light poles, people everywhere, moving constantly, marching, yakking, heads bent to phones, men, women, the wind rush of car noise, garbage trucks, laughter, the smell of curry from a restaurant. Hip-hop, Chinese, *New Yawk*. Fun fun fun. And better fun on foot.

The evening sun was sinking below the tops of the Midtown skyscrapers, casting sharp gold light down the Manhattan streets. The mood of the city was shifting, like a jukebox record cueing up to drop. Replacing the daytime bustle, the moneymaking drive, straight ahead, work work work, with that evening buzz. The animal hum, from deeper in the brain, from the loins, beginning to throb, ready to break free and roam, and rave, and *take*. That was straight-up anthropology.

You know this, totally, the driver thought. *All those library books, the ones you read in the back seat of the car on long road trips to the next place, the next town, the next home—those books that educated you . . .*

Bam, a man swept around a corner, and their shoulders collided.

"Fuck you, buddy," the guy said, looking up from his phone.

"Really?"

The guy kept going but did a double take, turning, looking over his shoulder, like, *Did I just make a mistake?*

You did, asshole. But there wasn't time to rectify it.

Nighttime was on its way.

Spinning around, making sure not to lose sight of the target . . .

Don't get distracted. The copycat sped up, bouncing, looking over the heads of the crowds on the wide sidewalk, these overconfident city people and the tourists, lost, wide-mouthed country goobers waddling along side by side, blocking the way, half of them with their heads tilted up to the rooftops, like *How could anything get that tall, Pa? 'Tain't natural.* Big Macs in their hands, maybe dripping out of their mouths.

Around the next corner, slipping between people, hurry hurry because . . .

The street opened up to the white-hot mechanical core of Manhattan. Times Square. Crazytown, an electric shriek. Packed with people. Electronic billboards twenty stories high. The NYSE ticker running along the side of a building. *Blade Runner.*

Exciting. Calming. Fit in with the flow.

There she was.

Heading south, the humid wind off the Hudson scudding between buildings, blowing the afternoon's heat in a swirl. The woman's hair lifted in shining waves. The copycat slid through the literally wall-to-wall crowd, past scaffolding and hoardings, huge billboards for TV shows. Along the angled path of Broadway. More people bumping shoulders, talking loud, shoving.

A perfect opportunity, most nights, to get your wallet stolen. Hands in pockets now, making sure that wouldn't happen. Eyes front. Following that bouncy hair, the knock-off bag on her shoulder, the tilt of her head. Flirty blouse, black jeans, boots. The woman was a next-gen version of Goode's beauties. Nose in the air. Strutting. Thinks she's all that.

An NYB—New York Bitch.

The woman was maybe twenty-two, and oblivious. Sliding through the crowds, aiming past the Army recruiting center, the NYPD station, and the bright, coldly inviting chain clothing stores. Swiveling aside to avoid hitting the bumbling ants that were crawling all over the street— people in suits and stinking sleeveless T-shirts, a guy in a backward baseball cap and thick gold chains, young women in towering heels and micro-shorts—oh, the panoply of humanity. The target was oblivious, yes, but experienced. She'd trained herself to slipstream through the stinking masses. Definitely a New Yorker.

She jogged down a staircase to the subway. Overhead, NASDAQ, Walgreens, a billboard with dragons, or maybe Godzilla. Always Godzilla.

Down the stairs, boots hitting the metal edges, into oppressive air. The NYB zoomed to the turnstile and through. The underground lair, Times Square station, was huge, echoing, everyone moving at twice the speed of people on the streets above. The roar of trains came from the tracks below. Follow her through the turnstile, across a low plaza, past musicians setting up by a metal pillar, buckets and drumsticks. Down another flight of stairs to the subway platform. People sweating, merging, trying not to touch each other in the awesome heat. The NYB ahead. Still not looking anywhere but up the black tunnel for the train.

It arrived. She got on. The doors closed. The NYB dropped onto a seat, earbuds in.

The copycat stood at the far end of the train car. This was the first chance to really look at her, while she was sitting still. Even under the harsh white lights of the train, against the reflective silver walls of the carriage, even with people getting on and off, it was a clarifying view.

The NYB was kohl-eyed and oblivious, scratching at her arms. Music in her ears, judging from the quick little way she rocked forward and back. Not so much swaying with a beat as twitching with it.

She got off in the Village. Up on the street, the sunlight had dropped to red. Everything blood-tinged now. Heavy traffic, cabs honking. The NYB turned a corner and scudded along the sidewalk.

The copycat followed, marking the path. Drawing with a Sharpie on bus stop benches and streetlight poles. Suppressing a smile. Humming, *I've got a little list . . . and they'll none of 'em be missed . . .*

The NYB walked to a pocket park where basketballs racketed through metal nets. The guy she met was already there, already deep into his evening business. She waited for one customer to finish a transaction, suddenly polite and reticent, then sidled up to the guy doing business.

Her drug dealer.

She must have ordered ahead, because she scored instantly.

Took it quickly, slipping it into her pocket, fist closed around it like it was the Hope Diamond. She swerved off, looking left and right, furtively, like a newb. From across the park, the copycat followed.

Ten minutes later, the NYB rushed through the door into a trendy Village bar. Through the big plate-glass windows, the copycat watched her wave to the manager and duck behind the bar. The manager frowned and tapped his watch. The NYB apologized.

Work. She was late for work.

Perfect.

Needing to score was perfect. Being late was perfect. It meant she'd spend the evening catching up, being watched, probably unable to sneak away to snort or swallow or smoke or shoot up. She'd be saving her bump for later.

Later, when she would really need it, want it, crave it. Seeing her sniffle and scratch at her arms on the subway had been a clear sign that she was a heavy user.

The plan took shape. Retreat, into the ever-lengthening shadows. Watch the basketball players in the park. Get a cappuccino.

And, when the NYB finished work, take her, take away her drugs, so that with every second that passed, the pressure she felt would become ever more intolerable.

The copycat settled into the shadows near the bar and waited.

14

The next morning, Caitlin had a fat stack of files on her desk relating to Efrem Judah Goode, and dozens more in her secure digital dropbox. She sat, tucking her white blouse back into her trousers, still not completely used to working in business attire. She'd worn a uniform for seven years, then, as a detective, had dressed in Northern California plainclothes—a Pendleton shirt with jeans and Doc Martens. Wearing a suit could still feel like playing dress-up.

It was okay. Play the part, be the part. Rainey came in, looking effortlessly chic, nodding over the lip of her steaming coffee cup as she passed. Keyes zoomed by, messenger bag over one shoulder, and hurried to his office as if he'd pulled something from the oven barehanded and was rushing to set it down before it burned his palms.

Caitlin opened her email and read the message from Detective Tashjian at the Brooklyn North Homicide Squad.

Emmerich was in his office. Caitlin tapped on his door. He waved her in.

"NYPD has officially asked me to profile their unsub," she said.

He took off his glasses and leaned back. "Excellent."

"I've been to the New York crime scene. It was forensically clean. No witnesses. And no video evidence, so far, linking a vehicle to the crime. That goes for all the dump sites and victim-encounter sites. Granted, the majority are in small towns or isolated spots. But that North Carolina bait shop is right out on the main road."

"That tells us something," he said.

"Yeah. Bold, willing to take risks, but cautious. Watchful. Picking the right moment. This killer is smart."

"Where were the nearest video cameras in that North Carolina town?"

"There's an ATM a quarter mile away."

"How many roads into and out of that town?"

"Two," she said. "The odds are strong that the unsub's vehicle got picked up on the ATM camera. Though the highway leads straight to a popular lake, so there's more traffic than the town's population would lead you to expect. But it'll be a start."

"Keyes can compare vehicles on the North Carolina camera with CCTV from Kentucky, Maryland, and Pennsylvania." He paused. "And New York."

"Daunting."

"*Daunting* is Nick's middle name. He'll take it as a challenge, like finding asteroids on a collision course with Earth, the way he did in Planetary Sciences at JPL."

"Undoubtedly," she said.

"You look excited but perturbed."

"I should put that on my card. It covers ninety percent of our work."

He nodded, perhaps with amusement.

"As for profiling the unsub, I need to dive into the original crimes. If I'm going to understand the copycat's behavior, I have to get to grips with Goode's."

"Copy that. Dive."

Back at her desk, Caitlin jumped in by reviewing police reports on Goode's crimes. After ninety minutes, she found herself astonished at how many times Goode had been pulled over, stopped on the street, and taken to jail. His jacket—multiple jackets, from a dozen states—covered more than forty arrests.

He always slid out from under serious scrutiny. He did two weeks for a bar brawl. Sixty days for petty theft. Six months for aggravated assault. A year for a gas station robbery. It never added up, because after serving short time, he always moved on to a fresh location. He would head across a state line to plant himself again like a weed. He subverted the ability to link him to his record.

That had let him commit murder and keep on moving.

In his wake, he left misery, emptiness, and fear. Caitlin shook her head. Seeing it all compiled was both maddening and heartbreaking.

But it also revealed something that extended across years and state lines.

A car.

One report described a "big old Caddy, rusted gold," seen at a riverbank where a victim's body was found. Another described an arrest during a traffic stop. The vehicle: a gold Cadillac.

A dashcam photo showed a 1982 Cadillac Coupe deVille. It was a supertanker of a car—boxy, ostentatious yet lumbering, with the Cadillac ornament standing proudly on a sun-faded hood.

Reason for the traffic stop: failure to yield at a freeway entrance. That told Caitlin the highway patrol officer who pulled Goode over may have been following him, and that something in Goode's driving had caught the officer's attention. Aggressive tailgating, speeding, swerving lane changes.

According to the report, Goode had refused to budge on a fast-moving freeway and forced a merging Volkswagen off the road into a ditch. He sideswiped the Beetle, which, weighing a fraction of the Caddy, caromed off like a hockey puck. At the bottom of the report, the arresting officer wrote *Road rage incident.*

Caitlin found vehicle information. The Cadillac had Iowa tags. It was registered . . .

"Huh," she said.

The car was registered to a woman named Corliss Yates.

A prickle ran up her arms.

She went to the conference room, spread printouts on the table, put electronic records up on the big screen, and dived deeper. She found another traffic stop, five years earlier. Same car, with Nebraska plates. Registered owner: Corliss Yates. And she discovered a reference in a stolen-property report. The victim said his stereo equipment had been ripped off by "Efrem Goode and a woman he ran with, 'Corless' or 'Corlise' (sp?)."

Goode was a drifter, but he had a road companion. A partner in crime. He had traveled with Corliss Yates for at least a decade.

Who was she?

Witness statements described Goode's companion as sexy. Sharp. "A redhead . . . you know, a handful." Caitlin, also a redhead, rolled her eyes.

A report written by an investigating officer in the Tennessee quadruple murders caught her eye. Marius Hayes had gone to Goode's previous addresses. Looking for family, for friends and confederates, for Goode's history. Interview notes from a trip to Alabama grabbed her attention.

Neighbor remembers Goode. 2008 or so. He rented a house at the end of a rural road. Lived there for approximately nine months. Drove a pickup truck, but the Cadillac was always parked in the driveway. Goode worked at the local lumber mill, seasonal labor. Neighbor says he was friendly, they'd see him working on the car, he'd wave, never talked about himself but was really interested in them. The neighbor now thinks Goode was fishing, angling to find out what they had worth stealing. But she says Goode mostly kept to himself—him and his family.

Family. What family?

He lived with a woman. The neighbor couldn't remember her name exactly. "Carly" something (maybe). Carly never talked to the neighbor. Stayed in the house or got in the Cadillac and roared off into town. She was midtwenties, a "real knockout," red hair sprayed tall, like a Nashville singer. Jeans sprayed on too. And blouses that revealed plenty.

Then the report listed a detail that set Caitlin's teeth on edge.

The neighbor also recalled that Carly had a little kid. They'd see her come out of the house holding a preschooler's hand, scooting the kid into the car with a pat on the behind.

The neighbor didn't know if the kid was Goode's. They couldn't remember seeing him with the child. What they remembered was that Caddy.

Caitlin pressed her palm to the page. A woman. A child. Goode had never mentioned either of them.

Where were they?

What had happened to them?

She read the report on Goode's arrest for murder. Spring River, Tennessee. He had been staying at a motel across the street from the sheriff's station. She saw nothing in the deputy's affidavit about a Cadillac or traveling companions.

Her stomach tightened. No family or friends had attended Goode's trial. His parents and older brother were dead. He claimed he had no next of kin, and nobody had stepped forward to claim otherwise.

A stunning redhead, patting a small child on the rear end as they climbed into the gold Cadillac that Goode liked to drive. An isolated "family," if that's what Corliss Yates and the youngster were—a kid whose name nobody knew. Whose parentage and even gender nobody knew.

What happened to that woman? That child?

Caitlin found the number for the Sheriff's Department substation in Spring River. The woman who answered the phone had an unabashed Tennessee drawl.

"Detective Hayes, please. Special Agent Caitlin Hendrix calling from the FBI."

"One minute, ma'am."

The woman's voice rose, possibly with surprise. It seemed the station didn't get frequent calls from the Bureau.

Caitlin gazed out the windows at the spring-green countryside. A group of Academy trainees in blue FBI T-shirts and khaki combats was jogging in an organized train toward the running trail in the woods. They looked fit and shiny and determined. She knew from experience that they would come back gasping and dirty and, possibly, proud.

After a few clicks, a man came on the line, his voice deep and confident. "Hayes."

Caitlin had the Sheriff's Department website up, with Hayes's photo. He looked about thirty, African American, clear eyed, built like a sequoia.

"Detective." She introduced herself. "I'm hoping you can help fill in some blanks about Efrem Judah Goode."

"Of course. Anything I can."

"You were the arresting officer."

"I was. Made detective nine months later."

"The car Goode was driving that night."

"Eighty-five Chevy Impala. It was stolen off a used-car lot in Chattanooga."

"Hot-wired?" she said. "Or did the thief break into the office and take the keys?"

"Hot-wired," Hayes said. "Door lock likely opened with a slim-jim."

Caitlin found a photo of the car. It was a dull blue. And it was clearly built on the same GM chassis as an eighties-vintage Cadillac Coupe deVille. Square, stolid—a cheaper version of the Caddy. A staple of police departments at the time.

"And Goode denied stealing it," she said.

"Up, down, back and forth, ten ways from Sunday." Hayes sounded weary. "But then, he denied everything. Everything except renting the room at the motor court. Clerk testified that Goode put down cash and got the key. Remembered him clearly."

"The motor court room."

Hayes sighed. Not loudly, more a heavy exhalation. She found the crime scene photos. Harsh flash of the official photographer's camera. A tatty room, small, worn green carpet, nicked bedside table with an old lamp, its shade knocked crooked. Thin, pilled synthetic bedspread.

Three duct-tape-entombed bodies, side by side on the double bed.

"Did you interview the desk clerk or other staff at the motor court?" she said.

"Interviewed them, yep. Know most of them. They live around here; some of them I grew up with."

"Did anybody mention a woman traveling with Goode?" Caitlin said.

"No. He's the only one anybody saw," Hayes said. "There was no sign of a woman in the room, either . . . I mean . . ."

"Aside from the victims."

"Correct." He cleared his throat. "No suitcase, no clothing, nothing in the bathroom or shower or closet that indicated a woman was there with Goode. It was him and his mummies." He was silent for a moment. "A couple of people quit right afterward. Woman who worked as a house-keeper—she cleaned the room—and the janitor. They did the work, then walked away. Didn't want anything more to do with that place. Burned their clothes, never looked back, and it's not like jobs are dropping from the trees around here."

"Goode drove a knife into the town, you're saying."

"Things are better now, but this place suffered. Bad."

"I hear you, Detective," she said. "I'm looking for information on a woman Goode ran with, long term. Going back years. She's referred to in your investigative report. Corliss Yates."

"That's her name?" Hayes said. "Redhead. Flashy, sexy. Stranger like that, she'd stand out in Spring River. But nobody saw anyone like that around here."

Caitlin thumped her knuckles on the table. "You saw Goode that night. Spoke to him."

"I did."

"What were your impressions?"

"Drunk off his ass. Stank of Crown Royal. Staggered like he'd shot-gunned the entire bottle. His story that he was roofied? Yeah. Sure."

"Why do you think he denied committing the murders?"

"Pride," he said. "He didn't want anybody to think he was honestly stupid enough to drunk-drive into a parking lot he didn't recognize as the sheriff's station, with Jayna Wizniak dead in the back seat. He couldn't admit failure."

"I think you're right."

"You get him for the rest of these murders, you let me know."

"Absolutely."

She ended the call. She'd heard the toll the case had taken on Hayes.

Spring River had been turned into a slaughterhouse. Horror and grief hung hard over everyone in the town, even now, long after the national news cameras shut off their lights and drove away.

Goode was the only one seen at the motel.

What had happened to his traveling companion? And to the child who once lived with them?

Caitlin thought of Goode's tattoo—his "long-gone baby." Sick dread whispered that he'd killed them.

Her phone rang, too loud. She nearly jumped. A New York number. "Hendrix."

"It's Greg Tashjian at the NYPD. We just fished a body out of the East River."

Her stomach sank.

"Homicide. Location matches the second spot Goode said he dumped a body."

She stood. "I'm on my way."

15

The victim's name was Chelsea Symanski, age twenty-three. She was yet another woman who was grabbed minutes after she left work, this time at a trendy Greenwich Village bar. Twenty-four hours later, her body fetched up beneath the Williamsburg Bridge, caught against a piling and tangled in debris.

Caitlin arrived late in the afternoon. She headed directly to the NYPD precinct where Tashjian was conferring with detectives from the Manhattan South Homicide Squad, who were charged with investigating Symanski's murder. The squad room was crowded with desks, detectives in suits, and a television playing Fox News. Same host as the TV in the Brooklyn squad room, maybe redder in the face. High windows caught the spring light.

From the doorway, she spotted Tashjian's hat with the red feather. He waved her to a desk where he was talking with one of the detectives. The man looked up languidly as she approached, visitor's badge clipped to her lapel, and returned to his conversation with Tashjian.

She waited, trying to sense the air—whether they were going to piss in a circle around the desk because she was a fed, or a woman, or whether they would toss her a bone. Tashjian looked semiwelcoming but didn't interrupt the Manhattan detective.

"Gentlemen," she finally said.

The man at the desk, wearing a silk tie and cufflinks, leaned back extravagantly, hands laced behind his head. "Good flight? Get pretzels? Or does the Bureau spring for almonds?"

"Gingerbread cookies. The air marshal dozed off, and I raided the cart." She extended her hand. "Caitlin Hendrix."

After a long pause, he rocked forward and shook. "Dennis Mancuso."

Tashjian said, "We have new photos. Autopsy's scheduled for tomorrow."

She nodded. "The Bureau's resources are at your disposal. We've got information from multiple cases. I can help you incorporate or eliminate evidence, history, theories. Put me to work."

"You bet." Tashjian pulled her toward an empty desk. "Don't mind Mancuso. He likes to keep investigations close to the vest. Not a task force kind of guy."

They weren't a task force, even unofficially, but Caitlin decided to play nice. "We'll work it out," she said with a breeziness she didn't feel. "Thanks for your vote of confidence. Being here lets me see the scope of the case more clearly."

On his phone, Tashjian brought up crime scene photos. They'd been snapped by a police photographer aboard the NYPD Harbor Patrol boat that fished the victim from the river. She lay faceup on a blue plastic tarp. She was fish-scale gray, her lips blue. Her wet hair lay in kelp strands across her face. Caitlin tried, too late, to slam the shutters on her emotions. The young woman's clouded eyes and half-parted lips seemed frozen with despair.

An orange lifebuoy was duct-taped to her chest. Dotted on her arms and shoulders were obvious electrical burns.

Caitlin held her voice even. "She was hit with a stun baton. Same as the copycat's other victims."

"What's your take?" Tashjian said. "What's driving this copycat?"

"Million-dollar question." She paused, feeling a frisson. "This unsub is meticulous. These re-creations. That could be obsession—and I think part of it is. But there's something cold about the killings. Something contemptuous in their presentation."

She scanned the crime scene photos. "This killing goes outside the parameters of the copycat's previous murders."

"How?"

"The victim was local—taken and dumped within a mile radius. And Symanski was much younger than the copycat's other victims."

"Was she a victim of opportunity? Or is he expanding his target pool?"

"Or refining it."

Something didn't sit right with her. She had learned to pay attention to these intuitions, as she would to a burr in her shoe. She tried to grab hold of what was bothering her, but when it didn't come crisply into focus, she stepped back mentally. *Let it stew. Don't stress.* She grabbed a notepad and scribbled, *"Duplication of Goode's killings—message, or taunt?"*

"What are you thinking?" Tashjian said.

She showed him the note. "Figuring it out."

"Here's a thing about the Symanski killing though." He scratched his nose. "Goode claims he killed a girl near the Williamsburg Bridge in 2008, a goth teenager."

Caitlin had Goode's sketch on her phone. "Liv."

"There's no record of a 2008 homicide fitting that description."

"You're kidding."

"Doesn't mean Goode lied. The victim could have floated into the Upper Bay. She could still be on the bottom of the river."

A uniformed officer led a man to Detective Mancuso's desk. Mancuso beckoned them.

The visitor was in his early forties, Latino, outdoorsy looking. And upset. In his palm, he clutched a memory stick.

Mancuso said, "This is David Garcia. Tell them what you were saying to me."

"I'm an amateur photographer," Garcia said. "Last night I was at East River Park, down by the Williamsburg Bridge. Testing a thermal-imaging system on my video camera."

"Thermal imaging?" Tashjian said.

"A black-and-white night-vision lens." Garcia raised his hands defensively. "Not spying. I was filming nocturnal wildlife. Owls. Foxes." He looked around at them. "You'd be surprised."

"Rats," Mancuso said.

"Plenty. Hence the owls, hunting. But that's not what I saw." He held out the memory stick.

Tashjian took it. "Sterile computer?"

Mancuso pointed at a terminal in the corner. A minute later, after running a malware scan, Tashjian put up a video on the computer's screen.

Caitlin asked Garcia, "What time was this?"

"Right around twelve thirty a.m.," Garcia said.

"Why so late?" Mancuso said.

"You have to wait for the basketball games to finish up. New York wildlife is bold, but instinct still rules. Better to let the place quiet down. And I'm a night owl. No pun intended."

Caitlin sensed his nervousness. Maybe he wasn't used to dealing with the cops. Mancuso wasn't setting him at ease. But from the way Garcia kept eyeing the computer screen, he seemed unsettled by what it would show.

"Let's see the video," she said.

Tashjian hit Play. The video opened on a walking path in the park between FDR Drive and the East River.

"I moved under the trees," Garcia said. "To be unobtrusive. Letting any animals that had gotten ruffled by my approach calm down and get back to being. Most wildlife knows the scent and sound of humans around here and doesn't get frightened off the way it might in the wilderness. There are white-tailed deer in the Bronx and Staten."

"Bambi Takes Manhattan," Mancuso said.

Caitlin watched the screen. The camera panned slowly, the focus and light settings changing as Garcia played around with the new lens. The leaves on the trees came off light gray. When he panned to the river, the lights of high-rises on the far shore in Brooklyn flashed phosphorous-bright. He kept panning. Squirrels scampered up a tree, hot white. Headlights in the distance, high in the air, crossed the Williamsburg Bridge.

"I was out of sight, that's the thing." Garcia's voice was strained. "There's a grove of trees behind the park benches. I was standing still, trying to blend. Let all the creepy-crawlies come out." He brushed his forehead with the back of his hand. "I mean, birds and predators."

The camera panned upriver. In the distance, a couple strolled away arm in arm, their forms burning white. The camera continued to pan.

Along the water, near the railing above the river, walked a ghostly human shadow.

Caitlin saw short hair, broad shoulders, slim hips—a typically masculine outline. A bouncing step, like a boxer's.

"*That*," Garcia said.

Everyone grew silent and intent. Something about the shadow seemed eerily *off*, but she couldn't put her finger on why. The figure—hot white, clearly delineated—walked along the riverbank at a brisk clip.

"Oh, no," Caitlin said.

The ghostly figure was keeping pace with a pale gray object floating in the river. It bobbed up and down, only partly visible, but its outline quickly became recognizable.

"That's a body," Mancuso said.

Caitlin felt a chill. "It's pale gray because it's cooling."

The thermal lens captured heat. Hotter translated as whiter. And she now knew why the killer had duct-taped the lifebuoy to her chest: to keep the body from sinking below the surface. To ensure that she was seen and recovered.

Garcia spoke tightly. "I noticed the man walking, but even at that hour, it's not unusual. I just kept filming. I didn't focus on the water at all, until the news broke this morning, about the murder. And when I took another look at the video . . ."

The video panned a little farther, skimming past the hot shadow walking downriver. The camera swiveled up to catch birds roosting in the treetops. When it swooped back down, the shadow was at the edge of the frame, walking more slowly than before.

The body in the river floated toward the Williamsburg Bridge. The shadow stopped to watch it drift away. Then put both hands together and raised them to the sky. In the shape of a heart.

"Jesus Christ," Caitlin said.

Tashjian hit Pause. There was no doubt. A heart.

He hit Play. The shadow turned, jogged to a park bench, and scrawled on it with a marker. Then he hustled past darkened basketball courts, ran across a pedestrian bridge that crossed the FDR, and disappeared amid apartment towers to the west.

Caitlin, Mancuso, and Tashjian exchanged glances.

Caitlin spun. "Thank you, Mr. Garcia."

They practically ran out the door.

16

At East River Park, the sun was beating down. The greenery throbbed and the asphalt shimmered with heat. The salty scent of the river kicked on a gusting breeze. Thunderclouds were rolling toward the city from the west, charcoal gray.

The Williamsburg Bridge loomed overhead, latticed with iron trusswork, droning with traffic, its approaches and anchorage piers pale brown stone. The park bench overlooked the Manhattan-side pier, where the victim's body had bumped to a stop.

Fishing rods rested against the railing above the river, lines trailing in the water. The fishermen sat on the park bench, two men in their sixties, leaning back, chatting in what sounded to Caitlin like Cantonese. When they spotted her and the detectives beelining toward them, they stood and meandered to their rods, immediately interested in not being there.

The graffito drawn by the unsub was clear and vivid. It was a foot tall, taking up several slats in the bench.

It was a broken heart. And a message.

GET IT?

Mancuso put his hands on his hips. "Ho-lee shit."

Caitlin took out her phone and snapped photos, getting down on one knee, zooming in. Mancuso called for patrol officers to close off the area, and a crime scene unit. Fingerprint, DNA, trace, he was saying.

Caitlin stepped back, riveted by the message.

"He's stepping out from Goode's shadow," she said.

The implications pressed in on her. There was no record of Goode leaving written messages at his crime scenes. He never taunted the police or public this way. The copycat was staking a claim to something here.

But, she realized, Goode had recently been sending *exactly* this kind of message. By drawing portraits. By labeling them. *Truck stop hooker, Paducah Kentucky 2003. East River, NYC, 2008.*

Tashjian stepped up. "What's going on in this guy's head?"

"I don't know if he's talking to us or to Efrem Judah Goode or to somebody else, but he wants us to see this."

"He didn't know he was going to be captured on video," Tashjian said. "Didn't know the victim would end up lodged against the bridge instead of floating into the Upper Bay or getting caught in a cruise ship's propeller."

"This is Goode's dump site. That's what counted," she said. "The copycat left a love note."

She turned in a slow circle, taking in the park. Then she headed for the pedestrian overpass, eyes on the ground for signs of anything the unsub might have left behind. For disturbances, for she didn't know what. The ringing noise of traffic on the bridge blended with the rush of tires on the FDR beyond the bike path. Yellow cabs, delivery trucks, shiny SUVs.

Tashjian caught up and they ascended the stairs to the pedestrian overpass, scanning the railing for graffiti as they crossed. Traffic whined past beneath them. They came down the stairs beneath the massive support ramp for the bridge.

Tashjian scanned the surrounding area. "He could have gone any direction. But he was escaping from a body dump. He headed for an exit. The subway, a cab, the spot where he parked a vehicle. All that's west of here. That suggests he continued up Delancey."

"Split up," Caitlin said. "I'll take the north side."

She ducked under the bridge approach and headed along the quieter surface street.

What the hell was this unsub up to?

Redbrick apartment blocks rose at the corner of FDR Drive. At a slow jog, she headed west. Trees shivered in the gusting wind. She passed playgrounds, newish parked cars, mothers with children in strollers, retired couples walking back from a market.

After a few blocks, she saw a bank. When she stepped in and showed her credentials, the manager stood, instantly energized.

"I'll be happy to show you our surveillance footage, Special Agent Hendrix."

Banks loved feds.

Caitlin felt a warm glow at his respect. She knew she should slip that feeling into her pocket so she didn't get attached to it. And so she could take it out and pet it when the NYPD tried to brush her off with a snide remark or failure to share information.

The manager led her to a security office. She gave him the time window and said, "I need the feed from cameras that overlook the street."

He quickly found the relevant footage. It showed the sidewalk and street illuminated by streetlights. Traffic on the Williamsburg Bridge was steady, even after midnight. The manager ran the footage at twice the normal speed. Caitlin watched for a person passing on foot.

"There. Stop," she said.

On-screen, the shadow jogged down Delancey, swimming into view beneath a streetlight. She asked the manager to rewind the video and run it at normal speed.

The killer ran in and out of the circle of light, a burst of 1940s noir but in fatigue pants, a black puff jacket, and athletic shoes. Pale hands, held in loose fists. His jacket topped a hoodie that draped over his face. She couldn't see his features. Passing beyond the light, he rounded the corner onto a cross street. Just a flash, three steps and gone. But the brief view set Caitlin's fingers tingling. The video was low quality, and enhancing it the way TV shows did was fantasy. But Keyes and the NYPD's techs could possibly scrape valuable information from it.

The unsub had left a virtual trail. And she was on it.

She phoned Tashjian. "Found him."

She asked the manager to download a copy of the video for her. She thanked him, made clear that the police would request an official copy, and told him not to delete it.

She headed back to the street.

The sidewalk was busy, the cross street busier. It was nearing

5:00 p.m. She wanted more video and wanted it now. She was hot, feeling the rush of the hunt. And with every hour that passed, more video systems were likely to erase footage. After twenty-four hours, plenty would be gone.

The cross street was lined with parked cars. Brick buildings stood packed cheek by jowl. Ahead was a massive apartment tower with cameras on the facade. When Caitlin went in, just a minute before five, the woman at the management office was locking up. Caitlin flashed her credentials. The woman told her, politely but firmly, that she would need a subpoena or warrant to view the footage. Caitlin didn't argue, just told her that one would be coming, and headed back out.

She went north to the next corner. Which way?

The killer could have gone in any direction, but the thermal-imaging video showed him pacing the floating body at the riverside. Caitlin felt sure the killer had a vehicle. Something easy to get victims into and out of. Something that gave him privacy and freedom of movement.

He had parked it. And after strolling alongside Chelsea Symanski's body, he ran back to it.

He'd been strolling south.

She continued north.

She crossed the intersection, eyeing businesses for cameras. A café. A shoe store. A church with freshly painted brick and white trim. She slowed. The paint was new but not new enough to keep graffiti from being scrawled on it.

Not tagging—a broken heart.

"You bastard."

She snapped photos. The wind gusted again, bending the branches of trees bristling with spring-green leaves. The sunshine dimmed as gray clouds scudded into view above the rooftops.

The graffiti had been drawn with a Sharpie. Maybe permanent ink, maybe not. She didn't touch it. But she couldn't trust it to last, not with rain coming. Or with the church's beautification committee turning up to erase it with whitewash or a bucket of soapy water.

She called Tashjian. "He headed north and kept drawing broken hearts. There's one on the wall at St. Sebastian Church. I'll talk to the people here, but you need to get this preserved as evidence."

"On my way. I'm a block behind you," Tashjian said.

Caitlin turned and saw him back toward Delancey, marching in her direction. She climbed the church steps and waved broadly.

Five minutes later, after speaking to the pastor, she rejoined Tashjian on the street. He opened a phone app that showed CCTV locations in the city. Caitlin thought that was a nifty little toy—if you were into building out a surveillance state. Her dueling angels of federal crime fighter and Berkeley civil liberties activist duked that out for a moment. Tashjian nodded up the block.

They each took a side of the street, heading north in parallel. Past a school and playground. Apartment buildings with black metal fire escapes. Tashjian ducked into a minimart. Minimarts always had surveillance cameras and stripes on the door jamb to indicate the height off the ground and tell how tall robbers were. After a minute, he beckoned Caitlin.

"They got him on camera. Just a glimpse of his legs, running past. Still heading north."

They were at a major intersection. She said, "Across Houston?"

"Yeah."

They waited for a break in traffic. When they crossed, she found a freshly drawn broken heart on a lamppost.

The clouds rolled past on a chilly gust. The trees cowered under the wind. Fat drops of rain hit Caitlin's face. Tashjian crossed to the far sidewalk and headed into an electronics store.

Soon, he stepped back out and whistled. "Jackpot."

The clouds opened as she crossed the street. People scurried for cover. Thunder cracked, shaking plate glass windows. It was just a cloudburst—the sky to the west was already clearing. But it changed the city's entire mood. And hers. She knew that any fingerprints left by the copycat on the copious locations where he drew graffiti might be washing away.

She hurried into the electronics store and dabbed rain from her face with the arm of her jacket. Tashjian was smiling. The store's camera had captured gold: the copycat jumping into an SUV.

The video was shot from about a hundred yards away. It was dim, showing the unsub from behind. But it provided a clear view of the vehicle. The shop manager sent the video to both their emails. As they waited by the door for the rain to ease, Caitlin phoned Keyes.

"Sending something your way. Priority is off the charts."

Keyes said, "Which chart? Astrological?"

In the background, Caitlin could hear classical music playing in his office. Soaring soprano voices, a whiff of Valhalla. Opera. Damn, Rainey had gotten to Keyes.

"Video for analysis," she said. "Color CCTV from a retail surveillance camera. Man getting in an SUV and driving away. Wring every drop of data from it you can."

"Yesterday, I presume."

"At the latest."

Outside, people ran past, some holding backpacks over their heads. A man with a pit bull on a leash ambled nonchalantly by. Rain splashed on the sidewalk.

"Thanks, Keyes." Caitlin ended the call. She thought for a moment. "This is the first direct evidence we have of the killer's crime scene behavior. It's bizarre. The question is, has he behaved similarly at the other crime scenes?"

"Does it matter?" Tashjian said.

"I think it does. Because it tells us whether the unsub screwed up last night, or planned to get his turn as a video star."

"What do you mean?"

As quickly as it had started, the cloudburst stopped. The wind dropped and sunlight split the clouds, turning the sidewalks silver, the lines on the road a burning gold. Caitlin and Tashjian stepped outside and walked in the direction the unsub had parked the SUV.

"I've had this uneasy feeling about what he did," Caitlin said. "'Uneasy' meaning I'm of two minds. What he did was horrific."

"And he did it in my town," Tashjian said.

"That's what's been biting at the back of my mind."

A cab splashed past, glistening a wet egg-yolk yellow in the sudden sunlight.

"This is the fourth murder linked to the copycat," she said. "The first where an abduction—and, presumably, the killing—took place in New York City. The second where a body was disposed of here. The previous kidnapping, murder, and dump sites . . ."

She stopped herself.

"I hate that term. *Dump site*," she said. "We're indicating how cruel these murderers are, treating human beings like trash. But when we use the term, it feels like we're adopting their mentality. We need some other shorthand to describe it. I can't even imagine how it feels for a murder victim's family to hear their lost child, or brother, or wife talked about in that way."

Tashjian shot a glance at her. "Agree. Didn't expect to hear a fed sound like such a warm, nurturing blanket."

"It matters." She shook her head. "The copycat disposed of his first victims in remote rural areas. His concern about being seen would have been minimal. But in New York?"

"He's following Goode's pattern. That determines his behavior," Tashjian said.

"That might determine the order in which he kills, and his decision about where to leave his victims' bodies . . ." She considered it. "Duplicating Goode's crimes would necessitate leaving the bodies in public places here in the city. The killer's willingness to do that says he's bold, confident, a risk-taker. What really cements that is all this video evidence. He followed the body along the river. Why? For entertainment?"

"You tell me. That's your department," Tashjian said.

"What gets me is the killer's willingness to be seen in the open, here." She swept her arm at the city. "So many eyes."

"Crowds create anonymity."

"So many cameras."

"He might not know that if he's from one of the rural areas where he started killing."

"True. Which brings me to my original point. Did he cavort around the streets here out of ignorance, or hubris? Or did he *want* us to find his graffiti and the videos?"

"The graffiti's too obscure. Too likely to be overlooked," Tashjian said.

"He was playing. His ego's enormous, and his sense of invincibility is growing."

"Let him rely on it. He'll make a mistake."

She had another thought. "I'm wondering if he's local. Because he's either scoped out his entry and escape routes from the crime scenes ahead of time—like a SEAL team infiltrating a terrorist hideout—or he's extremely familiar with the city. On the thermal-imaging video, after the killer made the heart hands, he headed straight for the pedestrian overpass. No hesitation. No hunting for it in the dark. He knew it was there."

"And that matters because . . ."

"He didn't double back. When people are in a new location—whether it's a theater, a hotel, or an airliner—if they need to get out fast, they overwhelmingly head for the door they entered by. They overlook the brightly lit exit sign or the nearby stairwell or the overwing exit. For somebody who's just committed murder and engaged in a public display that put him in danger of arrest, you'd think his first impulse, his second, and his last would be to escape. If he was at the park for the first time, that suggests his instinct would be to turn on his heel and race straight for the SUV."

They reached the spot on the street where the copycat had parked the SUV. It had now been eighteen hours at minimum, and the rain had cleaned the street of potential evidence.

"But the killer didn't double back. He headed at right angles to where it was parked." She pointed at the ground. "He maneuvered here indirectly, on a route he'd scoped out. He planned."

"That he did," Tashjian said. He checked his phone app. "I'll keep going north, check for more videos of the SUV."

Caitlin looked up and down the street. "I'll backtrack. See if I can find more graffiti."

A hundred yards back, across an intersection, she saw a business they had skipped past—a jewelry store. Cameras bedecked the premises. The owner, a suave older man who trailed the scent of cigars, happily let her look at his video. Jewelers—another group that, on the whole, liked law enforcement.

In his office, behind a steel door with electronic access almost as good as the bank's, the owner pulled up video that Caitlin could now give quick parameters for.

"That's it."

The store's street-facing camera caught the copycat passing by outside, jamming the marker in his pocket, and running across the street.

"Thank you." She repeated her spiel about expecting an official request to preserve and turn over the footage.

Outside, Caitlin hunted for what she was sure must be the killer's graffiti. She walked up and down the street. Lampposts. A bus stop shelter. The sidewalk. No sign of anything.

She was stymied. The jewelry store footage unmistakably showed the copycat stuffing a marker into a pocket. Why put it away unless he'd had it out, tagging?

Until she realized, it was daytime. Shops were open.

She walked to a bakery next door to the jewelry store. Looked up and saw a glint of silver.

She yanked on the bakery's metal roll-up door. Inside, the woman behind the counter called, "Hey!"

Caitlin stepped back.

When the metal door clanged down, the heart was right there. Three feet tall.

I ♡ HOMICIDE

Below that was written, GONNA GET IT GOOD.

17

"**G**oddamn," Caitlin said.

From inside the bakery came banging on the metal door. "What the hell?"

"FBI," she said.

The woman inside pulled the door halfway up. Caitlin held out her creds and said, "One minute. Please."

Skeptical but acquiescent, the woman let go, and the door rolled down again. Standing on the wet sidewalk, Caitlin snapped photos.

She phoned Tashjian. "Get back here." Her pulse was thudding.

I heart homicide.

Gonna get it good.

Good . . . *Goode.*

"What's going on?" Tashjian said.

"The copycat is playing some kind of game."

"On my way."

Caitlin's mind raced. She raised the roll-up door and thanked the proprietor. Then she frantically reviewed old crime scene photos. People passed her on the sidewalk, and cars splashed by on the glistening street.

It took her less than a minute. "God-*double*-damn."

There, on a bridge support at the 2005 North Carolina crime scene, nestled amid overflowing graffiti, was a small spray-painted heart. Her vision pulsed.

Another one at the 2008 Brooklyn scene, squirreled into an entire wall of graffiti.

At the Kentucky crime scene, a graffiti-laden bridge was visible far upstream from the victim's body—beyond the police tape and, thus, probably uninvestigated.

How could she and every other cop have missed this?

Tashjian jogged up. He had the same grimly eager look on his face that she imagined she had on hers.

"What's the game?" he said.

"Hearts." She handed him her phone. "Broken hearts."

Had Goode scribbled a broken heart for each of his "beauties?" For his long-gone baby? For his missing road companion, Corliss Yates?

Tashjian frowned, shaking his head. "Is the copycat playing with Goode? Against him?" He looked up at her. "Trying to outdo him?"

"Or playing with us. Or all of it."

Goode had hidden this under their noses.

The broken heart was a signature.

And the copycat knew about it.

These photos had never been released to the public, yet the copycat knew of the signature. This unsub wasn't some random fan of Efrem Judah Goode. The Broken Heart Killer had a connection to him.

18

In the Hudson Valley, the sun was going down. The narrow road wound through heavily wooded backcountry. Greenery flickered past. Power lines sagged under ivy. The last red dregs of sunset patched the asphalt as the Yukon curved along. Houses were intermittent, mostly whitewashed clapboard homes where American flags blew stiffly in the oncoming storm and where the occasional pickup rusted on concrete blocks on the lawn.

The Yukon passed a fire station that looked exceptionally tidy because the firefighters had nothing to do besides keep the building swept, their hoses stowed, and their pecs and delts popping for that Hudson Valley Firefighters Calendar. Every now and then, a long gravel driveway led back through the trees. Those were farms, generally old ones, with dairy barns, and cornfields in rotation with soybeans and red clover. The newer places, the vineyards and artisanal organic cooperatives, had handcrafted signs posted along the road, for the drive-by tourists.

Dropping down a long hill, the Yukon crossed a stone bridge over a creek. Shadows and cloud overtook the dusk. At a listing mailbox topped by a painted red metal rooster, a dirt driveway headed through heavy trees and overgrown grass and bushes.

The Yukon turned in. Creeping along the rutted drive, it followed a tunnel of trees, leaves brushing the roof, dandelion puffs swirling in the last orange flare of sunlight as the wind picked up. After several minutes at a near crawl, the driver got a glimpse of a dilapidated white farmhouse. A jolly red-painted door stood out like lipstick. Beyond it were overgrown trees, a rotting barn, and cornfields. This was it.

The driver turned off the headlights and eased the Yukon over the last stretch of the potholed drive. Downshifted to low gear to keep from using the brakes and lighting the trees with that insidious red glow. Do that, and you alert people on the property to the vehicle's approach. No way.

Inside the farmhouse, a figure was visible, watching television. Sitting in a sagging recliner in the living room, with the eerie blue light flickering across her face. She looked downtrodden. Yes, that was the word. She was watching the TV fervently, brow creased, as if whatever was on-screen had twisted her panties into a double-hitch knot. The driver let the Yukon roll to a stop, killed the engine, and climbed out to the frantic insect buzz that heralded the approach of rain. Rush of wind. The woman was fanning herself with a *People* magazine, scowling.

Well. This will be fun.

On the dusty drive, footsteps left no sound. The back door opened without a creak. The driver carefully shut it again and paused, listening. The TV show was *Forensic Files*. Cheesy, creepy synth music, a breathless narration. Some tale of a black-widow wife who poisoned her husbands, one after the other, with arsenic. So unoriginal.

At least it wasn't a news report on Efrem Judah Goode.

The driver walked silently into the living room. Stopped just beyond arm's reach of the recliner. The back of the woman's head was visible, her hair piled on top and secured messily with a rubber band. The driver breathed, and thought, and took another step. The floor creaked.

The woman continued to stare at the droning TV. "That you, Landry?"

Maybe this wouldn't be so much fun after all.

"The one and only."

She looked up sharply. Her face froze, perplexed. She frowned.

"Where'd you get those clothes?" Her eyes zipped up and down. "You look like Kurt Cobain."

The driver smiled. Better to smile than to tell her about the other clothes—the ones spattered with blood, stuffed in a New York trash can. "I'll change for dinner, Mom."

"Where you been?" The woman stood up. She tossed the *People* mag, stepped closer, and sniffed Landry's shirt. "Sneak out for sex?"

Yeah, it was one of those nights.

Take a breath. "Of course I did. Then stole his clothes, left him there buck naked, and ran." Landry winked and, when Mom snorted in amusement, rubbed her shoulder. Face mild, expression sensitive, attentive but not distressed. Calibrated. "Tough day?"

Mom sighed and plopped back in her chair.

Soothe her when she was like this—that was the best you could do. Mom got overwhelmed when she was alone. Overwrought. And she'd been alone for nearly a week this time. Landry knew not to let Mom get wind of anything. Landry treated her delicately, like a snake handler maneuvering around an agitated cobra.

People called Mom mercurial. Loving one minute, icy the next. She was what shrinks called impulsive borderline. Landry had looked it up. Capricious, seductive, a risk-seeker. A stranger to empathy, terrified of abandonment, full of dark energy that could suddenly flare—an emotional IED.

Important to know that, living with her. It made handling her safer. Less likelihood of getting bitten or blown up. Which kept things calmer, kept the questions to a minimum.

Mom could erupt, basically without warning. Like flipping a switch. But with everything the world had dumped on her, it was no surprise. Humiliation, hunger, loss—a whole laundry list of awfulness.

"Wanted to order art supplies but was afraid to use the card," she said. "It gets rejected, somebody takes down the address . . . Who knows what kind of trouble comes rolling up the driveway?"

Landry could remember being little and Mom counting out pennies to pay for their convenience-store bologna. A man behind her muttered, *Hurry it up, Lindsay Lohan.* Landry had cringed. Mom kept counting, ignoring the man, eyes on the change in her palm, but Landry had caught her infinitesimal pause. The psychic slap. It had stung, no doubt. And everyone else in line at the store had gotten the insult.

But up the sidewalk five minutes later, Mom swept serenely past the man, head high. Back at the car, she opened the wallet she'd lifted from his pocket. Inside was a hundred bucks. Tearfully she pulled Landry into her arms. A hundred bucks meant they would eat. For a week.

Mom had given Landry everything. Sacrificed everything. Created a much better life than so many other kids whose parents were poor and desperate ever got. Out of nothing, out of abuse and degradation, she had created a life of adventure, exploration, discovery. Road trips and libraries. Out in the barn was an entire suitcase full of library books they'd picked up over the years. Each one a universe, an education, an escape into wonder. Mom would do anything to give Landry a clean home, hot food, clothes, an education, even if it was unconventional.

Landry owed Mom everything and would take care of her forever.

All that mattered was that she not find the rolls of duct tape under the tarp in the Yukon. Duct tape set her off.

"You taught me that clothes are nothing but sleight of hand, right?" Landry squeezed her shoulder. "I'll heat you up a Lean Cuisine. Chicken pot pie?"

"With gravy."

"You got it, Corliss."

19

How did the copycat know that Goode drew broken hearts at his dump sites?

Back at the Manhattan South Homicide Squad, Caitlin pulled up every single image from both Goode's and the copycat's killings and began scouring them. The sun had sunk to a scarlet stripe on the horizon. Office windows reflected the ruddy gleam. Traffic rivered on the streets outside. She finger-combed her damp hair off her neck, twisted it into a low bun, and pinned it in place with a pencil.

Crime scene photographs popped up on her screen. Bodies of victims in situ. Along the banks of streams. In muddy storm drains. Pulled onto the bank of the East River in 2008.

Her gaze flitted across the photos. She was hopped up. *Calm down.* Deliberately slowing, she examined each one carefully. It took her less than a minute to find the first broken heart—at the copycat's dump site in Maryland, on the inner lip of the storm drain.

"Got you," she said.

She switched to photos of Goode's killing at the same location, fifteen years earlier. Graffiti was ubiquitous in that one; in the intervening years, the site had been cleaned up, or tagging had fallen out of fashion. Goode's victim lay facedown, one arm extended straight ahead. She'd probably been dragged by the wrist through the storm drain, then dropped. It made her look like a swimmer doing the crawl. Again Caitlin felt a pang.

The victim's autopsy showed that she had died before being taken to the ditch. Small comfort that she never knew the degradation Goode inflicted to eliminate trace evidence.

In the photo, gleaming water trickled from the storm drain. Caitlin saw no broken hearts on the culvert's concrete. Downstream, the creek's edges looked freshly cleared—brush and trees trimmed back, maybe as flood control. Trees in the distance had red spray-painted Xs on their trunks, marking them for trimming or removal. She refocused.

There it was. On the trunk of a sycamore twenty feet from the victim's body. Below the X was a red broken heart. The woman in the creek was aimed directly at it, as if she were stretching her hand to see what was broken.

"Son of a bitch."

After that, the hearts seemed to leap out at her. Kentucky. Arkansas. Maryland. North Carolina.

Tashjian appeared at her shoulder. "What's this?"

"I heart homicide. Countrywide," she said.

"Holy shit."

She leaned back. What about the Spring River victims? The duct tape mummies? The Chevy Impala had been exhaustively photographed. So had the motel room where the three side-by-side victims were found. No graffiti had been mentioned in any of the reports on those crimes. Was it because Goode had been caught before he could dispose of his victims?

"Goode left his signature at all these scenes, for years, and nobody noticed," Tashjian said.

"They blended. Just more graffiti. And without linkage, there was no way to tie this to any crime as his signature. Goddamn."

"What about the Brooklyn pier?" Tashjian said.

Caitlin pulled up the old and new crime scene photos.

"Shit," Tashjian said.

In the 2008 pics, the heart was simply part of a massive wall of graffiti. In the latest photos, it cleverly melded into a mural that faced the river.

"This wall is even on the Brooklyn Graffiti Tour," Caitlin said.

She got on the phone to Emmerich. He listened, his silence seeming to crackle.

"Is Goode purposely influencing the Broken Heart Killer?" he said.

"That's what I'm wondering," she said. "There's a connection. Information is flowing. *Nobody* knew about this signature. Only Goode or ..."

"Or who?"

"Somebody he told, clearly. Or an accomplice. Or someone so obsessed with him that they found this before we did."

"We need to know," Emmerich said. "Get back to Nashville. Go in with the Tennessee detectives. Resume interrogating him."

"On my way."

Ending the call, she stood and grabbed her jacket. She gave Tashjian a hot look, eager and uncertain.

"I'm going to Nashville," she said. "I'm going to put this together."

"Belly of the beast," Tashjian said. "Carry a spear."

20

A morning stillness lay across the green Tennessee hills. It took the edge off Caitlin's drive to the prison. Her eagerness to interrogate Goode was spiked with apprehension. The case had spiraled. The faces of victims lurked in the corners of her mind, watching her. A low whisper seemed to score the air. *Why did we die?*

She tried to shake off her dread-laden sense of urgency, talking on the phone with Sean as she pulled into the prison lot.

"I'm early. I don't see the local investigators." She parked and killed the engine. "And I'm glad I packed my running gear."

She was wearing a black suit with pencil slacks, a gray T-shirt, and loafers. No belt, but a sports bra. Visitors weren't allowed to wear any metal.

"Otherwise, I'd have to cut open my lace bra and rip out the under-wire with my teeth."

"I'd pay good money to see that," Sean said.

"Maybe for Christmas."

A Jessup County Sheriff's cruiser swung in and parked beside her.

"I'm up," she said. "See you tonight."

"Watch your six."

"Always."

She climbed out to greet the two detectives who exited from the cruiser. One was a pale Ichabod Crane of a man with long limbs, a sepulchral face, and deep-set eyes.

"Special Agent Hendrix? R. C. Pettibone."

She took the hand he extended. It was cold. "Lieutenant."

"You been here before, I take it."

His voice was reedy, with a drawl softer than a puppy's ears. A good voice for talking to victims' families. But his gaze was iron hard. He was sizing her up, maybe checking to see if her spine was stiff enough to handle the convicts inside a southern prison.

She held his eye. "I'm the one Goode gave his drawings to. And you're the one who asked my unit chief to send BAU interrogators."

He nodded curtly. The other man came around the cruiser, buttoning a jacket that barely contained his cannonball shoulders. African American, young, calm but looking ready to launch.

"Detective Hayes?" Caitlin said.

He tipped his head. "Ma'am."

"Never." She smiled. "Caitlin."

Marius Hayes, who had arrested Goode, looked ready to spar with him again. Psyched and champing at the bit. Maybe as anxious as she was. This case had shredded the fabric of the town he guarded, thrown him into the spotlight, scoured his mind and heart.

Pettibone smoothed his tie. "Seems we've all met Mr. Efrem Goode, the smug bastard. Getting him to admit a connection to the copycat killer—that'll be a trick."

"I want us to tag-team," Caitlin said, "You two lead. I'll lurk in the background. Let him wonder why I'm here."

Pettibone squinted against the morning sun. "He's going to think you're here out of desperation, hoping he'll give you more crumbs. He's going to be conniving and smiley."

"Like a snake that just swallowed a rabbit, I'm sure." She set her face flat. "I can play smug and smiley too."

Hayes said, "You want to be Bad Cop?"

"Just want to tip him off balance wondering what I'm going to do."

He looked amused. "Like the *Simpsons* episode with the Mafia squaring off against the yakuza. 'But, Marge, that little guy hasn't done anything yet. Look at him. He's gonna do something—and you know it's gonna be good . . .'"

"I'll be the little guy," she said. "Happily."

They eyed her. She was five ten, six feet in stack-heel loafers. As tall as Hayes, though several inches shorter than Pettibone, whose forehead could have scraped a low ceiling.

Pettibone nodded. "More like the Smoking Man from *X-Files*. Stay in the shadows until you're ready to slither out and strike."

She genuinely laughed.

"We'll work up to the copycat connection," Pettibone said. "I'll play dumb. Let him think he has the bit in his teeth."

In the interview room, under the racket of voices and slamming doors, smelling the faint aroma of pancake syrup, Hayes and Pettibone took seats at the table. Caitlin leaned back against the cinder-block wall. They heard clinking chains. A guard's face appeared in the door's containment-glass porthole. He opened it, and Goode strolled in.

"Strolled" about covered it. Considering his feet were shackled, he should have been shuffling. But his attitude was all strut. Pumped, plump with hubris, exuding feigned ennui.

Caitlin kept her arms loose, idly tapping her thumbs against the wall. Goode caught sight of her, didn't slow, no hitch in his stride, but his gaze sharpened and his shoulders lowered, just enough. An animal response. Perhaps ingrained through repetition, all those robberies, burglaries, murders—the criminal's fine-tuned reaction to a threat environment. He had adapted to the structure and rituals of incarceration with heightened predatory instincts.

He sat, studiously ignoring Caitlin as the guards shackled him to the floor. When they left, he rested his arms on the table and laced his fingers together, centered and calm.

Like a coiled viper. Again, she wondered, what was his game?

"You're at it so early," Goode said. "Y'all made me rush my breakfast." He slid a look Caitlin's way. "And here's my friendly fed. Don't stand in the corner, hon; the light's bad on your face."

Definitely feeling full of himself. Caitlin stared, dead-eyed.

Pettibone said, "How you holding up, Efrem? Getting enough exercise? Food okay?"

Goode said he was all right. The food sucked. Meals back at the Spring River jail had been better because deputies sometimes brought in Popeyes chicken. Hayes and Pettibone pretended to smile. They chatted for a bit; then Pettibone flattened his hands on the table.

"We want you to know that the information you gave the FBI has been helpful. We're getting someplace thanks to it. Let's keep going on positive terms."

Goode flicked a glance at Caitlin. "I gave. What do I get today?"

Hayes said, "The drawings helped verify some of the claims you've made. That's good, Efrem. That shows that your memories are accurate. But there's still a ton of missing information. Such as victims' names."

Goode hulked forward, shoulders bunching. "Why should I tell you?"

"It would be a win for you," Hayes said. "It'd affect your appeal."

Goode scoffed. "Doubt that. Besides, I'm here for truth-telling. On *my* terms."

"You a praying man?" Pettibone said.

"Never found that it got me much."

"You said the women you killed were angels. Did you think they'd fly to heaven, thanking God for meeting you?"

Goode scratched his cheek, raising both cuffed hands. "That's a pretty thought. Them telling God I sent 'em hurrying home."

"God knows their names," Hayes said. "We don't. Three victims are still unidentified."

Goode's lips retracted. It was almost a smile. "Then maybe *you* should pray."

Hayes's voice stayed steady, but below the table his right hand drew into a fist. "You don't want to tell us, okay. We don't need their names for a dance card. But there are families out there, wondering, Is that my daughter? My sister?"

"You crazy? You think Mama and Daddy want to know their baby's dead? Not a chance. They're living on hope. I ain't gonna ruin their fantasies. No names." He leaned back, seemingly disgusted. "Break their hearts? Fuck, no."

Caitlin stopped breathing for a beat. Hayes and Pettibone went silent.

She spoke casually. "About that."

Goode glanced up. "About what?"

"The broken hearts."

He blinked slowly.

Hayes shifted his shoulders. "The ones you spray-painted at crime scenes. On bridge abutments, overpasses. On the tree beside the Maryland storm drain."

Goode settled in the chair. He looked . . . satisfied. "Took you long enough to get it."

A nasty buzz started at the back of Caitlin's brain. *Get it? Good*, the copycat had written on the bakery door.

Her mind raced. Goode claimed he wanted to tell his story, wanted to expose law enforcement's failures—to crow that for twenty years the FBI missed his trail of murder. He had to wonder what they had discovered about him. She was convinced that fame wasn't his end goal. But his monstrous ego was ravenous for nourishment. If they offered to feed it, he might talk.

"You want to know what's happening outside, thanks to your confessions?" she said.

"Not really." His eyes said otherwise.

Pettibone shook his head. He had hangdog down to an art. "If you think those mamas and daddies aren't already heartbroken, you're mistaken." He sighed. "Aren't you sorry?"

Goode sneered.

Caitlin knew he felt no remorse. She assumed that Pettibone knew it too and was playing stupid.

In a bored tone, she said, "Sorry you got caught?"

At that, Goode laughed. "You think I got caught? Nobody could catch me. Not you, not any of my beauties . . ." His gaze drifted and his face darkened. "I got hooked. And handed in."

His response sent a jolt down her back. It wasn't what she'd expected.

How *did* Goode get arrested? He claimed that he was roofied and framed for the Spring River murders. The jury disagreed. They concluded that Goode killed his victims, wrapped them up, and planned to drop them in a series of isolated locations before continuing his road trip into darkness. But that he couldn't resist getting hammered before taking the first victim to a disposal site and ended up driving to the sheriff's station.

Goode insisted he had no memory of his arrest or the hours leading up to it. Was he lying? Or was there a real basis to his white-hot insistence that somebody set him up?

If so, who?

Caitlin thought of Goode's female traveling companion. The woman who owned that old Cadillac. Could she be alive?

"Who framed you?" she said.

"I have twenty years' worth of enemies. Could be any of them."

He was cagy, playing some infuriating game she couldn't decipher. Enemies. Did they include the woman? Did she set him up? Was he now after *her*?

Caitlin spoke with genuine curiosity. "What are you after? Is it the cash you stashed from your robberies? Or is it revenge against Corliss Yates?"

A veil dropped across his expression.

She didn't move from the wall. Not immediately. Then she stepped forward, hands loose.

"Well," she said. "Surprise, surprise."

She'd cornered him.

He tilted his head. Leaned back, breathing more heavily than before. The rattler eyes blinked. Then he sneered.

"Where's my book deal?"

She held his gaze but didn't immediately answer. He jumped into the silence.

"And no bullshit. Don't tell me a prisoner can't publish a book. Supreme Court says I have the right. Free expression. Publisher can put my money in a state escrow account, and if anyone related to my beauties has a complaint, they can sue. But I have the right. First Amendment." He glared. "I do my research, hon."

She took her time. "Here's the thing. A book's got to have exciting revelations. But we've figured out the broken-heart graffiti. If you want to sell your story, you need more. Something shocking I can offer a publisher. What can you give me?"

"No. First, the deal. You want me to talk, you better deliver on that."

He turned to Hayes and Pettibone, steaming. "Call the guard. I'm done."

Pettibone shifted. "Efrem—"

"I need to see the chaplain. Got a sudden case of spiritual indigestion. *Guard*."

In the lobby a few minutes later, Pettibone looked downcast. Hayes shook his head.

"Strikeout," he said.

Caitlin felt a restless energy. "No. That was helpful."

"Not so sure about that," Pettibone said.

"It was. Goode is deliberately influencing the Broken Heart Killer. I'm positive." She turned to them. "When he heard we'd discovered his graffiti, he lit up. It was more than an ego rush. He knows we're piecing something together. He knows that the broken hearts matter to us. That was valuable information to him." She paused. "That tells me he knows the copycat is acting in response to his confessions."

Hayes's eyes narrowed. "I don't want him lighting up. I want him shut down. We should make sure he doesn't give the copycat any more information."

"Absolutely," she said.

Hayes turned and walked to the desk. "We need to speak to the warden. It's urgent."

He made another fist. "Time to put pressure on Goode. Need to take away his computer privileges and cut his access to the outside world."

21

When Caitlin turned the key in the lock, the front door opened to the sounds of Muse thundering from the stereo. Outside, a deep blue twilight seeped up from the western horizon. Her suit was wrinkled, her feet tired, her knees sore from cramming into the back-row seat on the flight from Nashville. She kicked off her shoes, dropped her gear, and headed to the living room. She stopped. And laughed.

Sean hated working evenings—stakeouts and raids aside. He loathed spending what should be his off hours doing paperwork.

But paperwork was what covered the town house. "Supermassive Black Hole" pounded from the speakers. Case files were spread across the coffee table, the kitchen island, the counters. Crime scene photos. Images of bomb components. Stills from the raid on a cabin in the California desert, where coils of barbed wire had filled the interior. Photos were stuck to the bookshelves with tape. In the kitchen, his back to her, Sean leaned over a sheaf of printouts, engrossed. His ass, in those jeans, looked fantastic.

She considered sneaking up on him. But guys who dealt with *boom* for a living generally didn't appreciate that kind of surprise. He nodded absentmindedly to the beat. Her smile spread.

"I like this view," she called over the music.

He glanced over his shoulder and smiled. When she walked up, he pulled her tight and kissed her. Just long enough. His eyes were bright, his expression focused somewhere far beyond the kitchen. He was coming up for air to say hello, genuinely happy that she was home, but the interruption had knocked him off his stride.

She boxed his ear and stepped back. "As you were."

"Dive in," he said. "Join me. You look beat. You get dinner?"

She nodded. She'd scarfed a sandwich at the Nashville airport. She got a Topo Chico from the fridge, found a bottle opener, and popped the cap off.

"Bring me up to speed."

She knew what he was working on. The ATF was narrowing its hunt for the Temescal bomber.

After fifteen months, the Alameda County Medical Examiner's Office had finally identified the victim who was strapped with the bomb. Rebecca Green, age forty-six, was a Northern California recluse who lived in a faded Victorian in Red Bluff. She had no family. When her neighbors finally realized she was missing, nobody thought to look for her beyond the city limits. Certainly not one hundred eighty miles south in Oakland. She'd once been a lively student at Berkeley, before schizophrenia and poverty took their toll. How she ended up on the street near the University of California campus that night was still unknown.

Was Green a pawn of the bomber? An accomplice? Had he lured her there? They still had no idea how he turned her into his walking bomb vest.

Or even whether the Ghost was the bomber.

Sean was closing in—but with explosives, close could be dangerous.

His laptop was open on the living room coffee table. Caitlin saw a dozen small video windows open in a grid. Each displayed dark, gritty low-resolution surveillance camera footage.

"Your Oakland all-seeing-eye project," she said.

"You told me I needed a hobby."

He said it wryly, but his eyes held something fierce.

Convinced that the bomber had lurked near the hospital to watch his device explode, Sean had gathered hundreds of CCTV videos recorded near Temescal. It had taken months of legwork but—as she saw on his screen—had delivered a trove of potential evidence.

Analyzing it would require a nightmarish amount of work.

Caitlin chugged the sparkling water. Sean's ferocious energy was reviving her. "How do you hope to pick out the unsub from"—she gestured at the computer screen—"what must be thousands of other people in these videos?"

"Maybe ten thousand, given that the cameras cover an area three-quarters of a mile square, roughly, and run for more than an hour in some cases."

"Jesus, Sean."

He handed her a printed article from the kitchen counter. It was from a medical journal.

"Psychopathy: Neural Deficits in Reaction Response," she said.

"A psychiatric study on psychopaths."

She skimmed the piece. It was a neuropsychiatric evaluation of a large population—which Caitlin took to mean convicted criminals. It analyzed reflex reactions in individuals diagnosed with antisocial personality disorder or psychopathic personality disorder, or whose brain scans showed the neurological patterns associated with psychopathy.

"Their fear levels test far below nonpsychopaths," Caitlin read. "And ..." She looked up. "They have virtually no startle response."

Sean stood motionless, coiled, bright-eyed. "The startle response is involuntary. A defensive reaction to sudden or threatening stimuli. Noise, sharp movement, a flash."

"You mean it makes people duck."

"Yes. Recoil. Raise their hands to their face or the back of their head. It's meant to protect the eyes and the neck. It triggers an escape response. It's lizard-brain level."

She paused, taking it in. "Psychopaths lack a survival reflex?"

"It makes them fearless."

Excitement hit her. "And it's a *tell.*"

Sean nodded. "When the Temescal bomb exploded, all of Oakland shuddered. All except the psychopath who did it." He smiled. "He'll be the person on video who doesn't flinch."

22

The email arrived as Finch was walking home from her shift at the coffeehouse.

SUBJECT: Your MoreMatch DNA results

She clutched the phone tight, her throat instantly dry, and ran up the echoing stairs to the apartment. She kicked the door shut and sloughed off her backpack. Held her thumb over the phone and paused.

This was the big deal. This was something she would want to save, maybe hide, maybe—oh, crap, why would she hide it from her mom? This was the first real step on her self-directed journey (which Mr. Herrera had taught about in English class) toward agency and self-actualization. Like Arthur pulling the sword from the stone. Her stomach clenched. She headed to the living room, the big window overlooking the back garden. Breathed.

She opened the message.

The text seemed to throb before her eyes. Happy words, exclamation points. A map of the world with regions highlighted in bright colors. A chart with ethnicity estimates. Portugal. Scotland/Wales. Finland/Northwest Russia. South Asia, 3 percent.

The message included a link to see all the data online. The phone screen was too small. She booted her mom's desktop and opened the link on the big, sharp monitor.

The world came to her. She saw it, shimmering, and blinked away tears.

"Whew." Her voice sounded little. Her hummingbird heart drummed against her chest.

Her entire background was in here. And, critically, her actual DNA profile was now analyzed and available to her. Every chromosome, every amino acid base pair that told her tale.

That told the truth.

That was what she needed now. Because her mom refused to deal with it. Because, after promising to talk, Annie had practically barked at Finch.

"Your birth mother was not murdered by a serial killer. You're imagining something that isn't true," she said.

Finch had begged, "How do you know?"

Annie went cold. "Trust me." And shut her down.

Now Finch clicked the link to her DNA file. It was huge and, she saw, encrypted. It would be incomprehensible in its raw form. But it was the clue.

Her phone rang, jolting her. "Livin' la Vida Loca," the ringtone she used for her mom. A joke between them. Irony. *"She's into superstitions . . ."* It was one of her mom's favorite songs from the nineties but was the total opposite of her life. Kitchens at peak hours could be crazy, but Annie Winter was a no-drama mama. *"I feel a premonition—that girl's gonna make me fall."*

All at once, Finch felt guilty. She reflexively closed the DNA site, though the call was voice and her mom wouldn't be able to see it, *duh*, and what was the problem anyway?

She answered. "Hey, Mom."

"You home? If you chop carrots and onions and celery, I'll make coq au vin tonight." Annie's voice was light, with its usual shining edge.

Finch dug her thumbnail into the desktop. "What time will you be home?"

"Six thirty. We'll have an evening in. You can teach me how to play that game."

"*Red Dead Redemption.*"

"Yeah." There was a smile, even if rushed, in Annie's voice. "How was school?"

"You know. Hormones. Food fights. Musical theater numbers broke out in the hallway."

"Cheerleader smackdowns?"

"Chem lab explosion."

"Love you. See you tonight."

Finch ended the call and set the phone on the desk. The dryness in her throat had returned. She reopened the genealogy site.

Getting her results felt like hope . . . and betrayal. Fear and longing. The truth was actually out there. It was not simply a slogan. From More-Match, whose site she was staring at, *she could actually find people she was genetically related to. Cousins.*

That could mean people who had known her birth mother. Who had proof. But subscribing to Cousin Match meant paying up—*again.* And she wouldn't get paid by the coffeehouse for two more weeks. Even if she got extra hours, or babysat or dog-walked, it wouldn't be enough. Her stomach felt queasy. Even if she earned the money, the site wanted a monthly enrollment fee paid for with a credit card and all she had was debit, but thousands of new subscribers were joining every month, so getting just one snapshot result wouldn't be enough. It would lock her out when new cousins might be joining, and she'd never know.

She leaned back. *Slow down.* Why had she submitted her DNA in the first place? Because Agent Hendrix had told her, flat out, that DNA was the evidence the police would take seriously.

Now she had it. She found the agent's card. Squaring her shoulders, she typed an email.

At Quantico, Caitlin was on the phone with Detective Hayes when her computer pinged with incoming emails.

IN DC ON MONDAY.

It was from her mother. Caitlin wheeled back in surprise. Happy surprise. Mostly.

Mom. Coming. For work. From Berkeley. Caitlin hadn't seen her since the holidays. She estimated how long it would take to vacuum lines into the town house's carpet, which her mother wouldn't notice, because Sandy Hendrix never looked down, only straight at you.

Caitlin replied, Awesome!!

The second email was equally startling.

FROM: Finch Winter
SUBJECT: EVIDENCE

Hi Special Agent Hendrix,
I have received my full DNA profile from MoreMatch. The profile is ready to be tested for a match with the unidentified 2008 murder victim who Efrem Judah Goode killed and threw into the East River in Brooklyn.

"Dang, kid," Caitlin said.

Rainey passed by. "Did you just say *dang?*"

Caitlin spun her chair. "This teenager in New York is a terrier," she explained, shaking her head. "I'm impressed with the girl's initiative."

"What else does she have besides initiative and a DNA profile?" Rainey said.

Caitlin read the rest of the email with Rainey looking over her shoulder.

I know it seems statistically a small chance that the unidentified victim is my birth mother, but the DNA comparison would prove it one way or the other. I also found this photograph.

Rainey leaned closer. "Dang."

Finch had attached a scan of an old snapshot. The date in the corner was July 2007. Three young women—girls, really—leaning against the wall outside a diner. They were skinny, defiant, clearly posing but looking genuinely ballsy. And wary—at least the young woman in the middle. The one with the heart-shaped face and the torn Pendleton shirt that covered her arms despite what looked like a hot summer day.

The one who looked shockingly like a live version of the Brooklyn Jane Doe's autopsy photo.

And who looked exactly like the drawing Goode had made of the victim he claimed he'd kicked from the rotting pier.

It was the jut of the girl's chin, the flyaway blond hair, the dreamy desire in her eyes, underlaid with something hot and hungry.

"Jesus," Rainey said.

"The bastard really captured her."

"This is way more than initiative. The kid is onto something." Rainey scanned the email. "No other information about the photo though. She doesn't say who took it or where she got it—or even whether it's in her possession. Still, wow."

Caitlin picked up her desk phone and punched a number. "NYPD needs this."

"Tashjian," the homicide detective answered.

"Caitlin Hendrix. Got something you should see. I'm forwarding."

She stayed on the line. A minute later, Tashjian said, "Shit."

Finch had the vegetables washed, peeled, and chopped, physics problem set spread across the kitchen table—*done*—when the email arrived. The light outside the kitchen window was bending toward gold. She heard kids playing in the courtyard. She wiped her hands on a dish towel.

Dear Finch, the email began.

Crap. She'd started her own email with *Hi*. How stupid, how . . . *teenage*. This was real adult-world shit. Her stomach tightened.

Thank you . . .

Agent Hendrix went on, all official, all dripping thanks, Miss Honeybee, but blowing her off again. Again again again.

I have forwarded your email to the detectives investigating the cold case at the New York Police Department. The NYPD has custody of the victim's DNA. Before they can test it against anyone else's for a match, they need strong evidence that the member of the public who submits a profile is related to the victim.

"But ..."

The scanned photo you sent could provide this sort of evidence, but before the police proceed, they need further information.

Finch read the rest and got it. Got it cold. A faded old snapshot wouldn't cut it. The cops wanted the name of the photographer. Wanted a chain of custody. She'd learned that phrase in Civics, their module on the criminal justice system.

She didn't have any of that and couldn't get it unless she told Annie what she was doing (betrayed Annie—*say it*—been a sneak, violated her trust), and she didn't know how she could thread that needle. Not yet. She wanted to throw the phone across the room.

Instead, she slumped on the sofa and texted Zack. They're tuning me out again.

He didn't immediately reply. Ugh, he was at band practice. She leaned back against the cushions and stared numbly at the ceiling.

Ping. Zack responded. Don't let the bastards get you down. Find another path.

Another path. What? Where?

She pulled up MoreMatch again. *Cousin match.* She stared at it, frustrated.

Then it hit her. MoreMatch wasn't the only site out there, or even the largest. There were others. And some of them let you upload your DNA profile for free.

She sat up straight. Searched.

By the time she finished working at her mom's desktop computer, the sun had turned orange and sunk below the rooftops. The public genealogy site, YourGenealogy.com, was basic—no frills, no graphics—but it didn't cost anything. Finch uploaded her raw DNA profile.

Then she tried to swallow. Nobody, it seemed, wanted her to find evidence that proved who she was. But she would find it anyway.

She clicked through to other sections on the site. On its discussion forums, she found a section titled "Seeking Long-Lost Relatives."

She thought about it. She went to the kitchen and got a LaCroix, still thinking.

A key turned in the apartment door. Her mom came in, looking glad to be home, smiling. "Hope you're hungry."

Damn, no no *no*.

Finch took a step toward the computer, but Annie was already there, dropping her purse on the desk.

"What's this?" she said.

Finch felt herself sailing across the apartment, saw her mom lean on the desk, looking, saw her reach for the mouse, saw the colorful tattoo on her forearm—the songbird, the finch—saw her enlarge the computer window.

"It's nothing." Finch ducked in front of her, knocking Annie's hand off the mouse.

"Finch."

"It's just something I was looking at." Rapid-fire she closed the browser window and cleared her history.

Annie set her hands on her hips. Her jeans had flour on them. "Seeking long-lost relatives?"

"It's nothing. It's *curiosity*. Is that a crime?"

"If it's about the sketch that killer drew, then yes. It's about a terrible crime. And it's dangerous. Finch, you have to drop this."

"Why?"

Annie's face had turned white. "It's unhealthy."

"Bullshit."

"Hey."

"It's *necessary*. Finding out anything about my birth mother is *justice*." Finch's voice cracked. "If you'd tell me *anything*, I wouldn't have to do this. If you had a single scrap of evidence disproving the possibility. Mementos. Letters. Photos of her."

"No."

Finch turned so hot she thought her head would catch fire. Annie had just lied to her.

She backed away, shaking her head.

"Drop the topic," Annie said. "It's only going to take you somewhere bad."

Tears rose in Finch's eyes, blurring her vision. She turned, stormed to her room, and slammed the door.

A second later, Annie knocked. "Don't do this."

Finch flipped the lock. Annie had lied *to her face.*

No photos? What the absolute hell?

Leaning back against the door, Finch slid to the floor. She blinked away her tears. Taking out her phone, she went to the public genealogy site.

On the "Long-Lost Relatives" forum, she started a new thread.

Help me find my mother's killer.

23

The Georgetown restaurant was a low-lit Italian place with distressed brick and an open kitchen. It smelled like garlic, yuppies, and power. When Caitlin walked in, a woman jumped to her feet, face glowing. Her electric-green top drew the light like a gemstone. She didn't exactly bound toward Caitlin so much as teleport and envelope her in a hug.

"Baby girl," she said.

Her hair was the same auburn as Caitlin's, but threaded with silver. She leaned back and took Caitlin's face in both hands. Happy. And assessing.

Caitlin submitted to the examination. "Hey, Mom."

"Look at you, popping to this bistro straight from work in the nation's capital."

Sandy Hendrix was the human version of double espresso with a Red Bull chaser. Senior paralegal for an East Bay law firm, she had come to DC with a litigation team for depositions in a trademark case. They sat. Caitlin asked if she'd had a good day.

"Bitch-ass case, up against bitch-ass corporate attorneys, but it's all good. I got to the Air and Space Museum this afternoon, holy Jesus, that place. I ordered bruschetta. And calamari."

Her mom took her in greedily. She seemed to approve of Caitlin's teal suit with the sleeveless cream sweater beneath.

"Are you armed?" she said.

"Always."

My mother, the tornado. Caitlin described her mom as independent and nurturing. Sean generally added, "And feisty."

Sandy swept her hair back. "The FBI shouldn't have control over you twenty-four hours a day. You told them that the job stays at the station, right?"

"The FBI doesn't have stations."

"Smart-ass."

Having been married to a detective, Sandy hadn't been surprised that Caitlin followed her father into investigative work. She never tried to dissuade her from pinning on a badge. But she knew the downside. She'd seen the worst that cop life offered.

"The government doesn't own you," she said. "And promise me nobody here is trying to enforce any fascist loyalty oaths."

"No oaths except the one I swore to defend the Constitution," Caitlin said. "But I'm required to take my calamari with a side of Glock."

Sandy eyed her. "How'd my girl get so tough?"

You know how, Caitlin thought. One day when she was nine, she came home from school to find a patrol car outside and two officers in the kitchen speaking to her mom. Caitlin had careened in, sure that Mack had been killed in the line of duty, because what else but death brought a patrol car to a cop's wife?

But her dad wasn't dead. His partner was. The cops were there to tell Sandy that, crazed with grief, Mack had driven off a bridge. And Sandy, seeing Caitlin near panic, swept her into a hug. But her face remained calm, as pale as marble and just as solid.

Caitlin got tough by modeling herself on her mom.

The waiter brought their appetizers. Sandy talked, buzzing—her usual quantum state—then paused, leaned back, and patted Caitlin's arm.

Three, two, one . . .

"And?" Sandy said. "How are you doing?"

Sandy knew that the previous winter Caitlin had succumbed to the urge to cut herself. Caitlin never considered withholding it. Even if she'd wanted to, Sandy would eventually have seen her in short sleeves and noticed white lines on her skin that hadn't been there before. And she would have pounced.

"I'm fine." She smiled. "Seriously, I'm good."

The anxiety on Sandy's face was plain to see.

"I told you. I found a therapist. I'm learning healthy ways to handle stress."

"That sounds like a nice slogan."

Caitlin resisted the urge to retreat into a shell. Her mom liked to put all cards faceup on the table. Nobody played poker with Sandy Hendrix, much less charades. But Caitlin reminded herself she was ready for this.

"Dr. Silverberg works with first responders, special forces operators, and law enforcement. And with child social workers, and moms whose kids have special needs. All kinds of people facing all kinds of fires."

"I want to know how she's helping *you* move forward."

"Like a freight train. Coming down a mountain pass with the brakes off and horn blaring."

Sandy made a face. "How's work? You look tired."

"Bitch-ass case, up against bitch-ass bad guys, but it's all good."

Sandy scowled.

Caitlin put her hand over her mom's. "There aren't guarantees. But I'm okay."

Sandy held her breath, let it out, and dropped the tension she'd been holding. Caitlin knew what her mother feared: a spiral. Toward the demons that had latched on to her dad.

"I'm proud I got this job," Caitlin said. "Proud of the work I do. Dad—" Her voice caught. "Dad would be too."

Sandy's eyes looked wide and dark, flecked with pain.

Caitlin patched the crack in her voice. "I want you to be proud of me as well."

Sandy clasped her arm. "Oh, sweetheart. I couldn't be prouder of you if I tried."

Caitlin felt a wave rising, lifting her. *Chill*, she told herself. Then *Why?*

She squeezed her eyes shut and let tears roll. She wiped them away. Laughed.

She checked her fingers for smeared mascara. "And before you ask, stress management doesn't just mean going for runs with Michele or consciously separating myself from the people I investigate and the people they hurt. It means accepting that I can't fix the world or rescue everyone."

"I don't believe it. You might as well try to scrub off original sin."

"I've had to admit that I'm a single individual. Possibly human. That I get my turn up to bat. That if I close my eyes, the Earth won't spin off its axis."

"I did raise you to think the sun rose and set around your every wish."

"Like hell you did. And thank God for that." She squeezed her mom's hand. "I'll do my part. Hope I do it well. Remind myself the weight of the universe isn't all on me."

"Thanks for the reassurance," her mom said.

"Take it to the bank."

Sandy nodded, and her shoulders lowered. It looked as if she was getting ready to launch into something new. Caitlin raised an eyebrow.

"Yes?" she said.

"I want to bring up something that's been weighing on me." She tried a smile before her expression turned grave. "The Ghost."

Caitlin could feel her heartbeat in her throat.

"That's what you call him, isn't it?" Sandy said.

"I do. What about him?"

During the hunt for the Prophet, the Ghost had threatened Sandy. He pulled his truck up beside her car at a stoplight. Late at night, on an empty street. He honked, claimed she had a flat, and tried to talk her into letting him fix it.

He live streamed the entire conversation to Caitlin.

Sandy had barely escaped. No way in hell would she let a voice emanating from a darkened truck cab convince her to open her car door. But it had been too damn close. It meant he knew who she was and how to find her.

"Since that night," she started.

"I'm working on it," Caitlin said. "The Bureau's working on it."

"Of course you are." Sandy frowned. "That's not what I'm saying."

"Are *you* okay?" Caitlin said.

"Perfectly fine. Madder than a nest of hornets."

"Don't let it eat at you."

"I don't. But . . . I wonder *why* the Ghost became a parasite on the Prophet's killings."

That was the prizewinning question. The answer had eluded Caitlin for several years now.

"I wonder what he's after." Sandy paused. "Whether he'll come for you."

Caitlin wondered the same thing.

The Ghost had phoned on her first day at the BAU, to warn that her time was coming. His call was audacious. Arrogant. It told her he sought to control and destroy.

He was brash, confident, and full of rage and loathing. He had injected himself as instigator and accomplice to a garish serial killer. That told her he was a Machiavellian manipulator and charmer. He toyed with people, then killed them. Was she an avatar for his hatreds? Did he loathe authority? The "System"?

Because of his expertise with explosives, she'd spoken to FBI counterterrorism agents. They gamed out the worst-case scenario: that the Ghost was a bomber who could combine forces with hackers to carry out simultaneous attacks in the virtual and physical worlds. Attacks that might shut down a building's doors, elevators, communication systems, and fire-safety features. Or take down a 911 system while carrying out a physical atrocity. It would cause havoc.

She feared he was planning something big.

Sandy looked as though she was holding something back. Caitlin said, "Out with it."

From her oversized purse, Sandy brought out a spiral-bound notebook, royal blue, its edges curled. At the top was written HENDRIX.

Caitlin stared. Shocked. "Dad gave me all his notebooks. At least, I thought he did."

"I found it when I cleaned out my storage unit," Sandy said.

Caitlin ran her fingers over the name where he'd scratched it on the cover. She felt a welter of emotions. Mack had kept copious notes on all the homicide investigations he worked. But he had obsessed over only one.

"I suppose I shouldn't be surprised," she said.

Touching something she'd never seen before, something that had belonged to her father, felt like a weird gift. He wasn't here anymore. She didn't get new experiences with him. A bright aura seemed to surround her, the notebook, the table, her mom.

She guessed this mix of pain and joy was belated grief.

She opened the notebook. Her father's handwriting, tight and intense, filled the pages. These were notes on one of the early killings committed by the Prophet in the nineties. No—the first.

She looked at her mother sharply. "Wow."

Sandy leaned on the table, steepling her fingers.

The notes included detailed descriptions of the crime scene, a list of witnesses, names of the responding officers, and hand-drawn maps. This was her dad at his most thorough and meticulous, before the gears started to get loose. Along with the who-what-when-where, Mack had written pages trying to answer the question *Why?*

The first killing. Before anyone even knew what was coming. Before anybody understood that a serial killer was unsheathing his claws.

She read, shaking her head. "Dad had no idea what was ahead."

"He couldn't have. Nobody did."

Despite the impossibility of it, Caitlin wanted to reach through the pages, back in time, and grab her dad by his lapels. To whisper, *watch out.*

She turned the page.

March 20, 1994. David Wehner.

Caitlin remembered crime scene photos: a carnival funhouse, a cotton candy stand. And Wehner's body, propped in the seat of a Ferris wheel, suffocated with a plastic bag. A note from the killer was pinned to his shirt. *This is a sign of what was, and is, and is to come.*

It sounded like the ravings of a demented prophet and gave the killer his nickname.

Mack's notes tried hard not to veer into wild speculation. But the scene was so grotesque, so seemingly inexplicable, that he could do nothing else.

He couldn't have known that the Bay Area was in for hell. Again Caitlin shot a look at her mom. Sandy's lips had whitened to a grim scar.

"Keep going," she said.

Caitlin turned the page. Paper-clipped to the notebook was an eight-by-ten envelope full of photos. She slid them out.

"Holy shit."

There were dozens of shots snapped with an Instamatic camera. Caitlin set aside her plate and spread them out.

"Dad took these," she said. "They're not official photographs from the Sheriff's Department photographer or the medical examiner's office."

Mack had always snapped unofficial shots, rolls of them, at crime scenes. These hadn't been taken with the intent to enter them into evidence but because Mack saw something meaningful or that might turn out to be meaningful. They were all new to her.

She could see that her dad had snapped a series of shots to build a 360-degree panorama. Bright sunlight, shining wet pavement; it had rained the night before. The carnival rides looked wind battered. In the background, trees, a parking lot, big rigs. In the center was the Ferris wheel, with the car bearing the victim's body, surrounded by cops, the ME leaning over the horrific sight of the plastic bag on the man's head.

The waiter arrived and abruptly stopped. Caitlin swept the photos up and flipped them over. He looked off-kilter for a mere fraction of a second, then smiled smoothly.

"Another drink?" he said.

"We're good," Sandy said.

He disappeared. No surprise. In Washington, waiters saw all kinds of things they pretended not to. At least at this table, a congressman wasn't being seduced into a Russian honey trap.

Caitlin turned the photos back over. "These are what you wanted me to see, Mom?"

Sandy just stared. Caitlin slowed down to examine the photos further. In one, behind yellow police tape, curious bystanders crowded the background. Sandy pointed.

A young teen lurked at the periphery. He was blond, slim, intense. Thirteen, Caitlin guessed, not much more.

A cold feeling pricked the back of her neck, like a single drop of ice water hitting her and rolling down her spine.

She turned to the next page in the notebook.

March 21, 1995. Barbara Gertz.

A year after the first murder, Gertz was stabbed and her body left in a car wash. In the notebook, another envelope contained more Instamatic photos. This time, Mack's 360-degree panorama captured the car wash, a strip of businesses, and a church where live oaks dotted the property. This time, Caitlin knew what to look for. And she found it.

Under the trees, the same kid was standing in the shadows.

He was taller, more filled out—clearly a teen rather than a gawky boy who had just been hit with puberty. But the distant, hyperfocused intensity on his face was unmistakable.

The same boy was in both crime scene photos. He was a bystander gripped by horrifying serial killings. And more. He was a boy who could have grown into the man Caitlin had seen at a biker bar several years back. The man she later discovered was the Ghost.

She felt an electric thrill. "Oh my God."

24

Caitlin arrived at work early the next morning pumped up, still fizzing with shock at the information her mother had found. Sean had nearly spat coffee across the kitchen when she showed him. She scanned Mack's notebook and snapshots and sent them to Sergeant Joe Guthrie, the lead investigator on the Prophet/Ghost killings at the Alameda County Sheriff's Department—her former boss.

These were never logged as official notes or crime scene photographs, but my father signed and dated the photos. My mother can attest to an unbroken chain of custody, and they're now logged as in the possession of the FBI.

Joe, I'm going to work this from my end. I'll keep you updated. If you find anything, let me know how I can help amplify.

C.

She also sent Guthrie the FBI sketch artist's drawing of the Ghost. She had sent it before, but she wanted it right in front of Guthrie's eyes. He would jump on this. The possibility that the killer had lived in the Bay Area at the dawn of the Prophet's attacks would help focus and narrow the search.

She stared at the photo of the teen. Murmured, "I'm onto you."

The office was stirring to life. Rainey came in, chatting with Noriko

Sato. Emmerich swept by, phone to his ear, nodding as he passed. When Caitlin saw Keyes round the corner, coffee in hand, messenger bag over one shoulder, she caught his eye.

He was already heading for her desk. "I identified the SUV used by the Broken Heart Killer. It's a GMC Yukon. Dark sapphire blue."

"Excellent," she said.

He set his coffee on her desk. "Mind?"

She scooted her chair back. He leaned over her computer and pulled up a CCTV video showing the SUV driving away. The rear license plate was visible.

"Plates come back as stolen," Keyes said. "They were taken from a car parked on the street in Manhattan, the day of the murder." He hit a key and the location of the plate theft came up. "Still, those tags will show up on license plate readers in the five boroughs. I'll see if I can find the Yukon taking any bridges and tunnels into or out of NYC."

It was a solid lead and lifted her energy even more than the coffee. That sent her hunting for echoes between the old and new Manhattan murders.

She turned to a question that remained unanswered. Goode claimed he'd killed and thrown a young woman into the river in 2008—the goth teen named Liv. But New York City had recorded no 2008 homicides where a female victim washed up near the Williamsburg Bridge.

She needed to look elsewhere for confirmation. Maybe the death had been recorded as an accident. Or suicide. Maybe the young woman's body washed up outside the city limits.

Caitlin checked to see where a body dropped in the East River would likely be pulled by the current. *Oh.* The East River technically wasn't a river but a tidal strait. It connected the Harlem River with two fingers of the Atlantic Ocean—New York Harbor and Long Island Sound. The current shifted depending on the tides.

She leaned back, called to Rainey, and explained what she had discovered. "Liv's body could have been taken by the current to Connecticut, or into the Atlantic."

"Or Goode's lying," Rainey said.

"We have to check death records in three states, a dozen counties, I don't know how many towns with a shoreline." Frustration cinched around her. "I feel like I'm holding a frayed rope that has nothing on the other end."

Rainey thought for a moment. "In one sense, it doesn't matter whether Goode's telling the truth."

"Right. Either way, the copycat regards the location as significant because that's where he threw Chelsea Symanski's body in the river."

Her fingers drummed on the desk. "Gonna talk to Emmerich. I'll be more useful on the street."

"In New York?" Rainey glanced at her computer. "I'll join you if I can get there tonight."

Nodding, Caitlin headed to Emmerich's office. She knocked, and he looked up over his reading glasses.

"I need to take another look at the neighborhood where the Broken Heart Killer dumped Chelsea Symanski. There's too much that I can't interpret from photos or CCTV clips of the killer. I need to get back on the street. If I drive, I can be there early this afternoon."

"What in particular has you so wound up?" he said.

"Four killings connected to New York. Then, and now. What's next? I have an ungodly suspicion that the Broken Heart Killer is still in the city and stalking his next victim."

"Call NYPD. Let them know you're coming."

She appreciated the endorsement. "I can be there by lunch if I rocket."

"Go." He sent her off with a lift of an eyebrow that, for him, counted as a belly laugh.

In lower Manhattan, Caitlin parked the FBI Suburban by the Williamsburg Bridge. The noontime sun glazed the scene blue and white. She took a last bite of the pastrami sandwich she'd grabbed a few blocks back. When she got out, the breeze lifted her hair. She put on her sunglasses. Above her, the rush of bridge traffic blended into the city's relentless aural landscape.

She walked to the FDR and crossed the pedestrian bridge. She paused halfway, taking in the motorscape, the unnatural mix of cars, trucks, buses, and human beings on foot or bicycle, the presence of birds overhead.

The Broken Heart Killer had dumped Chelsea Symanski's body in

the river, then run, late at night. Almost everything the killer had done
so far had been under the cover of darkness. That, Caitlin thought, was
by design. To maintain anonymity. To facilitate escape. To surprise and
terrify victims, to confuse them, catching them with their defenses down,
giving himself crucial seconds to gain an advantage over them.

She crossed the park to the river. The water was turbid and slate blue.
Chelsea's face rose in her mind, wet hair shrouding her cheeks, dead eyes
despondent. She turned from the water. The park bench with the broken
heart was empty. It looked mocking.

She needed to absorb and observe, to be present, to see if she'd missed
anything on her previous search of the area. This dense, information-rich
3D environment didn't allow for seeing and understanding everything
that flooded in all at once. She hung her phone on a lanyard around her
neck and set it to record video. Then she retraced the killer's escape route.

He had taken this path as a getaway but had also used this neighborhood as a stage. Or a playground. A canvas. This was where he acted
out his elaborate, taunting postmurder behavior. She needed to analyze
and understand it.

When she reached the bakery where the killer had sharpied
"I ♡ HOMICIDE," she stopped. The block had low commercial buildings: florists, hardware stores, boutiques. Places that were all shuttered
at midnight. Again, she saw nothing exceptional about the bakery itself.
Had the killer chosen the roll-up door randomly, because it was bare of
graffiti—a clean canvas?

Inside, the proprietor was loading loaves of bread onto shelves behind
a glass case. Caitlin stood where the killer had, looking up and down the
street.

The bakery was near a corner. The Yukon had parked across the intersection, a hundred yards north. Thanks to the broad cross street, Caitlin
had a clear view to the river.

The killer must have driven as close to the water as possible, removed
the body from the vehicle, left it on the riverbank, then parked and returned on foot to roll his victim into the river.

Presuming he was alone.

Caitlin considered it. The Broken Heart Killer was working from Goode's playbook. But could he be working with a confederate? The video from the night Chelsea's body was dumped showed the killer walking alone along the riverfront. When he returned to the Yukon, he jumped in the driver's seat. She had seen no sign that another person was in the car. That didn't exclude the possibility, but it lowered it.

Keyes was going over hours of footage captured that night. The NYPD was hunting for video taken in Greenwich Village the night before that, searching for images of the killer stalking or abducting Chelsea Symanski. Facial recognition software could assist, but identifying the killer from among thousands of people on the streets of Manhattan would be a chore and a half, as her grandmother used to say.

But that was where big law enforcement agencies had an advantage. The FBI and NYPD didn't always have cutting-edge hardware, but they had brains who could weave and dodge and find important information. Brains like Keyes.

The smell of fresh bread and cupcake icing filled the bakery behind her. The proprietor saw her and paused, dismay on her face. The FBI swarming over her shop hadn't been fun. She raised her chin in brief acknowledgment. Caitlin waved but didn't go inside. That seemed to ease the woman's mind.

Caitlin turned. *Focus on the offender's behavior.* This location was an extended part of crime scene. The huge heart, and the message, had been left here. The wind cut around the corner. The view down the cross street to the water struck Caitlin as significant.

She pulled up the surveillance video captured by the jewelry store camera that night. She saw the unsub jogging along the street. Steady pace. Up on his toes, still full of energy a mile from the riverside spot where he raised his hands in a heart. He was fit. And he didn't slow to consider where to draw *I heart homicide*. Didn't look around. He came straight to the bakery.

Deliberately. He had the Sharpie out and raised before he got within fifty feet. He had been aiming for this spot. Caitlin turned slowly, pivoting her gaze toward the river.

Trees, cars, and the FDR obscured much of the view. But when she stepped away from the bakery door, she saw not only the water but beyond. She recognized something.

She recognized some*where*. A place she had been only recently.

Directly across the river, Goode's 2008 Brooklyn crime scene was visible.

She wouldn't have known it from fifty thousand other spots in New York City except for the two shining glass condominium towers that now flanked the location. She assured herself she was actually seeing it. Then she jogged along the cross street to another pedestrian overpass across the FDR. Looking back, the bakery door was absolutely in view. She ascended the stairs and walked to the center of the overpass. Loud traffic rushed past below her.

There was no doubt. The crime scene was directly across the river, at least two hundred yards away but plainly visible. It practically flashed like a strobe light. The rotting pier and vivid graffiti mural were unmistakable.

She caught her breath. The sight line to the 2008 murder scene and to its present-day duplicate both thrilled and unsettled her. She snapped photos and took a 360-degree video. Then, before leaving, she told herself, *Wait. Pay attention for just another minute. The killer was laying out signs, symbols, hints at meaning. Let them come to you.*

South of her was the Williamsburg Bridge. She let her gaze flow up the river with the water. Brooklyn construction. A ferry chugging toward a Manhattan pier. The bright wall of the graffiti mural, psychedelic, kaleidoscopic. It naturally drew the eye.

"What should I be seeing?"

She stilled. She saw the pier and leftover yellow police tape tied around a light post. That was chilling enough. But beyond the crime scene was something else she recognized.

Past the pier, across a vacant lot, was an old diner. Its red neon sign was familiar. It was the diner in the photo that Finch Winter had shown her.

"No way. You're shitting me."

But even as she said it, she knew it was true. A direct line ran between the diner, the crime scene, and the bakery where the killer had written "I heart homicide." Fire a harpoon from the diner's front step, and it would arrow past the pier and embed itself in the heart painted on the bakery's roll-down door.

She called Emmerich.

"Hendrix," he said. "You have something?"

"The kid, Finch, is onto something. We need to investigate this place, the diner," she said. "It's called Landry's."

25

The overhead lights at the Pop-In-Go buzzed spasmodically. Like a bug zapper, Tonya Pappas thought. The doorbell chimed and a customer clomped in, bringing along humid air, noise from the expressway, and an undercurrent of diesel exhaust. Behind the counter, Tonya flipped her hair over her shoulder, eyeing him. An overboiled frat boy in a too-tight golf shirt, yakking on his phone. He looked right through her. Headed for the refrigerated section and—oh, what a surprise—grabbed a twelve-pack of brews.

She was rocking a Spandex top with a wench-style lace-up front. But her leprechaun-green Pop-In-Go vest covered it, and that was what he saw. Like she was just a piece of equipment in the convenience store. She could have been a credit card terminal.

Fat frat boy grabbed a second twelve-pack. Go on, asshole. Drink till your shirt balloons over your beer gut, and your golf pants split up the ass.

She was forty-seven. But married only twice, no kids. Her jeans size hadn't changed in thirty years.

Look at me, you punk.

He dropped the beer on the counter, phone stuck to his ear. "He'll fold. Hammer him and close the deal."

She rang him up, glaring.

Pop-In-Go was steady work, a no-sweat job. But this guy. For some reason, he ground her gears. He just wouldn't frickin' look at her. Yammering into the phone, ignoring the total for the beer.

He didn't know about her online life. What she controlled. The connections she had. Who she was.

The woman who ran the Efrem Judah Goode Facebook fan page.

"Thirty-nine ninety-eight," she said.

He pointed at the shelf behind her. "And a fifth of Stoli."

Before she could grab the vodka, her phone buzzed in her back pocket. Her manager would disapprove, that pissant ferret, but she took the phone out. If Frat Boy could converse during their transaction, so could she.

There was a text. It was from an unfamiliar number. Frowning, she thumbed the preview.

Hey, T-bird.

Her breath caught. She stopped herself, swallowed the grin, fighting it. Only one person called her T-bird.

Still blabbing away on his sales call, Frat Boy snapped his fingers at her. She felt a wave of anger rise, then subside. Confidence swept in to replace it.

Fat Frat had no idea who he was dealing with. Who backed her up. And what her friend, the one who called her T-bird—the one, the only, the truly incomparable Efrem Judah Goode—could do to him given a chance. Given the word, from her. Well, she bet. If she asked, and right now, boy, did she feel like asking.

Tonya turned and walked away, not caring, going straight through the stockroom and out the rear door, into the alley behind the Pop-In-Go.

She could get Fat Frat's license number off the CCTV if she wanted. She felt a swell of power. *The bastard didn't know who I am.*

But Efrem did.

Lighting a smoke, Tonya leaned against the minimart's brick wall. She savored her first drag, waiting, letting the anticipation build. Then she opened the text.

New phone, the message began. COs put me in lockdown.

"Cocksuckers," Tonya muttered.

Reading on, she learned that purely from spite and meanness, the prison guards—correctional officers, COs—had suspended Efrem from exercise and from using the library and barred his usual weekly phone call. They were punishing him, for nothing. Just because he stood tall and looked them in the eye, and they couldn't take that, couldn't deal with a man being a man. It made her chest ache. Efrem was a caged tiger. Magnificent creatures like him weren't meant for captivity. The weak, small people who guarded him knew it. That made them all the angrier.

But, his message went on, he had outwitted them. Traded. Got this phone.

He had obtained a contraband cell phone. She blew smoke at the sky. Contraband—that was the word, right?

Tonya wanted to sound like a person who knew the prison system. She had never come out and told Efrem, or anybody who followed the Facebook fan page, that she hadn't actually done time, hadn't been an outlaw biker's old lady, didn't actually have a history as a sorceress, hadn't been a Vegas showgirl, because working as a waitress in Atlantic City was not precisely *that* close to dancing at the Bellagio. It was Facebook. You were who you said you were. And on the fan page, she said she was "Administrator, Interlocutor and Amanuensis" to the spirit of Efrem Judah Goode.

On Facebook, she didn't make change for fat frat boys. There, she was queen.

As proved by the message she held in her palm. It was like *The Bachelorette*. She'd been given the rose. Efrem Judah Goode spoke to *her*.

His text said the authorities had isolated him from the outside world. But he had outsmarted them. This phone was secret. Supersecret.

She felt a light-headed buzz. He trusted her with his supersecrets.

I need you to send a message for me.

Jamming the cigarette in the corner of her mouth, she thumbed a reply. Of course. Immediately. I will post news of your persecution on the fan page.

He replied in a flash. NO. If you post that on the fan page, they will know I am communicating with you. Then they'll toss my cell for the phone and put me in solitary.

Her skin went clammy. Losing touch with him would be like cutting off her airway.

On the screen, a bubble appeared. Efrem was typing. She shivered. The repetitive roll of the three dots felt like him petting her.

The message I need you to send has to get to the right people, and ONLY them. Listen carefully.

Inside the minimart, Fat Frat called, "Hey, I'm waiting here."

Tonya ignored him, ash dropping off the end of her cigarette. A new text arrived.

Fat Frat yelled, "I'm taking the beer. Your loss."

She read the text, tingling with excitement. "Oh, sweet lord."

It was a drawing. A new drawing, one nobody had seen. It was unlike any of his others, extraordinary, and she knew immediately it was precious, was vital, was a revelation.

Keep this secret, Efrem texted.

Tonya flicked her cigarette away. It spat red embers on the alley pavement.

Of course, she texted.

Good. Nobody sees it, Efrem replied. Until I say so.

26

Hiking back to her SUV through lower Manhattan, Caitlin phoned Detective Greg Tashjian.

"I'm sending you fresh photos."

She explained that she had discovered a direct line of sight from the *I heart homicide* site to the abandoned Brooklyn pier and the old diner named Landry's. Tashjian listened. Processing the information, dismissing it—she didn't know.

"He's putting a stamp on the connection between the old and new killings," she said. "That makes me think the killer isn't choosing victims at random. He may have a target list. If so, it relates to Landry's."

"I'll check the diner out."

"Chelsea Symanski was murdered just two days ago. The connection's here in New York City. I think the killer's here too."

It was just after 4:00 p.m. She had several hours of daylight left. She felt as if there were an hourglass looming over this case, draining inexorably toward the killer's next attack. She was here now. What could she do?

What was lacking in her understanding of the Broken Heart Killer?

He had tossed a young woman in the river and held a grotesque funeral procession along the waterfront beside her drifting body. If he had a target list, what had put Symanski at the top of it?

Chelsea had been twenty-three, white, tattooed, employed in a trendy bar, and according to a fellow bartender, an opioid abuser. What linked her to the other victims? How were they chosen? What led the killer to torture them repeatedly with a stun baton?

Victimology.

She was light on victimology. She needed to learn everything she could about the women the Broken Heart Killer had murdered.

And that required the painful task of talking to their families.

Crossing a street to her SUV, she inhaled and reset herself mentally. Tashjian was still on the line.

"Do you have contact information for Chelsea's next of kin?" she said.

She heard him typing on a keyboard.

"She has a sister. Aviva," Tashjian said. "She lives in the city. I'll send you the information."

Caitlin hopped behind the wheel of the SUV and opened her laptop to pull it up.

Tough as it was, facing grieving relatives wasn't merely part of the job. It was essential. A lot of homicide cops and prosecutors and medical examiners said, believed, and committed themselves to the idea that they spoke for the dead. And to do that, they had to speak to the heartbroken living.

Tashjian said, "Forwarding the info now."

"Thanks. Have you spoken to her?"

"No. Mancuso did. She sounds like a hermit. Tracking her down took work. Mancuso said she made the identification at the morgue. Left in shock. She hasn't been to the precinct."

The file arrived. Caitlin pulled it up. "I'll let you know how it goes."

Aviva Symanski. Age 36. Address in Brooklyn.

That was the first page of the file. But Tashjian had sent more. Aviva had a criminal jacket from her early twenties. Minor drug possession and drunk-and-disorderly arrests. Nothing in the past twelve years. She had been straight long enough that she now had a commercial driver's license and was a driver for a package delivery company.

That interested Caitlin on a purely human level. Female delivery drivers were a minority, perhaps a smaller minority than even female FBI agents. She scrolled deeper through the information Tashjian had sent and clicked a link. A driver's license photo popped up.

Caitlin stopped. She told herself she was imagining it. She enlarged the photo.

She wasn't imagining it.

She had seen that intense stare before. The woman in the driver's license snapshot was older, her hair now a natural brown instead of streaky home-dyed blond, her face softened and broadened by the passage of time. But not that much. The eyes, the hypervigilant glare, were indelible.

"Holy crap."

Aviva Symanski was one of the three women in Finch's photo.

27

Caitlin fired up the ignition, voice-dialing Tashjian as she swung a hard U-turn. The steering squealed, and she gunned the SUV toward the Williamsburg Bridge.

Tashjian picked up. "Two calls in three minutes? This isn't the slots in Reno, Hendrix. You don't win on volume."

"Pull everything on the sister, the next of kin." Caitlin barely paused at a stop sign. "Aviva Symanski. Check her driver's license photo. Compare it to the old snapshot that the girl—Finch Winter—found. Aviva's in that photo. Sure bet."

"What—"

"I'm going to Aviva's place. Not calling ahead. This needs to be face-to-face. Call me back when you get up to speed."

She ended the call without waiting for Tashjian's reply and swung onto the approach to the bridge. Mancuso had met the sister. Had he also seen the old photo? She couldn't believe he had, because the resemblance was so striking that she thought it would be impossible to miss. And right on time, a text came in from Tashjian.

What the f—

She accelerated onto the bridge. Subway tracks ran along the center of the metal roadway, and a pedestrian platform above the trains.

Linkage. Aviva Symanski, sister of the latest victim of the Broken Heart Killer, was in the photo Finch found, alongside the Jane Doe killed in 2008. Outside the diner visible from the spot where the killer had spray-painted *I heart homicide*.

Two people connected to that photo were dead. It couldn't possibly be coincidence.

Her suspicion that the killer was still in the city, pursuing his next target, now seemed a sick certainty. Caitlin dodged through traffic into the heights above the river. She needed to get to Aviva ASAP. The water shone, slate and silver, far below.

She was descending toward Brooklyn when Tashjian called her back.

"I called Aviva Symanski's employer. She's not on shift today. Try catching her at home. I can phone and check whether she's there."

The bridge led into a crowded neighborhood of refurbished brick buildings, stone offices with elaborate cupolas, walls painted with retro advertising for Peter Luger Steak House.

"Call to see how she's doing," she said. "Hold off mentioning that I'm on my way."

Tashjian ended the call. She drove past spring-green trees, new apartment buildings, old brownstones, coffee shops, cupcake boutiques, busy sidewalks.

The blocks were narrow, the city humming, gearing up toward rush hour. Sunshine poured down. On a playing field, softball teams warmed up. Schools had let out for the day, kids and parents on the street, bike messengers, taxis. They all slowed her down.

Tashjian called back. "Aviva answered. She's at home. She's not talkative. Got off as soon as possible. She didn't ask any questions of me. Which is . . ."

"Strange," Caitlin said.

"Let me know."

Caitlin crawled up a street past dry cleaners, chichi bistros, and a spacious carpet store featuring no customers, just scowling, heavily muscled men standing inside the doors. She shook her head. If criminals were going to launder drug money, they could put a little more effort into disguising the front. She turned onto a side street where older apartment buildings sat on a square around a shady park.

She parked, climbed the steps to Aviva Symanski's building, and rang the buzzer. Traffic hummed past. Children's laughter echoed from the park playground.

She buzzed again and glanced up at the windows above, hoping to see someone looking back. Inside the front door, footsteps clattered. But when the door opened, the woman who came out was Black and in her twenties, walking a mountain bike.

She gave Caitlin a considered look as she hoisted the bike onto her shoulder to hike down the steps. Took in Caitlin's suit and attitude, maybe deciding she was an official.

"You looking for Aviva?" she said.

"I am."

"About her sister?" The young woman ran a somber gaze up and down the suit again. "You with the city, or the funeral home?"

"FBI." Caitlin showed her credentials.

The woman scanned them. Then she pointed up the street.

"You just missed her. She passed me on the stairs two minutes ago. Said she had to make arrangements. She headed for the subway."

"What's she wearing?"

"Black sweater and pants. A yellow scarf tied around her hair."

"Thanks." Caitlin hurried down the steps.

The woman called after her. "Who killed her sister?"

Aviva's neighbor was young, hip, and in the killer's preferred age demographic, though not—so far—his racial one.

Caitlin turned. "Somebody extremely dangerous. Early twenties, Caucasian. Take care of yourself and keep your eyes open."

"I always do."

Caitlin nodded and jogged along the block. When she reached the corner, she saw, a hundred yards ahead, a woman in black with a bright yellow scarf tied around her hair. She was walking with grim determination toward the Metropolitan Avenue subway station.

Picking up her pace, Caitlin ran down the station steps thirty seconds behind her. At the echoing entry hall, she held out her creds to the woman in the ticket booth.

The woman said, "Fare's two-seventy-five."

Caitlin veered toward the turnstiles. Pulling her phone from her pocket, she tapped it to the digital payment reader and went through.

The walls of the station were tiled white with green accents. The tracks ran down the center of the station, platforms on the outer walls. The rush-hour bustle was growing.

Caitlin slowed on the stairs to look for Aviva. People flowed past her. The platform was almost two hundred yards long, with another entrance at the far end. Clearly, the station ran the length of the block beneath the street. She caught sight of the yellow scarf halfway along the platform.

She hurried down the stairs, keeping the scarf in sight. An overhead display flashed. **TRAIN APPROACHING**

Caitlin had grown up riding BART in the Bay Area, but the New York subway system still felt epic to her, even in its mundane mix of rush and wait, crowd and swerve. The pop culture image from eighties movies—graffiti, a bass beat of danger—was extinct. The platform was trash free, though the concrete had its share of paleolithic chewing gum ground in by passing feet. The wall tiles gleamed. The movie posters promised escape, action, love.

As she maneuvered through the crowd, a racket rose from the tunnel behind her. The arriving train sped into the station, still traveling at real speed. Cars slid by, silver, packed with passengers. The train stopped and the doors rolled open. People flooded out.

Popping up on her toes, she saw Aviva board a car in the middle of the train. Caitlin inched forward with a bolus of riders preparing to board.

She almost missed it. But even as her feet kept forward momentum, her eyes, and brain, locked in place.

On the nearest movie poster, in the middle of the action hero's forehead, was a freshly drawn broken heart.

It was about the size of a baby's fist, shredded down the center, just like the sure-handed hearts drawn at the riverside park in Manhattan and along Delancey Street.

People continued to fill the train. Caitlin felt a sharp throb at the base of her skull. She scanned the thinning crowd on the platform.

She saw a figure at the far end.

Short blond hair—extremely blond, and sticking up in an Ivan Drago macho do. A hooded puffy black jacket, baggy jeans, and a feral, concentrated stare. No longer a shadow, a white-hot grayscale phantom, but in full, weird color. He was a hundred yards away, but Caitlin felt goose bumps. She paused, watching. When he boarded the train at the front, his stride popped, like a boxer.

The sense of wrongness intensified, something twisting the air around him, a field distortion. The goose bumps sharpened, like static electricity running down her arms.

The killer was stalking Aviva.

28

The killer, diamond bright in Caitlin's vision, stepped through the doors of the front carriage, onto the subway train.

This wasn't coincidence. Not some weird cosmic fluke. The look on the copycat's face, the purpose and hungry desire, had been unmistakable. Caitlin jumped aboard at the nearest door, heart pumping. The doors shut and the train pulled out.

The car was air-conditioned, busy but not packed. As the train accelerated, she grabbed a pole for balance. They yawed out of the brightly lit station into the dark subway tunnel.

The car rocked on the tracks. Caitlin worked her way forward, again pulling out her phone, and was relieved to see she had a full signal.

She needed backup. But what kind, she wasn't sure yet.

The Broken Heart Killer had not, as far as she knew, ever attacked a target in the middle of a crowd. He waited until they could be taken alone, at night, when they were vulnerable and darkness concealed his approach. Five p.m. on a New York workday didn't fit.

His presence here told her that he was even more patient and tactical than she had imagined. He must be willing to spend hours—days, maybe—surveilling and following his desired victim.

"Excuse me." She swung past a tattooed couple who were sharing earbuds in the center of the car.

Her hands felt cold. First Chelsea Symanski, then Aviva. Why?

The train consisted of maybe—she hadn't counted—ten cars. She was in the last; the killer had jumped on the first. Aviva was somewhere in the middle.

Caitlin needed to reach her before the killer did, and keep him from getting anywhere near her.

Why? Was it a game to the copycat? Tag? Why was this killer after the second sister?

Caitlin reached the door at the end of the car. Blunt signs warned that it was dangerous to cross between cars while the train was in motion. She pulled the door open anyway, stepped into the passage, and was overwhelmed with noise, a shuddering, dark. She grabbed the door to the next car. The train entered a curve and she tipped sideways. Shit. She clung to the door, widened her stance, and forced it to slide open. She rushed into the next car.

This one was maybe three-quarters full, more people standing, most reading on their phones, a few holding shopping bags or briefcases. She ranked her goals by priority.

Keep Aviva safe. Keep everyone else on the train safe as well—if she showed her hand, or got Aviva out, it was possible that the killer might switch to target another potential victim. Keep him in sight.

Capture him.

For that, she needed help. Ideally, she would arrest and take custody of him on the train. She wanted to keep him from getting back onto a platform. Above all, she wanted to have the NYPD or transit police seal the exits to any station where he got off the train, to prevent him from reaching the street. But which station? The train was a moving target.

She hit redial on her phone. Tashjian.

He picked up with a jaunty tone. "Three times? You calling bingo now?"

She worked her way through the car. "I need backup ASAP."

She told him where she was and what was happening. "You know the right drill to call. Can you—"

"On it." His voice went coldly professional. "I'll alert the transit cops and NYPD units in the area. They'll send a broadcast to all stations on the G to cover the exits."

"You can't shut all the exits on the line yourself, can you?"

"No. That's done by station staff, by hand. It's not automatic."

She reached the door at the end of the car and, bracing herself, pushed through. The noise rose and overcame her ability to hear the phone call.

When she entered the next car, Tashjian's voice returned. "Tell me you didn't just—"

"Get backup. I'll stay on the call."

She didn't have a radio, so she jammed her phone in her front pants pocket and kept going, now running, dodging people. The train braked sharply and emerged from the tunnel into the bright light of the next station. The platform slid by fast, jammed with people. Behind them, Caitlin saw more slick white and green tile. When the doors opened, she stuck her head out. Aviva didn't get off. She ducked back in and continued heading to the next car as the train pulled out again.

They plunged back into the tunnel. The view outside went black. She wormed her way past riders, feeling the train bottom out and slowly climb uphill. Feeling it bank. She paused at the door, people's eyes now coming up, noticing her. The train decelerated. She pushed through the door and hurried into the next car.

It was packed. Seats full, people standing, holding on to poles and overhead bars. The train slowed. Caitlin lurched forward into a man who looked as though he had come off a construction site, wearing mud-splashed boots and a high-visibility vest.

He grunted and glared. She muttered a sorry and bumped past.

In the center of the car, she spotted Aviva sitting silently, head down, eyes closed. Through the door at the opposite end, she could see into the car beyond.

Standing on the other side of the connecting door was the copycat.

His face was obscured by dingy glass and glare. She couldn't see his eyes but could tell that he was staring into this car with predatory focus. His gaze was trained on Aviva.

Bracing herself, she worked her way toward Aviva. She kept an eye on the far door. The killer remained where he was in the next car.

Like a customer eyeing a piece of meat in the butcher's display counter.

Caitlin realized he was probably waiting to see if Aviva stayed on or got off at the next stop. They rushed into the station. As the train braked,

Caitlin grabbed the overhead bar and held on against forward momentum. They stopped. Passengers turned, shuffled, or stood and inched toward the still-closed doors.

Aviva opened her eyes and looked up.

The intense stare Caitlin had seen in the woman's photos was there, muted with sorrow. She seemed somehow adrift. She stood and turned toward the door, readying to get off.

The killer did the same.

Caitlin stepped up to Aviva and flashed her FBI creds. "Stay aboard."

The woman was short, compact, dressed as for mourning, though Caitlin sensed that black might be what she wore every day. When she saw the FBI ID, her distractedness vanished. She glanced from the badge to Caitlin's eyes.

"Why?" she said, low and serious.

"For your safety. Believe me."

Aviva searched Caitlin's expression, and her demeanor changed. She turned rock solid. She looked as if she knew when to believe that danger was nearby. Instinct, experience, history; a woman who worked alone, on the New York streets; a survivor.

The doors slid open. Passengers flooded off, a few eyeing Caitlin sharply as they passed. Through the doors at the far end, she saw the killer join departing riders and step off the train onto the platform. He walked toward the car in which she and Aviva waited. Caitlin motioned Aviva to sit, and to pull off her bright yellow scarf. Then she stood in front of her, blocking the killer's view of her as he passed the window. Caitlin waited a moment as he walked along the platform, bobbing, popping up on his toes, searching the platform crowd for Aviva.

Caitlin handed Aviva her card. "At the next stop, go to the ticket booth, get the cops, and *stay* there until I come back."

"What's going on?"

"I'll explain when I get back. And I will. Please."

Aviva's expression was ice cold. "Okay."

Caitlin ducked out with the last of the departing passengers, slipping through as the doors shut. She kept her eye on the killer, who was among several hundred people weaving their way along the platform toward the stairs at the distant end. More green and white tile. A yellow strip at the edge of the platform, to warn of the edge. Across the tracks on the opposite platform, two buskers had set up a tub drumming session. The noise echoed through the station. She pulled her phone from her pocket.

"Tashjian?"

"Here."

"Greenpoint Avenue. He left the train. I'm following him. Aviva is still aboard, and once the train departs, she'll be safe. He thinks she got off. He's looking for her."

She slid through the crowd. Fifty yards ahead, the killer flowed along with the swell of people on the platform, popping up on his toes, searching.

Tashjian said, "Hold on."

She heard him on another line, talking to someone in the field. He came back.

"Two squad cars are on their way. Which exit?"

She looked around. She had a good sense of spatial orientation but wasn't certain which direction she was facing or how to describe what Tashjian was after.

"I'm on the . . ." She searched the signage. "East platform? Does that make sense? Heading south, I think."

"Which direction were you heading on the train?"

"Toward Court Square. Now I'm walking toward the main exit from the station."

"Got it. I'll send the uniforms to the south exit and have dispatch alert the transit cops and see if they can hold people there."

"How far out are they?" she said.

"Five minutes. Don't lose him."

"I don't plan to."

The train pulled away, slowly at first, inching forward, then gaining speed. Silver cars slid by. The killer slowed, baffled. Aviva wasn't in the departing crowd ahead of him on the platform.

He turned to look behind him. First he gazed at the distant north exit. Then at the people coming toward him.

He saw Caitlin.

She felt adrenaline dumping into her veins, her skin and scalp prickling. She told herself to keep absolutely calm, keep walking, not to react. She let her gaze sweep across the killer's face and past, let her field of vision deepen to seem that she was eyeing the exit. Keeping the copycat in her peripheral vision. Knowing that her entire physical being had just jumped to heightened alert. Fight, flight, fucking attack.

She dressed like a fed because she wanted people to know she was a fed. *You will respect my authority.* Now she wished she were wearing jeans and a T-shirt.

In her pocket, Tashjian's voice emanated from her phone. *"Hendrix. Units are inbound. Four minutes."*

She kept walking. The copycat hovered in her vision, shimmering, again something *off* about his mien. Something aside from his being a killer.

He had gone totally still. It had been less than a second, but the way he abruptly froze, stony, his feral presence no longer searching—it had locked. On her.

She could sense it, see it peripherally. No point in pretending otherwise now. She let her gaze zero in on his.

"Hendrix, are you there?"

The copycat's utter stillness wasn't confusion. It seemed to be a reset. Calculation. Caitlin's heart ratcheted up to a machine-gun rhythm. The platform was full of people flowing toward the exit. More passengers were coming down the stairs.

The killer's target was gone. He had to know it. And to know that she was after him. And at least a hundred other potential targets or hostages were within his reach. Caitlin's mouth felt dry. She kept walking toward him.

Less than two seconds had elapsed. The killer didn't exactly move but seemed to gather himself. From beneath the puffy hooded coat came a surge of energy, the sense of an entity powering up, locking and loading. His gaze, absolute zero, black and sharp, bored in on her.

With a swift sweep of motion, like a scythe slicing across a field, he turned and leaped off the platform, onto the tracks.

29

The killer soared past the yellow warning strip painted on the edge of the platform. Lithe, determined, he never glanced along the tracks to see if a train was approaching.

"Stop! FBI!" Caitlin yelled.

People shied away from her. Someone shouted, "The fuck, man?"

The killer landed in a neat crouch and planted himself like a fullback, in a three-point stance. Then he burst into a run, straight across the tracks, aiming for the opposite platform.

Caitlin's backup was four minutes out. Nobody was there to seal the exits. Whether the killer wanted to out-gut her, outrun her, or out-crazy her, if he made it to the other platform while she stood still, he would give himself an unbeatable head start for an exit that she couldn't reach from where she was standing. She would be hopelessly behind.

If the killer made it to the far platform, he was gone.

She shot a glance at the arrivals sign.

1. Ⓖ Court Square 3 min

2. Ⓖ Court Square 5 min

In her pocket, her phone was still connected to the call with Detective Tashjian.

"Hendrix, do you copy?"

Taking a breath, she jumped from the platform onto the tracks.

She landed with a thud. Behind her, people gasped.

The ties were grimy, the tracks sleek and polished. She smelled grease and ozone. The opposite platform was twenty yards away. A short field goal.

An abyss. The killer was midway, jumping over each rail like a kid playing double-Dutch jump rope. Caitlin careered after him, eyeing the third rail. It didn't audibly hum, but it lay there straight and deadly nonetheless, a live steel snake, ready to strike.

The killer reached the far side and vaulted onto the packed platform as people shouted and backed away. He rolled and popped to his feet.

Caitlin maneuvered past the upright iron pillars, fuzzed with grease and dust, that divided the tracks. Ahead, the killer took off again, sprinting along the edge of the platform, high-wire agile, dancing along the eighteen-inch-wide yellow warning strip. Caitlin threw a nervous look to her right, up the tunnel, and saw only darkness. She jumped over the third rail, reached the platform, and scrambled up. People scattered. They had heard her yell "FBI!"

In her pocket, Tashjian's voice was a dull throb. "*Hendrix. What's happening?*"

There was no sign of uniforms, nobody here besides her. There wouldn't be, not in time. She jostled past people. The killer was twenty yards ahead of her and gazelle fast.

"*Hendrix,*" Tashjian yelled.

The crowd up the platform hadn't yet caught wind of what was coming. They milled and laughed. The tub drummers continued playing.

The killer ran toward a knot of people standing near the edge of the platform. He lowered his shoulder and plowed into a young mother who was pushing a stroller. Gasps and shouts rose from the crowd. The young woman flew off her feet and cracked her head on the concrete.

The killer kept moving. Off balance, he spun and shoved the stroller toward the tracks.

Before anyone could grab it, it toppled off the platform's edge.

People screamed. Caitlin's heart jerked. Pushing people aside, she rushed to the edge of the platform. The stroller had fallen onto the tracks, upside down. She heard a small child wailing.

And beneath the cries of the child and the battering echo of the bucket drummers, a deeper sound. It was noise in the tunnel.

She swung a frantic look at the arrival display.

1. Ⓖ Church Av 1 min

A train was sixty seconds out, rushing toward the station.

Like every New Yorker in history, she craned her neck to look down the tunnel. It was nothing but a black throat. No light, no motion. But that rumble was getting louder.

Caitlin leaped down onto the track. Ran the ten yards to the upside-down stroller and flipped it back onto its wheels. It took more effort than she expected. Inside, strapped tightly in, was a sobbing toddler. The little boy was red-faced and terrified but didn't look badly injured.

She shot a look up the track. On the platform, the display had changed.

TRAIN APPROACHING

Her vision throbbed. The stroller was bulky, and she realized that it was too heavy to lift quickly back onto the platform. The restraints in the stroller looked like a five-point seatbelt. She popped the clasps and wrestled the little boy out.

At the mouth of the tunnel, noise became a clatter. Chattering, banging. A harsh blast of air hit her, a hot sting of wind being forced from the tunnel by a pressure wave ahead of the train. She couldn't see the train, just its lights reflecting off the roof of the tunnel.

Cradling the sobbing boy to her chest, she stumbled toward the platform. Its four-foot height now looked like the Berlin Wall.

For a fraction of a second, she thought about tossing the toddler like a rugby ball. Then, unbidden, half a dozen arms reached toward her as people on the platform crouched down. She held the boy out and passed him to the phalanx of waiting hands above her.

The lights of the train shot from the tunnel. A horn blared and brakes shrieked. Everything became noise and electric fear. She clawed her way up as the horn blasted, lights flared, and the train screeched into the station. Silver, massive, hot, rushing past her with a mechanical wind like a threshing machine. Caitlin rolled onto her back, momentarily deaf with shock. Then she felt hands take hold of her, a man grabbing her forearm and pulling her up, another person squeezing her shoulder. An older man had the toddler in his arms, a portly African American guy who had set down his backpack to cradle the boy, and even in her stunned state, Caitlin knew that no New Yorker ordinarily did that, not even for one second. The man nodded somberly to her.

He bounced the sobbing boy in his arms. "He's okay."

She pitched toward him, even as she scanned the platform. The killer was still running—nimble, razoring through the crowd. The train's doors opened, and people flooded the platform. The killer elbowed them aside. Caitlin's stomach tightened. Who else would he hurt to get away?

She put her fingers to her lips, whistled, and hollered, "Look out!"

Then she looked around for the child's mother. The young woman lay flat on her back, unconscious. The sight hit Caitlin like a two-by-four.

She couldn't leave the little boy. Not even with a good Samaritan.

She held out her hands. "Thank you. I'll take him."

The man handed the little boy to her. The child was maybe two years old, with E.T. cheeks and chubby hands. He was hupping deep sobs.

She pulled him against her chest. "I gotcha."

But a man, another subway rider, wasn't going to stay a bystander. He gave chase.

"No—" Caitlin yelled, even as she saw that she couldn't stop him from leaping into the fray.

She wanted to race after him. It was almost physically painful to hold still. But she could not take a toddler even a single step closer to a murderer. She pulled her phone from her pocket and put it to her ear.

"Tashjian, he's fleeing toward the . . ." Which exit? "The north exit at the Greenpoint Avenue subway station."

"Where the f—" Tashjian started.

"I cannot pursue," she said pointedly.

"Fuck."

Down the platform, the bystander pounded after the fleeing copycat. He was burly, a charging spark plug of a man, and he was gaining on the killer.

The station exit had floor-to-ceiling bars, like a jail. The only way out was through a high entrance/exit gate, a revolving door–style turnstile with horizontal bars spaced six inches apart. The killer ran at it full speed. The pursuing bystander was a couple of feet behind. Caitlin held her breath as the toddler sobbed and squirmed in her arms.

The killer shoved into the revolving exit. The bystander lunged for him, missed, then grabbed the bars of the exit, hoping to stop them from turning, trying to trap the killer in the revolving door. But the man's momentum carried him forward, and he was pulled halfway through the turnstile himself. The bars at the front were still swinging around and gave the killer a gap. Maybe nine inches. He squirmed sideways, trying to slide through.

The bystander grabbed the hood of the killer's coat. The killer's head jerked back. Caitlin saw him twist, and her heart cramped. If he had a weapon . . .

The killer unzipped the puffy coat, twisted free, and squeezed through the exit.

Off balance, he spun around. For a split second, the copycat locked eyes with Caitlin. Then ran up the stairs to the street.

Gone.

Caitlin held tight to the crying toddler. She knew what she had just seen. Cold eyes. Calculation, desperation, and excitement.

A tight wife-beater. With a bra beneath.

She put her phone to her ear. "Tashjian. The suspect is out the exit. Blond, jeans, white tank top."

"Units aren't there yet," Tashjian yelled in frustration. "Anything else?"

"Yes," she said. "The killer is a young woman."

30

Transit police and NYPD precinct cops were swarming the subway platform. The young mother who had been knocked to the concrete sat on a bench while paramedics checked her vital signs. Her little boy sat beside her, clinging to her sleeve.

"I'm okay, really," the woman said. "Where's the stroller?"

It was the fifth time she had asked. The stroller had disintegrated when the incoming train hit it, and the paramedics were going to transport her to the emergency room with a concussion.

At the end of the platform, Detective Tashjian jogged down the stairs.

Caitlin's adrenaline jag had subsided, leaving her spent. But when she saw Brianne Rainey follow Tashjian down the stairs, she revived.

Caitlin gave the little boy a last look. He blinked up at her with red-rimmed eyes. His face was streaked with grease. She suppressed a resurgent spark of fear, waved goodbye, and headed up the platform.

Tashjian looked grim. His hat was tilted back on his head. His suit jacket flared as he walked up to her. "What happened?"

"Diversion. The killer tried to use a little boy as a human sacrifice."

He set his hands on his hips, disgusted.

Rainey's expression was buttoned down, but she had heat in her eyes. She looked Caitlin up and down and took in the grease stains on her knees and palms.

"You rock and roll?" she said.

"The killer shoved a stroller onto the tracks." Caitlin nodded toward the stairs. "Let's talk outside."

They climbed to the street, where a knot of NYPD blue-and-whites and a black FBI SUV filled an intersection. The street was made up of delis, bodegas, brick apartment buildings with fire escapes, a redbrick Catholic church with a looming spire. The afternoon sky was ripening to orange in the west. Pedestrians passed them, curious or deliberately uncurious, speeding by. The air had weight, heat, a breeze that couldn't chase away the humidity.

Tashjian turned to Caitlin. "I kept shouting to you."

Was he angry? Frustrated? Or had he actually feared she had gone down? "Next time, I'll narrate the pursuit in real time. Apologies, Detective."

He frowned, as if he didn't know whether she was joking. She didn't, either.

Rainey said, "I just got here. I've heard zip. Give me the highlights."

"The copycat's a woman," Caitlin said.

Rainey's eyebrows rose.

"Some things are clear that didn't make sense earlier," Caitlin said. "Tashjian—when we saw the original night-vision video of the copycat, I told you that something felt off to me. Now I know why. The killer's presentation was an act. The masculinity was a disguise."

Tashjian stared at the ground. After a second, he nodded. "You don't think this unsub is trans? Nonbinary?"

"I don't know anything for certain. I'm giving you fleeting impressions." She looked at her palms, blackened with grease, and tried to wipe some of it off. "The killer seemed committed to her—their, I don't know—public presentation. The projection of . . ."

She saw it.

"Forceful dominance. She was projecting forceful dominance."

"You said the same of Goode," Rainey said.

"Yes. Though his is organic. It reeks from his pores. From his psyche. He's a big man with an antisocial personality. And his charisma, his physical power, his refusal to acknowledge limits on his behavior, his complete confidence in his ability to wield violence to obtain his goals—they all meld into a persona that throbs with it."

The breeze blew her hair around her head.

"But the Broken Heart Killer doesn't have that complete package. Maybe it's age. She's young." She looked at Tashjian. "I'd say twenty-one. Maybe younger."

"We're pulling camera footage from both Greenpoint and Metropolitan Ave. And the train cabs. We'll see what we get."

"With the coat ripped off," Caitlin said, "her . . . *costume* seemed to be torn away. That might be it. She had put on the dominance persona—a deliberately male persona—and was taking it out for a spin. But it seemed that the costume wasn't exactly a full fit. Maybe it was her sex. With the coat off, I could see how slight she is. Wiry, strong, but not an overpowering physique—nothing that would intimidate a grown man on a Brooklyn street if he saw a young woman with empty hands challenge him to a fight." She thought. "She was trying on something big. She hasn't quite grown to fill it out. She was . . . callow."

"Callow," Tashjian said.

"Green. Inexperienced."

"Doesn't sound like it to me."

"I don't mean she's ineffective," Caitlin said. "Far from it. She's reckless, ruthless, devious, and willing to let even the most innocent die to achieve her goals."

"Hell of a profile. What is going on?"

"That's what I plan to find out."

Behind them, a uniform jogged up the subway entrance stairs and beckoned Tashjian. He strode over, nodded, and came back.

"We have the perp's coat. Nothing in the pockets, no ID, no little name tag sewn into the collar by Mommy, but crime scene will go over it for trace." To Caitlin he said, "We need more."

He stalked off, whistling to another detective. Rainey waited until Tashjian headed down the subway steps. Then her gaze calmly settled on Caitlin. It was solid, searching, but not worried. Instead, it held Caitlin steady.

"You okay?"

Caitlin exhaled, long and slow, and let a wave of tension roll down her arms and off her fingertips like water.

"Yeah. Just frustrated as hell."

"This was already weird. Now it's—"

"WFS," Caitlin said. "We need to talk to Aviva Symanski."

31

Caitlin and Rainey found Aviva waiting with a transit cop at the Court Square terminus of the G train. Her yellow scarf was wrapped around her throat, her arms folded over her chest. She looked as if she was trying to ball up and hide, like an armadillo. She glared at them, edgy.

"What the hell is going on?"

"We'll explain," Caitlin said. "Let's get you out of here."

Caitlin thought the killer had probably fled the area, but she and Rainey couldn't count on it. And they thought the unsub might try another attack on Aviva. They didn't want her to return to her apartment yet. They drove her to a coffee shop beside a Queens expressway and took a booth. A yellow slice of sunlight cut through the windows. Aviva hunched, wrung out.

Her voice was shaky. "You're positive it's a woman."

"I saw her," Caitlin said.

"She killed my sister, then came for me? Why?"

"That's what we need to figure out."

Caitlin grabbed napkins and wiped some of the grease from her palms, shuddering unexpectedly, then got her phone. She brought up Finch's photo of the three young women leaning against the wall outside Landry's Diner.

"This is you, Aviva. Isn't it?" she said.

Aviva's dark gaze zeroed on the screen. Surprise took hold. "Landry's ... wow, long time ago. Where'd you get this?"

Caitlin didn't answer. "Who are the other two women?"

She shifted defensively. "Friends who worked there."

A waitress came. Caitlin ordered coffee, Rainey a Diet Coke. Aviva asked for water.

The waitress left. Caitlin and Rainey waited.

Aviva inhaled. Then, her shoulders drooping, she pointed at the teenager in the center of the photo. Thin, blond, with a thirsty smile. It was the young woman Finch thought was her birth mother.

"That's Phoenix."

"Phoenix?" Rainey said.

Aviva nodded. Then indicated the third woman. "And Stinger."

Caitlin set down the phone. "Can you give us their real names?"

Aviva shrugged. "Never knew."

"Why not?" Rainey said.

Aviva leaned back against the red vinyl seat, frowning. "Because we didn't, that's why."

She was only five years older than Caitlin, but the lines between her eyes were heavy, and her world-weariness heavier.

"Do you really need to know?" she said. "This is about . . . What the fuck *is* this about?"

Caitlin kept her voice low and even. "It's about finding the person who killed your sister. And three others. And who came after you."

Aviva's jaw tightened. "You're *sure* this asshole was after me?"

Caitlin thought again of the jagged broken heart sharpied on the subway station movie poster. "Positive." She raised the photo. "Who were they? Who were you?"

"We were runaways. We didn't go by legal names. We were living rough, hustling to get by."

"Any story behind their nicknames?"

"Phoenix was from Arizona," Aviva said, with a *whatever* lift to her shoulder. "Stinger?" Her gaze seemed to fall into the photo, back in time. "Stinger had a scorpion tattoo."

Caitlin's radar warmed up. The Broken Heart Killer's first victim, the woman abducted from the North Carolina bait shop, had a scorpion tattoo.

Rainey grew focused. "Amber Roark?"

Slowly, with a distant expression that said she was running it through her memory, Aviva shook her head. "Not familiar to me. Is that Stinger's real name?"

Maybe, Caitlin thought. "Where was the tattoo?"

"Her lower back. Why? Have you seen it? Seen her?"

When Amber Roark died, she looked nothing like the young woman in the blurry, faded old snapshot. But Caitlin had seen the tattoo in autopsy photos. Her pulse ticked up. A dread-laced excitement prickled along the back of her neck—a sense that she was circling something delicate, some deadly truth.

"What does any of this have to do with me?" Aviva said. "And with Chelsea? Where'd you get that photo?"

Chelsea. Aviva. The diner. The copycat's tattooed victim. Connections.

Caitlin didn't answer Aviva's question. Instead, she scrolled through her phone and showed Aviva another image: Goode's drawing of Liv, the goth he claimed to have killed and dumped near the Williamsburg Bridge in 2008. The teenager whose murder Chelsea's killing duplicated.

Aviva eyed the photo for several seconds. She nodded again, slowly. "That's Rhiannon."

Caitlin sat up straight. She had heard that uncommon name recently. A relative, hanging on to a worn thread of hope, had sent a message to the FBI tip line, along with photos of a girl last seen in 2007 before running away to New York City.

"Last name?" Caitlin said.

"Griffith."

Bingo.

Aviva's gaze jumped between Caitlin, Rainey, and the photo. "What's going on?"

Caitlin maintained a calm tone. "Rhiannon Griffith."

"Yeah."

"Not Liv?"

Aviva shook her head. "No." She let out a *huh.* "Did somebody tell you that's her name?"

Rainey pointed at the drawing. "You know this woman's real name. No doubts?"

"Rhiannon never went by a street name," Aviva said.

Caitlin pulled up the photo Rhiannon Griffith's family had sent her—a blond, rebellious teenager. Full cheeks, round with baby fat. No makeup.

Aviva took a long look. "Guess so. She did *not* look like that."

"But this is the same person?"

"You tell me."

The waitress returned with their drinks. "Ready to order?"

"We need a minute," Caitlin said.

She turned back to Aviva with rising eagerness. "How did you know Rhiannon?"

"She worked at Landry's too," Aviva said.

This, finally, was something concrete. A connection existed between Goode's past victims and the present case of the Broken Heart Killer. From Rainey's alert stillness, she felt the same excitement.

But Aviva's eyes filled with alarm. "Will you tell me what's going on? Why are you asking me about Rhiannon? Why do you have that picture of her?"

"When's the last time you saw her?" Rainey said.

"Long time back."

"How long?" Caitlin said.

"I don't know. One day she wasn't around anymore."

"Was that notable?"

She shook her head. "Not really. People came—turned up in the neighborhood, if they made it past the Port Authority bus depot and didn't get swept up by the pimps. They took up space, and if we got to trust them, they hung with us. But we didn't take roll. People could be your best friend for six months and then hitch a ride out of town."

"Rhiannon?"

Aviva's forbidding glare centered on Caitlin. "Where did that drawing come from?"

Aviva was holding back. Caitlin knew that the woman was under incredible stress, but this was no time to withhold information. She held the sketch so Aviva had to look at it.

"What happened to her?" she said.

"I don't know. She melted away. People did back then." Aviva's hostility seemed to intensify. "Where'd you get the drawing?"

"A convict drew it. Efrem Judah Goode."

Aviva went still. "Goode." She blinked. "Did he *kill* her? Oh, my God . . ."

Caitlin swiped to another sketch: Goode's drawing labeled *Jane Doe, Brooklyn 2008*.

Rainey shifted, perhaps uncomfortably, at the aggressive approach.

Aviva paled. Hot patches reddened her neck.

Caitlin zoomed in on the drawing. Her pulse was pounding in her temples. She wanted to shove the photo right at Aviva's face. Rainey cleared her throat. Her eyes asked, *Why are you so wound up?*

People were dying, that's why. Aviva was grieving and shaken up yet holding back information that might help catch the killer. In her mind's eye, Caitlin saw autopsy photos, and a woman lying on her back in the mud, as if crucified. She saw Aviva's sister, Chelsea. Her wet hair and lifeless eyes.

She saw the little boy in the subway, grease on his face. Same as the grease on her hands. The roar of the arriving train filled her head again. Close. Too, too close.

Caitlin realized that her pulse was pounding in her ears. *What are you doing?* She stopped herself. Then she looked across the table and saw her fears staring back.

Aviva's toughness, her protective shell, was battered battle armor. She had survived the streets. Made a life. Lost her sister. And was now sitting with the FBI after a near miss with a killer.

The same killer who would have been happy to take Caitlin out too.

They were in this together. She had to reach out, not push.

She set the phone on the table. "Please." She softened. "It's important."

Aviva held her gaze a moment, then picked up the phone. She examined Goode's drawing of the Brooklyn Jane Doe.

Her voice went quiet. "It's Phoenix."

"You're not surprised," Caitlin said.

Aviva shook her head. Tears rose in her eyes. The waitress came toward the booth. Rainey glanced at her. She turned on her heel.

"Tell me," Caitlin said, more gently.

Aviva took a second. The slice of sunlight angled across the floor and hit her face, illuminating the gleam of her tears.

"Phoenix disappeared."

"When?"

Aviva gestured at the drawing. "Then."

"In 2008."

She nodded.

"Around the time Rhiannon Griffith melted away?"

Wiping her eyes with her palms, Aviva nodded again.

Caitlin spoke calmly. "You knew that Phoenix was the woman murdered at the pier? The one whose body washed up, wrapped in duct tape?"

Aviva flushed and gazed down at the table. "We didn't talk to the cops."

Caitlin tried to work it out. A nexus linked four teenage friends to the old and new murders. Phoenix was the 2008 Brooklyn Jane Doe. Rhiannon had been missing since then, now presumed murdered. Stinger was, it seemed certain, the copycat's victim number one.

And Aviva was the copycat's latest target.

The connection between Goode and the Broken Heart Killer had to run through this nexus.

But why these women? What was the Broken Heart Killer after? Caitlin didn't know, though she felt, more strongly than ever, that Goode had been lying and withholding information.

Aviva wrung her hands. "Why is this woman after my sister and me?"

Caitlin considered what to say. She didn't want to panic Aviva.

"Tell me about Chelsea," she said gently.

Aviva's eyes swarmed with emotion. Warmth. Melancholy. Emptiness. "She moved here after high school. She was a go-getter and loved the party life. Too much. She was a good bartender." Her voice strengthened. "But she was strong. Took no shit."

Caitlin spoke softly. "Did you ever see signs of—"

"She used. I knew. I pretended I didn't. Told myself I wasn't seeing it, because I hated it—lost too many friends to that fuckery—and wanted to deny that my baby sis had an issue with opioids. But hell, so do ten million other people. Nothing I could do. Nothing she was going to listen to." She shook her head. "That doesn't explain why she was attacked."

Caitlin nodded. She didn't tell Aviva what she knew: that Chelsea's tox screen, rushed through because of the case's urgency, showed a high residue of opioids in her system. She'd been a regular user, probably addicted. But she hadn't taken drugs in more than twenty-four hours. Either she missed her connection, or her hit was withheld from her—by the unsub.

Again, why? To inflict pain? Most serial killers had a sadistic aspect. This one, who repeatedly burned her victims with a stun baton, certainly did. Caitlin thought the stun baton was more than a retail choice. Tasers were harder to obtain, but the killer wanted personal contact. The *feel* of hurting her prisoners. It indicated volcanic anger.

But Caitlin wanted to know if the killer sought to torture information from her targets. In Chelsea's case, shocking her with the stun baton, while simultaneously denying her the drugs her body craved, could have driven Chelsea to tell the killer what she wanted to know.

And what did she want? Maybe the address of Chelsea's mistrustful, near-hermit sister. The one in the photo with two other people connected to the case. The only one still alive.

Finally, Caitlin said, "I think this person came after you, and after Chelsea, for the same reason. She wants information. She thinks you can provide it."

"Information she's willing to kill for."

"Unfortunately."

Aviva shut her eyes and breathed deeply. "You showed me that photo. You think I'm the one with the information the killer's after." She looked at Caitlin. "Chelsea was just a rung on the ladder to get to me."

Caitlin couldn't deny the possibility. "The photo. Did you work at the diner?"

Aviva shook her head.

"Did you live with any of those girls?"

No, Aviva said. Not regularly. She couldn't recall who had snapped the photo. She had never met Efrem Judah Goode. At least, not that she recalled. He could have been anybody. She had no idea why the killer would come after her.

That didn't diminish Caitlin's suspicion—the killer thought Aviva knew something valuable.

"Is your name in the phone book?" Caitlin asked.

"No. None of my information." She scraped her fingers through her hair. "I got used to being invisible on the street, back when. I don't like anyone knowing how to find me. I don't use social media. My phone and address are unlisted. I rent. I never even give out my email address, and certainly not my cell phone number."

Rainey said, "You're an information recluse."

"Some people call me paranoid. It doesn't seem to have helped."

"How about your sister?" Caitlin said.

"Social butterfly. Extrovert, life of the party, out there with everything she did. Constant poster. And she worked at a bar." The tears welled again. "It wouldn't have taken the killer ten seconds to find Chelsea."

"Did Chelsea know your friends from the old days? Have any connections to Landry's Diner?"

Aviva shook her head. "She was so much younger than me. From my dad's second marriage. She was just a toddler when I was on the street. It took a long time to build a relationship with her. These past couple of years. And I thought . . ." She trailed off.

"I'm sorry for your loss," Caitlin said.

Aviva got the tears back under control and seemed to deflate. "I'm getting out of town and going off the grid ASAP."

"We'll drive you," Rainey said.

"Hell, yes. Let's get going. Sitting here makes me itchy."

32

They drove Aviva to her neighborhood, where Rainey escorted her in through the apartment building's back door to pack. Caitlin walked to the park on the square across from the building's front entrance. On a bench beyond the playground, an older man sat sharing a sandwich with his young granddaughter. Caitlin circled the bench, examining it critically.

The man gave her a guarded look. "Something I can do for you?"

"You could stand up for a minute, if you don't mind."

After a moment's hesitation, he lumbered to his feet. He came to stand beside her. Together, they looked at the bench. They went quiet.

A broken heart the size of a bear's paw was drawn on the bench. Caitlin turned. There was a clear line of sight to the front door of Aviva's building.

She snapped photos with her phone. "I'm going to have to ask you to find another spot to sit."

The man stared at the heart as if it were radioactive, then took his granddaughter's hand. "Come on, precious. We're going home."

Caitlin called Tashjian. "The killer set up surveillance on Aviva Symanski across the street from her building."

"I'll send a uniform and crime scene unit."

The sun had dipped below the rooftops to the west. People were getting home from work. Evening was coming on. This wasn't her city, and Caitlin felt out of place.

She told herself what she always did in this circumstance: *Use it.*

Be situationally aware. Take advantage of having to evalu-
ate the architecture, the vibe, the scene, from a stranger's perspective.
There would be tons of customs and nuance she missed, but plenty
that the locals no longer paid close attention to. Like the spire of the
Empire State Building piercing the sky across the river, silhouetted,
proud, iconic.

"Have you pulled the subway station's CCTV imagery?" she asked
Tashjian. "Photos of the unsub?"

"Sending you some now."

She surveyed the scene. "The park's busy. The man who was sitting on
the bench saw the broken heart. Then he booked, with his granddaughter."

"If you're suggesting the broken-heart signature is going to become
public . . ."

"Inevitable."

"*Everything's* going to become public. You're already on Instagram.
Passenger on the platform filmed you running across the tracks like a high
hurdler. You truly wanted to stay away from the third rail, didn't you? You
were jumping like a spooked deer."

"Electricity arcs blue when it kills someone. You don't forget the smell
either."

That shut him up.

"Rainey and I will escort Aviva to the train station and make sure
she's not followed."

"Keep me updated," Tashjian said. "Sending photos of the unsub."

"Thank you."

The photos had been captured from an overhead camera at the Greenpoint Avenue station. Low resolution, washed-out color. They caught the
young woman in full flight toward the exit. Got several views of her face,
but from twenty or thirty yards away. One of them caught her profile as
she shot a look back over her shoulder.

Who are you?

The blue lights of a police car flashed along the street. Caitlin waved
at the officer and showed her the park bench.

"Cordon it off," she said. "Thanks."

Her phone pinged. Rainey. Coming down. Pull your Suburban around the corner. I'll follow in my SUV.

Caitlin crossed the park, aware of the bright laughter of children, the rush of the breeze through the leaves of the trees, the sense of quiet amid the turmoil of this great city.

The killer had struck here. And she had hit tiny towns, rural backwaters. She was comfortable and confident—and successful—in multiple environments. Caitlin told herself not to forget that.

And not to forget the killer's utter disregard for human life. Her confidence in her ability to survive, her risk-taking, her speed.

She drove around the corner from Aviva's building, where a narrow walkway led to the back door. As soon as she pulled up, Rainey stepped out the door, checked the walkway, and ushered Aviva into the Suburban.

Caitlin pulled out immediately. She headed for Grand Central Terminal. In her rearview, she saw Rainey swing the SUV away from the curb and follow.

Caitlin handed Aviva her phone, with the photos of the unsub.

"Do you recognize her?" she said.

From the passenger seat, there was portentous silence. Caitlin glanced over. Aviva looked transfixed by the images.

"I don't . . ." Her gaze, already dark, deepened. "She could be anybody. She could be all of us." She shook her head. "I'm seeing things."

"What do you mean?"

She frowned, then shrugged. "I don't recognize her. But if I see her on the street, I'm going to scream, and pick up the nearest blunt object, and bash her brains in."

New York, Caitlin thought.

33

aitlin pulled up to Grand Central Terminal feeling as if she'd just driven Fury Road. Midtown Manhattan traffic was packed with jockeying taxis, buses, police cars, pedestrians lined up ten across in both directions at every street corner, powering past each other when the light turned green in some mind-blowing game of red rover.

Rainey was directly behind her. They'd seen no sign of a tail—by a GMC Yukon, a taxi, or any other vehicle. Caitlin had taken an evasive route here, the Queensboro Bridge and a roundabout path through Midtown streets. She had slowed outside a police precinct on the chance it would cause a skittish follower to back off. But from everything she could tell, they were clear.

At Grand Central, she flashed her FBI credentials at the NYPD units parked outside. Units were always parked outside Grand Central. Anti-truck-bomb bollards ringed the building. She stepped into the peak crush of the city. People. Food carts. Tour bus hawkers. The Chrysler Building needled the sky.

She and Rainey escorted Aviva inside, scanning the scene. The echoing, soaring terminal—a civic cathedral, really—was a nightmare to surveil, people crisscrossing the huge central space in every direction. Aviva had a roller bag and that black glare. She walked with grim purpose beneath the constellation-spangled ceiling.

Bypassing the tunnels to the train tracks, they headed out of the building onto Lexington Avenue and walked Aviva to a nearby chain hotel.

Upstairs, at the door to her room, she paused. "Thank you. I guess. I mean, yes."

Her gaze hung on Caitlin. Caitlin took it as an opening.

"The photo taken outside Landry's Diner—you, Stinger, and Phoenix."

Three lost souls, found and bound to each other. Now brought back together under the specter of violent death.

Caitlin said, "Did Phoenix have children?"

Aviva blinked in surprise. "A little girl."

"How little?"

"Not a baby. Walking, talking. I don't remember."

"What was her name?"

Aviva shrugged and seemed to think about it. "I don't ... I don't think I ever knew, not really. I remember Phoenix calling her 'Sunshine.'"

Shrugging, she opened the door.

"Throw the dead bolt," Rainey said.

Outside, in the echoing canyon of Lexington Avenue, Caitlin and Rainey paused.

"What happened to Phoenix's child?" Rainey said.

At Manhattan South Homicide, Caitlin and Rainey found Detective Dennis Mancuso striding down a hallway toward his desk. He had on a wilted dress shirt and a tired expression. But he brightened when he spotted Caitlin.

"Hear you caught some action," he said.

"Is Tashjian still at the scene?"

"He'll stay until he scrapes the gum off the platforms if he has to."

Caitlin introduced Rainey. Mancuso led them to the squad room. The evening light was purplish, reflecting off the windows of the building across the street.

"Coffee?" he said. "It's shit, but it's hot."

"Thanks." Caitlin wanted nothing less, but she knew when to take an olive branch. "We just had a conversation with Aviva Symanski."

Mancuso poured coffee into Styrofoam cups, and Caitlin pretended to sip. They brought him up to speed. Caitlin sent Mancuso the photo of

Aviva with Stinger and Phoenix at Landry's Diner. He printed the picture and stuck it on the lead board.

Mancuso rubbed his chin, staring at it. "You think there's a solid connection between the 2008 cases and the copycat killings. Something besides random serial-offender shit."

"I do." She nodded at the diner photo. "The blonde. 'Phoenix.' We have two new pieces of information. One, she was from Arizona. And two, she was employed at the diner."

"Fifteen years ago. Sketchy."

"You're the NYPD. We're FBI. I bet we have the flex to fill in that sketch." She put up another image: the drawing of the Brooklyn Jane Doe. "Literally."

She knew that her next suggestion could be delicate. "I've spoken several times to the young woman who gave me the diner photo. Finch Winter."

She explained Finch's theory about her birth mother. "I'm far from convinced. But this photo, and Aviva's ID, convince me it's worth checking out. Could you expedite a DNA comparison between Finch and the Brooklyn Jane Doe?"

Mancuso thought for a moment. "Brooklyn North handled the case. I'll give them a kick in the pants about it."

"Thanks."

It was 6:00 p.m. The TV in the corner was, for once, playing the local news. She turned away. She didn't want to see herself on-screen, under a banner reading SUBWAY CHASE.

"I know you hate to let anybody hang around your squad room, but if we can borrow a desk for half an hour instead of hoofing it over to Federal Plaza, I'll buy you dinner."

"The falafel cart on the corner. I'll take mine with the works, plus fries."

Rainey saluted with an index finger. "I'll get it. Hendrix, you scrub the rest of the subway grease out of your lifeline." She nodded at Caitlin's hands.

Caitlin gave her some cash, then washed up, opened her laptop, and got Keyes on video at Quantico. He was his usual slightly overcharged self. That calmed Caitlin. She liked it when Keyes was on the case.

She had sent him the latest information. He slid into his Aeron chair and nudged close to the screen. "I've been collating police records, death records, arrest and missing-persons records. Looking at multiple databases and trying to cross-pollinate and find commonalities. So far, I've had no luck putting a real name to Phoenix."

"It'll be a long shot, but somewhere, she's in there."

"Don't despair." His eyes went bright. "I have news. The copycat's first victim. The one abducted from the bait shop in North Carolina."

"Amber Roark."

"I got the police report. And her criminal jacket. She had arrests for vagrancy and prostitution in New York City. Identifying marks include the scorpion tattoo," he said. "Multiple reports list her known alias as 'Stinger.'"

"So that's confirmed," Caitlin said.

Rainey came in with fat white food bags. She caught the excitement in Caitlin's eyes.

"Amber Roark is Stinger," Caitlin said. "The woman in the photo taken outside the diner."

Rainey unwrapped her shawarma and greeted Keyes on-screen. "What's up?"

"News. I only told Hendrix half of it. Data comes through again," he said. "I've made another connection to what you're calling the nexus."

Caitlin bit into her falafel as if she had killed it on the savanna. "Spill."

"The woman kidnapped from the Monongahela Valley and dumped at the Brooklyn pier was a high school classmate of Rhiannon Griffith."

"What?"

She said it sharply enough that Mancuso turned to look at her.

Keyes repeated, "Chely Ann McKee. She was born in the same town and grew up and went to the same high school as Rhiannon Griffith."

"Thanks, Keyes."

Caitlin ended the call, her mind churning. She had been searching for any indication why the killer would target both Symanski sisters. They had no connections that anyone could find with Efrem Judah Goode. Chelsea had no connections to the case, aside from her relationship to Aviva.

But every person attacked by the copycat, and every person killed by Goode in New York City, did have a connection. To Rhiannon Griffith. She was the nexus that every target, past and present, had a link to.

Caitlin stopped eating. "Mancuso."

"I heard you. Rhiannon Griffith." He dropped into his desk chair and clacked at his keyboard.

What had happened to Rhiannon?

Mancuso clicked and pounded, opening half a dozen databases.

"She's not in the NYPD system," he said.

"Not at all?"

"No criminal record by DOB, SSN, or driver's license in New York City. Or New York State. Or New Jersey, or Connecticut." He looked over. "The only mention of her name is in the email you forwarded to the NYPD from the FBI tip line."

"Any other sign she lived here?"

"It's getting to be a long time ago," he said. "If she didn't lease, didn't have a credit card—no credit history, no bank accounts, no W2 or employer wage reports—she could have slid along in the cracks. We think of the aughts as just yesterday, but even that recently it was easier for someone to live in the shadows. Especially if, as you say, she was a runaway."

"No footprint."

"If she was ever in New York, she left no official trace."

Turning to her laptop, Caitlin found the email to the tip line from Rhiannon Griffith's cousin. She wrote back, asking for more information. And asking whether the cousin would submit a DNA sample to test against Jane Does in the NYPD and FBI systems.

Mancuso got a call and left to go to the front desk. Caitlin sat thinking.

It seemed increasingly clear that the Broken Heart Killer was on a hunt. Her victims had all been taken and held for twenty-four hours to force information out of them.

She got up and crossed the room to the lead board. Goode's drawings of his New York victims were in the top right corner, above photos of the copycat's victims.

Caitlin took down Goode's drawing of the goth teenager labeled *Liv NYC 2008.*

Liv. Rhiannon. Two names, one girl.

Caitlin moved some charts and printouts around and put the drawing at the center of a web of connections that didn't yet make sense.

Then, staring at the drawing, it hit her with a sick thud. *Liv.*

"Damn it."

It couldn't be. Her face heated. Was it actually that obvious?

Rainey was typing on her laptop. Caitlin beckoned to her. She walked over, wondering why Caitlin was shaking her head.

"I can't believe it." Caitlin got her phone and dialed Emmerich.

Rainey said, "What are you looking at?"

Caitlin pointed at the name.

Rainey exhaled as if she'd been punched.

Emmerich picked up. "Hendrix?"

"Goode played us," she said.

She told him to pull up the drawing. When he had it, she continued, her face hot.

"*Liv*," she said. "That's not the victim's name."

"It's Rhiannon Griffith. Correct?"

"Yes, but there's a reason Goode signed the drawing that way. It's not because the girl in the sketch told him that was her name, or because that was a nickname he decided to give her. It's a signal that the woman in the drawing *lives*."

Rainey was shaking her head. "Mother Mary, it's right there and I completely overlooked it. And I'm the one with a background in psyops."

Emmerich was silent. Caitlin went on.

"Her name is Rhiannon Griffith, and she's *alive*. The drawing is a message. And Goode got us to publish it."

34

Up the Hudson Valley, the Yukon rumbled down the long hill and across the stone bridge over the creek. Dusk had come on. The headlights drilled the road ahead. At the mailbox with the red rooster, Landry turned in.

She gunned it down the rutted drive, through the tunnel of trees, gravel kicking up from the wheels and hitting the undercarriage like buckshot. The rows of corn scrolled past, gray in the twilight. Inside the house, behind the red door, the blue eye of the TV flickered.

Stopping outside the barn, Landry put it in park and sat, listening to the engine thrum. She didn't want to shut it off. Shut it off and she'd hear the silence. The accusatory silence. The stillness after hours of motion. The pause, the dislocation, that always signaled a coming storm.

When she finally killed the engine, she sat in the descending darkness. She couldn't bring herself to open the door and go inside the house yet.

She had failed on her mission.

She was angry. The dirty sludge of rage, which she had sublimated for the past two hours, began pumping through her veins. She felt humiliated. A fucking red-haired Feeb had stopped her from going the next step.

She slammed the heel of her palm against the dashboard.

She had been *that* close to grabbing Aviva Symanski. Aviva—a prize, a tasty, tempting morsel. It had taken days—no, a whole goddamned week—to find the woman. It had taken an oblique approach, through the woman's sister. All that stalking from the Upper West Side down through Times Square, having to put up with the crowds to tail the NYB, who then tried to hold out, who cried, and kicked, and spit, until Landry slapped a strip of duct tape across her mouth and jabbed her repeatedly with the stun baton . . .

Stop it.

Yeah, Chelsea Symanski had given up her sister's address—after twenty-two hard hours of enhanced interrogation and the hair-raising specter of opioid withdrawal. She had talked, thinking it was her ticket to a fix. It had been her ticket, all right. Her ticket straight to the river.

"Shut up, shut up," Landry muttered.

Reliving that win did her no good now. Finding Aviva had been the intermediate objective. And Aviva was now a loss.

Aviva, who might have been a font of information—a stepping-stone to her goal. Now the chance to interrogate Aviva was surely gone. She was thwarted on that front.

It was appalling.

That FBI agent. The woman thought she was all that. Clear from the way she shouted, the way her eyes drilled into Landry's with that federal gaze. But she hadn't been fast enough. She hadn't responded instinctively, hadn't insta-leaped onto the tracks. And she had reacted with a fatal weakness on the far platform. She had broken off the chase to yank the kid from the toppled stroller.

Yeah, that had worked. It told her the Feeb had a soft spot. Like a baby's fontanelle. Something that could be probed and poked and used to destroy her, maybe.

But distracting the Feeb on the platform hadn't gotten Landry any closer to her objectives.

And now time was going to get tight.

The camouflage was blown. Losing the coat had cost her. It had been a faultless disguise. Honestly, making people think you were a man was as near foolproof as possible.

People saw what they assumed they were seeing. What they wanted to see. What they needed to see to keep their minds from going to an uncomfortable place. She had learned to play on that, to perfection.

Until that asshole bystander on the subway platform came after her, bigging himself up to be a hero.

She had kept him from catching her, kept them all from capturing her. But she'd had to shed her skin. They knew they were after a woman now. They had seen her face, her form, maybe the tats. Identifying marks.

Now she couldn't show any of that again. Not for a long while, not in public.

She slammed her head back against the headrest.

They had beaten her. The fed had fucked up her plan. A-P-P-A-L-L-I-N-G.

The rage was practically visible to her, rising like a red flood, filling the car, the air, her lungs.

But she couldn't show any of that in front of Mom.

And the longer she sat here, the more it was going to make Mom think something was wrong.

She smoothed her expression. Took a deep, corrosive breath and let it out with a calming hiss. She told herself she was blowing away the rage, the rising flood. She was *being present*. And *present* meant floating in a perfect, clear, distilled vat of acid.

Another breath, and her head cleared—enough, at least. She wasn't out of the game. Not entirely. She just needed a plan. A plan to take her revenge on the bitches who would keep her from her objective. She inhaled again. Exhaled. Regrouped.

She opened the Yukon's door and climbed out into a night filling with stars and the comforting buzz of locusts in the trees. Dark and electric.

She was going to *finish this*. All she had to do was come at it from another direction.

35

iv.

Driving through Manhattan an hour later, heading back to DC, Caitlin once again kicked herself. Goode's sketch was a Bat-Signal: *The woman in the drawing is alive.* He drew it, counting on somebody to recognize her and to get the message.

Lights in skyscrapers rose around her. Headlights, taxis changing lanes like goldfish, darting, sliding, nearly taking the skin off city buses and bike messengers. As she drove, she tried anew to put the pieces of the case together.

Rhiannon Griffith had to be a key to the puzzle. She was alive. She was the link that connected old and new victims. But how did she connect to Goode? And to the Broken Heart Killer?

Was the unsub working for Goode, hunting Rhiannon down? And if so, why?

According to Aviva Symanski, Rhiannon had been a runaway, a street kid in NYC, hustling to get by. Caitlin took "hustling" to include petty criminality. Theft. Could Rhiannon have stolen Goode's ill-gotten money? He had a twenty-year career of armed robbery. Not just convenience stores and gas stations, but payroll deliveries, banks, and payday loan stores. He hadn't been living high on the hog when he got arrested. But he wore good clothes and kept himself fed and entertained while on the road, and he never seemed to lack for funds when he moved into a town. She couldn't believe he had hoarded enough to retire on. Criminal drifters generally squandered their spoils as fast as possible on booze, gambling, toys.

The infamous Los Angeles bank robbery boom of the 1980s was driven as much by cocaine and heroin addiction as by the proximity of freeways. Robbers stole to fund their next high, not a villa on the Côte d'Azur.

But plenty of thieves went to prison with a stash outside. And Goode . . .

He's sly.

Goode was all about power and possession. If he'd been sent away without his cache, he would never give up wanting to get it. Or, barring his ability to get it, determine how to distribute it—like an exiled king handing out spoils.

She stopped at a red light and stretched her shoulders. Rainey had gone to meet with the US Attorney's Office about another case she was working. Caitlin was wrung out, running on empty, but her mind wouldn't stop churning.

She knew that right now her thoughts about the Broken Heart Killer amounted to rank speculation. But even that beat drawing a blank. She let her ideas play out.

Maybe the unsub was working for Goode, hunting Rhiannon.

Perhaps Rhiannon Griffith had crossed paths with Goode in New York in 2008. Stolen his stash. Perhaps Goode thought Rhiannon's friend Phoenix was involved in the theft, and killed Phoenix because of it.

The unknowns were stacked a mile deep. But thanks to Finch's photograph, Caitlin had peeled back a few layers.

In fact, it was *only* thanks to Finch's photograph that she'd gotten this far.

Headlights flowed across the intersection where she was stopped. She reflected: She had been standing too far back emotionally to catch hidden messages and subtext vital to this case.

She should be listening to her intuition, including her sense that Finch was worth listening to. And worth being concerned about.

Finch was somehow connected to the nexus too, and that worried Caitlin.

She'd texted Finch and left a voice mail for her mother, but hadn't heard back. She drummed her fingers on the steering wheel, then punched a new address into the vehicle GPS. When the light turned green, she headed to Brooklyn.

Parking outside a stone apartment building, she climbed out into the cool twilight. The street was tree lined, a block off a busy thoroughfare but a world away from its bustle. She rang the buzzer at the street entrance, hoping that an adult would answer.

"Hello?"

It was a youthful voice.

"Finch? It's Special Agent Hendrix."

"Omigosh."

The lock buzzed open. Inside, as Caitlin started up the stairs, Finch called down to her.

"Here." Three stories above, Finch leaned over the railing, waving.

The girl greeted her at the door of a small but airy apartment with hardwood floors and a high-end kitchen. Bookshelves, modern art, a wall-mounted TV with a video game paused. The controller sat on top of a physics textbook. On the couch sat a teenage boy.

Caitlin nodded to him. He jumped to his feet and tried to neaten a wild head of dark hair under a slouch cap.

"Zack Arcega. How do you do?"

He stuck out his hand, awkward and abruptly uncertain where he'd placed his mask of adulthood. He was adorable.

Finch eyed Caitlin with bright, overt hope. "What's going on?"

"Is your mom here?"

Finch had been driving this bus, providing the impetus to investigate possible links between an unknown birth mother and the events of 2008. But the photo she had uncovered had almost certainly been obtained from her adoptive mom. Caitlin needed to talk to Annie Winter.

Finch shook her head. "She's out with work friends after her shift. At Axis. In Manhattan? Off Union Square? She's a chef."

Caitlin spoke casually. "I left her a message yesterday and haven't had the chance to talk to her."

Finch's shoulders tightened. "She's super busy. I doubt she got your message."

That was the first false note Caitlin had heard from this girl. The voice mail she left for Annie had been a house phone. Now she wondered if Finch had listened to it and deleted it.

Why did she get that feeling, and why would Finch do that?

Because maybe Finch hadn't told her mother she'd contacted the FBI or gotten a DNA test. Because Finch was an adoptee whose mother had spent her entire life protecting her from knowledge about her origins. And because Finch might be worried that she would hurt Annie by connecting with her birth family. Caitlin knew that such situations could be emotionally fraught.

"Do you have news?" Finch eyed her excitedly. "Otherwise, you wouldn't be here."

"When will your mom get home?"

"Not until late. It's classic movie night. A group goes out every Tuesday, hits something from the Criterion Collection that's playing in Manhattan. What's going on?"

"I really need to talk to her," Caitlin said. "Can you give me her cell number?"

Finch stuck her hands in her pockets. "I'd have to ask her permission."

"Finch."

"I can't give out her personal information. Not even to an FBI agent. Maybe *especially* not to an FBI agent." Finch's cheeks were turning bright red. "Not without her permission."

"Then please get it."

Caitlin could find another way to obtain Annie Winter's cell number. Seeing Finch squirming to keep it from her was practically as informative.

"Now, I need you to listen to me," Caitlin said. "I want you to be careful."

Finch stuck out her hip. It seemed a deliberate attempt to appear unconcerned and in charge. But under the force of Caitlin's gaze, she pulled back. She took in Caitlin's messy hair, the grime beneath her nails, and the dirty knees of her pants. A cloud came over her gaze.

"You'll see it on the news tonight," Caitlin said. "I got within a few feet of the killer we're after. She escaped. She's still at large."

"She."

"You'll see her photo on the news. Blond, a barber-style man's hair-cut. Athletic. She's extremely dangerous," Caitlin said. "You understand?"

Finch opened her mouth to speak, then gulped and nodded.

"I want you to tell me about the photo you found. Where it came from, how your mother got it. Because it belongs to her, right?" Caitlin raised an eyebrow. Finch didn't respond, which she took as a yes. "I need to know if it was given to her at the time of your adoption, and whether she has information about the people in it."

Finch's shoulders ratcheted upward. "I don't know."

Caitlin glared.

"Honest."

"Do these names mean anything to you? Phoenix. Stinger. Amber Roark. Rhiannon Griffith. Aviva Symanski."

At each one, Finch shook her head. She looked legitimately baffled.

Caitlin took a step closer to the girl. "I'm here to deliver a warning."

"What warning?"

"You need to steer clear of strangers who contact you about your birth family. Or about the murder case, or Efrem Judah Goode."

"Why would anybody even contact me?"

"Finch, please. I'm not the only one you've talked to about all this." She looked over Finch's shoulder. "Right?"

Zack shuffled and pushed his slouch cap down over his hair. "Uh."

"You've talked about it at school, online, social, everywhere. Don't pretend you haven't." Probably complaining about how her mother treated her like a little kid, and how the cops and the FBI were ignoring her. "This case is big, and active, and sprawling. You don't know who might get hold of a piece of information and use it to try to get access to you. Somebody who's a scammer, or a thief, or has even more sinister goals. Somebody who might manipulate or hurt you," Caitlin said. "If anybody—*anybody*—gets hold of you about your birth family, please, tell your mother. And call me. Immediately."

The excitement on Finch's face had turned to disappointment, then annoyance. The hip jutted more emphatically. She gave Caitlin an eye roll that belonged in the teenage hall of fame.

"If you'd tell me what's going on," Finch said, "I'd have a better idea of *how* and *who* to watch out for. And maybe I could help you with the case."

The girl tried to look bold, but her voice wavered. She was teetering on tears, desperate, and, somewhere maybe, fearful. Not fearful enough, Caitlin thought.

"I want information, not warnings," Finch said quietly.

"I understand," Caitlin said. "I do, truly." And she did. But she couldn't divulge her suspicions. "I can't reveal details of the case. I'm sorry."

"Sure."

"Please, Finch." As annoyed as Caitlin felt, she knew she had to keep the girl onside. "You're making a difference. Otherwise, I wouldn't be standing here. Trust me for now. I need you to be patient."

"It's hard. It's been so long already."

"I know. I promise that when it's possible, I'll tell you as much as I can."

"Okay." Finch stared at the floor, then nodded. "I'll be careful. But I'll hold you to that."

Out on the sidewalk a minute later, Caitlin phoned Keyes.

"I need a cell number," she said. "New York City. The name is Annie Winter."

"Have it for you in ten," Keyes said.

She walked to the Suburban, frustrated, feeling a cold drip of anxiety slide down her spine. She was heading into the Queens-Midtown Tunnel when Keyes came through with the phone number. She called and got voice mail. She left Annie a message to get in touch.

Finch stood at the window, watching the street long after Agent Hendrix passed out of sight beneath the trees below. Zack finally came over and draped his arms over her shoulders.

"Why didn't you give her your mom's cell?" he said.

"I can't. Not while Annie is lying to me."

Why, *why* had Annie lied about the existence of the photo? Finch felt a sharp fork in her belly, twisting her guts.

"You have to clear the air with your mom. You've practically been hiding from her."

"She lied to me. She might lie to Agent Hendrix too." Lie, and get information that Agent Hendrix was withholding from her because she was a teenager. "It would only make Mom spend even more effort to shut me down. To stop me from getting the facts."

Her throat tightened.

"Not yet," she said. "I have to find more information. So that when I talk to her"—confront her, she would have to *confront* her—"she can't wriggle out of telling me the truth."

Zack turned her toward him and pulled her into an embrace. He looked less annoyed than troubled. She pressed her face to his chest and hugged him.

"I have to find the answers first," Finch said. "There's no other way."

36

Morning sun was slanting through the shutters when Caitlin rolled over and squinted an eye open. She was alone in bed under tousled covers. She had arrived home near 1:00 a.m., kicked off her shoes, chugged a smoothie, then tumbled into the warmth of Sean's arms.

"Hey," he had murmured. "You good?"

"Solid gold. You?"

"I am now," he said, and pulled her on top of him.

Now, waking after a dreamless sleep, she grabbed her phone from the nightstand: 6:45 a.m. From the kitchen came the clatter of silverware and plates and the aroma of coffee and bacon. All at once, she was ravenous. She tossed off the covers and pulled on one of Sean's Cal T-shirts.

She found him at the stove—barefoot, jeans, no shirt—scrambling eggs in a skillet. Shadow sat alertly at his feet. Caitlin wrapped her arms around his waist and kissed his shoulder.

"Coffee's hot," he said.

She topped off his mug, poured one for herself, and caught the toast that leaped from the toaster. He heaped eggs onto plates for both of them, poured Cholula over his, and ate standing up.

She sat at the counter. "What's shaking?"

Sean didn't eat big breakfasts at 6:45 a.m. He rolled out the door with Shadow for a run, then hit the shower and drove to work with a fifty-five-gallon drum of coffee in the cup holder.

"I mean, bacon? Something big is going down." She gave him a cool look. "You didn't say anything last night."

"It was late."

And they had the rule. After hours, the badge comes off. Especially in bed. But Sean was clearly fueling up for something besides a Power-Point presentation at the office.

"Well?" she said.

He nodded at her slacks stained with grease balled up on the floor in the entry hall. "Well?"

"You can find a summary in the *New York Post*," she said. "Read up, and I'll fill in the gaps—after you tell me what the plan is."

He set down his coffee. "We have a lead. We're executing a warrant. Today."

It hit her like a jolt of electricity. "The bomber?"

Sean gave her the raider's stare. He was already mentally gearing up for something heavy. If she had been half-awake a minute ago, she was vividly alert now.

"It's come down in the last seventy-two hours," he said. "We've been back-tracing him via chemical forensics and sales records for electronic components. Yesterday, we managed to peel through a set of shell companies."

"You have a name and an address?"

"Donald Jameson Burkholder. Could be another alias, but that's the name on the deed for a property across the West Virginia state line. There's a trailer down a dirt road. ATF, SRT, and state troopers are gearing up. The Bureau's sending local agents and a comms command truck."

"When are you going?" she said.

He dug into the eggs. "Tonight."

The investigation had been at this point before. The previous December, they had traced sales receipts for bomb components to an address in Garlock, California. Sean had flown with SRT—the Special Response Team, the ATF's tactical unit—to the Mojave Desert and raided an old miner's cabin in the mountains north of Edwards Air Force Base.

The place had been filled floor to ceiling with coils of barbed wire.

Stuck to the barbs were photos. Snapshots taken in the aftermaths of bombings. They were scrawled over with notes written in silver marker. One message said, "Everything has a spark."

That photo showed Sean and Caitlin outside the bombed Temescal ER, jogging alongside Michele as she was taken to an ambulance.

The cabin had been rigged with trip wires on the doors and windows. It was an ambush.

This raid would be one too.

"Were you planning to go without telling me?" she said.

"Yeah." He looked at her. "Probably stupid to think I could actually do that, but I was."

She set down her fork. "Why?"

His expression clouded. "Because you're exhausted."

"I am not."

"You have dark circles under your eyes. You're talking in your sleep. You told your mom you're working a bitch-ass case. You have more stress than you need right now."

"That's not—"

"I saw you on Instagram. Playing chicken with six hundred volts and an oncoming train."

She held his gaze. "Managed risk." She paused. "I should go with you."

Sean kept the raider's stare. "No." Before she could argue, he raised a hand. "Let's skip to the end. Yes, the bomber has had eyes on us. We both think the Ghost is behind this, and the Garlock photo provides evidence to support that."

The Ghost had experience with explosives. He had rigged a murder victim's dead body so that when the cops entered the crime scene, a trip wire set off a horrifying pyrotechnic display. He had helped the Prophet steal, prep, and wire a massive cache of explosives, then had the knowledge and guile to sabotage it. He was an expert.

"He's the prime suspect," she said. "And I'm the one eyewitness who's seen him in person."

Sean took a slow breath. Before he could argue, she raised a hand.

"I should go. But I'm after a bitch-ass unsub. Fine, I'm stressed. I'm never getting near the subway again. But it's going to kill me to sit here while you take the bomber down. So keep me in the loop. Text, photos, video. I ain't gonna sleep tonight, and I might be able to ID him."

He gave her a gamma-ray glare, then put down his mug. "Okay."

She nodded. Her heart thundered in her chest.

37

At the Pop-In-Go, Tonya Pappas drummed her nails on the counter. She had three minutes before she was supposed to take her break, but the buzzing overhead lights were jamming her nerves. And she needed a cig.

Tonya put a Back in a Minute sign on the counter. In the alley behind the store, she leaned on the wall, facing the chain-link fence and the grasping green weeds that worked their way through it. She stood directly beneath the security camera so she wasn't visible, and lit up.

Then, like a sentry making her rounds, she slid her phone from her jeans pocket and checked Facebook.

She had put up a post an hour back. Typed it out *exactly* as Efrem Judah dictated it to her.

Live and let die. That's how it goes, right?

Twenty-three reactions. Not that high, considering the page had 4,200 followers. Most had joined in the past few weeks since Efrem made his revelations to the world.

Which, Tonya had to admit, bothered her. He hadn't consulted with her before giving his drawings to the Tennessee police and the FBI. She hadn't known that the drawings were coming. Seeing them on the news, knowing the FBI got them before she did . . .

It was only when Efrem sent her the new drawing, the *secret* drawing, that she got herself squared away with him again. Getting the secret drawing told her she was still his number one. The person he could count on. His biggest fan. No, not fan. Soul mate. Because honestly, who else did he have in his life? Nobody.

Twenty-three reactions. Likes and wows and hearts. Yeah, those hearts, they chapped her ass. Too many women thought they could sweet-talk Tonya into passing along messages of lust to Efrem, the bitches. Two comments. She always loved reading those. Usually. Some people thought if they followed the page, that made Tonya their best friend, and by some magic, that made Efrem their best friend too. Wackos.

Live and Let Die. Great song.

Is Efrem going to be in a band on the run? 😆

Asses, she thought. Two comments, both dumb. She flicked her cigarette across the alley.

Then she saw the little red flag. She had two private messages.

The first was from a snitch follower, a rando telling her that some teenage girl in New York was trying to get a campaign going to blame Efrem for her mother's death. Tonya didn't have time to deal with that, not when she had bigger fish to fry.

She opened the second message and gasped.

It goes Liv and let die.

"Sweet fucking Saint Joseph."

The message was from a woman named Sigrun Landry. Her profile pic was an eagle. No other information available. The message continued.

Need to meet.

Just the way Efrem had predicted.

Somebody might write back, he had told her. *Probably not a regular comment. A personal message. They might use their real name, probably fake. You got to play it cool.*

Now here it was, just as Efrem had foreseen. Because Sigrun? Was that even a name? Tonya licked her lips. Her hand trembled. She responded exactly the way he had told her.

Not so fast. What comes next?

She sent it and stood against the wall, quivering. What if her reply to Sigrun Landry didn't go through?

Then, on her screen, a check mark appeared beneath her text bubble. The message had been delivered. *Good, good.*

But it might be hours before somebody read her reply. Might be to-morrow. Or never. This sucked, this waiting. Did spies feel like this, waiting for other spies to send back coded messages? Because that's what she was now, Efrem's secret agent.

She looked up and down the alley. She'd been out here too long. She couldn't stand around waiting for Sigrun Landry to send the correct response.

Just as she stuck her phone in her pocket, it buzzed. A reply appeared. Freebird?

"Jesus Christ on shredded wheat," Tonya said.

Freebird. That was the answer Efrem had told her to watch for. She nearly dropped her phone typing OK.

Thank you, Sigrun replied. I will tell you everything. I will take you to meet Efrem.

Tonya felt a surge of excitement—and jealousy. Take her to meet Efrem? How could this Sigrun promise that? What kind of close personal bond did this woman have with him?

A red scrim appeared at the edges of Tonya's vision. She typed: Are you his wife?

The reply came quickly. Sigrun was on the line, ready to jump.

LOL no!

That was a relief. If you believed her. *Do you believe her, Tonya?* Not his wife. Could be his lover, mistress, side action, old flame, his favorite hooker. *Shit.* This was not okay, not at all.

Tonya typed, What, then?

Sigrun replied, I'm his descendant.

Descendant? What did that mean? Niece? Granddaughter? Efrem didn't have kids. He'd never mentioned one to her. Never mentioned any woman or family beyond his redneck father and drunken mother back in East Texas. It was just him. Him, and now her.

Her, Tonya. Not her, Sigrun Landry.

Tonya's heart clenched. She dreamed of marrying Efrem and hated the thought of others being close to him. But Sigrun had provided the right response, knew the password, was the one Efrem must have been telling Tonya to watch for. She was the secret agent.

And she was dangling entry into Efrem's private life. His *real* private life. In person, in the flesh. I will take you to meet Efrem. Did she know that Tonya couldn't afford a trip to Nashville, or that with Efrem under lockdown, everybody but immediate family was banned from prison visits? Was she secretly telling Tonya that she could help Tonya get in by becoming his wife?

She typed, Where?

Your bio says you're in New Jersey.

Yes. In Woodbridge, off the Garden State Parkway. Where are you?

Sigrun wrote, Can you meet today?

I'm off at 5. Meet at the bar at The Outback?

No. Not in public. What we have to discuss is extremely confidential. You don't want anybody to overhear or see us and put two and two together. This isn't a game. This is important.

Tonya blew out a breath.

Sigrun said, Please. You and I need someplace quiet and private. You can be such a help. Please.

Tonya decided. It felt absolutely right. Like nothing had ever felt so right in her life. Now was her time. It was here, and she needed to seize it.

She typed, My place.

38

The raid team rolled into West Virginia under cover of darkness. The landscape was hilly and densely wooded. The road curved through night-rich countryside that felt wild and empty, furtive and dangerous. Every time they passed a farmhouse or gas station, Sean wondered if local spies were taking note—people paid to call the bomber when unfamiliar vehicles drove by. Especially vehicles like the black Suburban he was driving. And SRT's armored command vehicle with a dish on the roof. The ATF bomb squad RV. The FBI communications truck with satellite uplink. Not to mention the Blackhawk helicopter that was staging with an assault team and medics at a regional airport twenty miles away.

They pulled off the highway at a tree-shrouded trailhead that led into the hills and got out into the starlit dark. The mood was electric.

The raid team leader, the SRT unit chief, Joel Segura, clapped his hands. "Gather round."

They assembled in a semicircle. SRT in tactical gear. Uniformed West Virginia State Police. FBI. Sean and his ATF team.

"We are here to execute a high-risk arrest warrant," Segura said. "Followed by a search of the subject's residence."

The raid team knew the plan. They had memorized the briefing and reviewed satellite overheads that showed the property in chillingly detailed resolution. A path ran from the trailhead through heavy woods to the single-wide trailer. There was a propane tank outside the back door. Mini satellite dish on the back steps. A motorcycle parked nearby.

Fifty yards of open ground surrounded the trailer. An infrared drone camera had captured the heat image of a person inside.

Segura raised his chin. "The person we are seeking is Donald Jameson Burkholder. We have no photo. Anyone on the property is subject to arrest. Anything on two, four, six, or no legs. People, dogs, snakes. Cuff them, take them out of action."

He nodded at Sean.

Sean panned the group, locking eyes with each of them. "Assume the subject will have an early warning system. Be alert."

"Saddle up," Segura said.

Adrenaline zinging, Sean popped the tailgate on the Suburban and put on his ballistic vest. The Velcro tightened with a crackle. The FBI comms team launched a drone. Its sullen buzz blended with the crickets and tree frogs. Sean turned on his body cam. He chambered a round in his duty weapon, holstered it, and slung a rifle across his chest.

He texted Caitlin. Up.

He put in his radio earpiece. He heard Segura say, "Roll."

Caitlin came out of the Quantico locker room with her gym bag over her shoulder, freshly showered after taking a run on the FBI Training Academy course and hitting the gym. She felt invigorated. She was going to get news tonight about the raid, one way or another, and didn't want to get it at home alone. She headed back toward the BAU, watching the dusk begin to twinkle with stars. Her phone vibrated in her jeans pocket.

She had a notification: The Efrem Judah Goode Facebook fan page had a new post.

Live and let die. That's how it goes, right?

She slowed. *Live.* Echoing Goode's code word, *Liv.*

The post struck her as suspicious. She checked likes and comments and muttered, "You sound fishy as hell, Tonya."

Was the post a new signal? She forwarded it to Keyes.

When she swiped into the building, the office was empty. She slid the gym bag beneath her desk.

Her phone vibrated again. She looked, and every nerve ending on her skin fired at once.

Up.

She peered out the windows, toward the west. Darkness had overtaken the view. She tried to see beyond the horizon, across the state line, into the threat-laden West Virginia forest. When Keyes texted back, it startled her.

Will investigate.

After a second, she walked around the corner. She found him in his office.

"Wondered if you'd show up," he said.

"I have a question."

The lights in his lair were low, blue-tinged, like a spaceship cockpit set for the dim reaches of the solar system. He turned to one of his monitors. "The ATF raid?"

"How'd you—"

"Emmerich. You spoke to him this morning about the warrant for the bomber." He ran his fingers over the keyboard. "FBI is running comms, and you can ID the prime suspect."

He hit Return. The big monitor switched to a multipanel view of satellite, drone, and body-cam feeds.

She grabbed Keyes by the shoulders. "My man. Thank you."

39

Tonya Pappas wanted a cigarette. She had just stubbed one out, but her skin, her veins, every cell in her body was screaming for another. Had been since she got back to her mobile home unit at Garden Terrace Village. She had vacuumed the rug, cleaned the litter box, wiped down the living room ashtrays, and set out snacks. She had put on good jeans and her wedge heels. Then she paced back and forth inside the living room window, waiting for the Descendant.

Outside, the evening was quiet. Nobody was sitting on their porch watching comings and goings—not even the old gossip in the unit across the way. That disappointed Tonya, because she was meeting privately with Sigrun Landry and truthfully wanted the world to know that she was about to be given entry to the holy of holies, the private, face-to-face world of Efrem Judah Goode.

In the kitchen, Winkie came through the cat door, slinking in from the alley like the tomcat he was. He sauntered in and rubbed against Tonya's calves as she stared at the street, craving a smoke. She reached for the pack on the coffee table and saw a vehicle turn the corner. Headlights high off the ground. Big SUV, dark. Her heart jumped.

She was waiting at the front door when the knock came. She opened it smiling. "Welcome to my home, Miss Landry."

The woman on the step eyed her alertly. Tonya felt a disconcerting nudge of surprise.

"Tonya. Thank you." Smiling brightly, the woman stepped inside and closed the door behind her. She clasped Tonya's hand like a long-lost friend. "It's wonderful to meet you," she said. "Good to be here."

Tonya felt confounded. Sigrun had to be Goode's kin. She'd said so in her message. But she looked nothing like him. Tonya couldn't stop staring at her.

Efrem Judah was massive and dark and had powerful energy in his black eyes. Sigrun had a colder, thinner sharpness. She was mannish, even with the black Spandex dress, the cosmetics-counter makeup, and the long red hair that Tonya thought might be a wig.

But her smile was warm and inviting, like a Marlboro. "Thank you for caring about Efrem."

"He's the thing in the world I care the most about," Tonya said. "Anything for him."

She gestured to the couch. Still smiling, Sigrun moved instead to the front window and drew the curtains.

"Do you mind?" she said. "I worry who might be watching."

"Oh," Tonya said.

"Your neighbors know about the Facebook page, right? And a quiet street like this, I presume they're only too eager to snoop."

Tonya should have thought of that. "Some of them, it's the high point of their day."

"I'd hate for strangers to use our meeting to their advantage," Sigrun said. "Post pics, try to go viral. I'm just concerned about protecting you. And Efrem, of course."

Tonya nodded. She clenched her hands and tried to tamp down her excitement. Why did she feel so jittery?

They sat on the couch, and Tonya gestured at the snacks she had set out on the coffee table.

"Help yourself," she said, then set a Dr Pepper and a Little Debbie snack cake on a napkin in front of Sigrun.

Sigrun smiled at the spread as she sat down. "This is really thoughtful of you."

She didn't touch anything though. Just smiled and stared at Tonya.

Tonya popped open a soda and smiled back. "So, who are you? Exactly?"

Sigrun folded her hands neatly on her lap, like Princess Di. "I hope you understand that before we talk—I mean, really talk, sharing confidential information—I need proof that you aren't shining me on."

Her gaze didn't have Di's fawn-eyed softness though. Tonya put down her soda.

"I'm not. Of course not. Haven't you seen the Facebook page? Efrem and I are close friends—"

Sigrun rested a hand on Tonya's knee. It felt hot. That didn't jibe with her cool appearance, her pale face, her ice-blue eyes. Under the surface, she was running like a Shelby Cobra.

"This isn't personal," she said. "Do you have evidence to prove your bona fides?"

"My what?"

"Something from Efrem you can show me as proof of good faith?"

Tonya sat straighter. Now she got it. She saw. Sigrun was nervous. And uncertain. Nervous and uncertain were good. It meant Tonya had the upper hand.

She played coy. "Maybe."

Sigrun's smile grew distant. "Has Efrem given you anything that you haven't posted on the Facebook page? A message? Maybe a photo? A drawing? Can you show me?"

"What do you want it for?" Tonya said.

Sigrun's lips opened, erasing the smile.

"I need your bona fides too," Tonya said.

Sigrun leaned back. For a fraction of a second, her eyes flashed hard. Tonya held her breath, going silent, so silent that she could hear the walls and the kitchen floor creak.

"For instance, what kind of name is Sigrun?" she said.

Winkie trotted up and jumped onto Sigrun's lap. He rubbed himself across her dress and swiped his tail into her hair. And *yes*, Tonya thought, that salon-style blowout was definitely a wig. What, was the woman losing her hair?

Sigrun didn't flinch at Tonya's ask though. Her gaze steadied. She actually seemed to relax.

"Fair enough," she said. "We're looking for someone."

That wasn't what Tonya had expected. "Who?"

"Someone who took from us. You can help us find her."

"Took?" Tonya said. "I don't understand. Took from Efrem?"

"If you could just reassure me, I'll explain. Everything."

Sigrun needed reassurance. Tonya liked that. Needing something from her—that was bona fides enough. Tonya got her phone and pulled up the drawing Efrem had sent her.

She paused. Always pause. She had learned from watching *Survivor*—make your decision but keep the audience hanging while you count to ten. She held the phone to her chest.

"Before I show you, I want to be sure we're absolutely clear. I'm doing this for Efrem."

The creaking sound returned. Footsteps thumped along the hallway. A voice rumbled.

"This isn't for Efrem, bitch."

Tonya spun. A woman boomed into the living room behind the sofa.

"Who the fuck are you?" Tonya said.

The woman was in her late thirties, redheaded like Sigrun, sexy as hell in a tight top and yoga pants. Her eyes fizzed with rage.

"Call me Corliss. The woman who's in charge here."

Tonya got halfway to her feet and saw a long black baton in Sigrun's hand. It had electrodes on the end. Blue electricity writhed between them.

Sigrun slammed the hot end of the stun baton into Tonya's chest. The living room flipped white. Pain jolted her. Her muscles locked and she crashed to the floor.

She couldn't move. Couldn't speak. She saw Sigrun looming over her.

"It's Old Norse," she said. "Sigrun. It means secret victory."

Winkie jumped off the couch, onto Tonya's stomach. Sigrun jabbed the stun baton at him. The cat went rigid, his hair standing on end, and toppled without a sound.

The Corliss woman came around the couch and stood over Tonya, watching her twitch.

"Get her in the car," she said.

40

They spread out and approached silently. SRT, Sean's ATF team, the state troopers, and FBI agents. Camouflaged by the woods and the night, they descended the hill toward the trailer. In the trees around them, an insect chorus rose and fell like an electric sine wave.

Sean caught a view downslope. Raising his left hand, he squeezed a fist. *Stop.* The two agents behind him halted. He crept to a boulder, raised the rifle, and scoured the hillside with the night scope, searching for booby traps, trip wires, sentries—any sign that their suspect had rigged an ambush or early warning system.

He saw nothing. He waved for the agents to join up. They settled on either side of him, gazing through the trees and across the clearing at the trailer.

The agent to his left, Conner, raised his binoculars. "He's there. Living room, on the right."

Sean saw him.

He was bent over a workbench. A young man, pasty, with sandy hair cut short, as if he'd buzzed it himself with clippers. A white T-shirt with a logo on the back. A band? An auto parts store? His arms, beneath the glue-white skin, were sinewy with muscle.

The agent to Sean's right, Yang, said, "Burkholder?"

Conner said, "Whoever. Look at the table where he's working."

The workbench was nothing more than a thick sheet of plywood set on two sawhorses. It was covered with electronic components, wire spools, a soldering iron—and more. The hair on the back of Sean's neck stood up. The work surface was heaped with . . .

"Fuck me," he said.

At his desk, Keyes zoomed in on a body-cam feed from the raid team. Caitlin stood behind him, eyes pinned on the monitor.

"That," she said.

On-screen was the trailer. Through a window, a tautly muscled young man worked with painstaking care.

"Fuck me," she said.

On the work bench sat a dozen bricks of plastic explosive.

Her vision throbbed. The man's back was to her. Was it the Ghost? She had his image clear in her mind: his low-key menace, his switchblade glare, and his sandpaper voice.

The man half turned his head, giving her a glimpse of his profile, then bent deeper over the bench.

Turn around, you bastard.

Sean keyed his radio. "We have visual confirmation. White man in the northernmost room, working with electronic components and plastic explosives."

"Copy," Segura replied.

"In position. Get off comms. RF hazard."

Radio frequency. Sean didn't know how the man in the trailer might wire his device to detonate, but from the components he could see on the workbench, the suspect might be preparing a bomb, or bombs, that operated via radio frequency. Sean didn't want the raid team's transmissions to trigger an explosion. The sounds in his ear went silent.

But from deep in the trees, a red penlight flashed on and off. It was Segura's signal.

Go.

Sean signaled with his hand, like a hatchet, directly ahead, and led Conner and Yang around the boulder.

The hillside was uneven and heavily thatched with ground cover.

Sean sidestepped, holding the rifle barrel down, index finger along the trigger guard. The agents closed up behind him. A hundred yards to his left, within the tree line, he saw Segura and his SRT unit.

This is it. Let's do it.

He advanced, scanning the ground for hazards, buried land mines—anything. Fifteen yards from the clearing, Sean signaled Yang and Conner to spread out and flank him. He kept eyes on the trailer. Once they broke from the trees onto open ground, they would have no cover.

They stepped cautiously, scanning the brush ahead and the forest floor. It came silently. Conner took one step too far.

He didn't step on anything, catch a trip wire, do anything wrong. He crossed an invisible border. And tripped a motion sensor.

In the clearing, an alarm sounded. It was a shriek, the kind that home security systems emit if a panic button is pressed. Piercing, swooping, overtaking the night. Floodlights erupted, lighting the ground around the trailer like a prison yard.

The man at the workbench jumped back, hands clenching into a boxer's stance, and jerked around. His mouth opened; his eyes widened. His profile was sharp.

Sean shouted from the edge of the clearing, "*Get back!*"

He spun and dived for the ground.

The flash came, white, turning the forest to a daguerreotype. His shadow threw itself spectrally onto the trees.

The blast wave came next. And the roar as the trailer exploded.

At Quantico, Caitlin and Keyes watched the screen. The drone feed bleached white. The raid team's body cams went to static.

41

Caitlin stood rigidly behind Keyes and scanned the screen. Whited out, scribbled with gray static. Her chest constricted.

"Keyes, can you get the feed back online?" she said.

He spun to another computer and pounded on the keyboard. The space-dim glow of the monitors was unearthly.

"The encrypted links to the satellite and comms truck are active. This is camera and radio interruption from the scene." He looked up at her. "Nothing I can do. We have to wait."

Sean hit the dirt facedown with his arms over his head. The smell of earth filled his nose as the pressure wave popped his ears, and the breath was smacked from his lungs. The boom rolled over him and echoed off the hills. In its wake came a heavy hush, insects falling silent. Then the vast cawing of crows taking flight from the darkened trees.

He raised his head. The night had bloomed orange with firelight reflecting off the leaves of the trees.

"Conner. Yang," he called.

"Here," Yang replied. Conner called out, "I'm okay."

Sean spun and got to his knees, rifle raised. In the clearing, the trailer had been obliterated. The walls had blown out and peeled open like an aluminum can. Flames shot into the night sky, yellow and orange, screaming, turning the clearing into an open furnace. The hideous heat was a wall against his face and chest, even seventy yards away.

Conner rose to his feet.

"Down," Sean said. "The propane—"

The tank went up in a white blast, sending shredded metal flying.

The drone feed remained blank. A body cam came back online. It showed a descending apocalypse.

Sean spun away as shrapnel spit into the trunks of the trees and shredded through leaves.

Flat on the ground, hands over his head, Conner said, "Copy getting down."

Sean blinked grit from his eyes, rose to a crouch, and took cover behind a tree trunk. He raised a hand against the fire's orange heat.

Yang ducked against a tree trunk beside him and squinted against the glare. "Is that real?"

"Too real," Sean said.

Rolls of concertina wire had erupted from the shredded trailer like spilled guts.

"Jesus," Yang said. "The explosion fried him, and that wire eviscerated what was left."

Sean keyed his radio. "Three from blue team returning to the staging point."

He stared for another second. "Let's go."

Caitlin watched the trailer turn into a burn pit. Her pulse thundered in her ears. It took a moment for Keyes's voice to cut through.

"I have him."

He raised the volume on a feed. She heard Sean's voice.

"All teams, retrace your steps to the staging point *exactly*. He may have planted trip wires or devices around the perimeter."

He sounded calm, and sharp as a razor blade. She sat down on the floor and leaned back against the wall. On the monitor, a dozen feeds now showed the blast's aftermath—a white-orange montage of destruction.

Keyes's dim space-capsule office felt comforting, like a chapel. Caitlin never wanted to see an explosion again. She wanted to outlaw anything that could ignite, including a match, a temper, or a fit of laughter.

Managed risk.

This was what Sean did for a living. This was the terrifying power he hunted and tried to subdue. A force that could vaporize lives, neighborhoods, and cities. Pride and fear blew through her like a burst of radiation.

Keyes turned silently to her.

"I'm good," she said.

It was half an hour later when her phone rang with a video call. She answered. Saw Sean at the staging point. His face was dirty. His eyes held a jagged light. Behind him, fire trucks and the ATF bomb squad headed toward the blast site.

"One dead in the trailer. Confirmed," he said.

"The firefighters saw the body?"

"Incinerated. County coroner's on the way."

Sean looked over his shoulder. Beyond the hilltop, a red glow lit the sky. "I could say we got him. Truth is, the guy got himself."

A man in SRT gear walked past Sean. His name tag read SEGURA. "Whoever he was, he's gone. He is good and got."

Sean clapped him on the shoulder. Segura touched two fingers to his brow in informal salute and headed for the SRT command vehicle. Sean turned back to Caitlin.

"No injuries. We got out clean."

"You're talking awfully loud," Caitlin said.

"My ears are ringing." He looked around. "Things seem bright." He glanced back through the mist-shrouded night. "The guy in the trailer screwed up. But we were still in the trees, and that helped stop the shrapnel."

She wanted to wrap him in her arms. She nodded instead.

Across the clearing, an ATF agent whistled and waved. "Rawlins."

Sean said, "Hold on."

A minute later, he returned to the call. "A video just posted. I'm sending it."

She turned to Keyes. When the link arrived, he loaded it on his monitor.

A graphic appeared: a red double helix twisted into a Möbius strip, with neon-blue corona spikes around the exterior. A Latin phrase ran below it. *Fiat justitia ruat caelum.*

Sean translated. "Let justice be done though the heavens fall."

"You speak Latin?" Keyes said.

"Science Latin. But I learned that phrase in a political history course. It's the belief that justice must be enacted no matter the consequences."

His tone suggested that the phrase had flown on banners supporting ugly causes.

The graphic cross-faded to a video camera view of a white drop cloth tacked up on a wall. The room was lit with an overhead bulb. A sliver of yellow sunlight penetrated the room through a window on the right.

From behind the camera, a man walked into frame. He posed in front of the drop cloth and glared into the lens.

"My name is Donald Jameson Burkholder, and if you're watching this, I'm dead."

"Here we go," Sean said.

The man had furious eyes and skin so pale that the hot patches on his cheeks stood out like cigarette burns. He was young, wearing a white T-shirt—a brilliant, bleached, freshly pressed white shirt. Sinewy arms. Short sandy hair.

It was the man Caitlin had seen in the trailer.

"I'm dead either by government-issued gunfire, corporate poison, or martyrdom. I may have been forced to protect myself and my knowledge by calling down the heavens. If so, I pray I brought the sky raining onto the poisoners and collaborators, with pillars of fire."

"A manifesto," Keyes said. "Nothing more charming."

"You want to know how I carried out the operations against your military-medical complex? Welcome to my fireside chat."

He smiled. It was the most ghoulish grin Caitlin had ever seen, soulless yet possessed.

"I am solely responsible for all instruments of rectification, including the warning device at New York Presbyterian Hospital. I placed the device outside the Defense Language Institute in Monterey. And at Warrington

Pharmaceutical in San Francisco. And I strapped the device to the body of the schizophrenic woman in Berkeley, who was the vector to transport my cleansing fire into the belly of the beast at Temescal Hospital." He leaned forward. "You're welcome."

"Jesus hell," Caitlin muttered.

Then Burkholder wound up and let loose.

He raged like an animatronic demon about plagues, the military, and a coming biowar apocalypse. Caitlin had no doubt that this abomination, this abortion of a soliloquy, had been recorded by the man in the trailer.

He jabbed a finger at the camera. "This I vow. Death cannot stop my work."

Then he lunged for the camera and shut the video down.

Caitlin stood for a moment, absorbing it. Trying to make sense of it. Accepting it.

She turned to Keyes. "We need—"

"To know everything about it. 'Everything' all caps. Instantly. On it."

She knew he would run with it. He would trace the IP address. He would identify the camera used to record this, down to the year it was manufactured and the factory worker who ground the lens. He would analyze the angle of the sunlight coming through the window, to figure out the camera's latitude.

New York. Monterey. San Francisco. Oakland. Garlock. West Virginia. Caitlin wondered where else the bomber had nested. And she wondered at the breadth of his movements, and the expertise and money required to carry out the bombing campaign.

She looked at Sean. "Was he acting alone?"

"Right. Cross-country campaign. Multiple properties, shell companies, diversions, purchase and theft of explosives. C-four," he said. "We'll find out."

Caitlin peered at the image of the bomber on the screen.

"Were we so wrong?" she said. "Was it confirmation bias, wishful thinking . . ."

"Or something else?" Sean said. "But yeah, no. That guy . . ."

"Isn't him. It's not the Ghost. Not even close."

She held Sean's gaze for seconds that felt eternal. Was she actually disappointed?

"I thought we had him," she said. "I thought we were going to close the case."

Sean looked into the distance. "I know."

Caitlin saw a van pull into the parking lot near him. It said HAWKINS COUNTY CORONER.

Sean rubbed his face. "I'll be here the rest of the night. There's a shit-ton to do on the right of boom."

When he arrived in West Virginia, Sean was left of boom—hoping to arrest the bomber. After the explosion—right of boom—he had a crime scene to dig through.

"See you at home," Caitlin said.

She ended the call, unsettled. The immediate threat had been neutralized.

The Ghost was still out there.

42

Finch woke to thunder, but by the time she dressed and got ready for school, the storm had blown east. Outside her window, puddles shone on the sidewalk and turned the street an oily gold. When she heard her mom start the shower, she slung her backpack over a shoulder, grabbed her keys, and headed for the door. She didn't want to see Annie.

Her phone pinged. She pulled it from her pack. She stopped. She had a notification from the YourGenealogy.com "Seeking Long-Lost Relatives" forum.

Across the apartment, the bathroom door opened. Her mom leaned out wearing a robe, her wet hair in a towel turban. "Hey."

Finch nearly jumped. She dumped the phone into her pack. "Hey. I'm meeting Luz and Shoshanna to work on our French class project. I'll see you tonight."

"Finch . . ."

"I have to go."

Annie stepped into the hall. Her face was pained. "I feel like we've let things get stressful. Let's do something this weekend. Go to a movie. Or the Kehinde Wiley exhibit in Tribeca."

Finch hesitated. "Okay. Yeah, that'd be cool."

She saw the house phone on the hallway table. A couple of days ago, she had erased the voice mails from Agent Hendrix before her mom heard them, but now the display said NEW MESSAGE. *Noooo*, she thought. She had forgotten to check the phone last night, and now there was a fresh voice mail and it was probably from Agent Hendrix and *no no no*.

Annie walked toward her. "Things have been ... strained. I hate that."

Finch set her backpack on the table in front of the phone. "No strain." She hurried toward her. "You're just a velociraptor before you have your caffeine. I'll make you coffee."

Annie seemed to relax. "Thank God I have a live-in barista."

She pulled her mom into the kitchen. "I presume you want yours with sour cream and two lumps of crab."

Annie smiled. It looked tentative. "The regular."

Finch brewed a pod in the machine and handed her mom the mug. "See you tonight."

"Thanks, love."

On her way out, she paused at the hallway table, unplugged the phone, and thumbed messages to "All read." She would tell her mom everything— once she got evidence. Then she would explain that she had defied her order to keep out of a mess involving a convicted killer. She would. When she worked up the nerve. When she figured out what could make Annie so insane that she would lie to Finch's face to keep her from learning the truth.

The NEW MESSAGE alert on the phone disappeared.

Downstairs, she headed into a sun-glazed morning, rushing up the sidewalk with the oil-gold street glaring in her face. The trees were budding, blossoms pinking up. She waited until she reached McCarren Park, then opened the message from YourGenealogy.com.

"Oh my God."

It was a reply to her plea to find her birth mother's killer.

I can help. Private message me.

43

When her phone rang, Caitlin was driving down I-95, with the morning sun painting the driver's window gold. She was sleep deprived but wired on adrenaline and espresso, feeling both relieved and uneasy. It was 8:00 a.m., and it was Emmerich's ringtone.

"Boss," she said. "I'm on my way. I'll fill you in on the raid."

"I got a preliminary after-action report from SRT," Emmerich said. "There'll be plenty to analyze. Especially to determine whether the suspect was a lone wolf, or had ties to extremist groups and funding."

In the passenger seat, Shadow stood and watched traffic, her tail going like a metronome. They were on the way to the dog walker. Caitlin reached over and petted her. "Right."

"But that's not why I'm calling."

Shadow licked her hand. Emmerich's tone turned her cold.

"The woman who runs the Efrem Judah Goode Facebook fan page," he said. "Tonya Pappas. She's missing."

Caitlin walked into the BAU conference room to find Rainey and Emmerich bent over photos and police reports.

Emmerich glanced up. His look lasted long enough to let her know he was assessing her emotional state.

"Tonya Pappas," she said.

He straightened. "I spoke to the detective handling the missing-persons case. Tonya didn't show up to drive her mother to a doctor's appointment this morning. Her sister went by her place, found the back door wide open."

"The detective didn't wait twenty-four hours to open an investigation," Caitlin said.

Rainey said, "The sister told him that Tonya runs a fan page for a serial killer."

Emmerich added, "Tonya's car was parked at home. Her purse was in the kitchen. It looked like she'd had a visitor or visitors. Food and drink were set out on a coffee table. Her cat was inside without food or water and acting strangely."

Rainey said, "Normally, the detective would think a grown woman with a crush on an incarcerated killer might have taken off to visit him. But all this, plus a neighbor described a strange vehicle pulling up in front of Pappas's unit."

"Tell me it was a GMC Yukon."

"A dark-blue SUV. The neighbor's looking at pictures of vehicles now."

Caitlin opened her laptop and loaded the Facebook fan page. "I know this might not be related to the Broken Heart Killer, but yesterday, Tonya posted this update."

She showed them the *Live and let die* post.

"There's something wrong about it." She turned to Rainey. "Have you checked on Aviva Symanski?"

"Spoke to her half an hour ago. She's still at the hotel. She's okay."

Emmerich said, "Thoughts?"

Caitlin gestured at the post. "This isn't coincidence. The post is couched as Tonya's own musing. Scroll back through the page—when she posts messages she's received from Goode, she identifies them clearly. 'This is from Efrem.' With a photo of his letter to her. Or 'Efrem dictated this to me on our phone call today.' 'He told me to let you know this.' She always advertises her personal connection to him," she said. "And when she posts her own thoughts, she either talks about Efrem's life or reminds people that he doesn't actually have access to the page—that she's his threshold guardian."

Rainey said, "Power and control. It's her patch of virtual ground."

"She never talks about song lyrics," Caitlin said. "Nowhere. Look back through two years of posts. This latest is a wild departure. And that sets off alarm bells."

"You think this was a message," Emmerich said.

"I think two things. One, damn right it's a message. The 'Liv' drawing was a Bat-Signal. This is a booster. It's an echo. Sent out, seeking a ping in response. And two, either Goode told Tonya long ago to put it out on a timetable, or . . .'"

Rainey pointed at her. "He's still communicating with her."

"The purse. The strange SUV. But above all, the snack buffet set out on the coffee table."

Emmerich said, "There was a diet soda on a napkin on a corner of the table. But it wasn't opened. And there are no fingerprints on it."

"Too bad." She tilted her head. "Again. Coincidence? Or the guest didn't want to touch it. And didn't want to leave DNA by opening and sipping on it."

"I sent the subway photo of the Broken Heart Killer to the township detective," Emmerich said. "He's going to show it to Pappas's neighbor."

"I don't want to get ahead of the evidence," Caitlin said, "but given Pappas's insertion of herself into Goode's world—even virtually—this is alarming. She's a groupie. And she's the person he uses as his conduit. That's where the voltage runs. And now, suddenly, it's been cut."

She looked again at the fan page. "Can we access her private messages?"

"Get started," Emmerich said. "Ask Keyes to talk to Pappas's sister and mother. Maybe they know her password."

"Bottom line?" Caitlin said. "I don't think Tonya Pappas has run off at Goode's behest to carry out some operation with the unsub. I think she's in trouble."

I can help. Private message me.

Finch felt hot and frozen at the same time. The message on her phone seemed to shimmer. Agent Hendrix's warning rose in the back of her mind. *Steer clear of strangers who contact you about your birth family. Or about the murder case, or Efrem Judah Goode.*

But this was urgent.

And what had the cops and FBI done? Nothing. It was up to *her.*

She looked over her shoulder. The park was empty aside from her. She typed a private message. How can you help? What do you know?

Ten minutes later, as she jogged up the steps to the high school entrance, her phone buzzed. She paused outside the door to read the message. Kids passed by, laughing, hurrying.

Her friend Shoshanna zoomed past, tugging her sleeve. "C'mon c'mon c'mon."

Finch bent over the phone. "Be right there."

A new private message was waiting for her.

I saw your message and the Jane Doe drawing. I know who that is.

The doors opened, noise pouring out. Inside, down the hallway, Finch saw Zack. Hands in his back pockets. Waiting for her. She held up a finger. *One minute.*

I'm listening, she wrote.

A reply came almost immediately. I am from the town where your birth mom grew up. I know the family. No joke.

Finch's chest tightened. How do you know?

I have been following the news since Efrem Judah Goode started confessing. I put two and two together. It blew my mind when I saw your message.

Zack spread his hands as if to say, *What's going on?*

Finch looked back at the phone. A new message appeared.

I can put you in contact with your relatives.

Finch waved at Zack to go to class without her.

I know they'll want to hear from you. I can try to set up a meeting.

Finch's breath would hardly come. *Go big or go home.*

The woman's screen name was Tonya P.

Finch typed, YES!!

Twenty-four hours.

Caitlin had been eyeing the clock since she learned that Tonya Pappas had been declared missing. Now more than twenty-four hours had passed. Cool morning sun bathed the view outside the windows at Quantico. There had been no word, no new information from the New Jersey police. No additional information about her Facebook fan page.

Keyes came by her desk, nudging his horn-rim glasses up his nose. "Tonya's relatives don't know her password. The local detectives are going to have to seek a warrant to access her private messages."

"How many hours will that take? All day?" She heard her own frustration.

"Nothing we—" His phone buzzed with a text. "Hang on a sec."

He opened it. His intake of breath was sharp.

"What?"

"It's from the FBI genetic genealogy unit. I asked them to look at Finch's DNA profile on the public genealogy site. Compare it with people in the system."

He turned his phone so Caitlin could read the message.

Finch Winter. Positive DNA match.

44

Keyes hustled back to his office to call the genetic genealogy unit. Caitlin phoned Detective Tashjian in New York, hoping he might also have the DNA results she had asked for. She got voice mail. She left messages, then called the NYPD Manhattan South Homicide Squad. Her pulse was zooming.

Detective Mancuso answered. "I don't have the data, and Tashjian's working another case in Brooklyn."

He didn't sound as eager as Caitlin felt. "If you hear from him, have him call."

DNA match. *I'll be damned.*

Finch was truly at the center of the nexus. Caitlin wouldn't speak to her until she learned what, exactly, the FBI's genealogy unit had discovered. But she wondered why she still hadn't heard from Finch's mother, Annie. She phoned the apartment. Voice mail was off. She tried Annie's cell. It went to a call-forwarding service, which said the voice mailbox was full. She phoned Axis restaurant. It wasn't open yet.

Something was moving. Beneath the surface, something was rousing itself and snarling.

She tossed her phone on the desk and dragged her fingers through her hair.

The coffee bar was on the Upper West Side. Poppycock's. Finch climbed to the street from the subway feeling as if she had already mainlined espresso. She was surprised that people on the sidewalk didn't hear her buzzing like a faulty electrical transformer.

Calm down, calm down.

She held her hands out. They were shaking, and not just because she was ditching English and AP Physics. Which, normally, she would never do. Like, *never*.

But this was different. This was . . .

Everything.

She hadn't known how much she wanted this. Or how afraid she would be.

When she was little, she had pictured her birth mom as a princess who had been kidnapped by aliens and taken to the far side of outer space, where she couldn't escape or even tell Finch how much she wanted to be with her.

Annie had always told Finch that her birth mom had given her life and had wanted her very much but couldn't take care of her. That vague assertion had only partially assuaged her. It had also left an aching sense of emptiness and helplessness. A lightless vacuum seemed to separate her from knowledge, from certainty, from . . . love. From a mother's touch. From the person whose kiss she barely remembered, so softly faded that it felt like mist.

Her birth mother hung in her memory, out of reach, a black hole, just *nothing*.

Finch stood rooted to the sidewalk. People rivered around her. Taxis honked.

She hadn't told Annie she was coming here. No way. The only person she had texted was Zack, and only after she got on the subway. But she couldn't lose her nerve now after coming this far.

The woman who had contacted her via the "Long-Lost Relatives" forum was named Tonya Pappas. She seemed like a weirdo because she had a Facebook page about Efrem Judah Goode, which gave Finch goose bumps and nearly got her to delete all the messages and shut communication down. But Finch decided to give her a chance (she'd never had a chance like this; she couldn't throw it away) and had messaged her back, asking for details about how she knew Finch's birth family.

The woman had explained everything. She had joined a prison pen pals initiative through her church. When she first wrote to Goode, she thought he was innocent. That was why she started the Facebook page. Then he began confessing, and she had to accept that he was guilty. But in a strange way, his guilt persuaded her heart even more deeply to maintain a connection with him. He was going to spend the rest of his life paying for his crimes. She had told him that the families of people he had harmed needed closure. They needed truth. That he had to tell it.

I know this might seem wack to you. I can understand how you might have reservations. But I grew up upstate and knew your family. Your mom was named Sigrun. Their name was Landry.

The *omigod* Finch dropped had echoed through the hallway. That tied the family to the diner. They owned it or knew the owners, or the girls in the photo took the snapshot as a joke, because of the name. Omi*god*.

I never knew what happened to your mom. But I do now, I'm sad to say. Here's the truth. I started the fan page because I met Efrem Judah Goode upstate, back when. I thought he was a normal person. I learned the hard way not to be naive. Finch, I'm sorry for what has happened to your mother and to you. I want to help make it up. And I want you to believe me.

Tonya sent an old snapshot. Of a tiny girl, maybe eighteen months old. I babysat you once.

The little girl was sitting on a woman's lap. The woman's face wasn't in the picture. Just the kid's. The kid with the stuffed lamb that Finch used to play with, which was now locked in the file cabinet in her Brooklyn apartment.

Omi-what-the-hell-*god*. Tonya was telling the truth.

Then, during first period this morning at school, Tonya had messaged Finch, saying she'd been authorized to pass along a request from Finch's relatives. They were in the city and wondered if Finch would be willing to meet for a cup of coffee. Tonya offered to come in from New Jersey to make the introduction, if Finch would feel more comfortable.

Finch thought about it and decided that actually, having Tonya there would not make her more comfortable. Tonya was legit, but inviting her to a family meeting was too much.

Having anybody there besides herself was too much. Even her girl-friends, even Zack.

But meeting the family wasn't too soon. It was a lifetime too long.

And now Finch was here, around the corner from the people she had pined for.

Here in this upscale neighborhood, about to walk into a public es-tablishment—a safe public spot—to meet with her long-lost family. She was wearing deliberately friendly clothes: a bright pink hoodie and a ball cap with a smiley face. She felt as if she had a wasps' nest in her chest. Vibrating, humming.

"You can do this," she said.

She walked around the corner and pushed through the door into the aroma of coffee. Chrome and ceiling fans, Broadway tunes on the stereo, baristas in black aprons.

In a booth by the windows, a girl stood up. She was pale and wiry, with voluminous red hair.

She and Finch stared at each other. Neither moved. Like gunslingers waiting for a countdown. *Is it her? Is it real?*

Then the red-haired girl walked straight at Finch. In a soft blouse and jeans, superstylish, with video-tutorial-quality makeup. Hands out, arms thrown wide.

"Finch," she said breathlessly.

Finch nodded. And was enveloped in the girl's hard, tight hug. She hugged her back.

"It's me," Finch said. "Thank you for coming, Landry."

The red-haired girl set her hands on Finch's shoulders, smiling with something like melancholy, her gaze poring over Finch's face. Her name was Landry Yates, which Finch thought was a cool way to pass down the family name to a new generation.

"I can't believe it," Landry said.

"Me, either." Finch's voice felt distant, as if she were underwater.

Then Landry laughed. It was a bright, tinkling sound. "Come on."

She led Finch to the booth by the window. She looked pumped, bubbly, anxious. "I don't know where to start. There's so much to talk about. *Oh.* Coffee. What do you want?"

She already had a frothy cold drink in front of her, covered with whipped cream and caramel syrup. It was a drink that, at the Brooklyn coffee bar where Finch worked, they called a Happy Meal. It was a reward drink. A comfort drink.

Finch nodded at it. "I'll have one of those."

Landry dashed to the counter and placed the order. She flipped her shiny hair over her shoulder when she slid back into the booth.

"I guess ... I need to start by saying thank you," Landry said.

"For what?"

"For being willing to take the chance and come here today. This is ... huge, and heavy. But I am *so glad* to finally meet you."

"Me too." Finch couldn't believe how nervous she was. How tongue-tied.

"I guess you want to know the basics first," Landry said. "I'm your cousin."

"Okay, yeah." Finch laughed nervously.

She realized she was looking at Landry's face for signs they were related. For things she saw in the mirror. Eye color. Cheekbones. Skin tone, that crooked tooth that her retainer couldn't quite control. Landry seemed familiar in some weird way, but it wasn't that she mirrored Finch. Maybe it was wishful thinking. The makeup and salon-style hair—maybe *that* was throwing Finch off. But Landry's sharp eyes, that cold pale blue, so clear and watchful ... Maybe her eyes reminded Finch of the photo she'd found, the photo with her dead mother. She was seeing her mom now, attenuated, *alive* somehow. Her breath caught hard in her chest.

"Cousin, right," she managed to say.

"Yes. First cousin on your mother's—your birth mother's—side."

"Yeah." Finch tried to keep from letting tears fill her eyes. She couldn't remember what she'd meant to say. It was all lint in her head now. She hadn't even asked Landry for an ID or anything. "I guess ... just tell me. Everything."

At the counter, the barista called Landry's name.

"Be right back." She hopped up and went to get Finch's drink.

Finch blew out a breath and spread her hands flat on the table. *Chill out. You have time. Landry's not going to vanish in a puff of smoke and take all the answers with her.*

The girl came back and set the molto caramel espressotini on the table. "With biscotti too, okay?"

Finch pulled the drink near, like a security blanket, and took a deep slurp from the straw. It was strong and sweet, with underlying bitterness. Which, she guessed, summed up her situation. Hey, she'd been paying attention to theme and metaphor in classical literature after all. Her English teacher would be so proud.

Landry settled across from her. A look both sad and excited filled her face. "I just can't believe it. You have to understand, the family's been looking for you for years."

"What?" Finch's chest heated. "Looking for me?"

That was far from what she had expected to hear. It was beyond her deepest, thinnest hopes.

"And I know you need proof that this isn't a scam."

Finch didn't want to say anything or even to react, because she worried it would frighten Landry off. Like a deer in the woods. But she felt relieved, and her face had to show it.

Landry's face softened. "Did you think I'd get huffy and storm out if you asked for evidence that we're related?"

"No." Finch attempted a smile. "Maybe."

She tore open the biscotto, then took a deep, comforting drink of the espressotini.

"We've been burned before," Landry said.

"What? When? How?"

"It's a sad fact that the world is full of duplicitous people," Landry said. "Some of them will prey on families that are desperate to find lost loved ones."

"That's . . . horrible."

Landry waved a hand. *Never mind.* "So I want you to understand that this is the real deal."

From her purse she took a Manila folder and brought out a drawing. It was a scan of a pastel sketch. She slid it across the table. Finch set down her drink, wiped whipped cream from her upper lip, and tried not to get a stomach cramp.

The drawing was a vivid, haunting sketch of a wide-eyed little girl.

A three-year-old with flyaway hair and wide, questioning eyes. With a rosebud mouth and long lashes. With a floppy stuffed lamb held tight in her small hand.

The shock and the tears came like a wave. They came with a crazy sense of surrealism. Finch had no doubt what she was looking at. The pastels, the art brut naturalism, the vivid colors, the haunting reflection of life in the eyes of the subject. This had been drawn by Efrem Judah Goode. It looked like all the other drawings he had given the FBI. Except this one looked . . . older. Rubbed down maybe. A little smeared? And it had never been published.

Landry leaned forward, hands steepled. "It's you."

Scrawled at the bottom was *NYC 2008*.

Landry leaned across the table, hands folded. Like a nun in prayer, the way she'd practiced it.

The girl was staring at the drawing as if she had just been given a map to the City of Gold. Landry could see it in her face. The shock. The longing, the slow dawn of understanding. The revulsion and the excitement. The drawing was a printout of the new sketch Goode had sent to Tonya Pappas. The oh-so-precious *I'm doing this for Efrem* prize that prissy, stupid Tonya had been trying to keep Landry from seeing before the stun baton made all her posturing moot.

Tonya's phone used face ID. As soon as Tonya had come around, Landry held the phone in front of her face, and *boom*, she was in and changed the password. Found the photo and printed it off.

Landry watched Finch put her fingers to her temples. She was about to cry. City kid, a girl used to fancy coffee drinks in a froufrou place like this, soft and gullible.

"I know it's me," Finch said.

Landry didn't move, except to adjust her expression. Holy compassion, eager love, something like that—she'd practiced it ahead of time. Thinking how useful Tonya's phone had proved. It contained Tonya's private messages, including one informing her that a teenage girl on a long-lost-relatives forum was blaming Efrem for her mother's death.

And that message gave Landry and Corliss a golden lead. With the phone in their possession, it was a piece of cake to spoof Tonya's ID and contact Finch with a sob story about Tonya being babysitter to the Landry family, and savior of convicted serial killers.

Hook, line, sinker. Everything but duct tape.

Landry smiled behind her steepled hands, then blanked her face again. She waited, knowing that in a second or two Finch would look up. Desperate for connection and explanation. She got ready.

Finch raised her head. "How?"

Finch felt the world around her contract to a bull's-eye. She needed an explanation, an anchor.

She looked at Landry. Landry reached out. Finch took her hand.

"Our family has had this drawing for years," she said. "It's more precious than anything else. It was a gift, something beautiful. Believe it or not, there was a time when this had no meaning beyond innocence. Efrem drew this. Of you. Before everything went wrong."

"Efrem Goode saw me in person? Omigod." Overwhelmed, Finch thought, *It's all true.*

It was just after 11:00 a.m. when Caitlin decided, *Screw it.* She walked to Keyes's office.

He didn't look up from his screen. "Nothing yet from the genetic genealogy unit. I've called three times."

"Give me the agent's number."

Keyes waved her off. "Hang on." He hit redial and put the call on speaker.

A man answered. Keyes said, "Special Agent Chao. Nicholas Keyes and Special Agent Caitlin Hendrix at BAU."

"You got my text," Chao said.

Caitlin said, "Positive DNA match. It's definite? There's a match between Finch Winter and the 2008 Brooklyn Jane Doe?"

"No. We don't have that woman's profile in the public database."

Caitlin stilled. "Then, what?"

"There's a DNA match between Finch and Efrem Judah Goode," Chao said. "Parental."

"What?"

"He's her father."

45

Finch clutched the drawing. Her heart felt about to jump out of her chest. "Goode saw me. He knew my mother. It's *true*."

The sketch wasn't signed. It didn't need to be. It was powerful and disturbing and *proof*.

Across the booth in the coffeehouse, her sleek red hair glinting unnaturally in the morning sun, Landry looked both eager and reserved. "You suspected Efrem was involved."

"Of course," Finch said. "That's why I got the DNA test and started the thread on the YourGenealogy forum." She clutched the drawing of the toddler girl. Of *herself*. "Once Goode started putting out these drawings, I knew in my heart that he was involved. Oh my God, this is . . . terrifying. But *perfect*."

She tried to catch her breath. (She knew—she'd wished, she'd dreamed—that her birth mother hadn't truly given her up. She knew it, hoped it, omigod . . .) The words tangled in her throat, then poured out. "My birth mom—we can get justice for her murder."

Landry didn't reply. Something dead calm entered her eyes. Finch didn't understand.

"That's what this is about. I mean, I can't believe this awful thing is what has finally brought us together. But . . ." Finch looked again at the drawing. "This is too incredible."

"It is."

"Justice. I mean . . . it's everything. Family is everything," Finch said.

"Absolutely."

Finch grabbed another biscotto and slurped her drink. She knew she'd said something to upset Landry but didn't know exactly what.

"Tell me everything. What happened? Tell me all about her, my mom. Please." Then she saw. "No—tell me about *you*. Omigod, I feel so rude. I want to know all about you and everybody in my family. I have a million questions."

"Slow down." Landry relaxed and laughed dryly. "We have all the time in the world now."

"We do, don't we." But Finch couldn't slow down. She felt giddy. Her excitement was spreading through her into a smooth sense of elevation. "Please. Tell me about you."

"I'm an artist. Ink and mixed media, mostly. Murals. Street art."

"That is so cool."

"Life studies, bricolage. It's . . . a calling."

"I can understand," Finch said. "Do you have brothers, sisters? Your mom, your dad . . ."

She had to pause to inhale. Landry's hair had a beatific shine. It seemed to cascade with goodwill. Finch wanted to laugh.

Smiling—she couldn't stop smiling—she said, "Who was related to my mom, from your family? I mean *our* family?" It still felt impossible to say those words. "Did they know what happened to her? Have you all been wondering all these years?"

Landry nodded soberly and said, "In good time. But I have more news for you."

"More? I don't know if I can handle that."

"This is good news. You're going to love it." She leaned in, smiling gently. "Your grandmother's alive."

Finch's heart swelled. "My grandmother."

She had never had a grandmother. No aunts, no uncles, no cousins, no nothing. She and Annie had been their own little nuclear unit. An island, self-contained, with no past, no roots, nothing but each other to anchor them. It had built rich soil for Finch to grow in but left the rest of the world looking inaccessible. Until now.

"Your mother's mother," Landry said. "*My* mother's mother."

"Where? Who?"

"I'm going to call Nana in a minute—"

Nana. It sounded gentle and warm, like cookies, like a cozy kitchen.

"She knows I'm here today. But you have to understand, Finch."

"What?"

"She's suffered terribly over the last fifteen years. Terribly."

"I can only imagine."

"Her heart has been broken again and again. Every time she thought justice might be served, and that it was possible you were alive and might be found and brought home to us. Every time her hopes were dashed, it got harder to hang onto the daylight. She's never given up. But it's come close to killing her."

Finch put a hand over her mouth. Her eyes were stinging.

"So," Landry said, "don't get upset that I didn't bring her with me. Or that I haven't planned a meeting with her yet. She needs confirmation that you're who you claim to be."

"I am."

"I mean, *proof* that you're not a scammer or a psycho. Which, now that I've met you, obviously you're not. But still . . ."

Finch grabbed Landry's hands. "Please. Don't make me wait. Don't make Nana wait any longer. Not a second more. I want to see her. Please. Have her come here right now—"

"That's sweet, but she's upstate."

"Then take me to meet her."

Landry tensed, her lips thinning. Finch held on.

"Please. I can take the train. Meet her in a coffee place wherever she lives. Public and safe. We can take it slow and easy. Please. You've met me. You see I'm for real. I've waited my whole life for this."

Landry squeezed back. "Yes. Yes, we all have."

"Great. Thank you. How far upstate? Do I need to plan for the weekend?"

Landry laughed. It was a birdlike sound. "Not far at all. There and back like that. You could dash over for another molto espressotini and pie, be back before dinner."

Finch held her breath. *I'm in now.* "Then let's go."

"What, now?"

"Why not? As long as I'm home by three this afternoon, I'm good."

"Well . . ."

Finch squeezed her hand again and held up the drawing. "We have no reason to wait."

"You're right." Landry rapped the tabletop with her knuckles. "Absolutely right."

She took out her phone. "Let me call and tell her to get ready. We can meet at Gertie's Bakery. It's the cutest place in town. You'll love it."

Finch's sense of well-being had begun to spread from her chest down to her fingertips. The sunlight felt golden, warm, and soft. It felt, coming through the window, like a beam of goodness shining through her skin and into her heart.

Landry was bent over her phone, texting.

Finch said, "I just need to call my mother—I mean, my adoptive mom—"

"No." Landry looked up sharply.

"What? Why not?"

"She's the reason we lost you."

"My mom? I don't understand."

Landry's gaze hardened. "She abducted you as a toddler."

46

"Her father."

At Keyes's desk, Caitlin stood stunned.

"Yes," Special Agent Chao said. "There's an incontrovertible match be-tween Finch Winter and Efrem Judah Goode. No chance it's mistaken. She's his daughter."

"Thank you." She ended the call. "Holy shit." She said it too loud, in a building where FBI decorum still held sway, though sometimes by only a thread. "Now I understand something."

She flashed back to her first prison visit with Goode. His words when she nodded at his tattoo and he said it was one of his beauties: "Long gone, baby" and "Mine, I said."

Rainey had said, "Killing something doesn't make it yours."

She turned to Keyes. "Goode said, 'Blood means mine.' He was talking about his child."

On her cell, she redialed Detective Tashjian. She walked to the con-ference room and put a display on the big screen—a digital version of the Broken Heart Killer lead board.

He answered. "Hendrix?"

"You're not going to believe this."

He didn't. She explained.

"We need to interview Finch's adoptive mother," she said. "See if it was an open adoption, get every bit of information she has—records, all of it."

She scrutinized the photos, dates, drawings.

"Goode has been trying to find his child," she said. "He could have simply announced that he has a long-lost daughter. But he didn't. He broadcast coded messages instead. If he's conspiring with the Broken Heart Killer to track Finch down—instead of announcing that he'd like to make contact—then he can only wish something bad for her."

"No shit," Tashjian said.

"I need to get back to New York."

"Come on down," Tashjian replied. "I'm heading off duty, but I'll be back tonight."

Ending the call, Caitlin left urgent messages telling Finch to contact her. She tried again to reach Annie Winter but had no luck. She left a voice mail at the restaurant where Annie worked, saying it was vital that they speak.

She turned back to the lead board, to the drawings and autopsy photos and cryptic links, the pictures of Rhiannon Griffith and Phoenix and a gold Cadillac.

The connection, the spark, the insight that would give her the Broken Heart Killer's identity had to be there.

She tried once more to get through to Finch. Yes, it was a school day, but she presumed that kids stared nonstop at their phones even in class. No luck.

Somehow, that felt . . . off. She headed for her desk. If she took the next flight to New York, she could catch Finch before school let out.

"Hendrix." Emmerich stood in his office door.

She walked toward him. "Finch Winter is Efrem Judah Goode's biological daughter," she said. "I'm going to NYC."

His expression became both sharp and remote. "Hold that thought."

She was too revved up. "No. Why?"

"There's been another murder."

47

"Goode's pen pal just washed up dead. Tonya Pappas," Emmerich said.

Caitlin's legs went as heavy as stone. "No."

"In the Cumberland River, outside the Nashville prison where he's incarcerated."

She looked at her watch. "Twenty-four hours after she disappeared?"

"Just over. The body was dumped before sunrise. The killer came and went in the dark," he said. "Killed by a gunshot to the back of the head."

Her stomach turned coldly queasy. "Escalation. Or more efficient lethality. Or both. Electrical burns?"

"Multiple." Emmerich's voice was flat, which, in Caitlin's experience of him, meant he was severely compartmentalizing his emotions. "More than any previous victim. It could indicate that the killer tortured her for information. But the torture devolved as the killer became enraged, or Pappas fought and thrashed, or both."

"If the killer was trying to get information out of her . . ."

"She may have given everything she had to give, and the killer kept on trying."

Caitlin bit back a firehose of profanity.

"There's one other thing. More than MO," he said.

"Signature?"

Emmerich paused, just half a breath. "The killer drew broken hearts on Pappas's skin with a Sharpie. Over each of the electrical burns. Including on the center of her forehead."

Caitlin leaned against the doorjamb and covered her eyes, sick.

She could have warned Tonya Pappas.

She had observed and kept track of the Facebook fan page. She could have done more. She could have told Tonya that it was risky to enmesh yourself with a convicted killer. And that it was always—*always*—beyond dangerous to try to become friends with a serial murderer.

"Hendrix?" Emmerich said.

She inhaled and corralled her emotions. "It's escalation, devolution, and more. Tonya's murder means that I misunderstood the dynamic between Goode and the Broken Heart Killer."

"How so?"

"Tonya was Goode's proxy. His voice. And the unsub slaughtered her and dumped her on his doorstep. It's a statement. *Fuck you.*"

"The Tennessee authorities are combing the area for tire tracks, footprints, trace, and searching CCTV footage for any signs of the GMC Yukon or another vehicle approaching the river upstream from where the body was found."

"We need to reevaluate the profile," Caitlin said. "The Broken Heart Killer doesn't fit any clear classification for serial slayers."

"She doesn't have to. She's got a unique imprint. And she's an antisocial personality who enjoys the sadism of these killings but is working toward a goal *outside* her personal fantasy."

"Right."

"I'm calling the Tennessee detective. Is it . . ."

"Hayes," she said. "Detective Marius Hayes."

She turned, trying to shake off the blow. Glazed, she walked back to the lead board.

Everything was there. It had to be. She just needed to rearrange the board into the correct picture to have it come into focus.

But after five seconds, she realized she was approaching this the wrong way.

She needed to do more than rehash the evidence. She needed insight into the unsub's mind and motive. What was driving these killings?

Blood means mine.

She felt bruised. If she had paid closer attention to Finch, she would have valued the gravitational pull of family on this case.

Finch didn't fear her history—she longed to connect with it. No, the one who feared her family legacy was Caitlin herself.

Daughter of Captain Crazy. Heir to legendary homicide detective Mack Hendrix. Mack, who failed to capture the Prophet and destroyed himself because of it, unaware that the crime scenes he had attended were toxic. That he'd been poisoned, literally, by his devotion to duty.

It had taken Caitlin two decades to restore a relationship with her father. Their reconciliation had come very late and left her bereaved.

Caitlin knew she could cross the line from relentless pursuit to dangerous obsession. Her dad had crossed it and spent decades lost beyond the border. Crossing that line and falling into the abyss was what she feared most.

She stepped back from the lead board and rubbed her eyes. Fear of repeating her father's mistakes was holding her back.

But instead, right now she should be embracing all she had learned from Mack in order to break this ungodly case. And she should be grateful for both the family she was born into and the one she now had the chance to build.

What she needed was the truth. There was one person she might wring it out of, if she played it right.

She returned to Emmerich's office and explained her idea.

He reached for the phone. "I'll arrange a plane. Go."

As she headed out the door, she texted Sean. Forgot to mention. Fucking love you.

Tunes were playing—Ariana Grande, from the car stereo. Finch sat in the passenger seat of a big SUV, a dark sapphire GMC Yukon. Sunk against the headrest, she let the music wash over her. It soared and swooped, but with a mechanical hum, dark, some laboratory frequency.

Landry drove. They were out of the city, heading up the Hudson Valley. Finch felt dizzy with shock.

Her mom, Annie, *could not* be an abductor.

But Annie *had* lied to her.

And Landry, apparently, had proof. *Abductor*. Finch fought a sob.

When Landry said that word at the coffee place, Finch had jerked back in the booth. "No."

"I'm sorry. It's true."

"That's crazy."

Her head had begun to spin. There was an explanation. Had to be.

"You lie," she said. "Annie adopted me."

Landry had looked at her with pity. And hurt. But mostly, definitely, pity. As if Finch was blind and refusing to see.

"What are you *talking about?*" Finch practically shouted.

"I'm so sorry," Landry said. "But what has your . . . What has Annie Winter actually told you about the circumstances of your adoption?"

Nothing.

Finch couldn't say that, but it rang in her head. *Nothing nothing nothing.* For years. *You had a tough start in life. A rough situation. Your mom couldn't keep you. It was unfortunate.*

"She was nineteen," Landry said. "A heavy drug user. A thief. She got to know your mom in New York City. Living in crash pads, filthy drug dens in lower Manhattan and Brooklyn."

The photo, Finch thought. The photo, shot outside the diner. *Jane Doe, Brooklyn 2008*—her birth mother—with two friends. Seedy-looking friends. Bad teeth, hungry eyes, the kind of thinness that came not just from malnutrition but from drug use. Was Annie possibly one of those two? Or was she the one who took the photo? Why hadn't Finch had the courage to ask her about it? Why had she hidden her quest from her mom?

"Annie was needy and jealous of your mother. And wacked out on meth." Landry looked at Finch searchingly, with worry. "You don't use, do you?"

"Of course not." Finch's head was throbbing. She didn't use drugs. Her mom didn't either. Even though the restaurant biz could be known for some crazy stuff, judging from what Annie hinted at, and from Finch's reading of *Kitchen Confidential*.

"This doesn't sound right at all," Finch said. "No way."

"I know you need evidence. This must be overwhelming. But for now, let me give you the basics, because you have to start digesting them." Landry's look of pity toughened into something rougher. "She was an unstable person. She ping-ponged back and forth between loving and envying your real mother, because your real mother had something precious and innocent to love. A baby."

No no no no no . . .

"She took you and ran."

At that point, Finch had started feeling physically ill. Almost dizzy. She felt tears rising to her eyes. Seeing that, Landry reached across the table, suddenly softer.

"Hey." She took Finch's hand and rubbed her thumb against it. "I'm sorry. You were hoping for a different story. You know this woman as somebody who has sheltered you. Whereas we—your real family—have spent a decade and a half desperately trying to find you. To know you're *alive*."

Even the floor beneath Finch's feet had felt like quicksand at that point. But she hadn't called Annie.

As her tears fell, Landry had come around to sit beside her in the booth. She put an arm around Finch's shoulder and led her out of the coffeehouse, waving to the concerned baristas. "It's okay. She just got some bad news."

Outside, in pinwheeling sunlight, Finch hesitated, wondering if she should really get on the train to meet with Nana today. But when she suggested postponing, Landry looked at her phone.

"Nana's already on her way. Please, Finch. Don't be scared. And please don't disappoint her. If you back out now, she'll never trust you. It will just be too hard. This is your chance."

Her chance. Her one chance?

Now, somehow, she was in Landry's SUV. It had been parked up the block from the coffee place, and Landry suggested that they drive because she was heading that way anyhow, and they could talk in privacy on the way, and then, after meeting Nana, she could drive Finch to the train station for the short trip back to the city.

Trees flashed by on the expressway. The music lulled Finch, sweet and smooth, easing the spiky anxiety that roiled her gut.

There was an explanation for what Landry had told her. There was a mistake. Annie wasn't a kidnapper. There was a perfectly rational explanation for everything.

She had to find it. Yes, Annie had lied to her, but why?

And the only way to get an explanation was to meet these people face-to-face and hear their stories, and challenge them.

Her phone pinged with a text. She took it from her pocket. The screen said *Caitlin Hendrix*.

Whoa. Crazy timing, or what?

Finch started to open the text, but Landry gave her side-eye. A definite frown, as though she thought Finch was trying something underhanded.

And, okay, Finch hadn't told Landry she'd been in touch with the FBI. That topic—for ... reasons, she guessed—hadn't come up. Mentioning it now, when this whole enterprise suddenly felt so rickety and weird, might put Landry off even more. The cousin she had only just met. Finch didn't want to throw cold water on the first meeting with her birth family. And she felt weirded out, super anxious, in a dreamy, distant way.

Landry's gaze felt like a hot iron.

Finch returned the phone to her pocket. She would get back to Agent Hendrix and tell her everything once she understood. And once the dizziness went away ... How strong was that coffee?

She closed her eyes.

When the guards brought Efrem Judah Goode to the interview room at Riverbend, Caitlin was waiting. She sat at the table, leaning back, tapping her fingers on the Formica. She hadn't asked for special lighting or to turn up the AC to a comfortable level. This was going to be down and dirty, an excavation.

As the guards prepared to shackle him to the ring in the floor, Goode eyed her up and down.

"Here for your sketch?" he said. "You got a light in your eyes today. Something hot."

She waited a second, letting him smirk at her. Then she folded her hands. "Sit down, Efrem. I have bad news."

48

Goode stood for long seconds after Caitlin told him Tonya Pappas was dead. He ingested the news silently. His flat eyes, his rattlesnake chill, didn't waver. But his breathing took an uptick. His chest rose heavily. The guards stiffened, sensing a shift in the air.

Caitlin gestured at the empty chair across the table. "Sit down."

Goode slumped into the seat with heavy menace. The guards locked his shackles to the ring in the floor. Caitlin held his dark gaze.

To the guards, she said, "I'll call you when I'm ready."

They stepped out and closed the door. The lock turned heavily. Caitlin waited another moment while Goode breathed audibly.

"You had no inkling," she said. "There's no view of the river from your block?"

His eyes didn't leave her, but a gray shadow seemed to shift behind his gaze. He couldn't have seen the body, or the police cars along the riverbank. But that kind of news spread through a prison with wildfire speed. She let the suggestion hang in the air: The cellblock grapevine hadn't passed the information along to him. That implied he was out of the loop, disconnected. Not top dog, not the powerful figure he hungered to be.

"When?" he said.

She had gamed out her interrogation plan with Emmerich. The strategy: Admit she was here to trade. Play it cool, and, if necessary, poke Goode. Emmerich reminded her that Goode saw victims as mere objects. Pieces on a game board. Goode would talk about them to serve his own interests and bolster his ego—an ego that craved power and domination.

"He wants to be the Big Bad," Emmerich said. "He loves to brag. He hates conceding failure. Get inside that loathing. If you can force him to admit that he's just taken a loss, he might respond by revealing information about things he considers wins."

Sitting across from him now, Caitlin spoke with legitimate sadness.

"Tonya's body was out there long enough that a guard spotted it in the water, and the county sheriff arrived, then the medical examiner. Then she was tentatively ID'd from fingerprints, and the ID was confirmed by her family, and the cops in New Jersey passed the confirmed ID to the FBI and to me. And I had time to travel here. It's been a while."

He digested that. Motionless but roiling. She got a sense of a great, dank engine grinding into gear deep inside him.

"How did Tonya die?" he said.

She didn't answer. He looked at the folder that lay on the table beneath her folded hands. From the eager shift in his shoulders, he thought the folder contained crime scene photos.

He wanted to see Tonya's body.

She spoke in a low, regretful tone. "The killer dumped Tonya on your doorstep. Like a cat that wanted you to see the mouse it tortured."

The unsub had killed someone who mattered to Goode. Tonya, his superfan, had been under his thumb emotionally. She had been an acolyte, his megaphone, broadcasting his every yawp. She had fed his ego and spread his word.

With her dead, Goode had lost a prized possession. Caitlin knew that Tonya's murder—her *taking*—would wound his pride and sense of ownership. But beyond the narcissistic injury, Tonya's death severely restricted his leverage in the outside world. He must have spent significant time and energy grooming her to be his mouthpiece. And the Broken Heart Killer had just erased that work, almost offhandedly.

He would want revenge.

Caitlin needed to turn that desire into truth-telling. She opened the folder and slid documents onto the table. The drawing labeled *Liv*. The police report naming Corliss as the owner of the Cadillac. A New York subway photo of the Broken Heart Killer.

Dealing her own hand, from a stacked deck.

Goode cast his gaze across the documents, breathing heavily. Caitlin let the silence settle. Her internal countdown clock was clacking. Events were churning in the black waters at the bottom of this case. The Broken Heart Killer had an endgame in mind and was getting ever closer to it. Minutes and seconds counted.

Goode's gaze settled on the police report. A photo of the Caddy. The highlighted name *Corliss Yates*.

The last time Caitlin was here, mentioning Corliss had set Goode off. Needling him with the suggestion that Corliss set him up for the Spring River quadruple murders had driven him from the room.

Losses. Humiliation. Caitlin saw it: Goode felt ashamed of the way he was captured in Spring River. To someone who couldn't admit weakness, his pathetic arrest represented a shattering blow to his ego. He'd rather say he was framed by shadowy, powerful enemies.

Which led her to wonder if a woman had outsmarted him, drugged him, and sent him swerving into the sheriff's station parking lot with a dead body in his back seat. If so, he couldn't take the emotional comedown.

She set her hands on the table like a blackjack dealer with the cards fanned across the felt.

"Your confessions, the drawings. What was the play, Efrem? If you wanted to hurt Corliss, it's not going to plan." She leaned in. "You need my help."

After a long, cold pause, Goode blinked. "You'll never find Corliss. She's a chameleon."

Caitlin didn't know if it was a boast, a warning, or a sad revelation of how his own fate had been sealed. This was the first glimpse into his mind that she had managed to get. She wanted to pump a fist. She held her chill.

And she held back her ace in the hole—that she knew he had a daughter. Right now she needed to wheedle him along.

"Even after all this time," she said, "you think she hasn't let her guard down?"

"It's in her DNA," he said. "Her way of being. She'll never let her guard down, especially now. She's been doing it for decades. It's a way of life."

"Tell me."

He paused.

"You want a ghostwriter?" she said. "A book deal? This is the stuff that you need to sell a book. And to sell me." She turned the photo of the Cadillac so he could see it more clearly. "Tell me."

He took one more breath, then straightened in the chair. And he talked.

49

"Corliss Yates."

Goode rolled the name around in his mouth before spitting it out. Round, then sharp, then sibilant.

"That's who you want to know about?" he said.

"You're the one who's got the stories," Caitlin said.

Eyes bright but remote, he settled forward, elbows on the table, his handsome face once again affable. Almost flirty. But with a killer, flirty was a breath away from threatening.

"How'd you two meet?" she said.

"Kansas City. Summer night, some honky-tonk. I walk toward the jukebox, the pool tables, and there she is, her ass, those jeans with the rip right below the crease. Leaning across the table to knock a ball into the corner pocket . . . The Bud I'm holding, it's ice cold, but nowhere near cold enough to keep my temperature from shooting through the roof. Instant fever," he said. "She knew the effect she had, boy howdy, did she ever. I think she saw me coming a hundred miles away. She had me in her sights like that eight ball and was lining me up for the drop."

Caitlin didn't take notes. She watched his body language.

"I stick a quarter in the jukebox for Guns N' Roses and let her watch me for a minute."

He was getting into the story. Shoulders relaxing, his head coming up. How much was true and how much was fantasy and lies, Caitlin didn't yet know. But she knew that he was tapping a vein of memory and emotion, and if she handled this right, she could pull from it.

"The dance," he said. "The ritual. Alphas, circling each other. The light was blue, I remember that. She saw me dark and shadowed, and that was how I liked it." He licked his lips. "Nineteen years old, skin as white as cream, a figure that screamed *I want it*. Hair like a forge." His eyes flicked up, momentarily focusing on Caitlin. "Like yours, but hotter red."

She took the remark as both a compliment and a dig. She suspected he was a pro at double-edged praise. She casually removed her phone from her pocket and held it up, with the record function showing.

He shrugged. *Sure.* "Couple nights in KC, and I was about to move on. I traveled considerably more in those days, you understand."

The affable smile widened, his teeth bright. He may be a scrounger and a killer, but he had grown up with fluoride. And he was making a joke.

Caitlin let her expression soften, let him see that she was dialed in.

"I know what they called me in the media. Drifter. Like that meant lowlife. Rootless." Goode snorted. "I prefer *rover. Plains warrior. Marauder.*"

He grinned, then dropped a mask back over his expression. It felt like a cold front passing through the room.

"She came with me. She had nothing keeping her in KC. No life, just stagnation, and for a woman like that, standing still is death. She has to move, has to surf the lip of the curl. So we hit the road and rolled through the Midwest."

"What was she like?" Caitlin said.

"*Like?* She was *hot* . . . and wild. Unpredictable." His gaze lengthened. His tone turned hypnotic. "Bewitching. She was a coin toss. Heads, loving. Tails, ice queen." The smile darkened. "She wants to own you. But get close, she claws loose, says she's suffocating. Give her space, she thinks you're quitting her. She's a have-your-cake-and-eat-it woman."

"Is that why she roofied you and got you to drive to the Spring River sheriff's station with your victim's body in the back seat?"

"She's a cunning little vixen."

Caitlin held utterly still. She had challenged him by saying "*your victim's body*," and he hadn't denied it. Hadn't called her a moron or blamed the woman's death on anyone else. Goode had finally, essentially, just admitted his guilt in at least one of the Spring River murders.

"Near twenty years we traveled together. I should have seen it coming," he said, and kept talking about Corliss—how he couldn't seem to get her out of his system, even though he left her more than once, and for more than a year.

"I always managed to find my way back to her." He'd leave, steal a car and drive halfway across the country, live in a Colorado mining town or an Idaho logging camp for a few months, thinking he'd find somebody new, somebody as enthralling and addicting as Corliss, but never managing it.

"New York?" Caitlin said.

"A few times. But Corliss—she was like quicksand. Like cocaine or an open cash register."

Caitlin thought, he would also find his way back when he was broke or when he needed to split because the heat was coming down on him. After he'd found some hookup who didn't rev his motor the right way, and dragged her lifeless body to a storm drain.

"Tell me about Spring River," she said.

"You know what happened," Goode said.

"I know the finale. Not what led up to it." Caitlin leaned in. "And at this point, the lead-up is what's driving everything outside. You're inside, and I'm all you've got left. Tell me."

She knew he would try to get one over on her. If she had been on his side of the table, she would too.

"You came to Tennessee with Corliss," she prompted.

"She thought Tennessee was going to be the end of everything," he said.

That was quick. He wanted to talk about it. Caitlin spoke coolly.

"She thought it was going to be the end of *you*."

"She'd been planning it a long time, clearly."

"Why?"

"Because she couldn't have pulled it off on the spur of the moment."

Caitlin held herself still. She needed him to keep his guard down for a few more minutes. He was a liar. A manipulator. He loved talking about himself, and he had opened a gate. Right now he wanted attention and sympathy, and as long as she gave it to him, or feigned it, she might keep him talking. She might get him to let his emotions roar and reveal something true.

"So," she said. "You did Nashville, then hit the road. Why'd you stop in Spring River?"

"Random. Was headed to Knoxville, and it was halfway."

"Good pickings?"

He half laughed. "Turned out that way at first."

She was prodding him, euphemistically, about both the criminal and sexual pickings. "How long were you in town before you went to the bordello?"

"A day."

"You never thought twice?"

He shrugged. "Things was bad between me and Corliss by that time."

"A fight?"

"Long running. Six months and six thousand miles."

"Over what?"

"Man-and-woman shit."

"Fair enough," Caitlin said. "What was Corliss doing during that time?"

"She saw the sights."

"Meaning?"

"She's a better thief than I'll ever be. She took it all. I mean, look where I am." He gestured ostentatiously at the locked room.

"So, we get to that hot little Tennessee burg, and unbeknownst to me, Corliss decides to spring the trap." He shook his head. "She knows how to bide her time. Fire and ice, I told you. That woman, she works on long timescales. Like a volcano building up." His tone turned mocking. "'Leave me alone.' 'Don't leave me.' 'You're stifling me.' 'Don't you want me?'"

Caitlin nodded, letting him ramble, suppressing the *tick, tick* at the back of her head.

"She has a way about her. Sneaky-like. Controlling, you know? How she freezes you out and punishes you until she needs you to love her again," he said. "And by the time we got to Spring River, she was ready to punish and control me for good."

"By getting you thrown in prison."

"'Bout the size of it."

"I hear a desire for righteous retribution."

Goode's reptilian gaze confirmed it. But there was something she didn't understand.

"Why didn't you just give the cops Corliss's name?" she said.

His smile spread and took on a gleaming edge.

Spring River, Tennessee, 2018

From his jail cell, Goode stared out the window at the Flying T Motor Court across the street. The motel where, until eighteen hours ago, he'd been crashing. And planning, and getting ready to hit the road for Knoxville.

The Flying T, the motel in this shit-water town where all he'd wanted was release. A night of need and pleasure, his for the taking. But he was the one who got taken.

Across the road, past the railroad tracks, the motel parking lot was crowded with black-and-whites and a coroner's van. In the afternoon sunlight, the hazy, lazy air, people buzzed in and out of the door like moths. The crime scene unit was tearing his room apart.

Inside, he was boiling. He'd gotten sucker punched.

How the fuck did he never see it coming?

Then, from up the street, a car came into view. Gleaming in the sunshine, hazy, lazy, shining. That heavy chrome Detroit majesty. It cruised slowly, moving at the speed of a parade float past the jail. It was a gold Cadillac Coupe deVille. Corliss was at the wheel.

Her red hair shone like a slow-burning flame. As she passed in front of the jail, she turned, sunglasses glinting, and seemed to stare right at him. On and on. Then she looked away. And drove off, out of sight.

Across the table from Caitlin, Goode looked ruminative.

"If I'd snitched on Corliss, nobody woulda believed me. Nobody in town saw her. It would've been the word of a drifter who got found with four bodies. They would've laughed."

She thought of the detectives from Spring River. Hayes and Pettibone might have at least listened to Goode's claim, but the prosecutor, judge, and jury would probably have scoffed.

Goode was right. But there was more to it, Caitlin thought. Psychologically, Goode sought power and domination. He wanted revenge on Corliss, and he wanted to control *how* it happened.

He didn't want Corliss locked up. He wanted her dead.

That goal was part of his game.

She tapped the drawing labeled *Liv*. The goth teen with the defiant expression. *NYC 2008*. The lie, the Bat-Signal. That drawing was also part of the game.

"Want to tell me why you claimed that you killed Rhiannon Griffith?" she said.

He wasn't expecting her to change course so abruptly. He leaned back, giving himself time, but didn't answer. It told her he was surprised that the authorities had seen through his ruse.

He was smart, but not that smart. He was ruthless and cunning and underhanded. He wasn't a genius, but he didn't need to be. He'd had a twenty-year run of death and misery. And by confessing to a string of murders, he had found a way to extend it. He had tunneled out of Riverbend prison, at least virtually. Caitlin had to shut that down. But to do so, she had to convince him that talking to her was his only hope for accomplishing his goals. Because Tonya was dead, the Tennessee cops wouldn't listen, and he had no other course.

Throw a punch.

"Efrem," she said. "You managed to communicate with Tonya after you were put in lockdown. Her Facebook post, 'Live and let die.' You dictated it to her. Tell me the truth now, and when I tell the guards you have a contraband cell phone, I'll say you voluntarily admitted it. Then, maybe, they won't send you to solitary confinement. They're going to roust your cell. My way, maybe you can keep your drawing pad and pastels, and have a chance to see the sun before your hair turns gray."

His gaze turned opaque. "You don't know that."

It was a decent front, the nonchalant dismissal. But from the tightness in his jaw, he did know it and did care. Still, he didn't give her anything.

Okay, time to convince him she wasn't a Barbie doll.

"All right," she said. "Here's how it looks—and when it comes to further prosecution, how it'll go down."

She spread the drawings and photos more widely on the table between them. Again she touched the drawing labeled *Liv*.

"Rhiannon's alive. You drew this sketch hoping that when it hit the news, Rhiannon would know that you're reaching out. That you're thinking of her." She said it snarkily.

He didn't reply.

"But Corliss is out there too. You knew she would also see the drawing. And that she'd know exactly what *Liv* meant. You wanted her to know it," she said. "Meaning that Corliss either suspected, or else was convinced, that Rhiannon was dead. The sketch sent a message. A big, flashing *nope*."

Goode was as still as a chunk of coal.

Caitlin tapped the photo of the Broken Heart Killer, the one captured as she fled the subway platform in Brooklyn. "Now she's after Rhiannon."

Goode's gaze hung on the image. Caitlin rested her fingertips on the photo.

"She's after Rhiannon. And whether you wanted it or not, she's after your daughter."

It was a guess. She was flying by the seat of her pants. She held his gaze.

The harsh overhead light cast Goode's face in sharp relief, angles and planes. His breathing deepened. His voice, when he spoke, was quiet.

"A long time ago, I told Corliss that Rhiannon and the kid were dead."

Caitlin's heart beat hard against her ribs. She had to play this right. She matched his tone of voice.

"Brooklyn, 2008," she said.

He nodded. "It simplified things."

"How, exactly?"

"The kid weighed me down. And Rhiannon could have turned . . . chatty."

The kid. Finch. His daughter. He had, what—abandoned her? Rhiannon, though—what was the connection there?

He was still holding back.

"Want to tell me what Rhiannon could have turned chatty about, and to whom?"

He snorted. "'Whom.' Sure, Miss Ivy League."

"Cal State Chico. Fine. Who was she to you?" Caitlin said. "What does she know?"

"She knew everything. She was a little lockbox of information."

"About you? Your crimes, your history?" She raised an eyebrow. "Give an inch and you'll get an inch, Efrem. Who was she to you?"

He leaned on the table, staring at the drawing he'd done. He began absentmindedly rubbing his forearm. The one with the tattoo. The gothic, filigreed letter "L."

His long-gone baby.

With the drawing of Rhiannon turned sideways, Caitlin saw, under the harsh lights, the outline of the same long, sinuous letter in the girl's black hair. It was subtle, and visible only now that the shadow fell from Goode's body across the top of the page.

With forced calm, Caitlin traced the letter on the drawing with her finger. "This sketch was a signal. Your daughter's alive."

She said it mildly, but her heart was drumming. Goode's eyes turned crafty. She was right.

And he was getting ready to dodge and lie.

He wanted Corliss dead. What did he want from Rhiannon? Why had he hidden the clue about his daughter's survival in that drawing? How the hell did all this tie together?

Chill. Play it cool. Stick with the facts you know.

"Rhiannon was friends with the 2008 Brooklyn murder victim," Caitlin said. "The young woman known on the street as Phoenix."

The stone face remained.

"You've confessed to the Brooklyn murder, Efrem," she said. "At this point, you can't turn shy about admitting you know the victim's name. Which makes me wonder what else Rhiannon knows that you're shy about revealing."

What was the connection with Rhiannon and Finch Winter? Did Rhiannon know that Finch was Phoenix's child?

Caitlin didn't know that herself. She forced herself to ease off the gas mentally. She breathed slowly. Under the glaring overhead bulb, Goode sat like a gargoyle. Death, money, family, an orphaned child. Somehow, both he and Corliss were interested in all that.

And if Corliss ended up dead, that would put him in sole position to control . . . a stash? An inheritance? Rhiannon? Finch?

"When was the last time you saw your daughter?" Caitlin said.

"You know how fire stations have those baby boxes?"

Caitlin did know. Safe haven baby boxes, installed in the walls of designated fire stations and hospitals, allowed desperate birth mothers to place their infants inside and surrender them without fear of repercussions. Baby boxes made it feasible for women unable to care for a newborn to place that baby in safe hands instead of abandoning it.

"You put a walking, talking toddler into a box designed for a newborn?" she said.

"Silent alarm trips when you open the box from the street. Firemen come running, lickety-split. Kid isn't in there long enough to start kicking."

"That's what you did?" she said.

"Why would I do something else?"

Because you're a stone killer, Caitlin didn't say. "You took the girl from her mother and gave her away?"

"Safer all around. Happier too. Cut the cord, give the child a chance at an ordinary life."

Caitlin would check NYFD records to determine whether any firehouses had received an abandoned child in 2008. Right now she played her cards from a new angle.

She slid forward the photo of the unsub, the Broken Heart Killer. "Who is she?"

"Can't say." Goode's eyes went flat.

Caitlin continued holding up the photo. He shifted, as if his clothes were suddenly itchy.

This was where she needed to break Goode's confidence. Until now, he thought he could manipulate the situation on the outside—including manipulating the killer. But he knew now that he'd backed the wrong horse. That he *had* no horse, because Tonya had been murdered by the Broken Heart Killer.

Caitlin was about to say, *she turned on you.* Something about Goode's discomfiture stopped her. She chose her words differently. "She blew up your scheme."

"Risk I took."

He said it too quickly and looked away. His expression betrayed contempt. Maybe self-contempt. And self-contempt was a feeling no psychopath could bear. They would lie and deny and scramble to hide their failures—from themselves and others.

Boom. Caitlin saw it clearly now. The Broken Heart Killer wasn't working for Goode. She was working for Corliss.

Caitlin held up the unsub's photo. "She played you, Efrem. She screwed you over."

He looked at her then. "You won't find her. Not as long as she's with the chameleon."

He was smooth but not impenetrable. She could see it now. Right up until Tonya was murdered, he had thought the unsub might be lured to carry out his wishes. He thought his Bat-Signal would activate her as his hit man on the outside and get his stash.

"Want to talk about your daughter's mama?" Caitlin said.

Goode turned to the door. "*Guard.*"

50

Thirty minutes after leaving the prison, her foot heavy on the accelerator, Caitlin pulled up at the Nashville airport's general aviation terminal. The FBI jet waited on the tarmac, the high sun glinting off its curved white fuselage. She jogged up the stairs and leaned into the cockpit.

"As soon as you're ready," she said.

The captain glanced back at her. "We should be airborne in fifteen minutes. Flight time to Teterboro is two hours, two minutes."

She gave him a thumbs-up, dropped into a seat, and pulled out her computer and phone. She was pumped. By the time the first officer closed the jet's main door, she was on her third phone call, urgently liaising with the BAU and NYPD. The engines started, and the jet swung around. Light arced through the cabin.

Her laptop chimed. She put in earbuds and opened a video conference window. Emmerich and Keyes appeared.

"You get my voice mail?" she said.

Keyes nodded. "It'll take me a couple of hours to find answers for you."

"Good. In two hours, I'll be landing in New York."

The plane swung onto the runway and lined up for takeoff.

"One thing," Keyes said. "I found a link between another victim and Rhiannon Griffith. Kimmie Koestler, the woman whose body was placed in the Maryland storm drain. Her family lived in the same neighborhood as Griffith when they were children."

"Keyes. Thank you."

Emmerich said, "I'll talk to the NYPD."

The engines spooled up and they accelerated down the runway. The jet's nose lifted. Caitlin's stomach dropped, and the jet soared skyward.

"This isn't what I was expecting," she said. "But there's a connection between Goode, the unsub, and Corliss Yates. We have to figure out how it links with Rhiannon and Finch."

"On it," Emmerich said.

Keyes had a manic intensity on his face. "Same."

They clicked off. The plane banked east. Caitlin watched the rolling countryside fall away below.

The Broken Heart Killer was working in tandem with Corliss Yates. Corliss, the have-your-cake-and-eat-it woman. Older, cagier, more experienced, and a master manipulator. Was she pulling the strings?

Two hours later, the sun gleamed through the cabin as the Gulfstream descended along the Hudson into Teterboro Airport. Manhattan passed by off the wing. As the jet touched down, Caitlin's phone pinged. The thrust reversers roared, and she swung forward against the seat belt.

The message was from Emmerich. It was evidence he had pushed the NYPD to expedite: DNA comparisons between Finch Winter and two of the women Goode claimed to have killed.

"Damn," she said.

She replied. Seriously—DAMN.

But as she thanked the pilots and ran down the stairs, she still couldn't reach Finch. Her stomach knotted. A rented SUV was waiting. She jumped in and took off for the city.

51

In the kitchen at Axis, off Union Square, Annie Winter walked along checking the prep stations and talking to the line cooks. Her white chef's coat was as bright as a klieg light. She took pride in looking sharp. She had worked too hard to get here, as a woman and a self-educated chef, to let anyone doubt she was in charge.

She stepped out to the dining room to speak to the hostess, get a sense of how many reservations they were looking at tonight. The restaurant was airy, with tall windows facing Fifteenth Street. Open brickwork, strategically placed flowers at the entrance. She loved it. Loved the buzz, the pleasure and nourishment the restaurant provided, the competitive adrenaline that surged through her when things got busy. She was an artist, a nurturer, but also a master sergeant, keeping the operation running. They were nicely booked. Thursday, people started ordering cocktails and wine more freely too. Thursday was a solid night at Axis.

She headed back toward the kitchen, greeting the bartenders as she passed. Her phone buzzed in her pocket. A call.

"Annie Winter."

"Ms. Winter? It's Zack Arcega."

Annie kept walking but felt a whisper of unease. Finch's boyfriend had never called her cell number before.

"Zack. Hey," she said. "What's up?"

"I know you're at work, and I'm sorry to disturb you. I normally, well, wouldn't." He cleared his throat. "But, oh, man, I . . ."

Annie's veins all at once felt full of acid. She pushed through the swinging door into the kitchen and kept walking straight out the side door, to the driveway that ran alongside the building. Her mother's instincts hissed, *Finch is hurt. Finch is drunk. Finch got scalded by boiling water at her coffeehouse job. Finch is pregnant.*

"Zack. What's going on? Why are you calling?"

He exhaled loudly. "I feel really bad about this. I feel like I'm ratting Finch out but also hurting your feelings."

Annie paused outside the door. "Zack. Stop. Just tell me."

"Yeah. She left school after first period. She said she'd be back in time to go over our history assignment. To meet her at your place at three."

"She cut class?" Annie said. "Why? Does . . ."

Jesus. Was this one of those bad-parenting moments, when it turned out the kid had been sliding and living a double life on the street for months and she never knew? She thought she was keeping a watchful eye on Finch. She hadn't seen any signs and hadn't given her any reason to go behind her back or . . . *Oh, my God.*

"Are you at our building now?" she said.

"I'm outside. She's not answering the buzzer, and she's not answering her phone."

Annie's stomach cramped. "Do you think she's home?" Good Christ, was Finch sick? Seriously ill? "Wait. She cut school why?"

"This is what I hate to tell you. And I'm sorry—I knew it, and Finch swore me to secrecy."

Annie closed her eyes. "*Zack.*"

"She went to meet her birth family."

The sound of traffic on the street, the echoes of horns and sirens off the tall buildings around the restaurant—all seemed to vanish in the thunder of blood rushing in her ears.

"Explain what you mean by that," she managed to say. "Clearly, in detail, from the beginning. Right this second."

"Since that FBI bulletin came out, she's been trying to get proof about her birth mother's murder," he started.

"Proof." The cramp sharpened and she nearly doubled over. "What kind of proof?"

"For the FBI. Because the NYPD ignored her," Zack said.

Behind Annie, one of the busboys came out, carrying a sack of garbage. Annie walked up the driveway away from the door. Zack kept talking, explaining what her daughter had been doing over the past few weeks. Her stomach sank.

"And the photo she found—and, Ms. Winter, I'm sorry to tell you about that. Finch felt really guilty."

That photo. Which she had saved all these years for . . . what? Evidence, should the day ever come? Nostalgia? No—as a reminder of what could be lost in a sickening moment. As a totem, an ever-lurking memento that whispered, *Be afraid. Stay sharp.*

She nearly heaved. The photo. Finch had asked about photos. And Annie had lied.

Now she knew why Finch had gotten so angry. It was her own fault.

Her rising fear joined her anger. "You're telling me the FBI has been in contact with Finch without my knowledge?"

"Yeah, about that."

The afternoon sun flashed from windows high in buildings overhead. Traffic rushed past on the street. Zack told her how Finch had pulled out the cord to the landline. That line had come with her internet and TV package. She kept it as a just-in-case number. It was meant for safety, not subversion. But now she understood why she hadn't received even a single spam voice mail in the past few days.

And if the authorities had obtained her cell phone number, any recent calls would have been forwarded to one of the voice mailboxes she maintained to keep people from tracking her down. She had skipped checking one of them in the past week. Damn it.

"She went to meet with somebody today, in person," she said. "Who?"

"A woman named Landry."

Annie stopped and leaned an arm against the brick wall of the building. "Where?"

"This place on the Upper West Side," he said. "She texted it to me, like, so someone would know. Poppycock's Coffee."

Every alarm bell in Annie's head rang wildly. *Finch, no.* "I'll call you back," she told Zack. "Be sure you answer."

She ended the call and phoned her daughter. No answer. She could hardly breathe.

From up the driveway, a voice called to her. "Annie Winter?"

She turned.

Walking toward her was a woman, tall and auburn-haired, with a confident stride, a no-nonsense expression, and FBI credentials clipped to the belt of her suit.

She locked eyes with Annie. "Or should I say, Rhiannon Griffith?"

52

For a second, Caitlin thought the woman was going to bolt. Ten feet ahead of her on the driveway next to Axis restaurant, framed by tall brick buildings and passing traffic, Annie Winter froze. Her eyes zeroed in on Caitlin, the creds on her belt, the diminishing distance between them. Annie was wiry, looked fit, with the white chef's coat and jeans. She had on running shoes. Caitlin tensed.

Then Annie straightened. Beneath her confident hipster look, Caitlin saw echoes of the rebellious teen in the old photo of Rhiannon, and the goth defiance in Goode's portrait of "Liv." She had lost the baby fat. Her face now had sharp planes and angles, mature even though she was just a few years older than Caitlin. She thought, *It ain't the years; it's the mileage.* And Annie Winter, born Rhiannon Griffith, had certainly traveled a long, hard road.

She was hiding in plain sight and had been for fifteen years. She held still, no longer ready to flee, but as tense as a coiled spring nonetheless.

"I just came from talking to Efrem Judah Goode," Caitlin said.

Annie shook her head. "Why?"

"I know he's Finch's biological father."

Annie said nothing.

"And I have DNA results. Finch is not related to Goode's Brooklyn victim, Phoenix."

Annie closed her eyes, just for a second, and exhaled. Then looked again at Caitlin. As if she had known this was coming for a long time and was bracing for still more.

"But she *is* related to you," Caitlin said.

Annie held back. Behind her eyes, emotions seemed to wrestle—fear, hope, and finally, resignation.

"Yes," she said. "I'm her aunt. Her biological mother's my older sister."

"Corliss," Caitlin said, finally understanding.

Annie raked her fingers through her hair, seeing the question on Caitlin's face. "I'll tell you, but first we have to find Finch. Her boyfriend just called. She went to meet with her birth family. She didn't come home. She's not answering my calls and texts. Please. I *cannot* let Corliss get her hands on her."

Caitlin pulled Annie toward her SUV, parked up the block. "Where did she meet them? When?"

"Poppycock's Coffee, West Eighty-Fourth. Noon."

Caitlin phoned Detective Tashjian. "Greg. Need your resources. Finch Winter is off the grid."

Annie's face creased with anxiety. Caitlin filled Tashjian in and ended the call.

"The NYPD is on it." She turned to Annie. "Talk."

"Wake up, sleepyhead."

Finch heard Landry's voice through what felt like soupy darkness. It sounded soft, gentle—and like an intrusion. The sound of the Yukon's engine had vanished. A disturbing absence had replaced it. She felt as if she had a weighted blanket on top of her, pressing on her chest, her shoulders, her eyes. She let herself slide back toward the deep call of sleep but felt a hand on her forearm.

"Finch."

Forcing her eyes open, Finch sat up, woozy and confused.

The Yukon was parked on a gravel driveway. Outside, she saw greenery. All around, heavy, throbbing in the afternoon sunlight. She brought her swimming vision into focus. They had stopped at a farm. A run-down house was surrounded by cornfields and woods.

"We here?"

Her voice sounded croaky. This didn't look like the charming artisanal town Landry had described. Where was Gertie's Bakery?

"This is Bearkill?" she said.

She tried to shake off the drowsiness. She felt weird—Benadryl-drowsy.

Landry's face swam into view. "Not yet." She smiled. "I wanted to save the surprise."

Finch forced herself upright. This was definitely a farm. A full-scale, hoedown, old-MacDonald-had-a farm.

"What surprise? Is Nana here?" she said.

Landry's smile was bright. "Had to make sure you were committed to us."

Committed. What did that mean? Finch tried to focus. Landry gestured at the farmhouse.

In the doorway, worn but lovely, stood a woman in her late thirties. She wore jeans—hip-huggers—and a tight white tank. Her hair was red like Landry's—no, not exactly, more like L'Oréal, less like a wig. She was too young to be Nana. She was gazing at Finch with the intensity of an acetylene torch.

"Who's that?" Finch said.

Landry put a hand on Finch's shoulder. "Your mother is alive."

At first, the words just slid off the leaden blanket of drowsiness without registering.

Then Finch reeled. "I thought . . ."

Alive. Her heart swelled. She felt the woman in the doorway's incendiary gaze. *Her?*

"I don't understand."

Landry said, "It's a long story. And she needs to tell it to you."

Landry leaned across Finch and opened the passenger door. Finch climbed down, dazed. The sunlight felt like a heat lamp on her skin, the afternoon abuzz with something beyond the cicadas razzing in the trees. She walked toward the house.

The woman in the doorway threw her arms wide. "Baby."

53

Caitlin and Annie got in the SUV. When the heavy doors thunked shut and the hush enveloped them, Annie lowered her shields and gave it to Caitlin unvarnished—quick, bitter, and urgent.

"All that matters now is Finch," she said. "That's what counts."

She looked at Caitlin's phone, practically willing the NYPD to call back.

"They'll call," Caitlin said. "Talk."

Caitlin knew she couldn't calm Annie's fears, but right now she had no indication that a crime had been committed or that Finch was in imminent danger. The girl was eighteen and had the right to meet with her birth family. But Caitlin felt unnerved. This news played into her picture of the case: something extraordinarily dangerous was going on.

"Okay." Annie raised her hands—a calming gesture. "Corliss and I grew up in the Monongahela Valley, town called Rylens Corner. Short form—alcoholic dad, doormat mom, drugs, beatings, evictions, younger brothers taken into foster care."

"What about you and Corliss?"

"We stuck it out into high school. Corliss left at sixteen, got married. They lasted just a year, but she kept his name. After the divorce, she hit the road. Someplace in the Midwest, she met this new guy at a bar." Annie looked at her. "Efrem Judah Goode, but you know that, right?"

"Kansas City, a honky-tonk, playing pool."

"She's not a shark, but she has game," Annie said. "It was some kind of chemical reaction. A corrosive bond. They got addicted to each other."

"And they had a child. Finch."

"Lissah," Annie said. "A combination of the names Corliss and Judah."

Saying the name seemed to take effort—like prying open a frozen lock.

"I can find that name on her original birth certificate?" Caitlin said.

Annie nodded. "Lissah Dove Yates." She pinched the bridge of her nose. "They came back to Rylens Corner after she was born. They'd lived in eight or nine places in two years. Efrem would get a job—construction, casual labor—find a crew to get in with, take down scores. Corliss . . ." She gave Caitlin a look. "What do you know about her?"

"None of what you're telling me right now."

"She called herself a full-time mother. She was also a full-time thief. She still is, I'm guessing."

"Does she have a record?"

"Criminal jackets in a few places. Couple of guilty pleas, deals knocking it down to probation or community service, one ninety-day stretch in a county lockup in Arkansas. Shoplifting, stealing from the till at retail jobs she worked, office embezzlement," Annie said. "But above all, she's a master pickpocket."

She sighed. "Classic moves, sleight of hand, a face everybody was entranced by, hips that swayed in a way that kept men's minds on her ass instead of what her hands were doing, sliding inside a jacket and lifting a wallet. I've seen her do it. She's magic."

A dump truck rumbled by. Annie said, "I was sixteen when she came back to Rylens Corner with Goode and the baby. They crashed at the house. I think Corliss expected Efrem to take Dad out, eventually. Kill him, or beat him into a vegetable, so she could live at the house, rent free, with Mom as her grateful servant. But Dad was a tough mofo. It was Efrem that got sick of him and told Corliss he was going to leave."

She clenched her fists. "Finch—Lissah—was nine months old. I knew if they left, I was going to split too. The only thing keeping me there was that baby."

"Your niece."

"She was Corliss's kid, but I loved her too. Loved her and worried about her." She looked pained. "Living with them was a nightmare, but having them go and take the baby . . . that scared me. Scared me thinking about her life on the road with those two—and thinking about myself home alone with my parents," she said. "I decided I was not going to take another beating from my old man. After they left, I waited for Dad to pass out, and I hit the road."

"To New York City. At seventeen."

"The streets here were better than that house."

Caitlin felt a pang. At seventeen, she had been angsty, introverted, inching her way out of the emotional pit caused by her parents' divorce. But she'd had a roof over her head. Had three meals a day, clean clothes, friends, school. She hadn't faced violence, hadn't been forced to risk home-lessness, exploitation, and death to save herself.

"I got by," Annie said. "Met people. Kept from being turned out. Crashed in people's apartments, garages, sometimes shelters, sometimes doorways. Did plenty to survive, and I mean plenty, but I kept my feet under me. A friend eventually got me a job washing dishes at a diner."

"Landry's? Who was the friend?"

Annie cut a glance at her. "Yeah. A friend I made on the street. We called her Phoenix."

She hesitated, waiting for Caitlin to say something, but Caitlin let her go on.

"I was okay. Until Corliss and Goode showed up."

Caitlin felt a charge in the air.

Annie rubbed her palms up and down her thighs, as if trying to clean them. "I made a mistake. I got to thinking about Finch—Lissah—and couldn't stand not knowing how she was. So I got in touch with Corliss," she said. "I hoped she might have got away from Efrem by then."

"You worried about the baby's safety, and your sister's?"

"Both. And Efrem's. They weren't just toxic together. They were ex-plosive. Like dynamite. It damaged them, and Finch, and anybody who came in contact with them. But Corliss and Efrem were tighter than ever. Like tangled vines." She knotted her hands. "I told her I was working in Brooklyn. And out of the blue one night, who walks in the door at the diner?" She shook her head. "I knew things were creepy, and I was screwed."

"Why?" Caitlin said.

"Because they never showed up anywhere just for shits and giggles. They didn't do loving visits. They drop in, it's because they want something and think they can get it from you, or at a minimum take over your place as base camp while they put some score into action. Sweeping up rich pickings from tourists in Times Square maybe." She exhaled. "But it was worse than that. From the moment they walked through the door at Landry's, I knew they were on a downswing. Those two fought and made up and didn't care who saw it. They loved the drama. Or at least Corliss did. The thing was, Finch was showing wear and tear."

She put her head in her hands. "Oh my God. Seeing her just killed me. She was three, should have been lively and pink cheeked and happy. But she was thin and withdrawn, and Corliss . . ." She squeezed her eyes shut. "Corliss seemed to loathe her."

Her voice broke. "She hardly even recognized me. Of course, I looked real different compared to the last time she'd seen me. I'd lost about thirty pounds and was very goth. But after giving me this scared look, real wary, I knelt down in front of her, and maybe it was the sound of my voice, but she jumped into my arms . . ."

"When was this?" Caitlin said.

"February 2008. It was cold. Finch just had on a hoodie and thin leggings, old shoes. Her hair was matted." She gave Caitlin a diamond-hard look. "And it wasn't because Corliss and Efrem were starving. Corliss had a good parka and boots. Efrem had new clothes too. And they were driving a fucking *Cadillac*. Excuse my language."

"You thought Finch was neglected?"

"Obviously. Corliss wanted a toy, not a responsibility. She wanted a child who would cling to her like a worshipper falls at the feet of a deity, showering her with love and bringing her compliments. 'What a beautiful little girl,' like it reflected on Corliss, like she was a shiny accessory. But Corliss didn't like the drudgery of motherhood, not when a kid got a fever and kept her up at night crying and didn't always express undying devotion. Finch was *three*."

"Had Corliss ever been reported to the authorities for neglect?"

"How would I know? She traveled the nation with Efrem. One place got hot, they moved on. And when they showed up, she fully expected me to feed all three of them. Gratis. Because she was my big sister." She leaned back against the headrest. "Sorry, I'm bitching, but I need you to understand, so you'll get it when you see where this is going." She looked at Caitlin's phone on the center console. "Nothing from the cops yet?"

Caitlin shook her head. "Keep talking."

"Then, one night, maybe five days after they showed up, I'm busing tables. Corliss and Goode are arguing in a corner booth. Finch is playing on the floor. Things escalate. Get loud. My boss was already annoyed that they hung out like they were the queen and king of the place, expecting free food," Annie said. "I knew things were heading toward the boiling point. They always did. Like a new season of the same show, but now it had sharper edges. Those two were harder, tireder; they knew exactly how to push each other's buttons. Efrem smacks her water glass off the table. Corliss storms out, dragging Finch. She was shouting. Saying, *I'm done with all of this. I can't even breathe.*"

She paused. Her hands were clenched. "Efrem stayed."

Caitlin said nothing.

"He stayed and watched Phoenix," Annie said.

A weight seemed to fill the Suburban. Phoenix. The girl from Arizona. The desperate, thin, hungry-eyed teen in the diner photo. The face in the drawing Efrem Judah Goode gave the FBI, labeled *Jane Doe, Brooklyn 2008.* The woman Finch had mistaken for her birth mother.

Annie whispered something. Almost prayerlike. Caitlin tilted her head. "Annie?"

Again, softly, Annie said, "This is the whirlwind." She hauled in a breath, as if to keep from crying. "I thought it had come and gone when Efrem was arrested in Tennessee. I shut my eyes to how heavy and huge it was going to be. But it's here now. Full force."

She looked at Caitlin. "After Corliss stormed out, big show, dragging Finch behind her, I got a broom and dustpan to sweep up the broken glass. I knew, if my boss saw the mess, I'd be in the shit," she said. "I get to the booth, and Efrem slides past me out of his seat, says nothing, just takes his heavy coat and walks, not even paying." Her voice rose. "I'm sweeping. I look over my shoulder. And I see Phoenix eyeing him before she turns and heads out the back door. Smile on her face. With Efrem right behind her. Smile on his."

She looked at Caitlin. "I knew what it meant."

"Had you seen them together before?"

Annie nodded. "Phoenix was sweet, but a mess. I knew what was going on. They were hooking up, and Efrem would pay her in cash or drugs."

She was clenching and unclenching her fists. Caitlin kept her voice level.

"You witnessed Phoenix's murder, didn't you?"

Tears filled Annie's eyes. She opened her lips, tried to speak, and covered her mouth with the back of her hand. After a juddering breath, she nodded. Caitlin didn't move.

"Heading home along the river," Annie said. "A couple hours later. It was freezing, a real bitch of a night. I was hurrying, hoping that when I got to the apartment, Corliss would be there, Finch would be tucked under a warm blanket. I was rushing, the path right along the river. And . . . I saw." She gulped a breath. "And . . . split."

She looked down, ashamed. "I dove to the ground, trying to get invisible, and I saw it all. Then I crawled backward, just desperate to get away, scared shitless. I backed over a piece of corrugated metal and it made a groaning sound. I thought I was hosed." Her chest rose and fell. "Then I got up and ran back toward the diner." She turned to Caitlin. "And found Finch."

Caitlin wasn't expecting that. "Found her where? How?"

"I turned the corner into the vacant lot behind the diner. There was a light over the back door. A bunch of trash bags piled there," she said. "Finch was crouching beside them, huddled there against the freezing cold."

Caitlin couldn't keep from letting out a hard breath.

"My niece. This precious little girl I'd loved since birth. Who I'd fed and diapered, nursed through fevers and bruises."

She gave a half glance at Caitlin at that one, and Caitlin got the message.

"Corliss had left Finch in the cold, alone in New York, by a *trash heap*," Annie said. "I was out of breath, crazy scared, ready to, to . . . I don't know what, but to hide, get myself safe, get *away* from my sister and her horror-show life and terrified by what I'd just seen. The hatred. The revenge. All I wanted to do was *run*. Even though running was chicken-shit, I hadn't helped Phoenix, hadn't screamed or called for the cops, just crawled away into the night."

She shook her head. "I know I couldn't have stopped what happened to Phoenix. I know that . . ." She tapped her temple. "Here. I've spent fifteen years dealing with it. I know with certainty what would have happened to me if I'd made any kind of a scene. I would have been dead within days. Instead of turning invisible for all these years . . . until that asshole put out the drawing of me and labeled it 'Liv.'"

She shook off a shudder. "And then I skid around the corner and I see that little girl all alone, shivering in the winter wind, waiting for somebody who's never coming back. Finch would have waited until she froze to death. You might not understand, but in that moment, when I was right on the edge, I saw light in the void I was in. I knew Phoenix was dead. Snuffed, like that." She snapped her fingers. "And I thought . . . somehow I could make up for running away from it. I could balance the scales. I picked Finch up."

She turned to Caitlin. "That's when Efrem showed up."

Even hearing it set the hairs on Caitlin's arms standing on end. "Had he followed you?"

"Yes."

"Did he know you'd witnessed the murder?"

Annie nodded. "I was terrified. Absolutely piss-my-pants, out-of-my-head petrified by the sight of him. I just clutched Finch to my chest and backed away, knowing he outweighed me by a hundred pounds and could run me down in three seconds flat."

"What did you do?"

"I said, 'I'll take care of her.'" Annie's face was dead pale. "It just came out. All I could think of that might keep him from killing both of us."

"And he didn't."

"No." She paused. "He said to take Lissah and go."

"What?"

"He said, 'Disappear. I'll tell Corliss you're dead.'"

Caitlin looked at her, surprised.

Annie continued. "He said, 'You ever come back, ever call the cops, you both die. Run.'"

This was a different story from the one Goode had told. Between him and Annie, Caitlin knew who she judged to be the liar.

"I took three minutes," Annie said. "Ran in the diner, grabbed cash—I knew I was going to need every damn dollar I could scrounge. Nobody saw me. I found Phoenix's backpack on a hook by the back entrance. I grabbed that too. Holding on to Finch. When I ran out the back door again, Efrem was gone." She lowered her shoulders. "Later on, when I finally looked in the backpack, I found Phoenix's ID. Her name was Annie Winter."

A big puzzle piece slotted into place. Caitlin nodded. But she couldn't see the whole picture yet. Why hadn't Goode killed her then and there? Was he worried that too many people had seen them together at the diner? That if Rhiannon's body was found, DNA would lead the cops inexorably to Corliss and then to him?

She said, "You ran but stayed in New York?"

"Where better to hide than New York City? In twenty-four hours, you can be somebody entirely new."

She said it without irony, and Caitlin believed her. But she also had admiration for what had to have been smarts, dedication, and incredible discipline—along with luck.

"Fair point," she said.

But there was one thing she still didn't understand: Why Goode had let her go. Caitlin was still missing something. She took in Annie's deep horror and ran back over her description of the murder. *Horror-show life. Hatred. Revenge.* Revenge against Phoenix.

It came to her with icy clarity. She turned and said, "Goode didn't kill Phoenix, did he?"

Annie shook her head. "No."

Caitlin said it quietly.

"Corliss did."

Annie broke down in sobs.

54

"It was Corliss," Caitlin said.

Annie sobbed, chest heaving. Then she grabbed the dashboard and, fighting for control, shut her emotions down. She gave Caitlin a dead-eyed stare.

"You got it right," she said. "That's who I saw."

New York City, 2008

She ran. Through the bitter cold, the air scoring her lungs, adrenaline pumping so hard that the ground disappeared and the night shimmered. Rhiannon sprinted along the river, the graffiti-covered walls blurring past, the black surface of the river writhing with Manhattan's lights.

Don't look back. Look back and they'll see my face. They'll know it's me. Know that I saw.

She looked back. On the rotting, abandoned pier, Phoenix sat bound and gagged with duct tape, whimpering for her life. A shadowed figure paced and ranted.

"Slut. Filthy succubus, stealing a man's lifeblood."

A streetlight caught the shadow's face. Corliss. Sister. Mother. Killer, bright-eyed and lethal.

Caitlin's mind spun. She should have considered this possibility. The Broken Heart Killer—the copycat—had disguised herself as male. But she was a woman. A woman working with Corliss Yates.

Corliss Yates, who had murdered under cover of darkness and disappeared, leaving everyone to assume that the killer was a man.

It was a strategy.

Caitlin eyed Annie Winter clinically. The woman was a mess, a ball of electricity, sizzling with fear for her daughter. Caitlin could take her to the NYPD, have them polygraph her. But right now she got the clear sense that Annie was telling the truth.

"You saw your sister kill Phoenix," Caitlin said.

Annie nodded. Then stared vacantly through the windshield. "I don't think it was the first time."

That knocked Caitlin back. "Why? Had she told you something? Had you seen evidence that connected her to other killings?"

Annie took a second to put it into words. "Her assurance. Her coldness. Her preparation. Her confidence. It seemed like a ritual of condemnation. She wasn't tentative." She looked at Caitlin. "She was having fun."

Williamsport, Maryland, 2006

Goode lay faceup on the back seat of the Cadillac. A woman rode him, moaning. The little checker from the grocery store, who he'd winked at earlier in the day when he went in to cool off. Hungry and horny and lonely, a tight little wildcat riding him like a bronco.

The car door flew open. Outside it stood Corliss. With a tire iron.

"Goddamn dirty whore," she said.

She dragged the cowgirl off of Goode, threw her to the ground, and swung.

In the Suburban, Annie turned to face Caitlin.

"With what I witnessed? And Efrem telling me to disappear? I couldn't let anyone know where—or who—I was. Because I couldn't let anybody know who Finch really is." She blinked her eyes dry. "What did Efrem say about me?"

"He told Corliss he killed you to eliminate a witness, because you could have gotten chatty. He never talked about Corliss and Finch in the same sentence. And so you know, he has no idea who or where she is."

"Thank God. But Jesus Christ."

"But that's not all. He never told me you had the child. He said he surrendered her to a safe haven baby box at a fire station in Brooklyn."

"Liar."

"I figured. New York City doesn't have safe haven baby boxes."

"He was trying to make himself look good," Annie said, then stopped. "But you already knew he was lying. Because . . ."

"Yeah. Finch ended up with you. A blood relative. Not an anonymous abandonment, which would have led to her placement with social services or an adoption agency."

"How did you find me? How did you put it together?"

"DNA. A cousin of yours provided a sample."

Her alarm was instant. "Who?"

"A woman named Ellen Griffith in Topeka. She alerted the FBI tip line to your disappearance."

She slumped and put the back of her hand to her mouth. "My mom's cousin. Probably the only person I remember as a kid who worried about me. Okay." She shook it off. "She didn't know about Corliss and Goode. Not that I'm aware of."

"It's not a trap, you mean?"

She nodded. Caitlin thought, time to check that out.

Caitlin said, "Today I got DNA comparison results I'd requested, between Finch and two people: Rhiannon and the Brooklyn Jane Doe."

"Phoenix," Annie said. "Finch became convinced that she was her birth mother."

"I was surprised that there was no match," Caitlin said. "And more surprised at the familial relationship between Finch and Rhiannon. I got your driver's license photo, but even then I wasn't certain you were her. Not until I walked down the driveway beside the restaurant. You haven't changed completely over the years."

"I tried. If I failed . . ."

"You haven't. If Goode knew who you are now, he would have put out the word." Caitlin turned to her. "Why do you think he told Corliss you and Finch were dead?"

"It simplified his life and gave him emotional power over Corliss."

That sounded exactly right to Caitlin.

She got her phone and showed Annie a photo of the Broken Heart Killer. Annie shook her head. "Never seen her."

Caitlin thought: Corliss was working with the Broken Heart Killer to find Finch—and to eliminate people who could connect her to unsolved killings she had committed. She was after her inheritance, in every sense. Destroying her legacy of murder and hunting for her daughter.

Corliss, from what Caitlin had gathered, flipped between love and hate. Feared engulfment and abandonment. It was how she related to Goode. And how she related to her little girl. That February night in Brooklyn, she had hated Finch. Felt consumed by her. So she abandoned her. But her personality issues went beyond that, into malignant entitlement.

Annie eyed her carefully. "You understand why I didn't go to the police, right? Either Efrem would have killed me and Finch, or the authorities would have taken her—to foster care or back to Corliss. I know it wasn't strictly legal. But I was not going to risk Finch's life."

"You saved her from being raised by two killers."

"And I won't let harm come to her now."

Caitlin's phone rang. Tashjian.

"I'm at the coffee place on the Upper West Side," he said. "Barista and the manager remember seeing Finch here a few hours ago. She had a big, emotional reunion of some kind."

Caitlin shot Annie a glance. "Okay."

"Got CCTV. Finch comes in, a woman runs up to greet her, hug, tears, then they spend half an hour in intense conversation at a booth by the windows. Before leaving together."

Caitlin's stomach tightened. She didn't want to alarm Annie. "And?"

"They walk up Eighty-Fourth Street and get in a GMC Yukon."

Caitlin didn't react. But a wave of nausea swept through her. Annie was pinning her with her gaze. Caitlin got out of the Suburban, mouthing, *One minute.*

She crossed the street and headed around a corner. "Thanks, Greg."

She ended the call and moved blindly along the street. Lightning seeming to fill the world, snaking, writhing, turning her inside out.

Finch got in the Yukon.

A roar rose in her throat. Approaching a construction site, she drew her knee back and kicked a garbage can into a retaining wall.

Finch. Why hadn't she grabbed the girl by the shoulders, shaken her, made her *see?*

She bent and put her hands on her knees.

Construction debris littered the sidewalk—sawdust and little kernels of broken safety glass. Sharp objects, glittering. Waiting for her to pick them up and run them through her skin. She hung her head.

Screw that. She straightened. After a moment, she texted Tashjian. Images?

Quickly, three photos came through. In the first, Finch was entering the coffee shop. In the second, she was extending her arms toward a young woman. Caitlin stared hard at the image. The flowing red hair, the high-fashion makeup, the soft blouse—all presented a package: upscale urbanite. But the woman's eyes, cold blue, had a predatory focus she recognized.

"I see you, copycat," she said.

Pausing a moment, calming herself, she walked back to the Suburban. She got in and showed the photos to Annie.

"Does she look familiar?" Caitlin said.

Annie stopped breathing for a moment. She slowly shook her head. "I don't know her. But she's doing a freaky imitation of Corliss."

"How?"

"The hair, the clothes. Jesus."

Caitlin looked longer at the photo and sent it to Keyes, texting, Facial recognition—compare this woman to the Broken Heart Killer subway photos.

Then she showed Annie the third photo: Finch getting in the Yukon.

"Oh, my God," Annie said.

"The NYPD is trying to track the path of the Yukon, but this was several hours ago."

Annie once again accessed "Find My Phone" for Finch's cell. This time, after she stared at it hard for a few seconds, a blue dot popped onto the screen.

"*There*. Got it. What the hell?"

The phone was north of them, up the Hudson Valley. Then the signal vanished.

Chilled, Caitlin phoned Keyes. "I need you to track a phone number via cell tower pings."

She gave him Finch's number, and he said, "On it. It'll take a while."

"How long?"

"Hour, ninety minutes maybe."

"Go." Hanging up, she called the FBI's Hudson Valley office and asked the agent on duty to contact local police departments to coordinate a search.

Normally, they had twenty-four hours to find kidnap victims before the Broken Heart Killer murdered them. But in this case, Finch was the prize. Caitlin had no idea whether that meant protection or danger, but she couldn't wait.

Annie's face was stretched tight with anxiety. Caitlin said, "I'm heading up there. I'll coordinate the search."

Annie said, "I'm going."

The last thing Caitlin wanted was a mother in the middle of an op. But Annie said, "Trying to stop me is a waste of time. So tell me how I can help."

Caitlin paused for a second, overcome with guilt, frustration, and urgency. She was about to shove Annie out the passenger door.

Instead, she started the engine. "Call and tell the restaurant you won't be cooking tonight. We don't have a second to waste."

She put it in gear.

55

The city receded as they crossed the George Washington Bridge, high on the span over the Hudson. Caitlin pushed the Suburban as the bridge flashed past and the water sparkled in the afternoon sun. They continued north along the Palisades and into the Hudson Valley. Knuckles white on the wheel, she checked in with Keyes, local FBI agents, and police departments, alerting them that Finch was in danger. Annie sat clutching her phone, willing her missing daughter to call. Willing the GPS locator on the girl's cell to come alive again.

Caitlin kept the pedal down as she put it together.

From the jump—from the minute the FBI put out its bulletin with Efrem Judah Goode's confessions and the drawings of his victims—Finch had been right. Her birth mother *was* involved in the 2008 slaying of the Brooklyn Jane Doe. But Finch's mother wasn't the victim.

She was the killer.

Corliss Yates, who possessively both loved and resented Finch—Lissah—had tossed the little girl aside in a snit, leaving her to freeze behind Landry's Diner. Caitlin didn't know if Corliss had intended for Finch to die. Maybe she thought somebody from the diner would come out and find Finch there. And that they would recognize the little girl and hand her to Rhiannon.

But Corliss was utterly indifferent to her child's fate.

Caitlin thought that Corliss had been playing a game. Drop-kick the kid, knowing there was a solid chance her runaway sister—her tough, loyal, loving younger sister, who had always picked Lissah up when she was knocked down—would do so again. That Corliss left her daughter like discarded garbage, satisfying an urge to be free of a clingy child, confident that if she came back in a week or a year, she could grab the kid and pick up where she left off.

But events intervened. After Corliss flounced from the diner, Goode left to hook up with Phoenix. Caitlin wasn't shocked. Humans had a capacity for depravity that was highly imaginative. She wasn't surprised that Goode—who had been living, thieving, traveling, and killing with Corliss at his side for years—might slip out to bang a near stranger only minutes after his life partner walked out the door. It was almost too perfect, a simian response.

But what Phoenix didn't know when she stepped outside behind Landry's was that Corliss was coming around the corner in the dark, probably to leave Finch there. That she saw Goode and Phoenix having sex up against the diner's brick wall.

And she stayed in the shadows and watched. And waited. Waited for Efrem to finish up and stagger away. For Phoenix to finish work and head home, alone. To get the duct tape from the Coupe de Ville and grab Phoenix as she turned a corner. To stick Finch by a pile of Hefty bags and head off to get rid of Efrem's hookup.

Corliss had tied Phoenix up on the rotting pier, berated her, then kicked her into the frigid waters of the East River. And—with Efrem—taken off again.

After, he told her that Rhiannon was the person she had heard in the weeds, that she'd witnessed the murder, but that he had killed her. And that Finch—Lissah—was dead too.

Two thousand eight had come into focus. It made sense.

But Caitlin was still missing pieces of the puzzle. The biggest: the identity of the Broken Heart Killer.

The unsub was tied to Corliss but killed with such utter rage and enthusiasm—what was her motive?

A smaller piece was also missing. Exiting onto a state highway, Caitlin glanced over. "I see how you assumed Annie Winter's identity. But how'd you pull off the 'adoption'?"

The road narrowed, trees arching overhead. Annie rubbed her face. No more defenses.

"Don't you know?" she said. "Phoenix had a kid."

Caitlin eyed her sharply. "A little girl. Aviva told me Phoenix called her 'Sunshine.'"

Annie nodded. "All I needed was Annie's Arizona ID, and I could get the daughter's birth certificate. And fudge it."

"Fudge it. Because their ages didn't line up?"

Annie nodded. "Phoenix's girl was a couple of years older. Scout Finch Winter. But . . ." she shrugged. "I edited the dates. Cooking wasn't the first skill I developed."

Caitlin looked at her. "So what happened to Phoenix's daughter?"

Annie looked grim. "I have a guess. It's not good."

New York, 2008

On the pier, Phoenix sobbed, "I have a kid. I'm all she has."

Corliss raised a boot to kick her into the river. "Not anymore."

Annie briefly closed her eyes.

Caitlin said, "You think Corliss took her?"

"Possibly. She knew where Phoenix lived."

"How?"

"Because I hung out with Phoenix, and one day Corliss gave her a ride home from the diner. She lived in a crash pad. It overlooked the street. When Corliss dropped her off, we heard a little hand patting the window upstairs. Phoenix's daughter was pressed against the glass. Phoenix smiled and waved."

Caitlin thought about it. Annie gave her a look of consternation.

"Don't think I left that little girl at the mercy of strangers. After I ran with Finch, the next day I called social services. Anonymously. I told them about an unattended child at the apartment. Of course, I never heard if they found her."

For a moment, Annie watched the countryside flash by. "Kids internalize adoption in predictable ways. It's unavoidable. When they start to believe that something about themselves caused their birth mothers to give them up, shame can take root." She shook her head. "Abandonment is brutal on a kid's heart. Even when it's unintentional."

Caitlin drove, leaving space for Annie to talk. Trying to listen actively.

"For some kids, it's a lifelong trauma. They never recover. Can't easily relate to friends, romantic partners ... or to their adoptive families. Some kids test their families, new friends, new partners, pushing to see if they might be rejected and abandoned again."

The pain in her voice was unmistakable. "Other kids acquiesce to whatever their new family and new friends ask of them so they won't lose those ties. They have an inner terror. They can mask it, present the world with a false self that hides their real feelings. Those kids can be even more messed up. Smiling, denying, and raging inside."

Caitlin held tight to the wheel. Shadows dappled the road.

She knew that Annie was talking about two daughters: hers and Phoenix's.

"So Finch came up with a story that helped her deny the truth. She wasn't abandoned. Wasn't mistreated. Her mother was stolen from her in the most violent and evil way," Annie said. "And I could never do what's healthiest in an adoptive family. I could never reassure Finch about her origins or tell her the truth, because that would have exposed her to extreme danger." Her voice caught. "I was afraid. And it's coming back to bite me."

She shook her head. "I shut Finch down whenever she brought up the subject. It built a barrier between us I was too afraid to breach. Even when the whirlwind descended," she choked. "I thought I could shelter her from the storm. Deny, deny, delay, delay ... Instead, I helped set this nightmare in motion."

She roughly wiped her eyes and straightened in the seat. "So now I have to stop that. I have to save my daughter from everything I tried to protect her from."

"Finch seems strong and well adjusted. You did a good job."

"A federal agent, approving of subterfuge and forgery?"

"I can't officially approve that you went to extralegal means to hide in plain sight. But count me impressed by your ingenuity." After a moment, Caitlin went further. "And your dedication and success in building a loving world for Finch. If you hadn't run across that vacant lot behind the diner, God knows what might have happened to her. But it wouldn't have been good."

"She might have turned out like Phoenix's child."

A couple of years older than Finch. Twenty, twenty-one. Caitlin thought back to her encounter with the Broken Heart Killer on the subway platform. That age, that youthful recklessness, fit the unsub exactly. Had Corliss abandoned one child only to grab another?

And turned her victim's child into a killer?

56

Forty miles up the Hudson Valley, deep into a landscape of lush, green hills and slate-blue rivers and lakes, Caitlin turned off the winding highway into the small town of Bearkill. She had Keyes on an earbud. He was telling her what he had managed to learn.

"I sweet-talked an NYPD techie into giving me temporary access to their CCTV and traffic camera app. I have my own software that let me accelerate the license plate recognition and vehicle recognition to find the GMC Yukon."

"Wizard," Caitlin said.

"I had to trade. App for app. Plus two tickets to the Yankees' opener, which I'm going to put on your credit card. I threaded CCTV images from the blocks around Poppycock's coffee and traced the Yukon leaving Manhattan via the GW Bridge and traveling north. They went out of range of the NYPD network, and it took me some time to track down cameras along potential paths the vehicle could take. Captured them on the interstate twenty-five miles north of the city. Then, the next camera, another thirty miles north. Nothing. The vehicle has turned off I-87."

That was incredible work in a short time under pressure, but Caitlin felt a crawling sense of unease. "That still gives us a massive area to search."

"Cell tower pings on Finch's phone get us ten miles west of the interstate," he said, "but they cut out after the vehicle headed into farm country."

"I'll call you back. Keep hunting."

Annie eyed her grimly. "Nothing more on the location of the phone?"

"Keyes will keep searching." She drove along a tree-shaded road. "Do you have any idea where this person named Landry might be taking Finch? Any family history up this way? Friends? Any links at all to the Hudson Valley?"

Annie shook her head. "None. We took a family trip through this area on our way to Boston when I was five. Aside from that . . ." She threw up her hands.

Cresting a wooded hill, Caitlin pulled into Bearkill. It was a town of twenty thousand spread across quiet, meandering roads, with a quaint downtown, some roomy suburban streets, and a vast tract of hilly, heavily wooded countryside, both within and without the city limits, dotted with farmland. But the town was too big for everyone to know every house or farm. Even the cops wouldn't be able to name all the townsfolk off the top of their head.

Caitlin pulled in at the small police station. Another SUV was in the slot outside—the vehicle belonging to agents from the FBI's Hudson Valley Resident Agency.

Inside, Caitlin introduced Annie and shook hands with a young local agent and the senior police officer on watch.

The cop, Sergeant Patrick Morris, was alert. "We've put out the BOLO. Patrols are on the watch for the Yukon. I don't recognize the photos you sent of the suspect. Nor do any of the other officers I've spoken to today. But that doesn't mean much in this situation."

Caitlin pulled up the most recent information Keyes had obtained. "We have a few pings from Finch's phone."

She showed the data to Morris. He answered thoughtfully. "That's useful. But once you get a mile past Main Street out here, cell towers are far between. Those towers—they're too far apart to triangulate with any exactitude."

Annie said, "'Exactitude' meaning what?"

"Pinpointing the phone's location from that data . . . sorry, it's impossible."

He looked at her calmly, then at Caitlin with an undertone that she interpreted as, *You brought the kid's mother?* And she couldn't blame him.

She said, "Ms. Winter wasn't going to stay in Manhattan when she learned that her daughter might be unwittingly in the company of a killer. She can provide us with information about Finch."

The FBI agent, Bill Williamson, said, "We have photos of Finch, the unsub, and the Yukon. And I brought something that can provide extra eyes." He cut a glance meaningfully upward.

"A drone?" Caitlin said,

"Yes, ma'am."

"Excellent."

Morris walked them to a wall map. "Let's organize a search grid."

57

The farmhouse kitchen was sunny. Finch sat across a wobbly table from the woman who had welcomed her with the most powerful hug of her life. It was like being drenched in emotion. Corliss. Her mother.

"You're everything I ever hoped to see," Corliss said. "You're so beautiful. My baby. I can't even believe it. Finally."

Corliss's voice was soft but bright, effervescing with joy. In the afternoon light, the wear on Corliss's—*her mom's*—face was obvious: lines around her mouth and at the corners of her eyes, and gray hairs amid the red. Her arms were tan, her long nails polished a deep violet, like a plum or a bruise. Finch couldn't stop drinking in everything about her.

Looking for signs of what she had never seen except in a mirror. Hoping, finding. The green flecks in Corliss's eyes, the fullness in her lips, the languorous way she inhabited her body.

All new, all unfamiliar. All so familiar.

Because Corliss was now telling her a story that upended everything she'd ever believed about her life. And she could no longer deny what she was hearing. What she knew had to be true.

Landry hovered in the background, pouring iced tea in big plastic glasses, putting out plates and forks and a hot cherry pie. She cut wide slices and set one in front of Finch, then scooped a heap of vanilla ice cream on top. It melted and skidded off the slice onto the plate.

Finch couldn't kick the drowsiness from her hard nap on the drive up. She feared her weird and unclear head had to do with what Corliss was telling her in an urgent, all-consuming rant.

"Let me tell you about you," Corliss said. "From the beginning."

The high-pitched hum rose and fell inside Finch's skull. This was exactly, and nothing at all, like her imagined, dreamed of, much feared reunion with her mother.

"I need to understand," Finch said. "The woman who died in the East River in 2008. She wasn't my . . ."

"No." Corliss's face went blank, like a wall.

It felt dreamlike. Like *Inception*, when the dream city is abandoned and crumbles into the thrashing sea. A weird pang went through Finch—a sense of being adrift, even though the woman across from her was telling her the origin story she had longed to hear.

The story wasn't a dream at all. It was a nightmare.

"You were born in Pennsylvania," Corliss said. "On a Saturday night. It was a hard labor, agonizing, but I didn't give up. When they said push, I screamed at them, I bit the nurse, but I gave in to your demand to enter the world." She laughed. "You little smoosh-faced critter, red, slimy, squalling—inconceivable. And all mine."

No mention of a dad. Something about the way Corliss said *all mine* kept Finch from asking about that. "When's my birthday?"

"Lissah Dove Yates. I named you when I saw you. I know instantly what name fits somebody."

The hum rose. Corliss's lips moved. When the hum fell, she was telling the incredible story about her drugged-out teenage sister abducting Finch as a toddler.

"I don't understand how that happened," Finch said.

Corliss eyed Landry, who stepped out of the kitchen and returned with an armload of photo albums. Real, stick-the-photos-inside albums. Corliss opened one.

There was Corliss, young and spent, in the labor and delivery suite at a Pennsylvania hospital, holding a baby in her arms.

Corliss, playing with the baby. The baby crawling. The baby pulling herself up. The little girl no longer a baby. Looking exactly like the drawing that Landry had shown her, and like the early photos she had in albums at home in her Brooklyn apartment.

These albums. Bursting with pictures of Finch. There was no doubt—none—that Corliss was her birth mother.

Or that the story Annie had told Finch her whole life was a lie.

Because in the depths of the third album was a photo of her, maybe a year old, in an old house much like this one, messy, faded. She was squirming on Corliss's lap. In the background, lurking in a darkened doorway, was Annie.

Or *not* Annie. Rhiannon. Blond, big-haired, wide-eyed. In a baggy T-shirt and cutoffs and a ton of makeup, glaring at the camera with something frightened and feral behind those eyes.

Finch said, "I just don't understand."

Corliss lowered her voice. "Meth does terrible things to a person."

But Annie didn't do drugs.

"She was uncontrollable," Corliss said. "Wild. Full of lies, selfish, and—I hate to say it—jealous of me. Over you. Because I had everything, I had this perfect ray of sunshine, and she had nothing but backseat fucks and weeklong highs."

Finch cringed. "This doesn't make sense to me."

"Because she's been lying to you," Corliss said.

"Where did Efrem Goode see me?" Finch said. "How did he draw that picture of me?"

Corliss sat back, exhaling, and pressed her lips white. Landry sat down at the table.

"This is the hardest part," Corliss said. "Rhiannon met him at a bar in the town where we lived. She used to play pool for money. She hooked up with him when he came in one night."

"No."

Corliss nodded. "She didn't know what he was. Not at first, anyhow."

No. No no no.

"So, you know him too?" Finch said.

"All too well, unfortunately. And we thought he was out of our lives. That he was safely behind bars. But now we see the truth. That one night when Rhiannon took you from your crib, she took off with him. To New York."

"I don't believe it."

Corliss's cheeks flushed. "You better believe it."

Finch shrank. She swallowed and felt a hard, unexpected knot in her throat. *Don't cry.*

"You have to understand," Corliss said. "I've spent the last fifteen years doing nothing but trying to find you."

The knot in Finch's throat got bigger. She blinked and felt tears rise.

"You have to believe that you—oh, sweetheart, don't cry. You are *everything* to me."

Corliss's eyes were kind. Finch nodded and wiped the tears away. Corliss's words felt overwhelming though. So big and powerful that they took all the oxygen from the room.

She didn't know how she could breathe under the weight of all this love.

"I just . . . I don't want to sound . . . weird or ungrateful or anything, but . . . I'm so confused about why Annie—Rhiannon—ran off with me." None of it made sense.

But Corliss's mouth went hard. And Finch's mind felt foggy. So she let Corliss talk, and cried, soaking up every drop of information she could. Corliss seemed unusually emotional, petting Finch's hair, gripping her hand and refusing to let go. It was a little creepy.

And Landry. Landry looked kind of stressed out. Uptight, like a sheet pulled taut by the wind. When Finch caught her eye, though, she smiled and pushed the pie closer to her.

Finch picked up her fork, but she had no appetite. She felt as if she was under a spotlight. Corliss and Landry were both staring at her with a bright intensity. It seemed to outshine the sunlight that shimmered through the curtains.

"I have this memory," Finch said.

Landry went still, even stiller than she had been.

"I don't know if it's real, or a dream," Finch said. "It's a snowy night, the snowfall fuzzing around streetlights. And somebody—my mom, I think—is holding me close and kissing me on the cheek."

Corliss blinked, her kindliness returning, but didn't respond. Finch forced a smile, hoping Corliss would remember, would say something, would even just nod. She didn't.

Finch felt the floor seem to soften beneath her. The snow, the kiss, the cotton candy memory, were what she had held on to her whole life. But it looked as if Corliss didn't remember. The air in the house felt still and stale. Finch decided she'd better change subjects.

"When Efrem Judah Goode was arrested, did you try to talk to him?" she said instead.

"Of course." Corliss sighed. "We contacted the prosecutors and the detectives in Tennessee. We hadn't heard diddly-squat about him since he drove off with Rhiannon and you. I told them he had helped spirit you away. But you know what I heard back?"

Finch shook her head.

"Jack shit. Efrem wouldn't talk. He never did, not while his trial was pending. He was Mr. Innocent, some white knight being railroaded by invisible enemies."

Corliss's face flushed. Landry put a hand on her wrist.

"It was later," Landry said, "after he was convicted, that we got a Facebook message from that pen pal of his. Saying to forget trying to talk to him. There was no point. Because it was a dead issue. That was the word she used. *Dead.* It meant he was telling us *you* were dead."

"Fucking liar," Corliss said.

Finch blinked. She wasn't expecting language from her mother. And something else. "The Facebook pen pal. Tonya, the one who put me in contact with you."

Landry smiled affably. Finch reached into her hip pocket for her phone. "There's something she said that—"

Her phone wasn't there.

She patted her pocket. All her pockets. She looked at the floor.

"Sorry, my phone," she said.

"Don't worry about that," Corliss said.

"No . . ." She stood up. "I don't know where it is."

"It's here someplace. Don't fuss. Have some pie."

But Finch felt a tugging tightness in her belly—a sign, she knew from too many years of anxiety, that something was getting her wound up. Maybe nothing. Maybe something wrong.

"Where is it?" Maybe it was in her backpack. She looked around. Her backpack wasn't in the kitchen. "Maybe it's in the car."

"Girl, chill, it's a phone, not a pacifier," Landry said with a laugh. "No need to grab it right now."

"I want to show you something," she said. "Just hold on a minute and I'll see if it fell out in the SUV."

"The Yukon's locked," Landry said.

Finch was on her feet. "If you can just unlock it, I'll check."

After what seemed like a long pause, Landry pulled the key fob from her jeans. She went to the window and pointed the fob at the car. Finch hurried for the front door, the old wooden floor creaking beneath her feet. She had her hand on the knob when Landry called to her.

"Hey. Is this it?"

Finch held on to the knob. Part of her, for reasons she couldn't explain, wanted to yank the door open, gulp a breath of air, and leave.

Then she turned. Landry and Corliss were standing in the kitchen doorway, watching her. Landry was holding up her cell.

"Where was it?" Finch said.

"On the kitchen counter. You must have set it down when you first came in."

That made no sense to Finch. She hadn't been holding her phone when she came in. She would have remembered . . . wouldn't she? The creepy vibe intensified.

She held out her hand and walked tentatively toward Landry. "Thanks."

Corliss's face froze in a cheerless smile. "You don't need it right now. I just need to know if you have face ID activated."

The phone looked as if it might be off. Or dead. The screen was black. Finch held out her hand. "Landry? Please. What's going on?"

Corliss's voice sharpened. "Landry."

Finch saw a change come over Landry's face. As if she were hearing Corliss's words as a command. *Heel.*

Landry's lips curled back, like a snarling dog's.

58

Annie paced in the small police station, biting her fingernails—an old, dirty habit she had given up a decade ago. She wanted a cigarette. A pack of them. She wanted Finch. She checked her phone again. No messages, no calls, no blue dot showing the phone's location. She wanted to text Agent Hendrix, but that would only slow down the search going on in the neighborhoods and countryside around her.

And somewhere out there, Finch might be face-to-face with Corliss. The binary star of her childhood and adolescence, the sun and black hole, shining, pulling, exploding, teasing, undermining, manipulating, begging her to hold on and love her. Sister. Enemy. Life force and bringer of death.

At a desk across the room, a uniformed officer was on a call. When it ended, Annie walked over. He was young and thin-lipped. His name tag said HEIN.

He looked up. "Ma'am?"

"Officer Hein," she said. "You don't look any happier to be sitting here than I am. We can add eyes to the search. You know the ground around here. I can identify my daughter."

He gave her a wary look.

"Otherwise, I'm going to call an Uber to drive me around town. But if I'm with you and see something, we can get on it immediately."

After a second, Hein stood. "It'll take twenty minutes for an Uber to get here." He called to the clerk at the front desk. "I'm taking a unit. I'll be back."

Outside, Annie jumped in the cruiser's passenger seat. Hein said,

"The other two PD units are searching for the Yukon south and east of us. We can head north and work our way back to the station."

"Good." Her voice was tight, her stomach knotted. *Finch, where are you?*

Hein drove north, past homes scattered in the wooded countryside. He radioed the other patrol cars. Two miles out, they reached a cross-roads. He looked left and right.

Annie said, "What's to the west?"

"Farms, fishing supply store, a paintball place."

They were looking that way when an orange Camaro raced into sight over the crest of a rise, riding the midline of the road. It roared through the stop sign ahead of them and kept going.

Hein flipped on his lights.

"Wait," Annie said.

"It's Wayne Tidro. Local asshole, and if he's sober, I'm Beyoncé."

"I'm getting out."

"I can't let you—"

"You can't take me on a pursuit. And I can't get distracted from looking for Finch." She opened the car door. "You're not letting me do anything. I'm taking a stroll. If I see the slightest sign of something suspect, I am calling 911. And you're calling all your backup, and Agent Hendrix, the FBI, the cadets down at West Point, Space Force, and Captain Fucking America. Fair enough?"

He paused a second. "Fair enough."

She got out. Hein hit the siren and floored the cruiser after the Camaro, out of sight.

Annie turned in a circle. She could head back toward the police station, but that was ground they had already covered. She raised a hand to shield her eyes from the sun. To the west on the crossroad she saw several mailboxes. She could cover that ground in fifteen or twenty minutes, she estimated. She started walking.

59

In the farmhouse hallway, Landry faced Finch. *No*, Landry thought, *Lissah. Lissah Dove.*

The girl looked stricken, guarded, and not nearly drugged enough. The phone. The stupid phone. When they left the city, it had been powered up and had a signal, so Landry knew that it had been connecting to cell towers on the drive up. It had been in Finch's back pocket, the far side, out of Landry's light-fingered reach. Only when Finch finally fell into a drug-sated sleep was she able to pull over, dig it out of the girl's jeans, and turn off GPS and location services before shutting it down. She couldn't dump it, not then, because she still needed it for scraping information, sending diversionary messages, and luring Finch's fake mom, Rhiannon, into the open. And after today, Finch wouldn't be with it, ever again. But here she was, freaking out over it, a real live *teenager*, and things were not going as smoothly as Landry had hoped.

From the kitchen doorway behind her, Corliss's breathing brushed the air between her shoulder blades. Her voice sharpened.

"Landry."

Landry heard the command. *Snap to attention, girl.*

Finch's eyes widened. Landry immediately blanked her face. But she had reacted to Corliss's words—a slip. Never react, not instinctively. Act always like the person you're presenting to the world. Sleight of hand, sleight of mind. Always, from the beginning.

She clamped down her emotions. But the tone of Corliss's voice was *that* tone. The one she had heard too often as a child.

Since this began—this, the post-Efrem's-confession world, the *they're alive* world, the hunt-the-friends-and-find-Lissah world, the world Landry had not known she was ready for but now knew she belonged in, freed, fiery, full of grace—she had been busy nonstop with planning, execution, interrogation, strategy, camouflage, escape, and entrapment. For this. For *now*.

But with *now* came *then*.

Memories. The old ones. The earliest ones. They had been playing in her head now for weeks.

Five years old. Dirty, hungry, huddled in a filthy NYC walkup, surrounded by stoned adults. Yellow afternoon light angling through the kitchen window. Then a woman appeared in the doorway. She sidled in, walking past people as if they were rat droppings.

Somebody said, "Who're you?"

"I'm here for Phoenix's kid."

Nobody objected.

Later that day, Landry sat in the backseat of a big, rumbling car. It was gold. Later, she learned to call it the Cadillac. A highway flashed by outside, noise and green treetops. She saw the back of the driver's head: dark hair, broad shoulders, young. Soon, she learned to call him Efrem. Corliss sat beside him, humming. She glanced over her shoulder. Gleaming eyes. A covetous smile.

She said, "Look what I got. Takeout from the diner. Landry. That's your name."

With Landry's memories came pain and anger. She was adept at masking all that from Corliss. She knew exactly how Corliss's rage could flare at the tiniest slight.

Landry's own rage could also flare. It was doing so now. It had been sparked by Rhiannon—whose current name and whereabouts she still didn't know. That was why she needed Finch, at least until Finch could give her the password or do the required open-eyed face ID for her phone. Landry had a text already in mind. *Mommy, help! Come get me!*

Rhiannon, long thought dead. Rhiannon, the runaway who Corliss had told her terrible stories about. The little sister who abandoned the family. Wanting to be a star, or rich, or at least a rich whore in New York City.

Lying, and living, all this time. While taking and keeping Lissah from her all this time. The sneaky thief of all thieves.

Landry knew that Corliss wasn't even that mad at Efrem anymore. But Rhiannon . . . She led Mom to do extreme things. After Lissah vanished, Mom had gone through all kinds of grief. At least, that was what Landry gathered from stories she had heard over the years. When Mom would say she couldn't take being abandoned again, losing her heart again, that Landry was all she had now. That Landry couldn't walk out—she would be killing Mom twice if she did that.

Then Efrem's drawings showed up on the TV. And the one—Liv— was the punch in the face. It was Efrem's way of hitting them with the truth. He hadn't killed Rhiannon. She had run off with Mom's firstborn.

What Landry glimpsed sometimes, in nightmares just before she awakened, was the memory of Mom walking into the drug den. That happened because of Rhiannon. If Rhiannon hadn't taken Lissah, Mom wouldn't have wanted another kid to take her place. Rhiannon caused everything that happened. And now she was alive?

Not for long.

Landry had taken the news about Rhiannon and Lissah with apparent stoicism. Mom wanted them found. By any means. If her sister had been skulking around for fifteen years, it meant that she had confederates helping her lie and hide.

Landry knew that Efrem had probably expected her to be on his side. Things between him and her had always been cool. She hadn't gone with him and Mom to Tennessee. She had stayed behind in Idaho, because she had a hustle going. When Efrem was arrested—in the stupidest way possible, for what, killing hookers? Addicts?—he ruined everything she had hoped he would teach her and give to her. Scores. Excitement. Shelter. She was done with his stupid ass.

The Liv drawing, she thought, was a signal that Efrem wanted her to contact him. He was hoping she could help him out. By killing Mom, no doubt.

But Mom needed Lissah. Oh my, did she ever. All her attention and joy and total mind-blowing energy became devoted to recapturing that shining little blond-haired demon she hadn't worried about in a decade at least. Lissah, alive and in Rhiannon's hands? Mom had a plan, and Landry was the one to execute it. Start with the people who had worked with Rhiannon at the diner. If they didn't have information, spread out. Get somebody from the old days, the hometown—the woman who went to high school with Rhiannon. The neighbor. Get information. Somebody had to have information. Track, take, torture, kill Chelsea Symanski for information. When Chelsea didn't know about Rhiannon, at the very least get the address of her sister, Aviva, who had hung with the drug whores back then.

And Landry had been getting closer, until the fucking red-haired Feeb had thwarted her on the subway platform. Luckily, Efrem had managed to get his pen pal Tonya to reach out. He'd sacrificed her, really—rook takes pawn—to try to draw Corliss into view. He had the right idea. Rhiannon and Lissah would be irresistible shiny objects that Corliss would try to capture. He hoped Landry would get the message and work for his goal. Offing Corliss Yates.

And here she was. Standing two feet from Corliss, in the hallway of an isolated farmhouse.

Landry was tough. But buried deep beneath the toughness was the terrified child who had been swept into Corliss's frightening embrace. And now Finch was here. The blood child that Corliss belatedly decided to retrieve. Mom's *everything*. Landry saw that she herself was merely a substitute, a toy that had been molded into a tool.

A tool that was ready to snap.

She could tell that Finch sensed something awry. The drugs she had put in Finch's coffee were wearing off. And Landry sensed Corliss preparing to bite, like the cobra she was.

"Landry?" Finch said. "What's going on?"

"Time for shit to get real, that's what." Landry backhanded her across the mouth.

As Finch stumbled backward, Landry turned to Corliss. "Mama."

60

The blow slammed through Finch's head. Stars flew across her vision. She was keeling back on her heels before the truth of what had happened reached her mind.

Omigod. Oh, hell no.

Get out.

Get out, get out, get out . . .

The words drummed through her mind, clearing her head, adrenaline emptying her veins of whatever had been slowing her down. Drugged—she'd been drugged. That *stupid* coffee, oh my God. That's why she had been reeling. *Do not operate heavy machinery* popped into her head as she fought to regain her balance. And heavy machinery was her life, her family, with gears and chains that were about to grind her up.

The stars dissipated, and she got a clear look at Landry standing in front of her. Behind Landry, Corliss hulked in the kitchen doorway.

Finch spun and lunged for the front door.

Annie walked up the narrow country road to a rutted driveway. Through the trees, she spotted a farmhouse. The late afternoon sun was cool on her face, a breeze rattling the new leaves. They seemed to whisper a warning.

She felt a trickle of fear. The road was empty, the driveway empty, the house seemingly quiet. Sticking close to the trees, she walked up the drive.

The home was dark. No car, no lights, curtains drawn. She listened for a minute, heard no sounds of human habitation. Checking her nerves, she jogged to the porch and looked through the glass in the door. Inside, the furniture was draped with sheets. She ran around to the back. The refrigerator door was open, lights off, empty. The house was uninhabited.

She headed back along the driveway toward the road, her stomach churning as she tried to stanch her rising panic and the sense that time was draining away.

Through the trees, she saw another house.

It was white, barely visible through the woods one property over from where she was standing. She'd seen a mailbox on the county highway out front.

She cut through the trees toward it. Halfway there, she slowed. Heeding an inner sense that she shouldn't approach the house directly, she circled and emerged from the woods behind a listing barn. Beyond it, a cornfield spread to the horizon. She tucked herself against the side of the barn and peered around at the weatherworn farmhouse.

The curtains were closed, but outside on the raggedy lawn, clothes hung on a line, swaying in the breeze. Crimson tops, white jeans, a zebra-print blouse. Not exactly farmer gear.

From this angle, she couldn't see whether any vehicles were parked in the driveway. She shoved aside a broken board in the back wall of the barn and crept inside. In the shadows and dusty sunlight, she ran toward the wide-open doors at the front. Hoes, pitchforks, and post-hole diggers hung from the joists. Shovels and axes were mounted on the walls. A tractor with a disc harrow attached was parked in the middle of the barn. She ducked around it.

A midnight-blue SUV was parked outside the front door of the farmhouse. She couldn't tell the make. She crept forward, her heart thumping.

She stopped. In the corner of the barn, under a tarp, was another car. Its boxy shape gave her a leaden sense of dread. She lifted an edge of the tarp.

It was a Cadillac Coupe deVille.

She pulled out her phone to call 911.

No signal.

"Shit."

She could backtrack, run to the road, get a signal. Call 911, then Agent

Hendrix and Officer Hein. He had to be the closest—maybe only a few
miles away. She needed backup. Firepower, literally. And seconds counted.

She retreated at a run toward the broken board in the wall.

She heard screams from inside the house.

Landry flew at Finch as the girl sprang for the front door. She grabbed
her by the hair.

"Come here, you little shit."

She slung Finch to the floor and dragged her toward the kitchen.

The girl was *running* from her? Running from Corliss, after all the
work they had put in, the hell, the death they had unleashed? She had
personally dodged across subway tracks, been forced to shed her disguise,
and had to abandon New York. And this brat was fleeing? *Deserting* them?

No way she was letting *that* happen.

Finch fought, kicking, trying to flip around and get to her feet, grabbing at Landry's hands.

"No," Landry said.

Landry was devoted to Corliss. Corliss, who rescued her from a drug
den. From hunger and filth. Corliss gave her clean sheets and hot food,
order and *purpose*. Corliss instilled the liberating message that you did
anything to protect your family. And you punished anyone who crossed it.

She feared and loved Corliss. Unlike Finch, who was failing to get
with the program.

Smack. She hit her again.

Corliss stepped aside from the doorway. Landry dragged Finch into
the kitchen and slid her across the floor. Finch hit the table and crumpled.

Then turned and got to her knees.

"Landry . . ." Finch mouthed, horror-struck.

She saw Landry's eyes, burning. The shock and pain had brought her
fully awake. She rose to a crouch. Landry blocked the doorway to the hall
and front door. Finch glanced peripherally at the kitchen door.

Corliss hustled over, flipped the dead bolt, and stood in front of it
like a bouncer.

Finch turned back to Landry. Her red hair was askew. The whole thing. It was a wig going sideways. Long strands fell in front of her face. But that wasn't what Finch really saw.

She saw the stun baton in Landry's left hand. The gun in her right.

And she saw Annie behind her in the doorway.

Who said, *"Run."* And swung a hatchet.

Finch bolted to her feet. She charged past Annie and down the hall to the front door. Behind her in the kitchen came a scream. Finch heard it as she raced from the house into the cornfield.

61

Caitlin reached the corner at a T-junction, creeping along at ten miles per hour, seeing nothing. She was driving the grid on the northwest side of Bearkill, out at the edge of the city limits, where the town's neat rectangular blocks broke into snaking roads with scattered homes nestled back amid the heavy, lovely, unhelpful trees. The sun was angling toward the west. They had perhaps two more hours of good daylight.

They had to find Finch before the sun went down.

But this quadrant had so far been a dead end. No sign of the GMC Yukon, of the redhead who was the unsub, of Finch. Caitlin's stomach felt cold. She slowed at the corner and called Special Agent Williamson, who was flying the drone. He was on the opposite side of town, working outward from the police station. He had nothing to report.

She hung up and put the Suburban in gear, and the phone rang.

A 917 area code. New York City. Something about the number was familiar enough that she felt a little shiver.

She answered. "Hendrix."

There was static on the other end, muffled noises. Someone was on the line.

She turned off the engine. In the quiet, she understood what she was hearing: agonized breathing.

"Who's there?" she said.

"Agent Hendrix . . ."

A woman's voice. Rasping. Caitlin inhaled.

"Annie?"

"I . . ."

Goddamn it. "Annie. What's wrong?"

"Farm," she gasped. "Highway northwest. Of town. West, a mailbox with. Rooster on it."

Caitlin started the engine and pulled up the GPS. "I'm coming. We're coming."

"Hurry."

The GPS showed the road Annie was talking about. There was a cut-through from the cross street where Caitlin was idling. It was less than half a mile away.

She jammed the pedal down. "I'm on my way. Hold on."

Racing along a back road, Caitlin frantically called Special Agent Williamson and Bearkill PD's Sergeant Morris. Both were miles farther away than she was.

"I need backup, but the situation sounds critical. I will recon and get back to you."

"I'm on my way," Morris said. "Fifteen minutes out."

She dropped down a hill, crossed a stone bridge, and spied several driveways up ahead. One had a mailbox with a rusting red rooster on top.

She turned into the rutted drive. Trees arched overhead. They gave her a looming sense of threat. She slowed and rounded a bend, pulse drumming.

Ahead, the woods ended and the driveway emptied at an old white farmhouse. Caitlin backed up and parked out of sight under the trees. She called Annie's number. It took five rings before Annie answered.

"It's Caitlin. I'm here."

"Please," Annie whispered. "They left. I can't go. After them. You have to."

Caitlin saw nobody outside the house. Didn't see the Yukon. A barn sat with its door wide, a tractor parked inside. Past that, a cornfield ran toward the horizon.

She climbed from the Suburban, silently shut the door, and ran through the trees to the rear of the house. Concealed within the tree line, she paused. Curtains drawn. Nobody visible outside. She put her phone to her ear and murmured Annie's name. The call had gone dead.

Gut check.

She ran across the back yard, past clothes swaying on a clothesline. The kitchen door was locked. She peered in. *Shit.*

She smashed a pane of glass with her elbow, reached inside, and opened the door. Heart pounding, Glock raised, she entered, sweeping the room.

A trail of blood ran from the middle of the kitchen floor into the hallway. She advanced, cleared the living room, and turned down the hall to follow the red slick on the wood.

At a bedroom, she cleared the doorway in vertical swaths. Nobody inside.

She walked three feet and swept right, following the blood trail through the next door.

Her heart thudding like a trip-hammer, she cleared that bedroom.

The bed, the desk, and the floor were covered with photographs of Efrem Judah Goode. Photo albums had been ripped and scattered everywhere. In all the photos, Goode's face was scratched out. On the floor in the center of the room, surrounded by the pictures, half covered in them, lay Annie.

Caitlin dropped to her side. "Hold on."

A broken heart was drawn in blood on her white chef's coat. It looked like a sacrifice at a shrine to hatred.

Annie peered up. "Finch . . ."

Her face was chalk white, her lips blue, her skin cold and clammy. Her chef's coat was soaked red along the hem. So were her jeans. There was a bullet hole near the zipper. Beneath it, a gunshot wound pulsed with every beat of Annie's heart, blood chugging out. With horror, Caitlin realized that the round had hit the femoral artery.

She holstered her Glock and put pressure on the wound.

Annie swiped at Caitlin's forearm. Her voice was a rasp. "Finch is running."

Caitlin's adrenaline surged, prickling up and down her arms.

"A young woman," Annie gasped, "went after her."

Caitlin pressed heavily with both hands on the wound, leaning into it. The blood slowed but didn't stop.

"Is Corliss here?" Caitlin said.

Annie shook her head. "Drove off. In the Yukon."

Keeping one hand on the gushing artery, Caitlin squirreled her phone from her pocket and called 911, her fingers slick with blood.

"I need paramedics." She gave her FBI badge number and the location of the property. "The mailbox has a rooster on it. Sergeant Morris knows I'm here. Hurry."

She hung up and pressed on the wound again with both hands. From the heat of the blood pulsing through her fingers, and the chill of Annie's skin, she knew that the woman was in desperate shape. All around, the grotesque display of defaced photos grinned at them—a circus of destruction.

Annie's hand slipped from Caitlin's forearm to the floor. "Go."

Caitlin shook her head.

Annie spoke louder. "Go *now*."

The passion behind Annie's thready rasp nearly sent Caitlin bolting after Finch. Tentatively she reduced the pressure on the wound. Blood instantly gushed again, in time to Annie's heartbeat.

Caitlin restored pressure, leaning down with both arms as if performing CPR. The gunshot was at hip level. Too high to get a tourniquet on it. She looked around the room for something she might use to replace the force of her arms on the wound. There was nothing—no object that could provide the directed pinpoint pressure needed to stanch the bleeding.

It was clear to her now. If she left, Annie wouldn't last two minutes. She would bleed out.

She was *not* leaving Annie to die. And she knew that Finch was fast, and gutsy. "When EMS gets here."

"No. Finch had barely any head start." Annie's gaze drilled her. "They'll catch her."

"They want Finch alive—"

"They dragged her across the floor by her hair. When I came in.

Landry had . . . a gun. Stun baton," she said. "Maybe they did want her alive. They don't now."

Heart thudding, Caitlin called 911 again. The urgency in her voice was hard to miss, but the dispatcher said, "The closest unit is ten minutes away, the ambulance maybe thirteen."

Annie whispered, *"Please."*

Caitlin didn't move. She pressed on the wound. Her hands were slick, wet, and hot. Annie's blood was puddling beneath her on the floor.

Annie put her hands over Caitlin's and looked her in the eye. "I need you to do this. But it has to be *now.*"

Caitlin held Annie's gaze. Annie, the woman who had escaped violence, toughed it out on the streets, rescued a youngster from horror, made a home for her, a life for her, remade herself, dedicated everything to creating a loving family while protecting Finch from danger—until now, when she'd thrown herself back into it. Annie's hands, on top of Caitlin's, were icy. Her skin had paled to the color of shadowed snow. But she was alive and impassioned, and Finch needed her. Caitlin needed her. Annie needed to live, not succumb to the sick hatreds of her sister and the Broken Heart Killer.

Annie's breathing was light and thready. Caitlin knew what she was asking her to do.

No. I can't.

Annie's eyes, though struggling to focus, were fiery. She tightened her grip on Caitlin's hands. "I heard the dispatcher. Even if you stay, I don't have thirteen minutes."

A sob caught in Caitlin's chest. Head ringing, she leaned close. She choked, "I'm here."

She released the pressure on the gunshot wound.

Annie exhaled. Caitlin wrapped her in a bear hug. She held Annie's head, pressed her own face to Annie's cheek, and held on tight.

She felt Annie's shallow breathing. Felt her heartbeat as their chests pressed together. Faster, lighter, like a sparrow taking flight. Every impulse in Caitlin's body screamed at her to press on the wound again.

The sparrow's wings fluttered and lightened and vanished. Skyborne, gone. Annie's chest stilled. Shaking, Caitlin clutched her tight.

The room felt airless, the light harsh and white—an X-ray.

Caitlin held on another aching second. Then, gently, she lowered Annie to the floor. A wrenching pain came over her. Annie lay still, staring at the ceiling, absent. Finished forever in a moment. Sent across the border that could be crossed in only one direction. Caitlin could hardly breathe.

She closed Annie's eyes. Then she stood up.

Backup was inbound. Ten minutes out. She knew that Corliss was after Finch—her legacy, her future, her victory over Efrem. Drawing her gun, Caitlin ran from the house toward the cornfield.

62

Finch fought her way through the cornfield. Its endless rows were green and heavy, taller than she was, thick—and noisy. She followed the furrows, arms up in front of her face, the skin on the back of her neck tight with fear. She heard Landry coming behind her. Another sob choked her throat. She kept going.

She'd heard gunshots.

Mom. The sight of Annie in the kitchen doorway, a hatchet in her hand, the look in her eyes—it was terrifying. As if a hole had been torn in the world, and chaos had screamed through, black and electric. Everything had shattered. Atomized.

But Annie. Annie had come. Somehow, out of nowhere, Annie had come and had a fucking *axe* in her hand, swinging it at Landry, and that was all Finch needed to know. Mom didn't come to play, and this was real, and she had to do what Mom said and *run.*

The corn went on and on. She was breathing hard. She looked back. Her footprints were everywhere. So was damage to the stalks.

Leave a trail, why don't you. Hansel and Gretel weren't this obvious.

She squeezed between rows of stalks and veered off at an angle, stumbling over the furrows. After a hundred yards, ducking low, she thought she saw light ahead. A break in the field.

She headed straight for it and burst onto a dirt track. Maybe six feet wide, it ran at ninety degrees to the furrows. Big ruts in the earth. It was a tractor path between fields.

Ahead was just more corn.

She paused, catching her breath, looking left and right. The tractor path ran for a couple of hundred yards in either direction. Then corn.

To her right, a car turned onto the path. It stopped. It was the Yukon. Through the windshield, she could see Corliss at the wheel.

Finch's skin seemed to jump. Her nerves, her blood. She charged into the next field.

Landry forged ahead through the cornfield. The girl, the little shit, was running like a crazy cow, blundering, damaging cornstalks, and leaving messy footprints.

Finch was heading for the dirt track that bisected the vast fields belonging to the farm. Landry plowed forward, pistol in her right hand, babying her left arm. Her forearm was pouring blood from a slash with the hatchet. It hurt like a bastard and degraded her ability to move.

Fucking Rhiannon.

The bitch had swung like a pro, and Landry had brought up her arm to deflect the blow. God*damn* the pain.

But there hadn't been a second blow, because a 9mm bullet beat even the brightest, keenest blade.

Landry pulled off her wig and tossed it away. Kept running.

She couldn't hear Finch blundering through the stalks right now. But to her right, she did hear the Yukon's engine gunning.

She crashed out onto the tractor path.

Corliss gunned up in front of her. From the SUV, she pointed at the next field. "Don't stand there, idiot. Go!"

Fucking Lissah Dove Yates.

Landry ran, diving into the next field. Behind her, she heard Corliss spin the Yukon's wheel and floor it into the corn.

63

Confronted with the massive cornfield, Caitlin stopped.

How would she find Finch and Landry on foot in that vast expanse? The breeze caught her hair. The sun shone off the tops of the stalks as they waved, a green sea.

Think. Look.

She swept her gaze across the field. She spotted footprints and bent cornstalks.

Bent cornstalks smeared with blood.

Running to the Suburban, she grabbed the shotgun. She had already checked the load. She stuffed extra shells in her pockets. She had a radio earpiece. She connected with Special Agent Williamson, and with Keyes at Quantico.

"Two female suspects pursuing Finch. They chased her into a cornfield. I'm in pursuit."

She plunged into the field.

On radio, Keyes came back, his voice tight. "Got satellite imagery of the farm. That field's three hundred acres."

Caitlin ran cautiously, the Remington aimed ahead of her. Cornstalks brushed at her arms, hissing as she pushed ahead.

"How big is three hundred acres? Give me distances."

"About two-thirds of a mile on each side."

"Damn."

"Divided midway by a tractor path," Keyes said. "There's no access to the field from the highway. Backup will need to ingress via the driveway at the farm."

Pushing through cornstalks, she told him, "Vector the cops and call in air support. State Police, whoever you can get. Williamson, are you close enough to deploy the drone over the property?"

Williamson's voice was rushed, and muffled by engine noise. "Not yet. Need to be within a thousand meters. I'm twelve, fifteen minutes away. Coming."

She couldn't wait for any of that. "Going silent."

She ran. Pushing ahead, she tracked crushed cornstalks and two sets of overlapping footprints. One set was small and light, one heavy and bloody.

She thought—hoped—Finch's prints were the light ones.

In the distance, she could hear engine noise and, even more faintly, sirens.

She reached the tractor path. She stopped and peered cautiously out.

Nobody was in sight. But across the path, a gaping hole in the corn marked where the Yukon had floored it straight into the next field, mowing down stalks in a swath six feet wide.

Keyes radioed: "Far corner of the field's bounded by a two-lane road and railroad tracks."

Caitlin dashed across the tractor path into the next field, following the Yukon's trail until she found footprints again. She paused, trying to orient the sounds she could hear only distantly. The SUV's big engine was moving, but near an idle, not racing. The sirens floated on the wind. The breeze set the cornstalks chattering, obscuring any chance she had to hear voices or the movement of people on foot. She couldn't tell how far ahead Finch and the unsub had run or whether the Yukon was closing on them. She kept going.

Then, after another hundred yards, the two sets of footprints reduced to one. She stopped, not wanting to overstep the trail on the ground, trying to analyze the story the tracks told her.

The small, light prints vanished. The bloody, heavy prints continued another twenty yards or so. Then they stopped, turned around, and backtracked to the place where the light prints had disappeared. At that point, Caitlin pushed aside a cornstalk and peered into the next row. The bloody footprints were there, veering off at a ninety-degree angle from their previous course. So were the light prints.

Finch must have jumped rows to try to lose the unsub. Smart kid.

Caitlin heard a rustle several rows away. She crouched, scanning. Sirens continued to float in and out on the wind. So did a train horn. She held still, eyes sweeping the green view ahead, hoping to see something out of place, a flash of movement—anything.

From the row of cornstalks behind her, a hand snaked out and grabbed her ankle.

She spun. Sweeping the barrel of the Remington around. She stopped short, heart thundering.

Behind her in the dirt, Finch lay flat.

The girl put a finger to her lips. Her wide eyes were hot with fear. Caitlin stilled, her pulse hammering.

They heard a voice on a phone, maybe fifty feet away. Not within sight, but hair-raisingly close. A young woman, her voice angry and ragged but full of cunning.

"Head due west. Meet me," she said.

Finch mouthed, *Landry*.

A second later, the Yukon roared. As the noise approached where Caitlin and Finch were huddled, cornstalks snapped and dust boiled up. Caitlin urged Finch to her feet, ready to retreat. Then brakes squeaked.

A woman shouted over the sound of the engine. "Why'd you stop?"

Landry said, "Zigzag. Mow in a grid."

Feet pounded on metal. Over the tops of the cornstalks, Caitlin glimpsed Landry climbing onto the roof of the Yukon, bloody, holding a semiautomatic handgun. Her short blond hair was instantly identifiable. She wore the soft blouse from the Upper West Side coffeehouse video, but her face and icy haircut revealed her unmistakably as the person Caitlin had chased across the subway tracks. She was the Broken Heart Killer.

Landry braced herself on the roof, feet planted wide. She had a wound on her left arm, blood draping down it like a sheet. The Yukon pulled out slowly. Caitlin leaned forward and glimpsed the driver. Corliss, face grim and focused, red hair piled on her head, scarlet lips pressed tight.

She accelerated, driving across the furrows at a forty-five-degree angle, crushing the field. Caitlin saw the plan. Corliss and Landry intended to plow the field under to flush her and Finch into the open.

If she and Finch stayed put, the Yukon would soon drive over them. If they moved, they would rustle the cornstalks, setting them waving like semaphores. And Landry had a high vantage point.

Caitlin considered her tactical position. Landry was out of range of her Glock. Missing with the shotgun would only blow a hole through the cornstalks and expose her location. De-escalation was off the table. She needed to retreat to safety to protect Finch, who was shivering and in tears, staring at the blood that coated Caitlin's hands.

Annie's blood.

The girl whispered, "My mom . . ."

Caitlin felt an electric jolt. She'd been so focused on getting to Finch, and now getting her out of here, that she had forgotten how she looked. She'd managed to bring a hard shield down on her emotions, but Finch wasn't ready for any of this. For her mom to be gone. Caitlin felt as if she'd had the breath punched out of her.

Finch's lower lip quivered. "My mom . . . I heard someone shooting a gun. Landry had the gun, I . . ."

Caitlin felt the black nowhere opening beneath her. Pain, guilt, failure. *Stop*, she told herself.

Finch's gaze drilled her. "Oh, God, is she hurt? Oh no, oh no, this is my fault . . ."

She turned sharply to look toward the farmhouse and nearly jumped to her feet, ready to run back.

Caitlin set her hands on Finch's shoulders and held her still. "Your mom sent me to get you."

Finch choked a breath.

"So we're going to do what she came here to do, and bring you home safe. Got it?"

After a second, Finch nodded, chin trembling.

Crouching low, Caitlin inched forward to a spot where she could see back across the field, toward the farmhouse. Her stomach tightened. The Yukon had mowed a wide swath of the field, a dead zone the size of a football field between them and the house, cutting off any return to the Suburban. They would have to head in a different direction, and do it so that they got as far ahead of the Yukon as possible before Landry, from her perch atop the SUV, could spot them. They had to be slick and smooth, moving through the field without leaving a wake of rustling corn-stalks behind them. And if at all possible, they had to blend in with their surroundings. Caitlin eyed Finch's pink hoodie and cap. Far too bright for camouflage.

"Listen up," she said.

She spoke quickly, explained, demonstrated, then gave Finch a solid look to confirm that the girl understood what to do.

"What I say. No matter what. And without hesitation," Caitlin said.

Finch nodded. Her young face had locked into a serious mode. The noise of the Yukon's engine was growing louder, mowing back and forth, now maybe twenty yards away in its zigzag pattern. Through thinning cornstalks, Caitlin glimpsed Landry crouched on the roof in a three-point stance, balancing herself as Corliss drove faster and harder.

Caitlin took a quick look at her phone—an overhead satellite view Keyes had sent her. They were two hundred yards from the northwest corner of the field, where the county road crossed the railroad tracks. In her ear, she had only poor radio reception, intermittent and crack-ling with static, but she got the gist. The state police were inbound from the west. But in these parts, on these winding roads, there was still too much time before they would arrive. Muffled sirens wafted through the trees and cornstalks—a hallucination of hope. Special Agent Williamson was on his way, and two police cars from Bearkill. But the one thing Caitlin and Finch could not do was wait. They had to move or die.

Corliss reached the far end of her track and swung the Yukon around

180 degrees. Dust flew in a widening pall. As she made the turn, Landry stood up and fired her semiautomatic into the corn.

Caitlin's skin shrank. Landry was trying to flush them from hiding.

"Behind me," Caitlin said. "Stay in my track. It'll minimize our profile through the cornstalks."

Ducking low, they ran toward the northwest corner of the field. Caitlin knifed through the cornstalks. She felt and heard Finch right behind her. The Yukon cut another swath and turned around again. Another gunshot came from Landry's pistol. She was firing randomly, hoping to spook them into the open. But random shots could still kill.

Then, abruptly, the view in front of Caitlin cleared as they reached the edge of the field. It was bounded by a low barbed-wire fence.

"Come on," she said.

Climbing over, they landed on a dirt path that ran alongside the railroad tracks. They were a hundred yards from the intersection with the two-lane road. Sirens were growing loud.

The train horn sounded again. Caitlin urged Finch toward the crossing. "Hurry."

As they broke into a run, behind them the Yukon's engine gunned. Cornstalks snapped; then posts ripped out and the barbed wire twanged and jumped as the SUV smashed through the fence.

Caitlin glanced back. A hundred yards behind them, the Yukon roared from the field onto the dirt track and skidded to a stop.

Up ahead, where the county road met the crossing, bells rang and the lights flashed. Glancing back at the Yukon as she ran, Caitlin saw Corliss at the wheel, staring at them, frozen with apparent confusion.

Caitlin's pulse surged. "Faster."

They dug in, sprinting, Caitlin holding tight to the Remington. The corn slashed past on their right, shivering in the wind. The sirens meant help, meant life, but they were still echoing and out of sight.

Caitlin ran, feeling as if she had a Day-Glo target on her back, because she was wearing Finch's pink sweatshirt and hat.

It was no real disguise. But from this distance, the color was what mattered. Distracting Corliss and Landry for even a few seconds might make the difference between escape and death. And she knew why Corliss was all at once left frozen. She and Landry didn't know there were *two* people in the field. They hadn't seen Caitlin arrive. Until now, they'd thought they were tracking a single unarmed teenager.

"Go," she yelled at Finch.

The road was forty yards away. If they could get there, get past the cornfield and the heavy surrounding woods, they'd be visible to the approaching troopers. She pumped her arms. Finch kept pace, her face hard and focused.

Caitlin heard angry shouts, looked back, and saw Landry swing down off the roof on the driver's side of the Yukon. Corliss threw open the door, then clambered into the passenger seat as Landry jumped behind the wheel.

Finch pumped her arms as she ran. Caitlin was breathing hard. Behind them, the driver's door slammed. Caitlin and Finch reached the road as Landry floored it.

Dashing onto the blacktop, Caitlin looked up and down the road. There was still no sign of the approaching cops. Behind them, dust flew and the SUV bore down on them.

At the railroad crossing, the gate arms swung down. In the distance, a massive freight train came into view. Then, across the tracks, the sirens rose, and Caitlin saw the state troopers closing in from around a curve, their flashing lights visible up the wooded road.

The Yukon roared toward the two running figures.

They were completely exposed. The cornfield wouldn't provide cover. Gunfire would cut through cornstalks like going through cobwebs, and the Yukon could smash straight back through the fence to run them down.

But there was one thing that might protect them: a mile of rolling iron. "Across the tracks. *Now.*"

The lights were flashing, the bells clamoring. Every instinct, every fiber in her body told Caitlin to back away. But she put her hand on Finch's back and ran to the crossing. The train was coming—long, massive diesel engines pulling destruction. It powered toward them, inexorable, headlights glaring, cab windows like narrow black eyes, hauling millions of pounds at velocity. The engines rumbled. The wheels of a hundred cars clattered and clacked. The rails on the ground in front of them rang with the noise.

Caitlin and Finch ducked under the gate arm and sprinted across the tracks. They got clear and ducked under the second arm. Flooded with adrenaline, Caitlin saw the world in a high-gloss shine.

She glanced back. The Yukon reached the road and swerved to face the crossing. The train was still seconds away.

"Keep running," she said. "Into the trees."

Finch accelerated. Got three feet.

A shot cracked the air.

Finch cried out and dropped to the pavement. Caitlin pulled up short. Flat on the ground, Finch gasped with shock, then her face crumpled with pain. The back of her khakis was blooming red. She'd been hit in the thigh. The train powered toward the crossing, huge, implacable—and, unbelievably, too late.

Beyond the tracks, the Yukon idled behind the gate. Corliss was leaning out the passenger side of the Yukon, gun in hand. Caitlin saw the anger on her face.

Read her lips as she shouted, "Shit. *Shit.* I missed."

Through the windshield, Landry's face, warped under the glare of the glass, seemed full of roaring calm. Pure, energized purpose. She stared at Caitlin, then at Finch sprawled helpless on the asphalt.

"*I* won't," she said.

Caitlin could run. Her nerves were firing, instinct shrieking at her to dive clear. But Finch couldn't. And there was no time to drag her into the trees.

Holy Jesus. She planted herself on the road in front of Finch. No cover. She raised the shotgun, walked toward the Yukon, and returned fire.

The Yukon's windshield spidered white. Corliss screamed and ducked back inside the cab. Landry didn't flinch.

The train bore down on the crossing. Landry stared straight at Caitlin through the fractured windshield. And floored it directly at her and Finch.

Sweet Christ.

In New York, Landry had dodged an approaching train. Could she beat this one too?

Caitlin kept walking. She pumped the action and fired again.

The train's horn blared. Its brakes shrieked. Landry crashed through the gate.

She almost made it.

64

Twenty-four hours later, the Bearkill farmhouse looked as if it had been hit by a tornado. Doors open, every square foot searched, forensic techs and state cops logging evidence. Bagging photo albums. Pulling down the wallpaper. Prying up the floorboards. A photographer snapped shots of the bloodstain that marked the spot where Annie Winter had died.

The farm was owned by a couple who had gone on a six-month tour of the USA in their Airstream trailer, towing motorcycles for backcountry rides. They had saved up for a once-in-a-lifetime vacation and hired a house sitter via Craigslist. They hadn't known that the house sitter's name was an alias. Corliss had all kinds of tricks in her hip pocket.

The shredded remains of the Yukon—a sight that Caitlin hoped never to see again—were found a hundred yards from the railroad tracks, flipped upside down in the woods. The smell of gasoline from the SUV's torn gas tank had penetrated Caitlin's head. She could handle that. The rest of the scene, she would try to burn from her memory.

She walked through the house. The afternoon light felt dim in Corliss and Landry's hiding place. In the back bedroom, where Annie had died, the cops had pulled apart the closet floor and found two hundred thousand dollars in cash—Goode's stash.

Sergeant Morris, from the Bearkill Police Department, was supervising. Caitlin glanced around. He caught her checking out the hidey-hole where the money had been secreted.

"The cash likely to be traceable?" he said.

"Maybe." She shrugged. "The FBI will check whether any of the bills were marked or in sequence and taken in a particular robbery."

He shook his head, half in admiration. "Two hundred grand. Most thieves gamble or snort it away before they accumulate that much."

Most armed robbers, maybe. The biggest thieves took their prizes other ways. In bribes, collusion, and stolen lives.

"Twenty years' worth of scores," she said. "Ten thousand a year. Goode had discipline. He's going to be extremely disappointed by this discovery." She paused. "Part of me wishes I could be the one who tells him he'll never get it."

Corliss had taken the money after setting up Goode's arrest in Tennessee. That helped explain why Goode never gave her name to the cops. He was an optimist. A conniving, unrealistic optimist with boundless ego and self-confidence. Now neither he nor Corliss would get to spend the cash.

From what Caitlin surmised, Corliss thought that by connecting with Finch, she could sweep the girl into her orbit and past the event horizon, pulling her irreversibly close, like a black hole—and then get Finch to lead her to Annie. Whose life Corliss had planned to strip-mine and destroy.

Sergeant Morris set his hands on his hips. "You heading out?"

"Back to Quantico," Caitlin said.

He nodded. "The girl was released from the hospital this afternoon."

Finch, fit and feisty, had been treated overnight. The family of her boyfriend, Zack, had driven up and taken her back to New York with them. Finch was suddenly more alone than she had been in a long time, more alone than she could ever have imagined. But she had people who had instantly swarmed in to take care of her. For the moment, she was safe and in loving hands.

She had texted Caitlin. Thank you. ♥

Wholehearted thanks. Caitlin intended to keep that one for a long time. And to reply in person.

"Tough kid," Morris said. He gave her an appreciative look. "Like you."

"Like her mom." Sunlight caught her in the eyes, causing a pang. She gave Morris a melancholy smile. "Keep me posted."

It was four days later when Annie Winter's memorial service took place, at a Brooklyn waterfront park looking out at the spires of Manhattan. Annie's neighbors attended, and her coworkers, and friends from across the city. The river gleamed. Finch had put the memorial together herself. Caitlin stood quietly at the back of the crowd.

The girl was grief-stricken but resolute. And grateful to her adopted mother. Afterward, Caitlin sought her out.

"You going to stay on with the Arcegas?" Caitlin said.

Finch nodded. In the distance, Zack's family huddled, a pack ready to step in if Finch needed them. Her new squad. It was going to be rough, facing young adulthood with all Finch had learned, and without her mom. But she wasn't alone.

Finch said, "I emailed the cousin in Kansas. The one who got in touch with you about Rhiannon."

"You did?"

"At a distance. I guess they're part of me. We'll see if I want to meet up. Later. Maybe."

She said nothing about Efrem Judah Goode. She had no plans to reach out to him. She had told the Arcegas and the police that she wanted protection against him ever contacting her.

She paused a moment. "I also tried to find out about the real Annie Winter. Phoenix." She swallowed. "I couldn't get much. I didn't contact her family."

"I recommend you don't. Not right now."

Caitlin did have information about the original Annie Winter. The young woman had run from a bad family situation in Arizona and eventually washed up in New York. When contacted by the NYPD, her relatives were flustered to be told that she was long dead.

They had never filed a missing-persons report. Never looked for her. They didn't even have the decency to be ashamed of that fact.

"Do they know about Landry?" Finch asked.

DNA had positively identified Landry as Phoenix's daughter. Caitlin nodded.

Finch said, "I took a close look at my birth certificate. The one my mom got from Arizona and edited."

"Right." Caitlin was wondering when she would get around to that, and how she would deal with it.

"The only thing Annie changed was the date. The year of birth."

"Yeah."

Finch looked at her. "The name on the certificate is Scout Finch Winter. That's not fake." She blew out a distressed breath. "That was Landry. She was Finch Winter. For real, she was me."

"She was not."

"But . . ." Finch's shoulders inched up.

"Landry wasn't you. You didn't steal her life. You escaped her fate. You are *you* and nobody else."

"I guess."

Caitlin glared. Finch smiled. It looked sad but sturdy.

"I know," she said.

Caitlin hugged her. "You know where you came from. Now you decide where you're going."

65

Home the next morning, with dawn inching through the shutters and spreading golden light across the bed, Caitlin lay in the crook of Sean's arm. It was the moment before the world crashed in. Birds sang outside. There was no chatter of news, no reports of death and destruction, no sirens to respond to. There were years past when Caitlin had hated this moment. It meant she was alone with herself, without distractions. Exposed.

She breathed.

Sean's arm was warm across her body. His breathing soothed and soon matched her own. She let her gaze absorb the morning light, and the rise and fall of his chest. She ran her hand across his cheek.

He didn't open his eyes. "You gotta give a guy at least three minutes to recharge, Hendrix."

She laughed. It felt good.

Two hours later, at her desk at Quantico, Caitlin wrote up her initial report on the Broken Heart Killer. Leaning back, giant coffee in her hand, she wondered, *What was Goode's real endgame?* It wasn't a book deal, which he was never going to get. Was it getting Finch under his thumb? Retrieving the money? Escaping and killing Corliss?

Emmerich's words echoed. *He's sly.*

She wondered if Goode was still after something. She emailed the warden at the prison, and Detective Marius Hayes at the Spring River Sheriff's Department, warning them to keep an ear to the ground.

As she hit Send, Keyes strode into the room, peering over the tops of cubicles, heading straight toward her. His energy was popping. He was snapping his fingers, bouncing on his toes.

"What's revving your engine?" she said.

He practically bounded up. "I analyzed the bomber's video manifesto."

She spun lazily in her chair. In the days since the West Virginia explosion, she had watched the manifesto dozens of times. Its eeriness hadn't diminished.

"And?" she said.

"It's a deepfake."

Her breath caught. All her nerve endings fired up.

He spread his hands. "You know, AI-generated counterfeits. Video photoshopping. Deepfakes put bogus words in people's mouths, put your face on a movie star's body or on Steph Curry draining a three-pointer."

"They're popular as revenge porn."

Keyes actually blushed. He cleared his throat. "It's not just about video anymore. Audio can be deepfaked. You can create 'voice skins' or clones of celebrities. Or of anybody."

"And?"

"The bomber's video has been manipulated to superimpose the dead man's face and voice over the original recording," Keyes said.

Caitlin's gaze extended—beyond her desk, beyond the windows, beyond the horizon. Since the explosion, she had felt unsettled. She'd had an inchoate sense that treachery ran through the events in West Virginia. An insidious subsonic echo. Beyond the fact of the weird manifesto. Beyond the exacting coincidence of an explosion that she couldn't help feeling was staged to look like accidental self-immolation—when too much spoke of an ambush. She didn't know what, exactly, had been eating at her, until now.

Keyes was saying he had analyzed the video backward and forward and employed new DARPA deepfake detection research, which used semantic forensics to expose manipulated videos.

It hit her.

When the ATF tripped the alarm outside the trailer, the man inside flinched.

He exhibited a startle reflex.

Certainly, he was reacting to the shriek of the alarm. The sound was meant to incite a reaction, and instantly. But the man in the trailer, bent over his incredibly dangerous work, hadn't simply reacted. He had jumped and cringed. Startled. That suggested that he *wasn't* a psychopath.

But the bomber surely was. Wasn't he?

Keyes waved her toward the conference room. "I'll show you. I reverse engineered the video to reveal the actual speaker."

He threw the manifesto video up on the big screen and pressed Play. The familiar face of the man in the trailer appeared.

"My name is Donald Jameson Burkholder, and if you're watching this, I'm dead."

Keyes paused it. "Now, with the manipulation removed."

He hit Play.

"I'm dead either by government-issued gunfire, corporate poison, or martyrdom."

The face, the entire body, of the speaker changed. The man on-screen, speaking words of death and hellfire and destruction, was young, white, and skeevy, with a raspy voice.

Caitlin froze. "Jesus God."

Keyes turned to her. He knew.

She had seen that man before. Heard him before.

"It's the Ghost."

Keyes paused the image. The man's eyes seemed to bore into Caitlin. She pulled out her phone and made a call. Her mouth was dry.

Sean answered brightly. "G-woman."

"I'm sending you something. Watch it this second."

She strode to her desk. The day all at once looked sharp and clear. She dug out the photos her mother had found, of the teenage boy at the Prophet's early crime scenes. She held them tightly and peered at his face.

She started hunting.

EPILOGUE

The cellblock corridor echoed with voices. Efrem could hear the guard walking along, patrolling, silently eyeing the men on this side of the bars. When he reached Efrem's cell, he paused. He admired the drawings of women that now covered every inch of wall space.

Efrem sat at the tiny desk, sketching a new portrait. This face was bright-eyed and vibrant, maybe sixteen.

The guard watched. "Who's that?"

Goode hummed. "My youngest."

She was his blood. She was out there, somewhere. And she had his eyes.

She had his heart.

ACKNOWLEDGMENTS

It takes more than a team to bring a book to publication—it takes several—and I am immensely grateful to all those who have helped this novel enter the world.

My heartfelt thanks go to Josh Stanton, Josie Woodbridge, Anne Fonteneau, Lauren Maturo, Stephanie Stanton, Greg Boguslawski, Michael Carr, Michael Krohn, and everyone at Blackstone who has supported my work with enthusiasm, dedication, and expertise.

Immeasurable gratitude goes to my agent, Shane Salerno—who has believed in me from the beginning and who has worked tirelessly to see that I write the best novels I possibly can, and that they're shepherded successfully to publication—and to Ryan Coleman, Deborah Randall, and the entire team at The Story Factory.

Many fellow writers have generously shared the word about my novels, have taken time to do book events with me, and have offered friendship, camaraderie, and writing advice. In particular I want to thank Stephen King, Don Winslow, and Jeff Abbott for their generosity and support.

Finally, I want to thank my family, who keep me going in every way: Katherine Lazo, David Lazo, Mark Shreve (who helped me make sure the New York City street geography in this novel was authentic), Nate Shreve (for insights into running a restaurant kitchen), and above all Paul Shreve—who listens to all my ideas, lets me choreograph fight scenes using him as an opponent, and who literally built a roof over our heads, out of ashes, while I was under a looming deadline. I couldn't do it without you. I love you all.